"*Celtic Empire* is some of the best work between Clive and Dirk Cussler in years—proving that Dirk Pitt, one of the thriller genre's premier heroes, has plenty more adventures left in him moving forward."

—*Crime Reads*

Intrepid heroes Dirk Pitt and Al Giordino embark on their wildest, boldest mission into the ancient world, unlocking extraordinary secrets and solving hideous crimes. Another fabulous read from the most beloved series from the #1 *New York Times* bestselling author.

During what was supposed to be a routine investigation in South America, NUMA Director Dirk Pitt finds himself embroiled in an international mystery, one that will lead him across the world and which will threaten everyone and everything he knows—most importantly, his own family. Pitt travels to Scotland in search of answers about the spread of an unknown disease and the shadowy bioremediation company that may be behind it.

Meanwhile, Pitt's son and daughter face a threat of their own when the discoveries they have made in an Egyptian tomb put killers on their trail. These seemingly unrelated riddles come together in a stunning showdown on the rocky isles of Ireland, where only the Pitts can unravel the secrets of an ancient enigma that could change the very future of mankind.

PRAISE FOR

Clive Cussler's Dirk Pitt Series

"This adventure series stands as one of the crown jewels in the Cussler empire."

—*Publishers Weekly*

"Exotic locations, ruthless villains, and many narrow escapes and derring-do by Dirk Pitt, oceanography's answer to Indiana Jones . . . Cussler's fans come for swashbuckling [and] he delivers."

—Associated Press

"Sketch out some exotic, ephemeral settings, make every villain as nasty as possible, and it's another of Cussler's cinematic-style entertainments spinning out at hold-on-to-your-hat speed."

—*Kirkus Reviews*

"Cussler speeds and twists through a complex plot and hairbreadth escapes with the intensity and suspense of a NASCAR race."

—*Publishers Weekly*

"Rollicking and exciting."

—*Library Journal*

"Enough intrigue to satisfy even the most demanding of thrill-seekers . . . An entertaining and exciting saga, full of techno details and daring escapes."

—*The Chattanooga Times*

"Fast-paced adventure."

—*Booklist*

TITLES BY CLIVE CUSSLER

DIRK PITT® ADVENTURES

Celtic Empire (with Dirk Cussler)

Odessa Sea (with Dirk Cussler)

Havana Storm (with Dirk Cussler)

Poseidon's Arrow (with Dirk Cussler)

Crescent Dawn (with Dirk Cussler)

Arctic Drift (with Dirk Cussler)

Treasure of Khan (with Dirk Cussler)

Black Wind (with Dirk Cussler)

Trojan Odyssey

Valhalla Rising

Atlantis Found

Flood Tide

Shock Wave

Inca Gold

Sahara

Dragon

Treasure

Cyclops

Deep Six

Pacific Vortex!

Night Probe!

Vixen 03

Raise the Titanic!

Iceberg

The Mediterranean Caper

SAM AND REMI FARGO ADVENTURES

The Oracle (with Robin Burcell)

The Gray Ghost (with Robin Burcell)

The Romanov Ransom (with Robin Burcell)

Pirate (with Robin Burcell)

The Solomon Curse (with Russell Blake)

The Eye of Heaven (with Russell Blake)

The Mayan Secrets (with Thomas Perry)

The Tombs (with Thomas Perry)

The Kingdom (with Grant Blackwood)

Lost Empire (with Grant Blackwood)

Spartan Gold (with Grant Blackwood)

ISAAC BELL ADVENTURES

The Titanic Secret (with Jack Du Brul)

The Cutthroat (with Justin Scott)

The Gangster (with Justin Scott)

The Assassin (with Justin Scott)

The Bootlegger (with Justin Scott)

The Striker (with Justin Scott)

The Thief (with Justin Scott)

The Race (with Justin Scott)

The Spy (with Justin Scott)

The Wrecker (with Justin Scott)

The Chase

KURT AUSTIN ADVENTURES
Novels from the NUMA® Files

Sea of Greed (with Graham Brown)

The Rising Sea (with Graham Brown)

Nighthawk (with Graham Brown)

The Pharaoh's Secret (with Graham Brown)

Ghost Ship (with Graham Brown)

Zero Hour (with Graham Brown)

The Storm (with Graham Brown)

Devil's Gate (with Graham Brown)

Medusa (with Paul Kemprecos)

The Navigator (with Paul Kemprecos)

Polar Shift (with Paul Kemprecos)

Lost City (with Paul Kemprecos)

White Death (with Paul Kemprecos)

Fire Ice (with Paul Kemprecos)

Blue Gold (with Paul Kemprecos)

Serpent (with Paul Kemprecos)

OREGON FILES

Final Option (with Boyd Morrison)

Shadow Tyrants (with Boyd Morrison)

Typhoon Fury (with Boyd Morrison)

The Emperor's Revenge (with Boyd Morrison)

Piranha (with Boyd Morrison)

OREGON FILES *(cont.)*

Mirage (with Jack Du Brul)

The Jungle (with Jack Du Brul)

The Silent Sea (with Jack Du Brul)

Corsair (with Jack Du Brul)

Plague Ship (with Jack Du Brul)

Skeleton Coast (with Jack Du Brul)

Dark Watch (with Jack Du Brul)

Sacred Stone (with Craig Dirgo)

Golden Buddha (with Craig Dirgo)

NONFICTION

Built for Adventure: The Classic Automobiles of Clive Cussler and Dirk Pitt

Built to Thrill: More Classic Automobiles from Clive Cussler and Dirk Pitt

The Sea Hunters (with Craig Dirgo)

The Sea Hunters II (with Craig Dirgo)

Clive Cussler and Dirk Pitt Revealed (with Craig Dirgo)

CHILDREN'S BOOKS

The Adventures of Vin Fiz

The Adventures of Hotsy Totsy

CLIVE
CUSSLER

AND DIRK CUSSLER

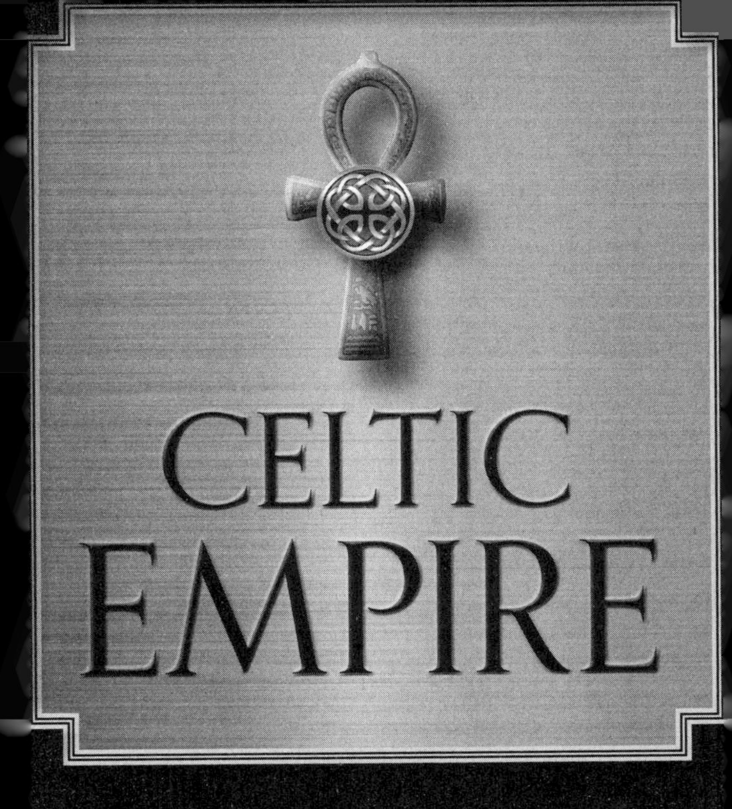

A DIRK PITT NOVEL

G. P. PUTNAM'S SONS
New York

PUTNAM
— EST. 1838 —

G. P. Putnam's Sons
Publishers Since 1838
An imprint of Penguin Random House LLC
penguinrandomhouse.com

The Library of Congress has catalogued the G. P. Putnam's Sons hardcover edition as follows:
Names: Cussler, Clive, author. | Cussler, Dirk, author.
Title: Celtic empire / Clive Cussler, Dirk Cussler.
Description: New York: G. P. Putnam's Sons, [2019] |
Series: Dirk Pitt adventure; 25
Identifiers: LCCN 2018056946| ISBN 9780735218994 (hardcover) |
ISBN 9780735219007 (epub)
Subjects: LCSH: Pitt, Dirk (Fictitious character)—Fiction. | BISAC: FICTION / Action & Adventure. | FICTION / Suspense. | FICTION / Thrillers. |
GSAFD: Adventure fiction. | Suspense fiction.
Classification: LCC PS3553.U75 C45 2019 | DDC 813/.54—dc23
LC record available at *https://lccn.loc.gov/2018056946*

First G. P. Putnam's Sons hardcover edition / March 2019
First G. P. Putnam's Sons international edition / March 2019
First G. P. Putnam's Sons trade paperback edition / December 2019
G. P. Putnam's Sons trade paperback edition ISBN: 9780593085714

Printed in the United States of America
1 3 5 7 9 10 8 6 4 2

Book design by Katy Riegel

Interior illustrations by Roland Dahlquist

CAST OF CHARACTERS

1334 B.C.E.

Meritaten Egyptian princess, daughter of Pharaoh.

Gaythelos Meritaten's husband.

Osarseph Prophet aided by Meritaten.

Ahrwn Osarseph's brother.

2020

NUMA Team

Dirk Pitt Director of the National Underwater and Marine Agency.

Al Giordino Director of Underwater Technology, NUMA.

Rudi Gunn Deputy Director, NUMA.

Zerri Pochinski Pitt's longtime secretary.

Michael Cruz Marine engineer and salvage expert, NUMA.

Dr. Rodney Zeibig Marine archeologist, NUMA.

Summer Pitt NUMA Special Projects director and daughter of Dirk Pitt.

Dirk Pitt, Jr. NUMA Special Projects director and son of Dirk Pitt.

Hiram Yaeger Computer Resource Center director, NUMA.

James Sandecker U.S. Vice President and former Director of NUMA.

Officials, Politicians, and Businesspeople

Loren Smith-Pitt Dirk Pitt's wife and congresswoman from Colorado.

Senator Stanton Bradshaw Chairman of the Senate Committee on Environment and Public Works.

Evanna McKee CEO of BioRem Global Limited.

Audrey McKee Field manager with BioRem Global Limited and daughter of Evanna McKee.

Rachel Associate of Evanna McKee.

Ross FBI agent protecting Elise Aguilar.

Abigail Brown Former prime minister of Australia.

Gavin Operative working for Evanna McKee.

Ainsley Operative working for Evanna McKee.

Irene Operative working for Evanna McKee.

Richard Operative working for Evanna McKee.

Historians, Experts, and Medical Professionals

Elise Aguilar Scientist with United States Agency for International Development in El Salvador.

Phil Scientist with United States Agency for International Development in El Salvador.

Rondi Salvadoran villager aiding the U.S. scientists.

Dr. Stephen Nakamura Epidemiologist, University of Maryland.

Dr. Susan Montgomery Head of the Environmental Health Laboratory, Centers for Disease Control.

Dr. Miles Perkins Scientist, Inverness Research Laboratory.
Dr. Harrison Stanley Emeritus professor of Egyptology from Cambridge University.
Riki Sadler Biochemist and archeologist and daughter of Evanna McKee.
Dr. Frasier McKee Biochemist and deceased husband of Evanna McKee.
Aziz Egyptian Antiquities Ministry agent.
St. Julian Perlmutter Nautical historian and longtime friend of Pitt.
Byron Lab Research director, Centers for Disease Control.
Dr. Eamon Brophy Former archeology department head, Dublin University.

Other

Manjeet Dhatt Father of ill boy in Mumbai.
Pratima Dhatt Mother of ill boy in Mumbai.
Ozzie Ackmadan Proprietor of the Abu Simbel Inn.
Friar Thomas Franciscan Friary of Killarney.
Captain Ron Posey Captain of the *Mayweather.*
Gauge Second officer of the *Mayweather.*

CELTIC EMPIRE

PROLOGUE

NILE FLIGHT

Escape on the Nile River

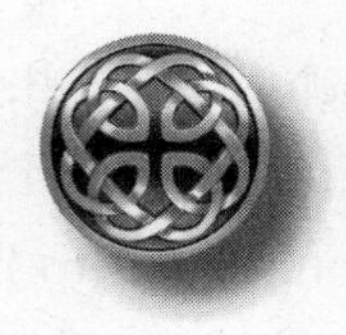

Memphis, Egypt

1334 B.C.E.

Wails of grief drifted over the city like a black aria. The mud brick dwellings burst with anguish, as the sorrow swirled into the night desert. But the winds ferried more than just the cries of mourning.

They carried the stench of death.

A mysterious scourge had descended upon the land, striking at nearly every household. The young were most afflicted, but not exclusively. The claws of death had grasped even the royal family, snatching the Pharaoh himself in their cold grip.

Crouched in the shadows of the Temple of Aten, a young woman tried to block the din and odor. As the moon slipped from behind a cloud, casting its glow over the landscape, she rubbed a heavy gold amulet on her chest and listened for sounds of movement. The rustle of leather soles on stone pricked her ears, and she turned to a figure running toward her across the temple's front portico.

Her husband, Gaythelos, was tall, with dark curly hair and broad shoulders. His skin was damp in the hot night air as he grasped her hand and pulled her to her feet. "The way to the river is clear," he said in a low voice.

She gazed beyond him. "Where are the others?"

"Securing the boats. Come, Meritaten, let us delay no further."

She turned to the shadows behind her and nodded. Three men emerged from along the temple wall, armed with spears and heavy *khopesh* swords. As she followed her husband, they took up a triangular defensive position around her.

Gaythelos led them away from the temple entrance and down a side street, their sandals kicking up dust. Despite the late hour, many houses showed the gleam of burning oil lamps through cracks in their shutters. The group moved at a quick pace, keeping silent as they crossed the former capital city.

The road sloped gently toward the riverside, where rows of small merchant boats were tied to a dock. As they moved along the bank, two men arose from the reeds. They wore long gray beards and were dressed in shabby linens.

The escorts raised their spears and sprang forward.

"Guards! Cease!" Meritaten cried.

The armed men froze.

She stepped past them and greeted the two men. "Osarseph, Ahrwn, what are you doing here? Why have you not departed?"

The younger of the two men stepped forward. His eyes held a determined look, shrouded by a weathered face. "Meritaten," he said, "we could not taste freedom without offering you our thanks. Your influence with Pharaoh was instrumental in his edict. I am saddened for you to learn of his passing at Amarna."

"My influence was debatable," she said. "What is not questioned is that Pharaoh's high priests are now in control of our lands—and have blamed the royal family for the sorrows brought upon Egypt."

"You are guilty only of having an open heart for the downtrodden." He slipped a goatskin bag from around his neck and passed it to her. "You saved us from the tainted waters of the Nile. I pray it is now time to save yourself."

"You took heed where Pharaoh did not. It is Gaythelos you should thank, not me." She nodded toward her husband. "He knew the power of the apium."

Osarseph turned and bowed to the man. "You will join us?" He waved an arm toward the river. On the opposite bank, the glow from a thousand campfires dotted the horizon.

"No," Meritaten said. "We will cast our fate to the sea."

The old man nodded, then knelt before her. "My brother and I shall carry your deeds close to our hearts. May you live in peace for the life of the stars."

"And you as well, Osarseph. Good-bye."

The two men climbed aboard a small raft, pushed into the dark river, and paddled for the opposite bank.

"Perhaps we should join them?" she whispered.

"The desert brings nothing but hardship, my love," Gaythelos said. "More hospitable lands await. We must delay no longer."

He led the company along the shoreline, turning away from the vessels at the town's landing to a trio of boats hidden in the reeds downriver. As they approached, they were challenged by armed sentries, who then guided them aboard one of the boats.

Meritaten and Gaythelos took a seat on a bench beneath the lone mast as the boat was released from its mooring. Crewmen rowed away from the bank, following the other two vessels to the Nile's center.

Meritaten cast an uneasy eye about the boat. It was less than 100 feet long and open-decked, with an upward-curving hull stem and stern. Pots and baskets filled with provisions littered the deck. Soldiers lined the gunwales, most rowing with short oars. The other two boats, veteran merchant ships that had crossed the Mediterranean many times, sat equally low in the water.

Square mainsails were partially raised and rigged fore and aft for maneuvering as the boats navigated north, propelled by the current. Small oil lamps dangled off the prows, providing faint light to the dark waters ahead. Leaving the city of Memphis in their wake, the boats sailed silently, except for the slap of water against their hulls and the dip of oars into the river.

Twelve miles downriver, murmurs rippled through the boats. Ahead, a string of lanterns had appeared. It was a vessel moored in the center of the river.

Meritaten squinted at the illuminated barge. Ropes stretched from it to either shore, to serve as a ferry during daylight hours, while at night it served as a tax station for passing merchant boats. But shouts of alarm from the barge revealed it was prepared this night for more than tax duty.

"Extinguish the lantern!" called the captain of Meritaten's boat, a gruff man with a clean-shaven head, and looked to the other boats.

Too late. All three had been seen. A team of archers assembled on the barge let loose a barrage of arrows.

Gaythelos shoved Meritaten to the deck. A crewman screamed and grabbed his neck where an arrow had struck.

"Stay down!" As two guards stood watch alongside, Gaythelos dragged a sack of grain across the deck and covered his wife with it.

Under the sack, she could only listen to the battle. The three boats turned to the far shoreline, putting as much distance as they could between themselves and the barge. The first boat approached one of the barge's ropes, and men with swords leaned over the bow to sever it. Several were picked off by the archers, others sliced the barrier free.

The three boats continued downriver, but the barge released a small chase vessel, filled with warriors and more archers. Putting oars to water, the pursuit craft made for the closest merchant vessel, the one carrying Meritaten and Gaythelos. It closed the distance quickly and pulled alongside. Its warriors swarmed over the side, expecting little resistance.

Gaythelos and the armed contingent sprang from the shadows, thrusting spears and striking their attackers with bronze swords. Hand-to-hand fighting spilled across the deck as every crewman fought to repel the boarders. Archers on the attack boat fired arrows into the melee, killing warriors on both sides. Bodies of the dead splashed into the Nile. The battle raged back and forth until the attackers seemed to gain the upper hand. Sensing defeat, Meritaten rose from her hiding place and picked up a dead warrior's sword.

"Seize victory!" she implored, plunging the blade into an attacking boarder.

The defenders rallied at the sight. Charging the attackers,

they drove them to the stern, killing them without mercy. The attack boat came next. The princess's raging swordsmen jumped into the vessel and massacred the remaining archers, then shoved the boat to drift away with its cargo of the dead.

Meritaten stepped to the bow in search of her husband. The deck was soaked in blood, dead and wounded men lay everywhere. Gaythelos appeared, holding a bloody dagger. She wrapped her arms around him.

"We are safe now," he said. "You have led us to victory." He turned to the captain, who sat at the steering oar, an arrow protruding from his shoulder. "Isn't that true?"

The man nodded. "There will be no more obstacles. We are nearly to the Delta—and multiple paths to the sea. By morning, Egypt will be in our wake."

The armada sailed through the night, squeezing down an eastern branch of the Nile Delta bordered by fields of ripe barley. The Mediterranean soon beckoned, and the three boats glided into the turquoise sea. They kept their distance from an approaching line of trading ships from the Levant as the sun brightened the morning sky.

Meritaten sat with Gaythelos as the Egyptian shore drifted away behind them. She clutched the goatskin bag tight to her chest, contemplating her future. While she had saved untold lives, she had also sacrificed everything she held dear.

Rising to her feet, she stepped to the ship's bow with a newfound sense of destiny. Facing the horizon across the open sea, she gazed toward the unknown world that beckoned her.

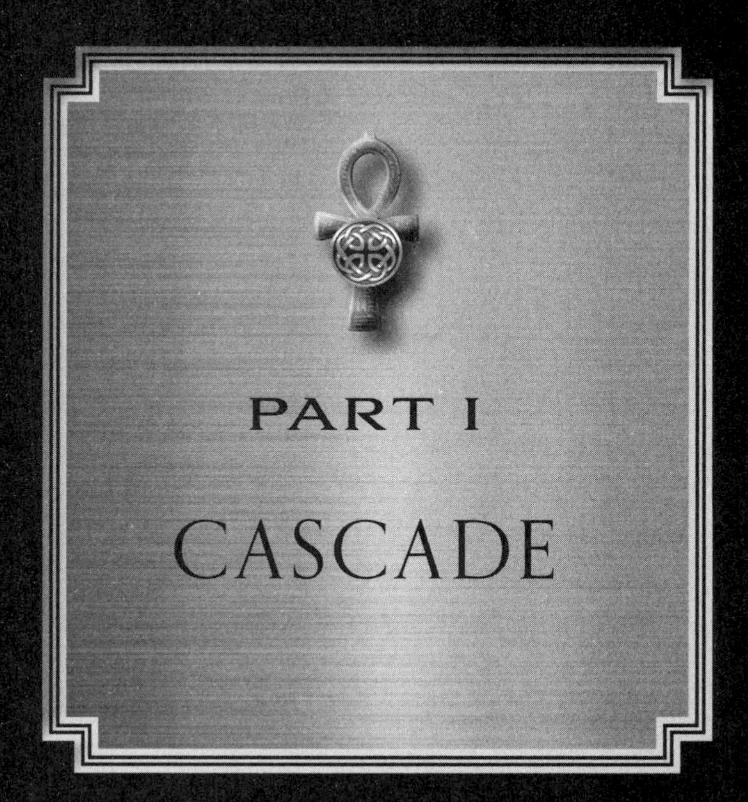

PART I

CASCADE

Cerrón Grande Reservoir

1

May 2020

Copapayo, El Salvador

Elise Aguilar watched with somber eyes as the funeral procession marched through the dusty village square. The four male pallbearers strode with downcast faces as they balanced a child's white casket on their shoulders. A small bouquet of yellow orchids had been slid across the lid, covering a hand-painted image of a soccer ball.

The dead child's family followed, weeping openly despite words of comfort offered by the townspeople.

Elise tracked the entourage until they disappeared around a bend thick with foliage. The town's tiny cemetery lay on a small hill just beyond.

She ignored a black Jeep that skirted the funeral procession as she turned and followed a worn footpath in the opposite direction. She walked past a handful of low-roofed, white stucco buildings that were home to the village's thirty residents. The path ambled downhill and opened onto an expansive view of a shimmering blue lake.

Cerrón Grande was a reservoir, the largest in El Salvador, built to supply hydroelectric power for the region. Hundreds of families had been resettled when the Lempa River was flooded in 1976, some to the hastily constructed village of Copapayo. Elise glanced at the lake. A fisherman in a canoe and a small workboat cruised across the waterway. To the right, a powder-gray concrete barrier marked the upper lip of the Cerrón Grande Dam that had created the lake.

Elise descended the path nearly to the water's edge. She stopped and wiped her brow in front of a large awning made from gnarled tree roots and covered with palm thatching. A half-dozen red tents were pitched in a semicircle around the awning's opposite side, facing the shaded interior. To either side lay a large tract of farmland, bursting with rows of green cornstalks.

Under the awning, fellow scientists from the United States Agency for International Development sat around makeshift worktables, performing experiments or computer analysis. The group wore shorts and T-shirts in the steamy climate.

A lanky man with thick glasses and a straggly beard looked up from a microscope. "Why the long face?" he asked in a heavy Boston accent.

"There's a funeral in the village today. The procession just passed."

"For the little boy?"

Elise nodded.

"Very sad. Rondi told me there was a sick boy from the village at the Suchitoto clinic. I didn't realize it was serious."

He shouted to a local teenage boy sorting stalks of corn from a bin. "Rondi, what happened to the little boy?"

The teen hurried over to the scientists. "He was *enfermo* for a short time. A doctor came and took him to the hospital last week, but they could not help him."

"What was the diagnosis?" Elise asked.

Rondi shrugged. "*Un misterio*. The doctors, they don't say. Just like the others."

"What others?"

"Three other children from the village have died in the past few months. Same thing. They get *enfermo*, and it is too late for the doctors to help them."

Elise looked at her colleague. "Phil, do you think it could be related to the food crops?" She pointed to the bin of corn Rondi had been sorting.

"Due to the genetically modified seeds we provided the farmers here last year?" He shook his head. "Not a chance. This variety is only engineered to withstand drought, and has been safely used all over the world."

She nodded. "It's just heartbreaking to see children get sick."

He shrugged. "We're agricultural scientists, Elise, not doctors." He glanced at the thriving cornfield. "And tomorrow, we need to pack up and move ten miles north."

He saw the disappointment in Elise's eyes. "Okay, maybe we can do more. I'll email our country manager and have her make a request to the World Health Organization. They have an established presence in El Salvador. I'm sure they can send someone to investigate."

"Thank you. The people here deserve to know what's creating the illness."

He nodded. "In the meantime, I need you and Rondi to assess the yields in Plot 17." He pointed to a diagram of the fields around the village. Plot 17 was a narrow field close to the lake.

"*Sí*, I know which one that is," Rondi said. He grabbed a canvas bag and looped it over his shoulder.

Elise followed him down a footpath through a neighboring cornfield. As they hiked, she kept thinking of the funeral procession and the small white coffin.

"Rondi, have there been sick children in the other villages, too?"

He nodded. "A cousin named Francisco. He died a short time ago. He lived in San Luis del Carmen, across the lake."

"How old was he?"

"Four, I think."

"I don't recall that village. Did we provide seeds to the farmers there?"

"No, they always have strong crops. But I did see the *científicos* there last week."

"What scientists?" Elise said. "Our team just arrived at Cerrón Grande four days ago."

"I don't think they were U.S. workers. Nobody seemed to know where they were from."

"What did they want?"

Another shrug. "They asked about the *niños* and took some food and water samples." He stopped at a plastic marker pinned to the ground with the number 17. "This is our plot."

Elise retrieved a yellow spool of string from Rondi's bag and strode a few yards into the cornfield. She uncoiled the string onto the ground, forming a square around a patch of stalks. With Rondi's assistance, she examined every stalk in the enclosure, recording the number of buds and ears forming on each. She jotted the figures on a clipboard, then moved the string to a patch several yards away and repeated the count. Back at the camp, she would calculate the predicted yield for the entire field.

"Let's return to the camp by the lake," Rondi suggested, once they completed their measurements. He guided Elise through the cornfield.

They emerged on a low bluff overlooking the reservoir. Less than a mile to their right was the eight-hundred-meter-long concrete wall of the Cerrón Grande Dam. They turned the opposite way and followed the shoreline toward camp.

Near the path to the village, Elise stopped to admire a small aluminum windmill on a concrete pad at the water's edge. An eight-bladed fan spun in the light breeze, and water sloshed beneath the structure's base. "I don't remember this being here last year."

"The village well was running low, so the government provided it. Now we can get water from the lake. Mr. Phillip helped us install it last year, after you left."

"The water is used to irrigate the fields?"

"*Sí*, and for the village. It draws water from a pipe that extends into the lake. We can direct it to the fields or to a filtered cistern that can be pumped into the village."

Elise gazed at the windmill, then turned to Rondi. "You have a boat, don't you?"

"Tied up just around the bend."

"Can you take me out into the lake? I'd like to get some water samples near the inlet pipe."

"I'll get the boat and be right back."

Elise jogged to the camp and dropped off the duffel bag and yield records. In its place, she grabbed a satchel with a half-dozen test tubes secured in Velcro pockets. She returned to the shore and waited until Rondi motored up in a small aluminum boat.

"Sorry." He gave a toothy grin. "The engine, it does not always like to start."

The dented, oxidized craft was powered by a little six-horsepower outboard that was older than Rondi and smoked as it idled. She tossed the satchel onto a bench, shoved the prow from shore, and hopped aboard. Rondi reversed into deeper water, then turned and motored offshore. They traveled just a short distance before he killed the engine and let the boat drift.

Rondi eyed their position relative to the windmill. "The pipe opening is about here."

Elise took two of the test tubes from the satchel, removed their stoppers, and dipped them into the cool, clear water. As she capped them, she noticed a dead fish floating nearby. "Do you see many dead fish in the lake?"

Rondi delivered another shrug. "I've seen some by the dam."

"Will you show me?"

Rondi tugged on the outboard's pull starter a dozen times until it rasped to life. He aimed toward the dam, passing an old fisherman in a canoe who was pulling in a purse seine net. They approached the dam's safety barrier, a simple steel cable stretched just above the water. Rondi cut the motor and allowed the boat to rub against the cable. Bobbing in the water were dozens of dead fish, their bloated white bellies turned skyward.

Elise snapped some pictures with her cell phone, feeling sick at the thought of the village people drinking untreated water from the lake. She collected two more samples, then looked across the reservoir.

"Let's go north toward San Luis del Carmen. I'd like to collect one more sample near there."

As Rondi nodded, three sharp, deep rolls of thunder echoed from the opposite side of the dam. Elise and the teen looked at each other—and a deep rumble burbled up beneath them. In a slow cascade, the center face of the concrete dam in front of them crumbled away with a roar.

Elise screamed as Rondi tried to start the outboard. The motor coughed to life, and Rondi turned the throttle full over. The little boat surged away from the collapsing dam, gaining a dozen yards, before losing headway. The tiny motor wailed, but the boat went nowhere.

"What's happening?" Elise cried.

"The current . . . it's too strong." Rondi looked at her with large eyes, his hand on the tiller trembling.

Behind him, the dam was disintegrating into the ravine a hundred meters below as the flow of water accelerated.

Squeezing the throttle until his knuckles turned white, Rondi stared back at the watery edge and shook his head.

He and Elise could only watch as the boat was drawn backward to the widening gap in the dam and the deadly waterfall just beyond.

2

The rumble echoed across the reservoir.

"What was that?" Dirk Pitt raised his head from behind a pair of computer monitors where he'd been watching a sonar image of the lakebed. He peered across the cramped wheelhouse of the workboat at the short burly man piloting the vessel.

"It wasn't thunder." Al Giordino glanced out the side window at blue skies. "Or my stomach, despite our meager excuse for lunch." He crumpled a potato chip bag and tossed it onto the dash, then shifted his gaze out the windscreen.

He suddenly sat upright. "Oh, brother, take a look at that. It's the dam."

Pitt stood, stretching his six-foot three-inch frame, and looked off the bow. Less than a quarter mile ahead, the rim of the Cerrón Grande Dam stretched across the reservoir. But now the structure had a huge gap at its center. Two small boats were just in front of the opening, being drawn into the void.

"The dam's given way," he said, "and those boats are going with it."

Giordino jammed the throttle forward. The thirty-foot workboat surged ahead, driven by a twin set of 250-horsepower outboards. Rather than turn away from the danger, he aimed straight for the havoc.

He glanced over his shoulder across the open stern deck to a taut blue cable that trailed in the frothy wake behind them. A hundred meters back, a yellow sonar towfish broke the surface and bounded through the water.

"No time to reel it in," Pitt said, reading Giordino's thoughts. He stepped to the rear cabin door. "Get as close as you can."

Pitt stepped onto the open deck, retrieved a life ring from the bulkhead, and tied it to a coil of line stored in a bucket. He moved to the transom and tied off the free end to a stern cleat. Looking over the side toward the dam, he wondered if they would get there too late.

ELISE DIDN'T NOTICE the survey boat charging toward them. She focused on the old fisherman in the nearby canoe, fighting for his life. Despite his fierce attempt to paddle clear, the narrow wooden craft was quickly being drawn backward toward the cascading torrent. The old man's skinny arms flailed with hard, even strokes, but he was powerless against the gushing force.

"Rondi, can you help him?"

She had to yell over the roar of the falling water. The teen winced, then adjusted the tiller, angling the boat toward the fisherman's path.

Elise slipped the satchel over her neck, then grabbed the side of the canoe and pulled the two boats together. The fisherman nodded thanks—and continued to slap the water on the opposite side with his paddle.

It was a losing battle. Both boats were sliding toward the abyss, now less than a hundred feet away.

Above the din of the waterfall, Elise noticed a new sound: the whine of large engines. The survey boat was charging toward the dam at top speed.

The boat curled around in a wide arc, trailing a blue cable, then slowed as it pulled just in front of them. A tall man with black hair standing at the stern tossed them a line.

"Tie off one of the boats," he yelled. "We'll pull you clear."

The rope landed on the aluminum boat's bow, and the fisherman grabbed it. Rather than tie it to one of the boats, he wrapped it around his waist and jumped into the water.

Elise couldn't believe her eyes. She glanced back and saw the plunging water was less than fifty feet away. The draw of the falls was getting stronger, even as Elise let go of the canoe.

But the survey boat was following their position, its pilot feathering the twin outboards to stay near. On the stern, the tall man furiously pulled on the rope until the fisherman's head bobbed alongside. He yanked the old man from the water and freed him from the line. Gathering the rope together, he again tossed the line toward the boat.

"Tie it off," he shouted.

As the line flew through the air, the aluminum boat pivoted in the accelerating current. The line went high and to the side, but Rondi grabbed for it anyway. "I've got it." He stood and stretched over the side.

A few feet ahead of him, Elise attempted a similar move. With both their weights shifted to the starboard rail, the boat dipped to the side, and the top of the gunnel kissed the water.

Elise tried to jump back. It was too late. The water poured in, flooding the interior, capsizing the boat.

Elise instinctively grabbed onto the boat, but it pulled her under as it sank. She let go and flailed to the surface. Gulping for air, she glimpsed Rondi rushing by, clinging to the line. With a flash of terror, she realized it was he who was stationary. She was the one speeding through the water.

With renewed panic, her heart pounding, she tried swimming away from the dam. The swift current drained her strength as she heard and felt the rumble of the falls closing in behind her.

Stroking harder, her arm slapped into something. Someone else was in the water with her. For an instant, she hoped she had reached Rondi and the line. One look above the surface told her it wasn't so. Instead, she found the dark-haired man from the survey boat next to her.

He wrapped an arm around her waist and pulled her tight against him. Confused, she continued to kick and stroke. Then she heard his calm voice. She stopped and looked up into his face.

"Hang on tight to me and take a deep breath." He winked at her through the greenest eyes she'd ever seen.

Adrenaline overtook analysis, and she did as he said. There

was nothing else she could do, as they'd reached the edge of the falls.

He raised a finger in the air and twirled it as she wrapped her arms around him and took a last breath.

Then gravity took command and carried them over the falls.

3

Elise felt the sensation of free-falling in the river's flow. With her eyes shut tight and her breath held, she clung in a bear hug to Pitt. His arms were wrapped around her, his legs bent and squeezed together. Amid the rushing water, Elise could feel something slipping across her legs and back.

They seemed to fall forever. She tensed for the anticipated collision with the rocks at the base of the dam. The impact didn't arrive. Instead, she felt a jolt from Pitt that nearly ripped her from his arms. Something had stopped their descent.

She caught a fistful of his shirt and pulled herself back to him. It took a herculean effort against the water's battering. She felt like the Empire State Building was falling on her, one floor at a time.

Pitt again pulled her close, and she clung tight against the relentless pressure.

She opened her eyes for an instant, saw only a violent froth of white water rushing past. As her racing heart slowed a beat, Elise realized she needed to breathe. It had been only seconds since they were drawn over the top, yet the exertion had been intense.

Her mind raced. What would become of them, suspended in the falls? She told herself she wasn't going to inhale the water no matter what. She'd hold her breath until she passed out, then accept her fate.

The force of the water tore at her limbs, taking her mind off the fear of drowning. Her arms ached, but losing her grip on Pitt would mean instant death. Yet she felt no such fatigue from the sinewy man who clutched her. He felt like a statue, his arms firm around her, despite the weight of the water on them.

The water pressure jostled them about, banging them against the dam. During one collision, Elise's leg slid against its surface. Oddly, she felt the wall fall away from her. Somehow, they seemed to be sliding *up* the face of the dam.

Again, she needed to breathe. Her head was pounding and her lungs ached for air. Elise began to have thoughts of simply letting go. Then her legs scuffed over the jagged top of the dam, and the tumult from the rushing water lessened.

She opened her eyes, surprised to encounter a few feet of visibility. The current was still strong, but not as heavy and not as frothy. She could now see that Pitt was grasping a small blue cable coiled around his leg, ending at a yellow tube-shaped device beneath his feet. The nose of the object had stopped their descent, and he had wedged his feet against it.

Elise's lungs felt like they would explode. She looked up to her rescuer. He had a hardened yet handsome face that had seen many hours in the sun. His eyes were open, and he looked at her with confidence and intelligence. Once more, the green orbs winked at her, telling her to hang on, they would soon be safe.

The force of the water diminished, and Pitt freed his legs from the towfish and kicked upward until they broke the surface. Elise gasped, filling her lungs with deep breaths as the pounding in her head slowly lessened. The current still pulled at their bodies, and she kept a firm hold on Pitt, whose arms were outstretched gripping the cable.

Elise looked ahead and saw the survey boat. On its stern deck a curly-haired man with Mediterranean features quickly pulled in the blue cable with his thick hands and arms. In the water nearby, Rondi grasped the taut rescue line tied to the survey boat's stern.

"That was a shower for the ages," Pitt said. He turned to her and grinned. "You okay?"

Still gasping, Elise nodded and gave a weak smile.

Giordino pulled them alongside the corner transom, keeping them away from the churning outboards that held the survey boat in place. He reached over and lifted Elise onto the deck with an effortless grab. Pitt climbed aboard on his own and waved to the old fisherman who was manning the helm. Then he pulled in the remaining cable and towfish.

Giordino offered Pitt a crooked grin. "I suggest you consider using a barrel next time you decide to jump over some falls."

"Barrels are for sissies," Pitt said. "But thanks for the lift."

Giordino stepped to the opposite corner of the stern and began pulling in Rondi. "I was hoping you wouldn't slip to the end. Glad the towfish held its bite on the cable."

"You and me both," Pitt replied. "I'm afraid that cable might be stretched a bit longer than it was when we started."

"I think our survey work is done for the day." Giordino nodded toward Elise and the old man, then yanked Rondi aboard.

The teen stood there, shivering, and stammered, "Miss Elise . . . I thought you were gone . . . over the dam . . . for good."

"So did I." Elise turned to Pitt. "I don't know how to thank you."

She stepped closer and awkwardly shook his hand. "My name is Elise Aguilar, with the U.S. Agency for International Development. I was trying to collect some water samples with Rondi when the dam gave way."

Rondi, calmer now, followed Elise's lead and shook hands with Pitt and Giordino. "I don't think the dam collapsed. I think it was blown up."

Elise looked at him. "Rondi, who would blow up a dam here?"

Rondi shrugged. "I don't know, Miss Elise. It just sounded like some explosions before it fell down."

They all looked aft at the remains of the dam. The reservoir had lost twenty feet of depth, exposing a wide, jagged opening in the concrete. The water drainage was slowing, but the impact was evident. Wide swaths of muddy ground lay exposed on the reservoir's shore. The survey boat pulled forward as the draw from the falls abated.

Giordino found a thermos of hot coffee for Elise and Rondi, then stepped to the wheelhouse and relieved the fisherman at the helm. Easing ahead on the throttle, he guided the boat away from the dam.

Elise slowly sipped the coffee, passed it to Rondi, then looked at the sonar towfish on the deck. She turned to Pitt. "What are you doing on Cerrón Grande?"

"We were attending a subsea technology conference in San Salvador and had a free afternoon. Thought we'd try out a new sonar system and see if there were any monsters or shipwrecks at the bottom of the lake."

"Monsters or shipwrecks?"

"Al and I work for the National Underwater and Marine Agency."

Elise was familiar with NUMA, the U.S. scientific organization tasked with monitoring the world's oceans. Pitt was in fact the agency's Director, while his age-old friend Al Giordino headed the undersea technology division. A marine engineer by trade since a stint in the Air Force, Pitt had a lifelong fascination with the sea, being drawn to underwater exploration at every opportunity.

"Yes, I know NUMA," Elise said, "though I doubt you'll find either monsters or shipwrecks in this lake. By the way, I thought all of NUMA's vessels were painted turquoise." She patted the white bulkhead of the survey boat.

"A rental from a local engineering firm," Pitt said. "Lucky for us, they didn't skimp on the outboard motors."

He looked over the rail at some mud-encased tires along the exposed shoreline. "What did you say you and the boy were doing out on the water?"

"I'm here as part of a scientific team assisting local farmers with their agricultural yields. Besides helping with crop rotation, irrigation, and fertilization techniques, we're introducing new crop strains that might be more productive. Our team has been assisting farmers throughout El Salvador and Guatemala."

She pointed to some distant cornfields. "The output in some of the villages has more than doubled in just three years."

"Sounds like a worthy endeavor," Pitt said. "But I'm not sure I see how that's a reason to sail in front of a collapsing dam."

"In the past months there've been unexplained child fatalities in the area. Rondi said some of the villages draw drinking water from the reservoir, so I thought I'd collect samples." She patted the soaked leather satchel that still hung from her neck.

Giordino looked over his shoulder from the wheelhouse. "Where would you like to be dropped off?"

"As close to that windmill as you can get." Rondi pointed to the western shore.

Giordino turned the boat, slowing as the depths shallowed. When he could see the bottom, he cut power and raised the propellers, letting the boat drift until its hull scraped. "Close as I can get. Watch out for quicksand."

Elise, Rondi, and the fisherman offered thanks once more, then climbed over the side and waded toward shore. Elise took a moment to stop at the water's edge and wave at the NUMA boat, then joined the others hiking across nearly fifty yards of mudflats and sand.

Pitt and Giordino watched until the trio was safely ashore. Elise and Rondi turned south, while the old fisherman hiked north. "Call it a day?" Giordino nodded toward the sun that was tickling the horizon.

"Sure," Pitt said. "We may be in for a muddy hike of our own back at the dock."

He slipped over the side and shoved the boat toward deeper water as Giordino lowered the props and eased on the motors. Once Pitt was aboard and they'd cleared the shallows, Giordino applied full throttle. But soon Pitt tapped him on the arm.

"Cut the motors!" Pitt shouted.

Giordino instantly obliged. The high-riding boat sagged to the flat surface as the motors fell quiet. He turned to ask Pitt why, then saw for himself.

Where they'd dropped Elise and the others was aglow with flames and rising black smoke. The sound of gunfire echoed across the lake.

Someone was attacking the U.S. aid camp.

4

Elise and Rondi had been onshore just long enough to stomp the mud off their feet when a loud explosion shook the ground. Past an adjacent cornfield, a cloud of black smoke mushroomed into the air.

"It's from the camp," Elise said. "Hurry!"

She sprinted down a path, Rondi following close behind. But her strength quickly ebbed, and she was winded by the time they reached the field's far edge. The sight of the camp just beyond made her stop in her tracks.

The palm-thatched awning around the camp, or what remained of it, was billowing with flames. Beneath it, the benches and workstations had turned into a black, smoldering mass. The nearby tents had mostly disintegrated.

Phil staggered from behind the ring of tents, his clothes singed. Specks of blood peppered his face where he'd been hit by debris from the explosion. He didn't notice Elise, instead raising his hands to someone across the camp to halt.

Two people stood on the opposite side of the crater left by the explosion, facing him. They weren't part of the aid team, nor were they villagers. Each wore dark clothes, with low-slung ball caps and sunglasses concealing their faces. It wasn't their attire that caught Elise's eye. It was the assault rifle each carried, balanced on the hip with the barrel thrust forward.

One of the weapons spit fire, and a bloody seam appeared on Phil's chest. The scientist staggered backward, tripped over a tent stake, and fell to the ground, where he lay motionless.

"Phil!" Elise tried to take a step toward his body. Something stopped her. It was Rondi, grabbing her arm and pulling her in the opposite direction.

"Run, Miss Elise, run!" The teen yanked, then shoved her toward the cornfield.

In a daze, Elise yielded to his urgings, turning and streaking toward the field. From the corner of her eye, a light flashed on the lake, but her attention was consumed by more gunshots. She and Rondi had reached the first row of cornstalks when the fusillade began. Rondi pushed her ahead as the bullets chewed up the ground at their feet, then struck flesh.

"Go," Rondi gasped, as a half-dozen rounds tore up his back.

Elise felt a sting in her arm as she staggered forward. Her eyes tracked Rondi as he fell in a heap. She kept moving, driven by the clatter of automatic rifle fire and her pounding heart. The gunfire ceased for a moment as one shooter ran closer, then fired again. Bullets whizzed over Elise's head and shredded the cornstalks beside her.

She diced through the rows, feeling woozy as blood dripped down her arm. She was in no condition for a footrace. As she jumped over a small irrigation ditch, she saw a pile of dried husks in a clearing. Elise burrowed in like a rat, tucked into a fetal position, and froze.

In the distance came the screams of others and more bursts of gunfire. But it was the closer sound of swishing cornstalks that made her hold her breath. Heavy footsteps entered the clearing, then paused. The crunch of husks underfoot told Elise the killer was circling the pile.

A shrill whistle sounded from the camp's direction. The gunman hesitated, then fired a short burst into the husks. He waited and watched for movement, then turned and bolted for the camp.

Under the husks, Elise fought to keep from trembling. Dried stalks near her face had disintegrated under the gunfire. Somehow she escaped harm. The footfalls had retreated. Was the killer waiting? She could do nothing but lie as still as possible, taking slow, shallow breaths.

Minutes passed. She heard a car start and drive away. She waited a bit longer, then began inching from beneath the stalks. Light-headed from blood loss, she fought to keep from passing out. She was nearly free of the pile when she heard a rustling. She tried to scramble back under the husks. It was too late.

"Elise?"

She turned to see Pitt step into the clearing. He rushed to her side and pulled her from the pile.

"Looks like you got a little nicked up." He tore off his shirt and wrapped it around her arm to stem the flow of blood.

"Two gunmen attacked the camp," she rasped. "They shot Phil and the others."

"Who were they?"

Elise shook her head, and her eyes turned glassy. Pitt slipped his arm under her and raised her to her feet. She regained her balance, and he led her to the shore, where Giordino came from the camp.

"Anyone else?" Pitt asked.

Giordino shook his head.

"Rondi? What about Rondi?" Elise asked.

Giordino just stared at the ground.

"No . . ." she moaned, tears welling in her eyes. She sagged against Pitt.

"She needs medical attention," he said. "Best to take her by boat back to Suchitoto."

Elise stirred. "The water sample."

Pitt and Giordino looked at her quizzically as she patted the satchel around her neck and passed it to Giordino.

"Please hold on to this. Keep it safe." She barely got the words out before losing consciousness and falling limp into Pitt's arms.

A HALF MILE AWAY, a woman in the passenger seat of an idling black Jeep watched the exchange through binoculars.

"They aren't police. They don't even appear to have weapons." She cursed. "The woman is still alive and just gave them a satchel."

"I lost her in the cornfield," said the driver, a square-jawed man with cropped black hair. "You called me off before I could find her."

"I saw a flashing light on the boat. I thought they were police." She shook her head. "I was fooled."

"We still have all of their computers." He jerked a thumb over his shoulder. The backseat was littered with half-melted laptops. "If it's a concern, let's go back and finish the job."

"It's too late, they're returning to the boat. But it does appear the woman is wounded."

"There's only one place they can take her for medical treatment. Suchitoto."

"Yes." She lowered the binoculars and flashed him an angry look. "If we want to be there to greet them, then I suggest you step on it."

5

With its twin outboards churning the water at maximum revolutions, the workboat leaped across the shrunken reservoir at close to forty knots. Elise had regained consciousness soon after Pitt had carried her onto the boat's deck. He broke open a medical kit and applied clean bandages to her wounds, while Giordino steered for the town of Suchitoto, radioing ahead for medical assistance.

They reached the town's lakefront a few minutes later. With a deeper channel fronting its small marina, Giordino was able to run the boat aground just a few yards from the lone pier. Pitt jumped over the side, and Giordino passed Elise to him. He carried her to the wooden dock, where a faded green flatbed truck with a red cross on its door waited. Two young men dressed in white rushed over with a stretcher and loaded Elise onto it and onto the truck.

Pitt looked to the driver. "She needs immediate attention."

The man nodded. *"La clínica está justo en la ciudad."*

Pitt watched the ambulance rumble off the dock toward the town. Had he looked to his left, he might have spotted a black Jeep sitting behind a large boat trailer. A dark-haired man climbed out, then the Jeep followed the ambulance into town.

Giordino crossed the dock with the boat keys in hand and approached Pitt. "Hope she's going to be all right."

He nodded. "She looks to have lost some blood, but I don't think her wound is serious."

"Seems like a nice kid."

"We can check on her after we return the boat."

They hiked along a dirt frontage road lined with local townspeople gawking at the shrunken reservoir. At a wood-frame building that faced the lake, Pitt and Giordino entered a door beneath a sign marked DARIEN CIVIL ENGINEERING. A heavyset man at a desk was hanging up the phone.

"Thank heavens you're safe." The man looked out the window at the boat grounded by the pier.

Pitt gave a wry smile. "And your boat, too."

"I heard some boats went over the spillway and I feared the worst." He gave Pitt a sideways look when he noticed his clothes were wet.

"We got close to the action to help some people, but your boat was never in peril."

Eduardo Darien shook his head. "I relayed to the authorities your call about the attack on the aid workers' camp. The town police are on their way, and an army drug enforcement helicopter from San Salvador is also en route. Can you describe the attackers?"

"I'm afraid we didn't see them. They were apparently well armed with explosives and automatic weapons."

"While this is a peaceful area, the drug gangs in our country are out of control. A territorial dispute, I fear. I am sorry the U.S. aid team was involved and that you were placed in danger."

"I just got an unplanned swim in the lake," Pitt said. "What happened to the dam?"

The civil engineer shook his head. "I'm told the upper half of the main spillway gave way. Funny thing is, that section just underwent a thorough inspection three weeks ago and checked out perfectly."

"Sabotage?" Pitt asked.

"It's possible. There were a lot of displaced people when the dam and reservoir were built. And you never know what twisted motivation one of the drug gangs might have."

"We heard a few loud rumblings before it gave way," Giordino said. "Sounded a lot like explosives."

"There will be a full investigation." He looked at Pitt. "Did you find what you were looking for?"

"We just wanted to test the sonar by dragging it over some of the settlements that were flooded when the dam was built. We got a nice look at a submerged village just east of here." He motioned toward the reservoir.

As he did, a thundering explosion erupted outside, rattling the office windows. Pitt turned to see the grounded workboat explode in a fireball, raining bits of debris in all directions.

"My boat!" The engineer leaped from the desk and bolted out the door.

"My sonar," Giordino said. He beat Pitt out the door, following Darien to the shoreline, where they watched the remaining hull disintegrate under a veil of black smoke.

"How could this happen?" the engineer asked.

Pitt kicked at a smoldering piece of fiberglass near his feet. "That was too massive an explosion to be an accident."

"Fuel tanks were about run dry," Giordino said.

Darien stared at the debris. "Who would do such a thing?"

"Likely the same people who blew up the dam and attacked the aid team." Pitt wheeled around to see who was nearby.

The gathering of villagers stared at the boat like it was a fireworks display. They all looked shocked.

Pitt, noticing his rental car was blocked by the spectators, turned to Darien. "The girl we brought ashore might be in danger. Can you take us to the clinic?"

The engineer fished through his pocket and handed Pitt the keys. "I'm going to call the police, then see what I can salvage from the boat. You can take my truck. The clinic is a yellow building at the far end of town."

Pitt and Giordino found the engineer's pickup truck parked behind the building. Pitt took the wheel and drove the single-lane dirt road toward town. The road wound around a forested hill, then into Suchitoto. It was a small, quaint colonial village with cobblestone streets and a tall whitewashed church at its center, La Iglesia Santa Lucía.

As they entered the town, they passed a well-dressed man wearing a hat and sunglasses walking along the road. Pitt drove past him, took a careful look, then stomped on the brakes. As the truck shuddered to a stop, the man produced a handgun and pumped two quick shots into the cab, then fled down an alley.

Fired at an angle, the bullets had ripped through Pitt's door, passed beneath his arm on the windowsill, and struck the dashboard. Pitt jammed the truck into reverse and floored it, backing up just enough to turn and pull into the alley.

"How did you know?" Giordino asked as the truck raced after the fleeing figure.

"His shoes. They were covered in fresh mud. He didn't exactly look like he was dressed to go clamming."

They gained on the man until he turned the corner into a narrow side street. Pitt threw the truck into a slide to follow, but then stood on the brakes and jerked the wheel to one side.

Filling the cobblestone lane, a half-dozen small boys were engaged in a game of soccer. The speeding truck ground into the stucco side of a corner building, stopping just short of the nearest boy. A few yards ahead, the gunman had already threaded his way past the boys. He glanced toward the damaged truck and ducked into a long brick building.

Giordino flung open his door and jumped to the ground. "Glad to see the team didn't lose a man. I'll see if I can cover the back door." Then he was gone, sprinting around the rear of the building.

With the driver's door wedged against the wall, Pitt slid across the bench seat and climbed out. The foolishness of chasing an armed man through town flashed through his mind. Maybe the assailant didn't know he was unarmed. Pitt glanced into the back of the truck, scooped up a hammer lying in the bed, and turned up the street.

The boys playing soccer stared at the tall stranger as he approached the building and paused beneath a hanging sign marked FÁBRICA DE VIDRIO. Pitt stepped to the entrance, eased aside the door handle, and then burst inside.

6

Pitt had lunged into a showroom lined with high wooden shelves, each overflowing with glass objects: vases, dishware, drinking glasses. The Fábrica de Vidrio was a factory that produced colorful tableware for local use and souvenirs for the tourist trade.

The showroom was empty, save for a young girl cowering behind a counter, staring at Pitt through frightened brown eyes.

"*¿El hombre?*" Pitt asked.

She pointed at an opening that led to the factory area. Pitt slipped around the corner and was instantly met by a gust of hot air. The back of the building was a high-roofed production bay, constructed around a mixing furnace, an open-air reheating pit, and a drying kiln. More shelves of glassware filled the sides, with stores of sand, soda ash, and limestone.

Two workmen sat on stools beside the open-air firepit, shaping balls of molten glass on the ends of blowpipes into small vases. They stood and shouted as the fleeing gunman sprinted past, kicking over a rack of animal figurines. The assailant ignored the workers and weaved his way to a heavy metal door at the rear.

Pitt entered the bay as the man reached the back door and twisted the handle. He got no farther. Giordino had just made it to the other side and rammed the door into him as it opened. The unexpected blow flung the gunman backward onto the concrete floor. Recovering quickly, he thrust the gun forward and fired two shots at Giordino while climbing to his feet. Both shots went high, but forced Giordino to duck behind the door. Pitt intervened before the man could fire again.

From across the bay, he wound up the claw hammer he'd taken from the truck and flung it. The tool spun through the air and struck the gunman's back shoulder. Dropping to one knee, the man gasped in pain, but only for a moment. Then he was up, backtracking across the bay.

Pitt was still on the move. Approaching one of the glassblowers, he plucked the blowpipe from the worker's hand and hurled it like a javelin at the gunman. The spear struck the assailant's outstretched arm, enveloping his hand in a glowing blob of molten glass. The man screamed as it torched his flesh. Shaking his arm, he flung the gun and most of the glass off his hand and onto the floor. Then he staggered toward the entrance, avoiding Pitt by skirting the far side of the reheating pit.

The second glassblower decided to follow Pitt's lead. He stood and with a strong arm flung his glasswork at the fleeing man. It struck him on the hip, but glanced off and fell to the ground.

Disoriented, the gunman wobbled into a storage rack of glass goblets, which showered onto him. He staggered to the side, tripped, and fell into the open firepit. Surprisingly, he didn't scream.

Pitt and the workmen rushed over and pulled him from the burning embers before his skin was charred. He didn't move a muscle as Pitt rolled him onto his back. His head and torso were covered in white ash.

"*Está muerto,*" one of the glassblowers whispered.

Pitt, too, saw that the man was dead.

"One of the glass goblets." Giordino approached and pointed to a gash in the dead man's neck.

Pitt saw it now, a short but deep gash below his ear that had been cauterized in the firepit. Beneath the ashes, a thick layer of dried blood streaked across his back.

"A shard struck him in the carotid artery," Pitt said. "He must have fallen into the pit unconscious and died before the fire got to him."

"*¡Un accidente!*" shouted the worker who'd pitched the blow. "*Un accidente.*"

"*Sí,*" Pitt said, "*un accidente.*"

Giordino scanned the dead man. "Who do you think he is?"

Pitt searched the man's pockets. "No wallet or identification, but plenty of cash." He produced a thick fold of U.S. dollars, used as currency in El Salvador. He threw it to the ground beside the body.

"All the markings of a professional," Giordino said.

"One who probably isn't working alone." Pitt gazed at Giordino with concern.

"You think someone else is still after Elise?"

Pitt nodded.

"Let's go."

Pitt told the workers to call the police, then sprinted out of the building with Giordino at his side, hoping that his gut instinct was wrong.

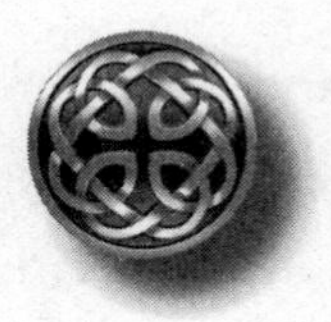

7

The black Jeep had kept its distance behind the ambulance, then stopped a block from the medical clinic at the edge of town. The driver, an athletically built woman with dark red hair and an angular face, watched as Elise was hurried into the building on a stretcher. She drove casually past the entrance, then continued toward the main road to San Salvador.

She circled back, drove to the rear of the building, and parked under a tree in view of the service entrance. Her partner had claimed he'd shot Elise before she disappeared into the cornfield. Maybe she'd die on her own, but it couldn't be left to chance.

It had been several minutes since the explosion at the lakefront, and she looked down the road for a sign of her partner. He was nowhere in sight. A small laundry truck approached the clinic and backed up to the service entrance. The driver hopped out, rang the buzzer, and an orderly propped open the door.

The woman smiled and reached for a small case. Inside was a makeup kit and a black wig. She applied a darkening cream to the naturally light skin of her face, neck, and hands. Then she pinned up her hair, slipped on the wig, and inserted a pair of brown contact lenses. Next, she slipped on the black ball cap she'd worn earlier and pulled the brim low. The final touch to distract from her natural features was a heavy pair of pink-framed eyeglasses.

She waited until the deliveryman entered the building with a load of clean laundry, then she ducked through the open door. The doorway opened into a cramped, dim stockroom. She stepped behind a tall shelf stacked with sheets and blankets. The deliveryman was retrieving bags of dirty laundry that lined the corridor. When he stepped outside with a load, she snatched a remaining bag and pulled it to her hiding spot.

She rifled through a twisted pile of patient gowns until she spotted a green doctor's smock. She ditched the ball cap and pulled on the smock, finding it close to her size. She rose with the bag as the deliveryman reentered.

"*Uno más.*" She handed it to him and turned on her heels.

Exiting the storeroom, she snatched a clipboard hanging on the wall and entered the hospital's main corridor.

The clinic was larger than she expected, with more than fifty beds. That would help protect her anonymity, but would make it harder to find the woman from the boat. She walked toward the entrance of the building, holding the clipboard to her nose whenever an employee appeared. Near the front desk, a pair of swinging doors plastered with red stripes marked the emergency room. She opened one of the doors and peered inside.

It was empty except for an orderly cleaning up a treatment table. Moving back down the main corridor, she found another door marked CUARTO DE RECUPERACIÓN. Entering the room, she encountered a leather-faced nurse.

"*¿Está de servicio?*" the nurse asked.

Unsure of her Spanish, the woman simply nodded, then scanned the recovery room. It held a half-dozen beds, each shielded by hanging drapes. Just two were occupied. The nearest held an old man surrounded by family members. At the far corner, behind a half-closed curtain, lay Elise.

The woman brushed past the nurse, strode to Elise's bedside, and pretended to study her medical monitors. The American aid worker's arm was heavily bandaged, and she appeared sedated.

The woman glanced over her shoulder. The duty nurse had taken a seat by the door and was typing on a computer. She pulled the curtains around Elise's bed, turned down the volume on a beeping heart monitor, and stepped to the head of the bed. Beneath her smock, she felt the grip of a handgun, but felt no need to use it. In Elise's unconscious state, she could be smothered quietly and without protest.

The woman reached for Elise's pillow, heard the curtains draw back. She wheeled to face two flushed and breathless men, one tall, the other short.

"Is she all right, Doctor?" Pitt asked.

The woman eyed Pitt's damp clothes, recognizing the duo from the boat. "*Sí.* Surgery was a success," she said in a gruff voice. "The young woman, she needs rest. *No molestar.*" She raised her clipboard and tried to shoo the men away.

But Giordino had already plopped into a chair beside the

bed. "We're not going anywhere until she's well enough to walk out of here."

Pitt nodded. "Her life may be in danger. Can you call for security protection?"

Time was short. She saw the determination in both men's faces and realized she couldn't coerce them away. She gave a frustrated glance at Elise and nodded.

"Yes, I will take care of it." She turned away quickly and strode out of the room.

"Something funny about her," Pitt said.

"What's that?"

"The page on the clipboard looked like a stockroom inventory sheet."

"Maybe somebody's been pilfering her supply of white stockings."

The two men were eyeing Elise's first stirrings when a bearded doctor entered a moment later with a nurse at his side.

"*¿Cómo está nuestro paciente?*" he asked.

"She's well, according to the other doctor," Giordino said.

"What other doctor?" the man asked in English.

Pitt described the woman, the doctor shrugged.

Pitt and Giordino looked at each other, then motioned toward Elise.

"Her life is in danger from an outside threat," Pitt said. "Please call security and post a guard with her."

He bolted for the door with Giordino right behind. Pitt motioned toward the clinic entrance. "You try the front, I'll check the back."

He sprinted down the corridor, peering into each side room

for the woman in the green smock. He reached the storeroom at the back of the clinic, ducked inside, and saw an open door to the parking lot. Outside, a car's engine revved.

He stepped into a cloud of dust as the black Jeep roared out of the lot.

Giordino ran up to him a minute later. "Got away?" he asked between heavy breaths.

Pitt motioned down the road. "A black Jeep."

"I think I saw it by the waterfront."

"Guess she decided to leave her bomb-throwing friend behind," Pitt said.

"They were certainly serious about putting Elise and the aid team out of business. I wonder why?"

"Maybe the water specimens. Did they survive the glassworks ordeal?"

Giordino smiled. "You dare doubt Al the Magnificent?"

He pulled open his windbreaker, revealing the four test tubes Elise had given him, intact in his shirt pocket.

Pitt grinned. "Better than pulling a rabbit out of a hat."

They waited at the hospital another hour until a NUMA helicopter arrived, summoned by Pitt from a research vessel working off the coast. A now conscious Elise was whisked aboard for a short ride to Comalapa International Airport near San Salvador, then onto a U.S. military transport bound for the States.

Pitt and Giordino remained there to brief police and embassy officials before they hopped their own commercial flight to Washington the next morning, leaving behind the unanswered mystery of who destroyed Cerrón Grande Dam—and why.

8

The city lights of Detroit glistened off the black river like crystalline stars in the night. Bounding waterfront skyscrapers of illuminated glass and steel showed a vibrant defiance to the recent economic struggles of the old industrial city. Captain Ron Posey glanced from Detroit's shining aura off the starboard bow of his ship to a similar, smaller radiance off the vessel's port side. In the midnight hour, Windsor, Canada, countered with an equally warm glow of buildings and homes. Posey rubbed his eyes and refocused on the black ribbon of water between the cities that funneled into the narrows of the Detroit River.

"Sir, why don't you get some shut-eye?" said his second officer, a cheerful young man named Gauge. "Traffic looks light on the radar."

Posey had stood on the bridge for the better part of the past two days, ever since the *Mayweather* departed Thunder Bay on

Lake Superior's west coast. The 12,000-ton tanker was laden with Alberta tar sands crude oil, bound for a refinery in Quebec.

Posey hated to give up command, yet he knew he wasn't superhuman. He'd been officially relieved by the second officer hours ago, but continued to pace the bridge. He stopped and gazed out the window. "I'll turn in once we kiss the waters of Lake Erie."

The entrance to Lake Erie was just twenty-five miles away. The remaining path wound through the narrow confines of the Detroit River. The waterway often bustled with traffic, even at this hour. Posey knew there'd be no sleep for him until the tanker reached the safe expanse of the lake.

The second officer ordered the helm to reduce speed as the ship approached Grosse Pointe. The tanker eased closer to the Michigan shore as it approached Peche Island and the onset of the Detroit River. Near the turn of the last century, this short stretch of water had been the world's busiest commercial riverway. Times and industry had changed dramatically, but the river still held economic prominence for the upper Great Lakes.

A flashing light dead ahead signaled the approach of Windmill Point. Beyond it, the river split in two around Belle Isle, a picturesque state park. With the main shipping channel along the island's eastern border, the helmsman prepared to ease the tanker to port.

"You've got a large vessel incoming," Posey said.

Gauge followed Posey's gaze to the radarscope, which showed a white linear shape moving off the center of Belle Isle. A notation on the screen indicated the vessel as the MV *Duluth*, traveling north at ten knots. The second officer looked out the bridge window, saw only a dark shadow.

Captain Posey had already reached for a pair of binoculars and was scanning the route ahead. "The fool has his running lights turned off and is steaming up the west side of Fleming."

Fleming Channel was the dredged passage east of Belle Isle designated for commercial traffic.

Gauge reached for the radio and hailed the *Duluth*. There was no reply.

"Looks to be a bulk freighter, nice-sized one at that." Posey lowered the binoculars and shifted his gaze to an overhead monitor that displayed a digital chart of the river. A moving white rectangle represented the *Mayweather* as it approached the northern tip of Belle Isle. The *Duluth* appeared as a yellow triangle approaching at an angle from Fleming Channel.

On the current course of both vessels, the *Mayweather* would be boxed out of entering the channel, unless it made a dangerous pass across the freighter's bow to the east.

Gauge read the captain's thoughts. "Looks like we should either hold position until they pass or duck into the western channel."

Posey nodded, his anger at the other vessel receding into concern for his own ship's safety. "Let's steer clear of the idiot. All slow and easy toward the west channel until he passes."

Gauge relayed the order to the helmsman, and the tanker's bow nudged right, toward the lights of Detroit.

Posey shook his head as the black outline of the freighter drew closer, holding its aggressive course. Due to the nature of the waterway, the *Duluth* was heading directly for the *Mayweather*.

A mountain of white water was breaking off the other ship's bow, and Posey asked Gauge her speed.

"She's up to fourteen knots," he said with tension in his voice.

The two ships were now nearly perpendicular. The freighter, closing fast, cleared the tip of Belle Isle and should have begun a turn to starboard. But it didn't.

"Sir, she's turning into us!"

There was no hiding the fear in Gauge's voice. Radar showed the freighter was veering sharply to port and meant to strike the tanker.

"Hard right rudder!" Posey shouted. "Engine full astern."

The helmsman yanked the rudder control hard over. There was no time for the tanker to respond. The freighter bore down on the 300-foot ship, its bow aimed square for the tanker's midsection.

Seconds from impact, a sharp crack sounded from the *Duluth*, and the freighter's pilothouse erupted in a fireball. Posey could only stare in wonder at the spectacle before bracing for collision.

The freighter struck amidships a moment later, driving halfway across the tanker's deck before losing momentum. On the *Mayweather*'s stern bridge, the crewmen felt only a slight jar, but they heard the wicked screech of steel slicing through steel. Only a few yards away, they saw and smelled the smoldering remains of the *Duluth*'s bridge.

As alarm bells sounded, Posey ordered his second officer to assemble the crew. The *Mayweather* had been dealt a mortal blow, nearly cut in two. The captain already felt a severe list to port as he stepped onto the bridge wing to observe the damage.

The *Duluth* had somehow broken free and was churning

upriver toward Grosse Pointe. A speedboat appeared and pulled alongside the freighter. Posey barely made out a rope ladder dangling from the freighter's railing, with a long-haired figure climbing down it to the water. The speedboat plucked the person from the ladder, then turned and roared away. Like the freighter, it motored into the darkness with no running lights.

Posey turned to the remains of the *Mayweather*, which was losing its fight with the river. Miraculously, no one on his own ship was injured. The tanker's small crew assembled behind the base of the bridge and climbed into an enclosed lifeboat. Posey was the last to enter, closing the hatch, then jettisoning the boat off an escape ramp.

The lifeboat struck the water and motored a short distance away as the *Mayweather* rolled heavily to her side. Posey looked at the scene and held his head in his hands. Thousands of gallons of gooey crude oil were now leaking into the Detroit River from the ship's ruptured tanks—potentially the ugliest environmental marine disaster in years.

His concentration was broken by a muffled thud that echoed over the water. A few hundred yards upstream, the *Duluth* had carved through a small marina filled with pleasure boats, then run aground at Windmill Point Park.

Posey stared at the rogue freighter with a mix of dread and fury. What could explain its actions? The only reply came not from the freighter, but from his own wounded ship. With a gurgling protest from its flooded holds, the *Mayweather* somehow regained its upright position, then promptly sank to the river's bottom.

9

The jetliner touched down on the east runway of Washington Dulles International Airport, jarring Pitt awake. He and Giordino shook off the effects of the early-morning flight from San Salvador, collected their bags, and drove to the NUMA headquarters building on the banks of the Potomac River. In the foyer of Pitt's ninth-floor office, they were welcomed by Rudi Gunn.

Pitt's Deputy Director, Gunn was a slight, wiry man who wore horn-rimmed glasses and tight-cropped hair. Bearing the erect posture of his days as a Navy commander, he brought a cerebral bearing and wit to the task at hand. He eyed the duffel bags the men had dropped in a corner of Pitt's office and shook his head. "I'm not seeing our prototype multibeam sonar system that you departed with."

"We left it in El Salvador," Giordino said, "in about a thousand pieces."

"It's bad enough you desecrate the landscape of a friendly nation, but did you have to destroy our latest survey equipment in the process?"

"None of it was our doing, Rudi." Pitt plopped into his desk chair.

"There is some good news for the accounting department, though," Giordino said. "The guy who blew up our chartered boat did so after we returned the keys, or we'd be on the hook for that, too."

"The State Department has indicated the Salvadoran government is requesting assistance from the FBI to investigate the matter," Gunn said. "They believe the Cerrón Grande Dam was blown up intentionally, in conjunction with the murder of the U.S. agricultural team."

"That much we figured," Pitt said. "The question is why."

"The local authorities are operating under the assumption a drug gang is responsible. The aid team may have camped in a drug transit zone, or one of their local support personnel may have been connected to a rival gang. But I'm not sure how that plays into blowing up the dam."

"For what it's worth," Giordino said, "our mad bomber friend and wannabe glassblower didn't look like a local."

"And," Pitt said, "the phony doctor at the clinic was a sophisticated play."

"I'm told the Salvadorans have been unable to identify either one," Gunn said. "The black Jeep was found semisubmerged in a river near San Salvador. It had been stolen a few days earlier from an airport car rental lot."

"Again, that sounds a bit more professional than a local drug gang," Pitt said. "Have you heard how Elise Aguilar, the agriculture scientist, is doing?"

"After you had her airlifted to San Salvador, I pulled some strings to get her on a military flight to Andrews Air Force Base. She's an Army vet, so that made things easier. She arrived last night and was checked into Walter Reed. At last report, she's doing fine. I had a message from the hospital staff saying that she asked about some water samples."

Giordino motioned toward one of his bags. "From the reservoir. Might be a clue as to why somebody wanted the team murdered."

Gunn pulled a slip from his pocket and handed it to Giordino. "If you have them, they are to be sent for analysis to a Dr. Stephen Nakamura at the University of Maryland's epidemiology department."

"I'll send them by courier after we're done here. I presume we have bigger fish to fry."

Gunn nodded. "You got my message and have probably seen the news reports. The situation in Detroit is not pretty. We've got a major environmental disaster on our hands."

"Isn't that the EPA's problem?" Giordino asked.

"The President wants NUMA to oversee the sequestration and salvage of the sunken tanker. It's well beyond the capabilities of the local authorities or the EPA. I've got an advance team en route and have scheduled a flight for the three of us first thing in the morning."

"Al and I will be on that plane. You best stay and deal with the media and political blowback. I'd prefer you tame the lions here rather than have the entire circus descend on us in Detroit."

"Can do," Gunn replied.

"How bad is the spill?" Giordino asked.

"Initial reports suggest the tanker may be leaking several thousand gallons of oil per hour."

"What's the local impact?"

"The Detroit metro area draws its drinking water from the river. The city's had to shut down their water draws and are scrambling for alternate sources. The taps may soon run dry. The President naturally fears the political tempest if that happens."

"We can address the salvage, but what about the cleanup?"

"The EPA is on-site. The problem is, tar sands crude oil is mixed with clay, sand, and various other hydrocarbons. It's more difficult to deal with than medium or light crude, as it's heavier than water. If it mixes with the river bottom, that sediment will have to be dredged. But at this point, they just seem focused on trying to siphon off the contaminated surface water."

Giordino slowly shook his head. "Good luck with that."

"I just fielded a call from the head of BioRem Global Limited, inquiring about cleanup efforts." Gunn paused to see if Pitt or Giordino had heard of the company.

"I know of BioRem Global," Pitt said. "They're a biotech firm that produces bacterial organisms for use in cleaning up industrial spills. The process is called bioremediation, hence the company name. They're one of the sponsors of the Ocean Preservation Society," he said, gazing at his desk calendar, "which happens to be hosting a fund-raiser in town tonight."

"They have a reputable track record dealing with oil cleanups in the North Sea," Gunn said. "The company was called in late on the Deepwater spill in the Gulf a few years ago. I'm told their product was found to be quite effective at consuming the oil where it was applied. The owner said they had a product suitable for attacking the tar sands oil—and they could deploy it rapidly. But they don't yet have federal approval to field-test the product in U.S. waters."

"Yes, as the Deepwater spill was located outside of territorial waters," Pitt recalled.

"I've got one of our scientists investigating a test sample that was sent over."

"The stuff could prove critical in limiting environmental damage in a confined location like the Detroit River," Giordino noted.

"Agreed," Pitt replied. "Who's the head of the company, Rudi? Maybe it'll be worth a swing by the gala tonight to talk with him about getting their product on-site."

"Not him," Gunn said, "her. Evanna McKee is her name. She mentioned that she was in Washington, so she must be here for the event."

"I'll see what can be done. In the meantime, we have a major salvage operation on our hands."

"How big a tanker are we talking about?" Giordino asked.

"The *Mayweather* is just under three hundred feet, a typical Great Lakes tanker."

"We'd better scour every available salvage resource in the area," Pitt said, "and get them to Detroit as soon as possible."

"I'm already on it," Gunn said.

A pert woman with long fawn-colored hair entered the office, balancing a thick stack of mail. "Welcome back to the fray, boss," Zerri Pochinski, Pitt's longtime secretary, said with a warm smile.

"Thanks. But I'm beginning to think I should have stayed in Central America."

"And leave all the fun to Rudi? By the way, I was reviewing your calendar and see that you have a staff meeting scheduled for three o'clock and an R and D strategy review at four. Shall I reschedule those, in light of the Detroit incident?"

"Yes, they'll have to wait. And can you leave a message with Loren's office and ask if she can accompany me to the Ocean Preservation gala tonight?"

"Certainly. You sure you're up for adding a Washington fund-raiser to your plate?"

Pitt shook his head in mock distress. "Not really. I don't know which will be worse—attending a charity event filled with venomous politicians or cleaning up a toxic oil spill."

"They both entail hazardous duty, but I think you ultimately were correct." She turned with a swivel of her hips to exit the office. "You'd have been better off staying in Central America."

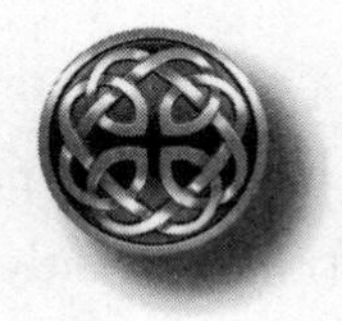

10

After coordinating initial plans for the *Mayweather* salvage operation, Pitt borrowed an agency Jeep and drove to Reagan National Airport. He parked next to an abandoned-looking hangar at the edge of the airfield, disabled an alarm, and entered the building.

Its dilapidated exterior stood in sharp contrast to what met Pitt's eye inside. He flicked on the interior lights and faced a bright, open floor crowded with a gleaming display of transportation from yesteryear. A beautifully restored Pullman railroad car stood on tracks at one side of the building, while a polished aluminum Ford Tri-Motor airplane poked its nose out of a corner. A rare jet-powered Messerschmitt Me 262 sat next to a bathtub rigged with an outboard motor, all mementos of past exploits. But most of the floor space was filled with Pitt's collection of classic automobiles from the first half of the twentieth century.

Pitt lugged his bags past the marvels of steel and chrome, then lingered a moment by a freshly painted chassis and a stack of primed body parts. Pitt had recently acquired the components of a 1925 Isotta-Fraschini in Bulgaria, and he silently lamented not having more time to restore the classic Italian auto.

He climbed a spiral staircase to an upper apartment, showered and dressed, and returned to the ground floor. He eyed several vehicles near the door, then plucked a set of keys off a workbench and approached a rakish cream and lime green roadster.

He slipped behind its broad steering wheel and cranked the starter a few times until the engine fired to life. A 1931 Stutz DV-32 Speedster, it had a custom-built body by the coachbuilder Weymann, featuring swoopy low-cut doors and a tapered boat-tail rear end.

Pitt drove the car outside, locked the building, and raced off across the airport grounds. The Stutz was powered by a 156-horsepower straight-eight engine with dual overhead camshafts and four valves per cylinder, giving the light-bodied car plenty of juice down the road. Pitt easily melded into traffic on the George Washington Parkway and soon crossed the Arlington Memorial Bridge into Washington, D.C. Passing some gawking tourists on the Washington Mall, he motored up to Capitol Hill and pulled to a stop in front of the Rayburn House Office Building.

A security guard eyed the idling car and signaled Pitt to move but was waved aside by an attractive woman who had stepped from the building. “It’s quite all right, Oscar. That’s my ride tonight.”

“Yes, Congresswoman.” The guard tipped his hat. “Nice car, whatever it is.”

With her high cheekbones, violet eyes, and lean figure

swathed in a form-fitting Prada dress, Loren Smith-Pitt could still pass for a *Vogue* model rather than the veteran representative from Colorado.

She rushed to the car, where Pitt gave her a hug and a kiss. "I missed you," she whispered in his ear.

Though not married long, they had a lengthy romantic history. Juggling the demands of their careers was a challenge, but they always carved out time for each other, and their passion still burned brightly.

She smiled at Pitt as he slipped behind the wheel. "I should have known you'd arrive in something that would devour my hair."

"We don't have far to go. Besides, you look sexy windblown."

He eased the Stutz into gear and roared away from the curb. Just a few blocks down the Mall, Pitt turned into a reserved parking lot for the Smithsonian National Museum of Natural History. Arm in arm, they walked toward the building, where a large gala was under way in the lobby.

"Any news of the killers in El Salvador?" she asked.

"Local authorities believe it was a random incident related to turf wars among local drug gangs." He neglected to voice his own skepticism.

Loren shook her head. "The Foreign Affairs Committee is up in arms over an attack on U.S. aid workers and is looking for answers."

"I'd be happy to discover a few myself. What else is happening in your bastion of democracy?"

"Our Environment Subcommittee hearing was hijacked by last night's Detroit incident."

"I'm heading there in the morning. We got called in by the President."

"Smartest thing he's done in weeks. The staff at EPA doesn't know how to do anything but sue people." She snuggled close to him. "Though I'll be sad to see you leave so soon."

They entered the museum's south rotunda, where a throng of politicians and power brokers stood swilling cocktails amid a low din of conversation. Pitt couldn't help but notice that many of the attendees resembled the stuffed and wrinkled bull elephant mounted in the lobby. "Some shindig," Pitt said as he steered them to a bar at the side, where an ice carving of a whale encircled a large punch bowl.

"Funded by donors, I'm sure. The Ocean Preservation Society is one of the few nonprofits that actually seem to do some good, in an area you can appreciate. I have it on good authority that none of their managers even draws a salary from the organization."

"Bully for them," Pitt said.

His wife was recognized by a slew of lobbyists and quickly surrounded. Pitt grinned at Loren as she tried to fend off the attacks, then he slipped over to the bar and ordered a Don Julio Blanco tequila on the rocks. He was sampling some smoked salmon when she joined him a few minutes later.

"Thanks for abandoning me to the sharks," she said as he passed her a glass of champagne.

"These are your waters to navigate," he said with a smile. "How did you lose them so quickly?"

"I said if they didn't let me go get a drink, I'd be proposing new legislation banning all lobbyists from the District of

Columbia. That, and I pointed out the arrival of the House Minority Leader. They scattered like flies."

"I thought they'd know by now that beneath your seductive exterior lies a pillar of virtuosity."

"Doesn't stop them from trying."

Pitt noticed a heavyset man with combed-over silver hair weaving through the crowd. He wore an insincere grin, and his eyes constantly darted around the room.

"Don't look now," Pitt said, "but a great white shark is headed your way."

Loren turned and extended her hand. "Senator Bradshaw, how nice to see you again."

Senator Stanton Bradshaw, chairman of the Senate Committee on Environment and Public Works and a well-known backroom dealmaker, shook Loren's hand with his plump mitt.

"How are you, Congresswoman? You look stunning tonight."

"Very well, thank you. I think you know my husband, Dirk?"

"Yes, of course." He swung his hand toward Pitt while keeping his eyes locked on Loren.

Pitt shook it, leaving behind a remnant of smoked salmon.

The senator now looked at Pitt and smiled. "Didn't you have something to do with preventing that terrorist incident in Baltimore last year?"

"I had a small role."

"Then we all owe you a debt of gratitude." He wiped his hand on his leg and promptly turned his back on Pitt.

"You know, my dear," he said to Loren, "the Senate just passed the bio cleanup bill, which your House committee is about to take up. I trust we'll have your full support in the measure." He grinned, exposing a mouthful of whitened teeth that reminded Pitt even more of a shark.

"I haven't studied the bill's content yet, so I'll have to reserve judgment for the time being."

"Its passage would be an important victory for our party." He turned and nodded at Pitt. "I'm sure your husband can appreciate winning one for the team."

"Actually, Senator," Pitt said, "if the team in question is one of our major political parties, I'd rather take a rusty knife to the spleen."

Loren choked on her champagne, stifling a laugh, before glaring at Pitt. "Well . . . I promise to give the bill a fair review," she said to the senator.

Bradshaw turned red for an instant, then resumed his polished ways. "Of course you will."

"Senator, do you happen to know Evanna McKee, the CEO of BioRem Global?" Pitt asked. "I believe she's a patron of the Society."

"Of course. She's a dear friend, and the sponsor of tonight's event." He scanned the room, spotting a figure in a flowing white gown near the back wall. Bradshaw grabbed Loren's arm. "Come along, I'll introduce the two of you."

Pitt grabbed a refill of tequila and joined Loren, following the senator to an attractive older woman standing by herself. She was lean and fair-skinned, and she enhanced her elegant dress with a scarab pendant dangling from a gold necklace. Platinum hair outlined an expressionless face marred by just the first hint of a wrinkle or two. Her ice-blue eyes seemed to absorb everything around her. To Pitt, they displayed both coolness and mistrust.

"Evanna McKee, may I present Congresswoman Loren Smith and her husband, Dirk Pitt, the head of NUMA," Bradshaw said. "Evanna is the generous sponsor of tonight's gala."

"A pleasure, Ms. McKee." Loren reached over and shook hands. "Thank you for your support of the foundation. These days too few people seem concerned about the health of the oceans."

"I'm happy to help," McKee said with a faint Scottish accent. "Truth be told, the cause is an important part of our business."

"Evanna is the head of BioRem Global," Bradshaw said. "They're doing some remarkable things in the fight against ocean pollution."

McKee's lips tightened as she shook hands with Pitt. "Did the senator say you were the head of NUMA?"

He nodded. "When I'm not looking after wayward members of Congress."

"I just spoke with one of your managers, Rudi Gunn, about the tragedy in Detroit."

"Yes, I was hoping to speak with you tonight. Rudi said your firm has a product that may assist in the cleanup."

"Our company develops microorganisms for pollution control. We have a proprietary bacteria that feeds on hydrocarbons, such as those the *Mayweather* was carrying. I'm afraid it has not yet been approved for use in the United States, but we've had excellent results in Europe and Asia."

"Since the Detroit spill occurred in a heavily populated area, quick abatement of the spill will be critical," Pitt said.

"Our BioRem product is both safe and effective, and we are ready to help. But time is of the essence."

"Is there anything I can do to help greenlight its approval?" Pitt asked.

"The senator has been assisting us in accelerating the process."

"The bureaucratic cogs move slowly at the EPA, but we're making progress," Bradshaw said. "I'm sure with the crisis in Detroit, we can get things streamlined. In fact, I'm planning on placing a temporary waiver on the EPA director's desk first thing in the morning."

McKee looked at Pitt. "Perhaps a word of support from NUMA wouldn't hurt."

"I'd be glad to help," Pitt said.

"Completely unnecessary, my dear," Bradshaw said to McKee. "I'm quite certain you'll have approval tomorrow."

"I've already arranged to have a vessel reach Detroit by morning with a stockpile of dispersant. If approval is granted," McKee said, "who should we contact to arrange delivery and deployment?"

"You're looking at him," Pitt said. "I'll be in Detroit tomorrow taking over the salvage operation. Your field staff can coordinate with me, if the senator delivers, and then we'll see what we can do to help the people of Detroit."

"Excellent. I'll notify my field manager in the morning. It's wonderful we had this chance to meet."

"I agree."

"Ms. McKee, I believe I owe you an apology," Loren said. "Aren't you the director of the Women's Governance League?"

"Why, yes. It's something of a pet project. We support women in leadership roles in all walks of life and provide an excellent networking system. I'd take it as an honor if you would consider joining our organization. Your achievements in Congress are an inspiration to women all over the world."

"I just realized you had invited me to speak at one of your gatherings in Paris last year, but I was away in Bulgaria at the time. I'm afraid I didn't make the connection."

"We're always looking for accomplished women to provide support to our younger members. In fact, we're holding our annual meeting in Scotland in two weeks. I would be delighted if you could attend. I can even arrange air transport. You can come, too, Mr. Pitt. There's marvelous fishing in the Scottish Highlands to occupy yourself with while we keep your wife busy."

"I may still be fishing for that tanker in Detroit, but thank you all the same."

An imposing black woman in a gray suit appeared at McKee's side and whispered in her ear.

"I'm sorry, but I must excuse myself to take an international call. It was lovely to meet you both." She turned to Loren. "I'll look forward to seeing you in Scotland."

Pitt watched as she strode away with practiced elegance to a private office in the museum.

"Lovely woman," Loren said.

"Yes, and quite persuasive," the senator said. "You'd be wise to join her group. She's *very* influential."

"I may just do that."

Loren and Pitt excused themselves from the senator as the chairman of the foundation took to a stage to introduce a short movie. It showed dramatic footage of polluted seas and ailing marine life, followed by news of research taking place to preserve the oceans. As the credits rolled, Pitt noticed it had been produced by BioRem Global.

They mingled with a few of the charities' board members before Pitt steered his wife toward the exit.

"There now, that wasn't too painful, was it?" Loren gripped Pitt's hand as they walked to the parking lot.

"Life did improve, once we lost the senator. It does seem a worthy foundation. And well-supported, it would appear, by your new Scottish friend."

"One of the board members said her company had made a substantial donation to the foundation and looks to be a partner going forward. It's obviously good publicity, but I'm sure gaining entry into the U.S. market has a lot to do with it."

"What do you know of this McKee woman?"

"Just that she inherited the company from her late husband, supposedly a brilliant microbiologist. I'm more familiar with her influence on women's rights. She's active in global legislation to protect women from violence and injustice, and in promoting women to positions of political leadership. But I don't know much about the Women's Governance League. I've heard rumors it's some sort of female trilateral commission, filled with women of power, and all very hush-hush."

"I guess this means if you join, you won't be sharing the secret handshake with me."

Loren laughed. "Of course not." She squeezed his hand. "You're not one to be trusted."

"I should have known . . . So, are you in for the Scotland trip?"

"The House goes on recess in a week. If you're still tied up in

Detroit, I think I will go. And if you're done in Detroit . . . Well, the fishing *is* supposed to be marvelous."

They reached the Stutz and drove out of the lot, turning west onto Constitution Avenue. It was an unusually warm May evening, and the scent of lingering cherry blossoms filled the air as they circled past the Lincoln Memorial. At that late hour, Pitt raced the car across the Arlington Bridge through minimal traffic. Finally free of the day's obligations, Loren smiled as the wind blew through her hair.

"Nice evening," Pitt said. "Care to go for an extended drive?"

"You're leaving tomorrow. I'd rather spend the time at home in other activities." She snuggled close to him on the bench seat.

Pitt gave a faint nod and steered toward the hangar while gently pressing the accelerator to the floor.

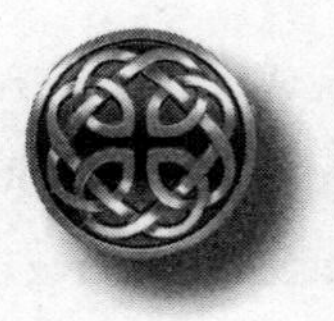

11

The square white blockhouse of the *Mayweather* stood out from the surface of the river like a cheap roadside hotel. Pitt eyed a swirl of waves breaking on the back of the structure as the waters of the Detroit River barreled into it. While the hull of the ship was hidden underwater, the shallow river hadn't been deep enough to swallow the ship's tall bridge housing.

"I guess we won't have to worry about any decompression dive stops," Giordino said. He was steering a small runabout they had picked up at Detroit's Harbor Hill Marina. Guiding the boat around the tanker's sunken stern, he headed for a large work barge moored in the river to the east.

"The charts show maximum depth is only thirty feet in this section of the river," Pitt said. "Aside from the current, life doesn't look so bad."

"Except for the Capitol Hill firing squads that will have us in their sights if we don't get it cleaned up quick."

"Since when are you worried about political fallout?"

"Since I looked at my pension fund and realized I need to work another twenty years before I can retire comfortably in Bora Bora."

Giordino pulled alongside the barge, which lay within spitting distance of an empty tanker moored upriver. A bearded, bear-sized man in a NUMA ball cap tied off the boat's lines and helped them up onto the barge.

"Welcome to Camp Maui," Michael Cruz said. A marine engineer and salvage expert with NUMA, Cruz had led the advance team.

"Camp Maui?" Giordino asked.

"Our little island paradise sandwiched between two big, ugly wrecks."

Giordino eyed the barge's weathered housing structure and grease-stained decks. "Not exactly my idea of paradise."

"Best we could do on short notice," Cruz said with a laugh. The husky engineer wore a constant grin beneath his thick beard, and his eyes crinkled with mirth. "Come, let me take you on the Grand Tour."

Cruz showed them to their cabins, then reconvened in the makeshift conference room. Underwater photos of the damaged tanker lined the walls, along with a large, hand-drawn rendition of the vessel. Cruz pointed to a nautical chart of the Detroit River on the table that was marked with the two wrecks.

"The *Mayweather*, carrying a full load of tar sands oil from

Thunder Bay, was approaching Belle Isle just after midnight. The *Duluth*, a ninety-meter dry cargo freighter, was running upriver at speed and veered across sharply, striking the tanker amidships. The *Mayweather* sank quickly, while the *Duluth* somehow broke free and continued upriver before running aground at Grosse Pointe."

"We took a spin by her before arriving here," Pitt said. "Looks like some tugs are ready to pull her off."

"That's right. She's headed for a city dock downriver off Grosse Isle, where she's to be impounded by the FBI."

"Why's the FBI involved?" Giordino asked. "The news accounts I saw called it an accident."

Cruz shook his head. "It was no accident. The *Duluth*'s captain and several crewmen were killed in an explosion on the bridge just seconds before impact."

"We noticed the charred exterior," Pitt said.

"Morgue and forensics people were there all night, removing the crew's remains. Reporters haven't picked up on it yet. The authorities are trying to keep a lid on it while the investigation gets under way."

"If it was a terrorist act," Pitt said, "it was more effective than most. Any suspects?"

"Not that I've heard, but I'm out of that loop. Got enough to contend with here."

"Tell us what we're facing with the *Mayweather*."

"The ship's still in one piece—just barely. The *Duluth* cut across her at a sixty-degree angle, opening her up like a sliced melon."

"Leaking heavily?"

Cruz nodded. "It's less evident on the surface. ROV cameras showed heavy plumes at the lower depths."

Pitt motioned upriver. "The empty tanker. Is she ready to evacuate the undamaged storage compartments?"

"Yes. We got lucky there. She happened to be crossing Lake Huron with bone-dry tanks. The *Mayweather*'s owners chartered her for a pretty penny. They hope to recover the bulk of the cargo."

"A few empty storage compartments will make things easier for our recovery." Pitt turned to Giordino. "Time we take a look downstairs?"

"I thought you'd never ask."

Cruz led them to a dive shack, where all three donned hazmat dry suits and collected scuba equipment. The men assembled on a dive platform off one end of the barge and put on their gear. As they prepared to enter the water, a crewman handed each a motorized underwater scooter.

"I was hoping we wouldn't have to thumb a ride back to the barge," Giordino said.

"You'd end up in Lake Erie without it," Cruz said with a grin.

Pitt adjusted a headlamp above his face mask and turned it on. "Let's start down current at the bow and work our way upriver." He bit into his regulator mouthpiece and stepped off the edge of the platform.

The May waters of the Detroit River were brisk, and Pitt shivered until the air pockets in his dry suit warmed from his body heat. While lacking the purity of an Arctic glacier, the river was clearer than Pitt had expected, offering almost twenty feet of visibility.

He flicked the scooter's throttle to low and tilted it forward, letting it pull him down until the river bottom appeared. With a visual frame of reference, he could see the strength of the three-knot current.

He waited until spotting the approaching headlights of Cruz and Giordino, then proceeded across the river bottom to where the towering mass of the tanker appeared. The black-colored hull had settled evenly, the white-painted Plimsoll line missing the mark by several meters. Pitt drifted with the current, sliding past the bow plates, until he reached the bulbous nose of the prow.

With Giordino and Cruz at his heels, he turned upriver to where the *Duluth* had struck the tanker. Pitt swam along the angled interior, peering at the sides of the corrugated storage tanks that had been sheared open. The water grew darker as black streams of oil swirled from multiple fissures in the bulkheads. Pitt ascended to the main deck, where he could see the freighter had come within ten feet of splitting the ship in two.

Pitt throttled the scooter and took a full spin around the sunken vessel before surfacing and motoring to the barge. As he swam up to the platform, a pair of soft, feminine hands reached down and took the scooter so he could climb aboard.

Pitt climbed onto the platform to face a red-haired woman in a tight-fitting jumpsuit. She stood with a confident bearing, and wore a petulant look. "Are you boys done with your swim so I can attack this oil spill?" she asked.

Pitt pulled off his mask and grinned at her forwardness. As

she looked into his eyes, she fumbled and dropped the scooter to the deck. Pitt stripped off his dive tank and weight belt as she retrieved the scooter, then he stood and shook her hand.

"Yes, we've completed our survey. And thanks for the assist. I'm Dirk Pitt."

"Audrey McKee, field manager with BioRem Global. The barge supervisor told me you were inspecting the *Mayweather*."

"McKee? You must be the daughter of Evanna McKee. I just met your mother last night."

Audrey squinted at him. "She's in Washington," she replied. "We just flew in this morning."

Giordino and Cruz surfaced and climbed aboard, and Pitt made the introductions.

"I hope you brought a big bag of hungry bacteria with you," Giordino said.

Audrey pointed to a small freighter moored on the Canadian shoreline. Two large stainless steel tanks were visible on the forward deck.

"We are fully stocked with a supply of bioremediation agent designed for tar sands oil, which we're ready to deploy."

"Live bacteria?" Cruz asked.

"Several proprietary varieties of microorganisms, actually, that feed on hydrocarbon molecules."

"Aren't they dangerous to marine life?"

"Not at all," she said. "They are completely safe to marine animals—and the environment. Sort of like the good bacteria that live in your stomach."

"Any word," Pitt said, "on its approval for use in U.S. waters?"

"A special waiver was signed by the EPA this morning. We now have authorization to operate in the Detroit River."

"That's good news," Giordino said. "How do you plan on deploying the stuff?"

"We'll run hoses to the ruptured parts of the ship and slowly disperse the agent with fresh water. The microbes will attach to the oil and break down, then, ultimately, metabolize the pollutants. Unfortunately, the current will make it impossible to fully contain the contaminants. But if we can pinpoint the spillage areas, we can effectively treat a high percentage of the oil."

"We have a pretty good idea where those are." Pitt turned to Cruz. "Mike, how soon can we get the evacuation tanker online?"

"We can begin sucking out the undamaged storage areas this afternoon, starting with the stern section. Probably take two days to get everything evacuated. I've got my team split into three units so we can run around the clock."

Pitt turned to Audrey. "Looks like we may not need your hungry bugs for very long."

"I don't like seeing the river polluted with oil any more than you do." She pointed toward the *Mayweather*'s submerged bow. "We'll set up just downstream and begin running dispersal lines to the damaged areas right away."

"I think we have the makings of a plan," Pitt said.

"I can communicate with you here on the barge?" Audrey asked.

"Al and I won't be aboard much, so you best coordinate with Mike."

Cruz gave him a quizzical look. “You’re not managing operations from our luxurious river barge?”

Pitt gazed at the *Mayweather*’s exposed blockhouse.

“Nope,” he said, with a shake of the head. “Al and I will be spending our time in the river, cutting that big, ugly beast in half.”

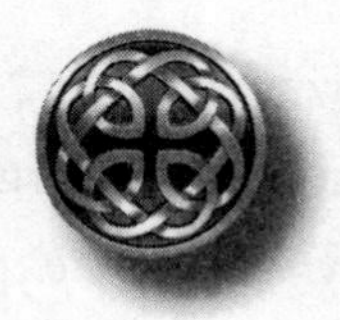

12

The underwater cutting torch burned with the brightness of the midday sun. Steadying himself against the hull with a large suction device, Pitt guided the torch across the *Mayweather*'s half-inch-thick outer steel hull. Thirty feet away, but on the ship's interior side, Giordino was duplicating the cut, slicing through a slimmer inner hull. Working off a surface-supplied air source, the men had worked nearly two days straight to dissect the sunken tanker.

With his knees resting on the river bottom, Pitt sliced down to the sediment, reaching the horizontal cut from the other side. Through his faceplate, he called to a control team member on the barge to cut the torch's oxygen supply and electric power. The fire at the tip was extinguished, and Pitt raised the eye shield from his faceplate.

Satisfied with his work, he coiled the exothermic torch, swam up the outer hull, and set the device on the deck. Then he dove down the opposite side, dropping into the open interior. As he approached Giordino from the side, his partner cut a final opening through the inner hull.

As his torch was shut off, he looked at Pitt and nodded. "I do believe that makes two pieces," he warbled through their underwater communications system. "If you want three, I'll need a new set of arms."

"I'm not sure there's enough cutting rods left in Michigan to burn any more," Pitt said. "Let's go have a beer."

They ascended to the surface, where their support crew pulled them by the powered cables back up to the barge.

Cruz greeted them as they climbed onto the deck and removed their dive helmets. "Well, it's the mad butchers. How goes the cutting?"

"Like a sliced loaf of sourdough," Giordino said.

"You're through?"

Pitt nodded. "We've got clean cuts through both the inner and outer hulls."

Cruz shook his head. "That was quick work. I figured it would take you another day."

Pitt unzipped his dry suit and stepped to the rail. The scene around the sunken ship was one of mass congestion, accompanied by the din of multiple generators. The *Mayweather* was surrounded by work vessels, the barge and evacuation tanker positioned on either side, while the BioRem freighter was moored to the south. Hoses dipped over the sides from the latter two vessels, converging on the wreck.

Pitt looked upriver at a new visitor to the site. A massive lift barge was standing by, ready to hoist the bisected ship.

"What's the status of the oil evacuation?" Pitt asked.

"The stern section is nearly dry," Cruz said. "We can start on the forward section once the stern is lifted."

"As soon as you're ready, have the lift barge come alongside," Pitt said.

"Will do. I'll have my team set the lift cables in the meantime. We should be set to pull it up by morning."

"Better advise the BioRem vessel of our lift plans. They'll want to pull their hoses until the stern section is clear."

"I'll let Audrey know. Reports from a monitoring station downriver suggest a decrease in detected river oil. Their little bugs must be working."

"Glad to hear." Pitt surveyed the wreck. "With a little luck, we might have both sections off the bottom by tomorrow night."

Cruz agreed with a nod. "We might just be saying aloha to Maui sooner than I thought."

By three in the morning, the lift barge had been positioned off the *Mayweather*'s flank and lift cables secured. At dawn, Pitt gave the go-ahead to proceed with the lift. The cables were pulled taut, and the *Mayweather*'s stern was hoisted high enough for an Army Corps of Engineers flatbed barge to be slipped beneath it. A pair of tugs then pulled the barge, with its massive cargo, down the Detroit River toward Cleveland and a waiting marine salvage yard.

"We're halfway home," Pitt said with satisfaction.

"The bow section should go quicker, as it has fewer oil compartments to evacuate," Cruz noted.

The tired crew shifted their focus to the forward half of the wreckage, working without letup. The evacuation tanker was repositioned alongside the *Mayweather*'s bow, with Cruz overseeing pipeline access. Meanwhile, Pitt and Giordino set about rigging the lift cables to enable the raising of the section. Downriver, the hum of generators on the BioRem freighter indicated Audrey had deployed new feeder lines for deploying the bacterial agent.

At dusk, Pitt called a status meeting, over barbecued ribs and beer ferried from a restaurant on Grosse Pointe.

"The evacuation tanker is running at full bore," Cruz reported. "The last of the storage tanks should be dry by midnight."

"That's when our next Army Corps barge is due in," Pitt said. "We'll turn things over to the second shift and get some shut-eye. Let's reconvene at midnight and see if we can rig for a predawn lift." He turned to Audrey. "How's our bioremediation stock holding up?"

"We have plenty on hand to see us through another day or two," she replied, stifling a yawn.

Cruz nodded as he finished the last of the ribs. "Sleep sounds good, but I think I'll take a quick survey dive to make sure we're pumping clean."

"Why don't you take Al with you?" Pitt said. "A solo night dive in this current is not advisable."

"Not necessary, I'll be in and out before your heads hit the pillow," Cruz said with his usual grin. "I'll see everybody at midnight."

A few minutes later, Cruz grabbed an air tank, squeezed into a dry suit, and slipped over the side. He switched on his underwater scooter's headlamp and motored the short distance to the *Mayweather*'s bow. He skimmed above the top deck, slowing to see through the murky water. He had to bob and weave to avoid the maze of pipes and catwalks that crisscrossed the tanker's deck.

Near the inshore rail, he stopped at a thick white hose that wiggled from the surface. It was connected to an inlet pipe, which ran to one of the *Mayweather*'s storage tanks. Through it, the thick tar sands oil was being sucked into the evacuation tanker. An ROV was perched on the deck and aimed at the hose, its cameras providing a live feed to crew members on the tanker. Finding no leaks, Cruz gave the camera a wave, then turned and headed forward.

Red ribbons tied to two remaining valves indicated there were just two tanks left to empty. The oil removal process was right on schedule.

He crossed the deck, returned to the serrated midsection, and descended to the riverbed, examining the sheared sides of the exposed storage tanks. He hesitated at a pair of yellow Bio-Rem hoses, spaced several feet apart, clamped to the edge of a ruptured and leaking tank.

Cruz inched close to the nearest hose and waved his hand over the nozzle, expecting to feel the flow of the microorganism dispersant. He felt nothing. He moved to the second hose, which was similarly inactive. Cruz followed the hoses across the river bottom as they snaked along the forward hull. About twenty feet past the tanker's bow, the hoses came to an abrupt end.

Cruz examined the open hose ends, weighed to the riverbed with rocks, then aimed his scooter toward the surface.

The dark outline of the BioRem freighter was faintly visible overhead. Perhaps the crew was changing the outlet hoses. Then Cruz noticed two thin lines extending from the ship, running aft. He cut the scooter's throttle and let himself drift with the current until he could identify the lines as a pair of black hoses. They led to the bottom, but trailed in the opposite direction from the *Mayweather*.

Cruz engaged the scooter and followed the hoses. Nearly two hundred feet downriver, the hoses slithered over a rocky berm and ended at a wide metallic grate set in concrete. Their nozzles were clamped to the grate, and when Cruz waved a hand in front of them, he felt a rush of fluid being discharged.

There had to be an explanation. Cruz didn't know what it was. Waste discharge? He'd radio Audrey McKee when he got back to the barge.

He advanced the scooter throttle to overcome the current and turned upriver, retracing the path of the hoses.

As he neared the BioRem ship, two small lights appeared in the water. Drawing closer, he could see a pair of divers about ten feet apart heading for him with similar scooters. Cruz slowed as they approached on either side, realizing too late that they were towing an object between them.

It was a mesh net, and he motored right into its center. He flicked the scooter over his head to try to slide up, but the divers were already converging behind him. One reached over and knocked the scooter from Cruz's hands, while the other inserted a plastic tie into the netting at his back and cinched it tight.

Anger flared through Cruz as he tried to kick clear of the net.

One arm broke free, and he reached over and grabbed one of the divers.

As he pulled him close, Cruz felt a cold blade slap the side of his neck—and he drew a mouthful of water. The other diver had cut his air hose from behind and was pulling him toward the bottom.

Cruz reached for the first man's throat. He had only one arm against two, and the other man twisted free.

Anger turned to panic as the struggle to breathe overcame all senses and he fought to free himself. The two divers were now at his back, and they forced him face-first into the river bottom.

Driven into the mud, he fought with all his strength to break free. It was to no avail. Out of breath and pinned to the bottom, he sucked in a mouthful of river water and faced his death amid a black cloud of silt.

13

Mike has gone missing."

The words stung Pitt like a punch to the midsection. "How long?" he asked, rising from his bunk and shaking off the cobwebs.

"He left the barge an hour ago," Giordino said. "The deck watch reported him missing ten minutes ago. He's in the water on a tank, no communications system. The extrusion tanker reported seeing him on their video feed about twenty minutes ago."

"Could be stretching his air, but let's get every available diver in the water. And now!"

"I'll have a deckhand position a tender off the *Mayweather*'s bow, just in case."

While Giordino made the call, Pitt gathered the four other NUMA divers and formulated a search plan. A few minutes later, he led the divers into the river.

Rainstorms to the north had added runoff to Lake St. Clair,

casting the nighttime waters dim and murky. Pitt used the lighted scooter to speed across the *Mayweather*'s upper deck. He surveyed around the evacuation hose, then descended along the blunt face of the sheared vessel. He searched methodically along the serrated bulkheads, then turned to face a light in his eyes.

The petite form of a female diver approached. Audrey McKee gave him a blank look, pointed at the riverbed behind her, and shook her head. Pitt aimed his light down and found a black object that contrasted with the sandy bottom: a dive fin.

Pitt moved past Audrey and angled his scooter's light into the next compartment. It was a ruptured storage tank that revealed a jagged open seam across its center. The still water in the interior was clear, and Pitt's light found a body in a blue wetsuit wedged inside.

As Audrey joined him with her light, he squeezed into the tank and swam face to face with Cruz. The NUMA engineer's unblinking eyes stared right through him. Cruz's buoyancy compensator strap was caught on a mangled piece of steel, holding the dead man in place. His regulator hung limp across his chest. Pitt noted both it and the attached dive console appeared brand-new.

Pitt left the diver in place and searched the storage tank with the scooter light. Then he squeezed back out to where Audrey waited. A new pair of lights cut through the murk, and two of the NUMA search divers appeared. Pitt pointed to the storage tank, then indicated he was surfacing. Audrey followed as he ascended and crossed over to the barge.

Giordino stood on the dive platform, suiting up. He helped Audrey out of the water, then turned as Pitt climbed aboard. Giordino could tell the news was not good. "You found him?"

"One of the ruptured storage tanks. It appears he was investigating the interior, and his gear got caught up on some debris. Couldn't free himself and ran out of air."

Audrey shook her head. "How horrible."

"How could it happen?" Giordino said. "Mike was highly experienced."

Pitt nodded.

"It looked pretty confined in there," Audrey said, "with plenty of jagged metal sticking out. He might have kicked up some sediment and lost his visibility. I've done some cave diving, and I know how easy it is to become disoriented."

"He was exhausted, too," Giordino said. "Like the rest of us."

Pitt stared at the deck. Cruz was a good diver. Too good.

"We'll suspend operations until we get him ashore and call in the authorities." Pitt turned to Audrey. "Best make sure your divers don't operate alone."

"I'm very sorry." She offered Pitt and Giordino a hug, then climbed into an inflatable and returned to her ship.

An hour later, members of the Wayne County Sheriff's Marine Unit brought Cruz to the surface in a body bag and transported him to shore. After a half-day delay for a safety review, the newly arrived lift barge was positioned alongside the wreck, and the bow section of the *Mayweather* was raised. It followed the stern section on a flat barge to Cleveland, while the remaining vessels cleared the area. Audrey radioed Pitt that the BioRem freighter was departing to Ontario, and she wished him and Giordino well.

"A tug will be here in an hour to pull our barge to shore," Giordino said. "Or we can jump ship in the tender right now.

Rudi has us booked on an evening flight that departs in three hours."

Pitt shook his head. The fatigue of the past few days showed on his face, but his eyes remained determined. There was no sense of accomplishment on the salvage operation, which had been completed faster than anyone anticipated. The only thought on Pitt's mind was the loss of Cruz.

He retrieved his gear. "I'd like to take a last look at the site." Pitt gazed at the river before stepping to the dive platform.

"I'll see that the rest of the equipment is stowed," Giordino said. He could tell his old friend wasn't looking for company.

Pitt entered the water with the scooter, dropped to the bottom, and propelled himself upriver. He reached the flattened section of riverbed where the *Mayweather*'s stern had rested and began to cruise back and forth, letting the current push him downriver. The visibility was marginally better, allowing him to hover five feet off the bottom.

He passed over the area where the bow had rested, then continued downriver. His mind began to wander as he stared at the featureless bottom, drifting over discarded tires, beer cans, and other debris. After a few minutes, he turned upriver and accelerated the scooter against the current.

He was about to adjust his path toward the barge when he eased off the throttle. A bright-colored item caught his attention. It wasn't just another piece of discarded junk. It was a familiar object that had been lost very recently. Pitt paused a moment, then plucked it from the sand and returned to the barge.

14

Senator Bradshaw gazed out the window at the Washington Monument, watching the red aviation warning lights atop its apex twinkle in the approaching dusk. He had to admit, the Thomas Jefferson Suite at the Willard InterContinental hotel offered an impressive view of the monuments along the National Mall and beyond. Taking a sip of iced bourbon, he turned from the suite's picture window and faced his host.

Evanna McKee, seated on a red sofa, studied a bound report with an official seal on its cover. "This is the committee's approved bill?"

"Yes, the Senate Environment and Public Works Committee. We'll still have to confer with the House when they pass their version."

"I'm counting on your influence there."

"I'll do what I can," Bradshaw said. "Representative Smith, whom you met the other evening, heads the subcommittee reviewing the proposed legislation. Unfortunately, she's a tough nut to crack. But the bill is written in a muted manner. It's only deep within the fine print that you'll find the language that opens the door for unlimited use of your bioremediation products in U.S. waters. It's what you asked for."

"And what you're getting paid for. Tell me more about this congresswoman."

"Loren Smith—or Smith-Pitt, as she now goes by—is a long-term representative from Colorado. She chairs the House subcommittees on Environment and Water, Power, and Oceans, and she also sits on the Foreign Affairs Committee. She's widely respected for her knowledge on legislative matters—and for her high ethics and nonpartisanship. She's authored several high-profile pieces of legislation promoting veterans' care and women's rights. Unfortunately, she's not known for succumbing to the usual congressional backroom dealmaking."

"I see," McKee said. "It would appear I may need to exert some additional influence. I will call her directly and invite her again to my conference in Scotland. Given the right sway, she could become an important ally." She set the report on a coffee table. "Thank you for pressing the EPA for approval in the Detroit incident. There will be something for you in your Dubai bank account."

Bradshaw finished his bourbon and bowed to McKee—as gracefully as an aged, overweight, tipsy senator could muster. "Thank you, Mrs. McKee. As always, it's a pleasure doing business with you."

"Rachel will show you out."

The large woman he'd seen at the charity event entered the

sitting room and nodded at him. The senator followed the broad-shouldered woman to the door.

A few seconds later, Audrey McKee entered from a back bedroom. She'd arrived from Detroit an hour earlier and was freshly showered and dressed in a blouse and slacks. "How can you stand to do business with that pig?" she asked.

"Because he will do anything for money. I prefer to hire people who will sell their soul for money, and let them do my bidding."

"He's still a pig."

"As are all men. Some serve our purpose, as muscle or marionettes. With his help, we will soon be able to operate throughout the U.S."

Audrey nodded. "We've already begun infiltrating the world's leading cities. New York and Los Angeles would be optimal additions."

McKee opened a second binder and examined a map inside. Major port cities across the globe were highlighted, with various codes assigned to each. She looked from the map to her daughter.

"What did we deploy to Mumbai?"

"The last stocks of our second blend, the EP-2 mix," Audrey replied. "When it was shipped, we still had hopes of minimal side effects. But as we discovered in El Salvador, that is not the case."

McKee nodded. "Well, we knew the first blend carried the original attributes, so we tested it where no one would know the difference. Kenya, Tanzania, Nigeria. Dr. Perkins gave us hope for benign effects of the second blend when we began deploying it a few months ago. We now know he was wrong."

"We're lucky no undue suspicions have been raised. The fatalities in the other Third World countries where EP-2 was deployed haven't received any attention."

"The risk of exposure is still there," McKee said, cutting her daughter a sharp glance. "And it is the western deployments that will be scrutinized."

"True, but the risk profile has changed with the new release. Our initial deployments of the third blend, EP-3, have occurred without issue."

"No adverse reports from Detroit?"

"None," Audrey replied. "The product is proving indiscernible. We can accelerate dispersal without concern. Our only delay may be in increasing production, due to limited source matter."

"An additional source sample may soon be at hand."

McKee stood and gazed at the darkened skyline. "We are on the verge of a triumphant moment. In a matter of weeks, there won't be a major metropolis beyond our reach. The global tipping point will soon follow."

"All before anyone will have attempted to create an antidote. You'll have done it, Mother. Changed the face of humanity forever."

"Yes," she said softly. "Within a generation, we will turn the planet's population upside down." McKee relished the thought a moment. The hardened veneer cracked, and she allowed herself a smile. "Now tell me, how did things go in Detroit?"

"We started by treating the oil spill, then deployed the EP-3 product as the tanker wreckage was cleared. It was salvaged quicker than expected, so we only had a day or so of active dispersant once the city began drawing its water from the river again. There was one slight problem. One of our underwater cameras caught a NUMA diver investigating the dispersal lines beneath our ship."

"Did he see anything?"

"He had no opportunity to tell anyone. We took care of him before he could."

"Did you eliminate him without suspicion?"

She nodded. "It was made to look like an accident. Fortunately, it happened just as the job was winding down."

"It will probably be best if you return to Scotland with me tomorrow." She paused. "We do have, however, one more loose end. I learned from the senator that the U.S. aid scientist from El Salvador is here in Washington. Her name is Elise Aguilar."

"I tried to dispatch her in El Salvador."

McKee gave her daughter a stern look. "Your operation in El Salvador was a fiasco."

"We were just following up on the EP-2 deployment," Audrey said. "We didn't know the U.S. scientific team would be there testing the water. We thought it best not to take chances."

"Take chances? They were an agricultural team helping farmers. You created an international incident."

"We know they took water samples—or at least the woman did."

"If she had been killed with the others, then at least there would be no worries now."

"There's . . . something I need to tell you about that," Audrey said. "The man who rescued this Aguilar woman at Cerrón Grande was the same person from NUMA who raised the *Mayweather*."

“He was at Cerrón Grande? You are certain of this?”

Audrey nodded. “His name is Dirk Pitt. He is the Director of NUMA.”

“Yes, I met Pitt at the gala. Did he recognize you?”

“No.”

“Well, he should be no bother now.”

“I’ve heard he’s quite accomplished.”

“I may need his wife, but not him.” McKee turned and admired the lights of Washington. “I have two people in-country to take care of Aguilar. If Pitt chooses to interfere, it will be his misfortune.”

15

It was customary for Rudi Gunn to find a stack of correspondence waiting on his desk when he arrived at NUMA headquarters in the morning. What wasn't usual was the extra-large paperweight he found awaiting him this day. It was a slightly used yellow dive scooter, with NUMA lettered in turquoise, parked on the center of his desk. Wrapped around it was a dive regulator. Gunn studied the object, then carried it down the hall to the corner office of Dirk Pitt.

"Warranty problem?" He set the scooter down and took a seat.

Pitt was examining a sheriff's report from Detroit. "It was Mike Cruz's."

Gunn nodded, still not sure why it had ended up on his desk. He waited for Pitt to explain.

"I found it on the bottom of the Detroit River. About two hundred feet from Mike's body."

"He might have lost his grip on it and it propelled off without him."

"No, the device requires pressure on the throttle. Otherwise, it stops."

"Perhaps the river carried it. I know you were working in strong currents."

"Mike was roughly at the center of the ship, near its keel line. The device would have to move fifty feet abeam of his position, take a ninety-degree turn, then proceed downriver. I know strange things can happen with underwater currents, but I'm not buying it."

"So what are you saying?"

"I think Mike was murdered."

Gunn considered the comment, his studious blue eyes refusing to blink. "I just read the Detroit Sheriff's Office's preliminary findings." He nodded to the report in Pitt's hands. "They call it an accidental drowning, pending autopsy results."

"Mike was too experienced."

"Disorientation and panic can strike even the most seasoned diver," Gunn said. "He was in nighttime conditions with a strong current and low visibility. A dangerous mix for a diver all alone. There was also the fatigue factor."

Gunn was probably right, Pitt thought, and that's what stung. He shouldn't have allowed Cruz to dive alone, regardless of his experience. Pitt felt the guilt of his death, and he hoped it wasn't clouding his judgment.

"He was in shallow depths. If his tank got entangled, he could have ditched it and kicked to the surface. Yet there was no evidence he even tried. Besides the location of his scooter, there's the matter of his regulator."

Gunn examined it. "Doesn't appear damaged. In fact, it appears brand-new."

"Too new. And it's not the make we carry on our projects."

"Someone swapped his regulator?"

"Possibly."

Gunn glanced at the regulator, then back at Pitt. "If he was murdered, why leave his body in the wreckage? They could have let him drift downriver where his remains might never have been found."

"It could be either to make it look like an accident or to discourage anybody searching downriver."

"That could explain a motive, but who would have done it?"

Pitt shook his head. "The big unknown. I checked with the captains of all of the vessels working the site. None saw any unknown boats approach at the time of Mike's dive. But, it was late at night."

"That leaves," Gunn said, "a finite number of divers on the assigned vessels."

"Eleven that I could determine. Six NUMA divers on the barge, including Al and me, three divers on the BioRem freighter, and one auxiliary diver each on both the lift barge and the evacuation tanker. Our divers were all on board during Mike's dive. The other vessels reported the same."

"Then someone's lying or it was indeed an accident. Be difficult to prove either way."

Pitt looked at Gunn with a steady gaze. "I'd like you to find everything you can on BioRem Global."

"A hunch?"

"If even that. They were the only ones downriver of the *Mayweather*."

"I'll do it, and monitor the autopsy findings from Detroit."

Gunn started to leave when Zerri Pochinski poked her head into the room. "Sorry to bother you two, but there's an unscheduled visitor outside. Would you have time to see one Elise Aguilar?"

"Of course," Pitt said. "Please show her right in."

He met Elise at the door and received a friendly hug. Dressed in a Elie Tahari business suit, with her dark curls neatly subdued in a low ponytail, she looked nothing like the waterlogged scientist Pitt had rescued in El Salvador.

"Now this is what I call a pleasant surprise," Pitt said. He introduced her to Gunn and offered her a seat. "Not only am I surprised to see you so soon. I'm surprised to see you looking so well."

Elise blushed. "I do feel pretty good. Two days at Walter Reed was enough motivation for me to heal quickly. I'll just be stuck with this a few more weeks." She raised her left arm, revealing a soft cast. "The doctors promise it will be as good as new."

"That's terrific news," Pitt said.

"I read in the papers about your salvage work in Detroit and was hoping you were back in the building. I wanted to say thanks for what you did to save my life."

"I'm sorry we couldn't help your colleagues."

"Part of the reason I stopped by," she said. "There's a local memorial service scheduled next week for my slain friends. I'd be grateful if you and Mr. Giordino could attend."

"We'd be honored," Pitt said.

"Dirk told me about your swim over the dam," Gunn said. "Could I ask if there was anything of interest in the water samples you collected from the reservoir?"

Elise smiled. "The third reason for my visit. I understand Mr. Giordino sent the samples to Dr. Stephen Nakamura at the University of Maryland. He's a professor of epidemiology in their Department of Environmental Health and a key research consultant to our agency. He left me a message this morning that he'd tested one of the samples and made an odd discovery."

"What was that?" Gunn asked.

"He didn't go into detail, only suggested I come by to discuss it."

"Do you think it could be significant?"

She nodded. "He said he was sending one of the remaining samples to the Centers for Disease Control in Atlanta and the others to a research institute in the UK. That tells me there's something unique in the water, perhaps something that prompted the attack on our camp." She turned to Pitt. "Would you be interested in coming with me to College Park? Since you helped save the samples, I thought you might want to know what's in them."

"If there was something in the water that led to the destruction of the dam and the attack on your people," Pitt said, "then I'd like to know about it." He eyed her cast. "On top of that, driving one-handed in this town is inviting a return to Walter Reed." He rose from his desk. "Rudi, mind the store."

Pitt borrowed an agency Jeep from the basement garage and drove them across town to the Maryland suburb of College Park. The Maryland University campus featured a mix of red brick Georgian buildings sprawled across thirteen hundred acres of neatly trimmed grass. Elise guided him to the north side of campus, where they parked next to the more contemporary School of Public Health building.

"Dr. Nakamura has an office next to a research lab in the basement," Elise said, as she guided Pitt down a stairwell off the main foyer. They had arrived during class sessions, so the corridors were quiet. As they reached the lower level, they passed a well-dressed man and woman heading up the stairs. One lugged a thick valise, while the other carried a pair of FedEx packages. Elise said hello, but they ignored her, staring coldly at Pitt as they passed.

Elise led them down a long hallway, passing three labs, each marked ENVIRONMENTAL HEALTH EPIDEMIOLOGY RESEARCH—NO ADMITTANCE. At the end of the corridor, Elise stopped at an office and tried the handle. The door was locked. She knocked twice. There was no answer.

"That's funny." She stepped back to make sure the nameplate next to the door read DR. STEPHEN NAKAMURA. "Maybe he's in the lab next door."

As she pulled out her phone to call him, a janitor exited the office across the hall and glanced their way. "Do you need to get in there? I guess the professor is getting hard of hearing in his old age." He selected a key card and unlocked the door.

"Thank you," Elise said.

"No problem. Not the first time today."

Elise pulled the door open and stepped in. Pitt followed, allowing the self-closing door to shut behind them. The office was long and narrow, with bookshelves lining the walls on either side. A small, round conference table was wedged into the middle of the room, with the professor's paper-strewn desk at the far end. A side door next to the desk led to the adjacent lab.

Nakamura sat at his desk with his back to them, his head tilted to a phone wedged against his ear. As Pitt and Elise stepped closer, she whispered, "Hello, Dr. Nakamura?"

She waved to get his attention. He remained still. She started to step closer. Pitt grabbed her arm and pulled her back.

"What is it?" she said.

Pitt didn't answer, but she heard why he had stopped her. It was the busy tone emanating from the receiver, signaling a phone left off the hook.

Pitt eased past Elise to where he had an unobstructed view of Nakamura. The scientist didn't move, and Pitt saw why. His face was ashen, his eyes were fixed open, with a neat red bullet hole perforating his temple.

16

Elise ignored Pitt's warning and observed Nakamura's wound for herself. She screamed.

As Pitt tried to calm her, his eyes scanned the scene. A file drawer sat open near the professor's feet, a gap revealing a missing file. Also at his feet was a sealed cardboard box with no label. Papers lay strewn about the desk. An electric cord for a computer dangled from an outlet, but no laptop was visible. In a plastic outbox sitting atop a pair of FedEx receipts, Pitt spied a set of car keys with an attached key card. He glanced back at the professor. A trickle of blood around the entry point was still wet. He'd not been dead long.

"There's nothing we can do for him." Pitt shuffled Elise away from the desk. "Let's go call the police."

He froze as two muffled pops sounded from the other side of the office. A piece of the door lock fell and rolled across the floor. Pitt shoved Elise behind a file cabinet as the door was kicked open, and the woman they'd passed in the stairwell stepped in. She had short hair, dark eyes, and held a black pistol fitted with a suppressor. Looking toward Pitt, she raised the gun and fired.

Pitt dove past Nakamura's desk. As the shot zipped by, he reached out and flicked off the wall lights. With the office dark, he jumped to his feet and groped about the professor's desk. He found the keys, and the papers beneath them, then felt his way to the side lab door.

Two muzzle flashes lit the far end of the office, and shots smashed into the wall behind the desk. Pitt reached out and found Elise, pulling her toward him. He held up the key card and heard the lock click, then pulled open the side lab door and pushed her through. At the far end of the office, the woman found the other light switch and flicked it on. She had just an instant to see Pitt follow Elise into the side lab and slam the door.

The lab was absent students, but filled with computers, microscopes, refrigerators, and an array of high-tech equipment. Elise had shaken off her horror and was scrambling past several crowded workbenches, making her way toward the back of the lab—and an exit.

Pitt lingered long enough to slide a rack of computers in front of the door and turn off the lights. He had followed Elise to the middle of the lab when they heard two more taps. The door opened a fraction, banging hard into the rack. The armed woman shoved again, knocking one of the computers onto the floor.

They wouldn't make the exit in time, so Pitt pushed Elise

behind a workbench and dove down alongside her, sliding against a small refrigerator. As the assailant banged against the computer rack, Pitt searched for a weapon. Finding nothing obvious nearby, he opened the refrigerator. Inside, he found some cans of soda, several small packages of perishable materials, and a gallon bottle of alcohol. He grabbed the cans and the alcohol and turned to Elise. "Turn on that heating plate above your head."

She reached up to an electric hot plate on the workbench and turned the dial to high. At the same time, Pitt crawled to the aisle and twisted off the cap to the alcohol bottle. He lay the bottle on its side, gave it a shove, and watched it roll down the aisle, spilling its contents along the way. It clinked against the far wall just as the woman pushed the rack aside and entered the lab.

"Stay low and try to get out the back door," Pitt whispered.

He retrieved a roll of paper towels from the bench and held one end to the red-hot burner. Another pop, and a small chunk of the corner bench disintegrated next to his hand. Pitt could hear the woman moving closer as the paper ignited. He held it to the spilled alcohol until it began to burn, then tossed the flaming roll toward the intruder.

The alcohol on the floor ignited in a low flame that burned across the lab to the bottle, which flared in a small blaze. The woman had to dodge the incoming paper towels, then stomp at the fire around her.

Pitt turned to Elise. "Go!"

He flicked the hot burner over onto a plastic lab tray, then popped up and hurled the two soda cans. The first missed, but the second clipped the woman on the side of the head. Pitt used the opportunity to move closer to the exit, diving over the next lab bench while knocking a computer monitor to the floor.

The distraction allowed Elise to sprint to the door and burst into the hallway as the armed woman regained her composure and squeezed another shot off at Pitt.

The burner melted the plastic tray and began filling the lab with thick black smoke. Pitt used the cover to crawl along the next workbench, grab an armful of glass beakers from above him, and wing them in the shooter's general direction. One shattered against the wall next to the intruder, temporarily halting her. The smoldering tray finally activated a fire alarm, which began blaring throughout the building. The woman froze.

Pitt knew what was coming next. It would be his only chance to escape. He crawled to the end of the workbench and peered at the exit less than ten feet away. Just beyond the door sat a cart overflowing with testing equipment.

Palming the last of his beakers, he hurled it blindly toward the woman, trying to buy a few more seconds. It took longer than he hoped, but at last the burning plastic did its work. With a sudden swoosh, the overhead fire sprinklers engaged, dowsing the bay in a heavy downpour of water.

Pitt bolted for the door, then ran past it to the cart of equipment. He ducked behind it, gave it a quick shove down the aisle, and reached for the doorknob.

The assassin squinted through the streaming water and fired

three shots, which were all absorbed by the equipment rolling toward her.

Pitt pushed open the door and burst into the hall. He managed only one step before halting in his tracks.

Elise stood a few feet away. Her chin was raised high, but her dark eyes pleaded with Pitt. She tried to speak. No sound came from her lips. For around her neck was the arm of the assailant, locking her throat in a tight chokehold.

17

Pitt needed only a second to take in the scene. He ignored the thundering fire alarm and flashing red lights and focused on the man gripping Elise. He was the man who'd been carrying the two packages, which now sat on the floor next to the thick valise. Lean, but powerfully built, he had short hair, a trimmed beard, and impassive eyes. What he didn't have was a weapon.

"Keep her," Pitt said, reaching down to pick up the two boxes.

The assailant muttered, "No." He eased his hold on Elise and reached out to snatch the boxes ahead of Pitt.

Pitt had anticipated the move. He sprang up into the man, launching his left fist in a powerful uppercut that caught the man squarely on the jaw.

The man's head snapped back, and his knees quivered. Still clutching the packages, he freed his grip on Elise as he sank to the floor.

Pitt grabbed Elise and pulled her down the corridor. The fire alarm had sent students and faculty scurrying, and a small crowd converged on the stairwell. Pitt knifed through the crowd, dragging Elise with him. Once they were on the steps, he glanced back and saw the armed woman burst from the lab—and holster her gun at the sight of her disabled partner and the crowd. Pitt kept pushing Elise forward, and they raced up the stairs.

An even larger throng congregated on the main floor. Pitt and Elise followed the herd outside, crossed the street, and moved east. They hesitated at the sound of a muffled explosion that seemed to originate from the basement. Following a small group of students down the street, they entered the grounds of an animal husbandry farm and slipped into a barn filled with goats.

Pitt watched to see if they were being followed, then guided Elise to his Jeep in the nearby parking lot. Once at the vehicle, he made two phone calls. The first, to the campus police, reported the murder of Dr. Nakamura and provided descriptions of the assailants. The second was a brief call to Gunn at NUMA headquarters.

As he started the Jeep, he turned to Elise.

"Are you all right?"

She nodded without conviction.

Pitt took an indirect route around the campus football stadium, eyeing the cars behind him. Satisfied no one was tailing them, he caught the Capital Beltway to return to Virginia.

"I can't believe Stephen is dead," Elise said. "Why would somebody kill him . . . and try to kill us?"

"I think we'll find that the explosion came from his office,"

Pitt said. "The sealed box next to the professor's desk, I'd guess. That's why the assassins returned. They were afraid we might discover and disable it."

"But why? What did Stephen do?"

Pitt kept his eyes on the erratic freeway drivers. "It has to be the water samples. Those two had a similar look and vibe, and I couldn't help thinking he was the guy who tried to kill Al and me in Suchitoto. I think the FedEx boxes held the remaining samples. They probably took Dr. Nakamura's laptop to capture his test results."

"What could be so important about those samples?"

Pitt shook his head. "I don't know. Whoever they are, they may have been tracking you."

Elise shuddered. "Horrible people. I hope they are satisfied now, if that's what they were after."

"Dr. Nakamura had all of the reservoir samples?"

"Yes."

"And there's no other means of duplicating them?"

"With the destruction of the dam, any tainted water has likely been washed away." She stared out the side window as they skirted the Potomac River. "I can request some additional samples be taken from the reservoir. That might take a few weeks. If the source is still active, there's a chance the results could be duplicated."

She thought a moment. "Wait! Our clothes. Have you had the ones you wore in the lake laundered?"

Pitt nodded.

"Mine were discarded at the hospital. But not my shoes." She pointed to an exit sign for Arlington, Virginia. "Could you take me by my apartment? When I went into the water I was wearing some trail runners, which should be absorbent. It's possible a residue or bacteria might be identifiable on the material. I'd like to have them tested."

Pitt smiled. "Better your gym shoes than mine . . . Tell me where to go."

He followed her guidance to a red brick garden apartment near Arlington Cemetery and accompanied her to the unit. "You should pack a few overnight things," he said as he waited in the living room. She returned a few minutes later with a small suitcase. And a sullen face.

"Did you find the shoes?" Pitt asked, taking her suitcase and carrying it to the Jeep.

"They're bagged up inside." She looked at him nervously. "I think someone was in my apartment. I can't tell for sure. A few things seem out of place. Could it be my imagination?"

"Maybe, but more likely it's good intuition. That's why we're going to move you somewhere safe."

At NUMA headquarters, they found Gunn in Pitt's office, talking with an FBI agent.

"You two seem to be a recipe for trouble," Gunn said. He introduced them to the agent, a broad-shouldered man named Ross.

"I'll be your liaison during the investigation," Ross said. "I've made arrangements for the young lady to stay at a secure town house in Georgetown for as long as necessary."

"Thank you," Elise said. "I think someone may have already broken into my apartment. Do you know if the Maryland campus police caught the two intruders in Dr. Nakamura's office?"

"No word yet," Ross said. "After the explosion, there was a good deal of confusion around the Public Health building. Campus security video should prove helpful."

He turned to Pitt. "The explosion was centered in Dr. Nakamura's office. Is that where you found him?"

"Yes," Pitt said. "I suspect they tried to make it look like an accident to hide his murder. We happened to traipse in at the wrong time."

Ross set up a small audio recording device. "Can I capture your immediate recollections of what happened? We'll need to take full statements as well, at your convenience."

Pitt and Elise provided a capsule of the events at the university. But Elise soon grew quiet and slumped in her seat. Ross turned off the recorder. "How about I take you to your safe house now?"

"I'd like that. One thing first." She opened her suitcase and handed Pitt her bag of shoes. "Can you send them to Dr. Susan Montgomery, head of the Environmental Health Laboratory at the CDC in Atlanta?"

"Certainly. Is she the same scientist Nakamura was sending the water samples to?"

Elise nodded.

"Then I think I have her address." He gave Elise a hug. "Try and get some rest."

"Thank you, Dirk." Her eyes glistened with exhaustion.

Gunn and Pitt escorted them to the elevator, then returned to Pitt's office.

"Poor girl looks like she's been through the wringer," Gunn said.

"She wasn't expecting the Cerrón Grande incident to follow her to Washington. Neither was I."

"It's clear someone didn't want those water samples identified and was willing to kill to prevent it."

"In two countries. I think we've got a potential motive, at least, for the murder of the aid team in El Salvador."

"What's in the bag?" Gunn asked.

"The shoes Elise wore in the lake. She hopes they might yield something."

"Good idea. By the way, how did you know the scientist's address?"

Pitt reached into his pocket and pulled out the two FedEx forms he'd grabbed from Nakamura's desk. The top form was addressed to Dr. Susan Montgomery. He passed them to Gunn. "Nakamura was sending the water samples to two other scientists, one at the CDC and one at a lab in the UK."

"There are phone numbers on the forms." Gunn glanced at a ship's chronometer on the wall. "It's too late in the UK. Atlanta might be home."

Pitt dialed the number, and Dr. Montgomery answered on the second ring. Pitt spoke with her a few minutes, then hung up.

"She knows nothing about the samples Nakamura was sending. They apparently exchange samples all the time for independent testing. Most are viral cases. She was shocked to hear he died."

"It's unfortunate they hadn't spoken." Gunn looked at the second FedEx form, and his brow wrinkled. "Dr. Miles Perkins of Inverness Research Laboratory," he read aloud.

"You know of him?"

"Not him, but the Inverness Research Lab. I ran across the

name earlier today. They're involved with biotechnology research."

"Anything intriguing in that?"

"Not in and of itself. It's just the coincidence of their ownership." Gunn's eyes narrowed as he handed the slip back to Pitt.

"Let me guess . . ." Pitt said. "An affiliate of a certain Scottish company of renown?"

Gunn nodded. "You got it. They're a wholly owned subsidiary of one BioRem Global Limited."

PART II

AMARNA

The Tomb at Amarna

18

Manjeet Dhatt heard his sobbing wife even before he opened the door to their house. Entering the one-room tenement in the Dharavi slums of Mumbai, he found her seated on the floor, rocking a young child in her arms.

"What is the matter, Pratima?"

The woman looked up, tears on her cheeks. "It is the baby. He has been violently ill all day."

Dhatt examined the child. Just under the age of two, the boy was hot and limp in his mother's arms. His bulging eyes were dull and listless. Dhatt touched his son's head and then pinched his arm, noting the skin felt hard and rubbery.

"We must take him to the clinic."

The weary man, who made his living driving a tuk-tuk on the streets of Mumbai, helped his wife to her feet, taking the child in his arms. They exited their tin-roofed house and trudged down a muddy lane littered with trash and reeking of assorted foul odors. Six blocks across the dirty streets of Dharavi, they reached a small clinic. Passing through its glass doors, they were aghast to find the entrance crammed with people.

Dhatt recognized a neighbor among the throng, nearly all clutching a baby or toddler. He made his way to the small admissions counter.

"My son . . ."

"You'll have to wait." An elderly woman behind the counter cut him off. She waved a hand toward the waiting room. "They are all sick."

Dhatt signed an admittance sheet, then shuffled back to his wife, who had found a spot on the floor to sit down. They waited nearly an hour before a young woman in a white coat appeared from behind the counter and began examining the patients in the waiting area. "There is no more space in the examination room," she announced. "Just stay where you are, and I'll come to you."

The room had swelled to overflowing by the time she reached the Dhatts. The doctor took their son's pulse, then called to an assistant. An intravenous solution bag was brought over, and the doctor injected a peripheral line into the boy's arm. "Hold this up," she instructed, passing the bag to Dhatt.

"The boy . . . Will he be all right?" Dhatt asked.

"Yes, I think so. You are lucky you brought him when you did. We will run out of medical supplies before long."

"Is it cholera? We are careful with the water."

The doctor nodded. "Careful does not matter in this instance. The entire city seems to be infected, even Bandra. And more lethally than usual." She motioned her eyes toward a woman behind her in a green shawl, then quickly moved on to the next patient.

Dhatt sat with his wife on the floor, keeping the IV bag elevated. As he waited to see signs of improvement in his son, he glanced at the woman in the shawl.

She was sitting on the floor across the room, mumbling to herself, while rocking an infant in her arms. Dhatt caught a brief glimpse of the baby and saw with sadness that it was dead. The mother had refused to give it up, however, and just sat there, rocking, for hours.

It would not be the last dead child he would witness. A steady stream of parents left the clinic in grief, unable to save their young from the quick-striking disease. Their anguished wails mixed with the cries of the suffering children.

The overworked doctor circled back sometime later and removed the empty IV bag. "Your son looks better. I'm afraid that is all I can do for you. Take him home. And keep him hydrated."

"Thank you, Doctor."

Dhatt studied his son with relief. His eyes were fully open now, and he seemed to have more strength. He would be one of the lucky ones. Dhatt just felt it in his soul.

The tuk-tuk driver helped his wife up and stepped to the door. Something had bothered him ever since he had arrived at the clinic, and he hesitated at the door in search of an answer. He looked around the crowded room, studying the parents and their sick children. It took a moment to realize what was wrong. And then it struck him.

All of the sick children in the clinic were boys.

19

Egypt

"Is it really a funerary boat?"

Dr. Rodney Zeibig rose from a dusty pit, where he'd been hunched over an exposed wooden beam delicately scraping away hard-packed sand. A portable canopy overhead blocked the intense rays of the Egyptian sun. Even in the shade the temperature hovered around the century mark. A hot breeze off the nearby Nile River didn't make things any more comfortable. Zeibig removed an Indiana Jones fedora and wiped his forehead, then looked up into the soft blue eyes of a young blond woman standing above him.

"It wasn't built as such, by my reckoning." He pointed to a parallel pair of trenches that extended from the square pit. Aged wooden planks embedded in the bottom sand stretched more than fifty feet.

"This has all the makings of a *sekhet* boat, or work barge, likely used to haul granite or alabaster from quarries upriver. It's heavily constructed, has a flat bottom, and even a hint of green paint on its sides." He looked at the beam. "The classic funerary barges were unpainted, and along with the royalty ships, were built with curved hulls in the shape of the earlier Egyptian reed rafts." He smiled. "But I'm just a visiting marine archeologist who arrived on the site yesterday. With the other team members off for supplies, you best consult your eminent Egyptologist and fearless expedition leader."

He turned to a tanned, older man in khaki who was directing a pair of laborers across the field. "Harry. Your benefactor would like to know where the tomb is."

With a jolly grin, Dr. Harrison Stanley, emeritus professor of Egyptology from Cambridge, scurried over to the pair. "Now, Riki Sadler, I didn't mean to lead you astray last week when I told you there may be a tomb here. That's just a hunch."

"Mr. Zeibig says this is a cargo vessel, not a funerary boat." She spoke in the same refined British accent as Stanley.

"Well, I happen to think it is both. But Rodney is quite right, it does appear to be a *sekhet* used to haul stone from Aswan. The question is, why did it end up here, near a residential palace? The answer may lie in the discovery we made off its bow, which makes for an interesting interpretation."

He hopped into the pit and waved for Riki and Zeibig to follow. The lithe young woman climbed down after Stanley, with Zeibig right behind. Stanley trekked along one of the narrow trenches, following it through a ninety-degree bend into an enlarged pit. He took an additional step down and stopped in front of a partially exposed slab of limestone. Riki crept alongside him and peered at the artifact.

Barely two feet square, the stone slab's upper and lower

surfaces featured carved bands of hieroglyphics. The center section's bas-relief depicted several animals, some pots and jugs, and a round loaf of bread. Beneath the carvings were two small indented basins, and between them the image of a boy standing on a vessel.

"Is it an offering table?" Riki asked.

"Well done!" Stanley said.

Riki stuck out her chin. "You may forget, Professor, that I have degrees in biochemistry and archeology and worked extensively in the field at your Thebes site."

"Of course. You were there when we found the mummified body of the child. Your stepfather always overshadowed things. Frasier was such an important benefactor and participant in the field excavations, I tend to forget events without him. I am grateful your family supports our work, and I am thankful for your presence here."

"We all harbor a keen interest in the reign of Pharaoh Akhenaten," Riki said, "and are excited at the prospect of another tomb discovery."

"You may well be disappointed," Stanley said. "As you know, the royal tombs of Amarna were carved in the valley several kilometers east of the city. One wouldn't expect to find a tomb of significance where we stand."

"You just did."

Stanley flashed a wide grin. "Perhaps, my dear, perhaps. Offering tables have been known to be placed above ancient tombs. Many were in fact found during the early excavations here. Of course, those were associated with the temples, and they were made of ceramic. Still, there is the inscription on this one. So just perhaps."

"Harry," Zeibig said, "what's your interpretation of the markings?"

Stanley pulled a small notebook from his chest pocket. "It follows the standard offering elements. My field translation is 'A gift that the King gives to the Ruler of the Two Horizons, so that he will give a voice offering in bread, ox, fowl, and every good and pure thing, on behalf of the son of Henuttaneb, beloved sister of the King.'"

"So the table itself," Zeibig said, "is an offering for the dead?"

"Yes, for the unnamed nephew of the Pharaoh. In the Old Kingdom era, the offerings of food were made literally to nourish both the gods and the deceased on their journey to the underworld. By the time of the New Kingdom, when Amarna was built, the offerings were made figuratively. In the same period of Akhenaten's rule, the offerings were made through the king, or pharaoh, who was the sole intermediary with the gods."

"This deceased boy," Riki asked. "Could he be the nephew of Pharaoh Akhenaten?"

Stanley's eyes glistened. "That's what makes this so intriguing. This would appear to be a royal—or at least a noble—offering table. We know Akhenaten had a sister named Henuttaneb, but there is no record of her offspring. What's curious is the carving of the ship with the boy. That's an image I have never seen on an offering table. It would be difficult not to assume a connection with the vessel buried behind us."

"Perhaps the young man had a love of boats," Zeibig said. "Or died on one."

Stanley nodded. "Entirely plausible."

"What is your plan for excavating beneath the table?" Riki asked.

"Well—"

A gunshot rang out from the opposite side of the field. Stanley turned to see a man walking toward him with a clumsy gait. An Egyptian Antiquities Ministry agent assigned to Amarna, he frequently visited the site. A neat red mark on the front of his white shirt blossomed into a bloody crest, and he staggered and fell.

"Aziz!" Stanley cried, climbing from the pit and running toward the stricken man. He halted when a gunman emerged from the far trench and fired in his direction. The bullet struck just ahead of Stanley, spraying sand onto his shoes. The archeologist froze and slowly raised his arms.

There were three gunmen, each dressed in loose-fitting white cotton trousers and shirts. To conceal their identities, each wore a headscarf and sunglasses. Armed with automatic pistols, they rounded up Riki and Zeibig and marched them with Stanley to the large open pit where the boat's stern had been exposed. A huge mound of sand, overburden that had been scraped away with a tractor, towered over the back of the pit, blocking the view to the Nile.

The two laborers had already been forced into the pit and were trembling at the prospect of being killed and buried there.

One of the gunmen, wearing a checked headscarf, turned to face Zeibig. "Who are you and what are you doing here?"

"My name is Rodney Zeibig. I'm a marine archeologist with

NUMA, working on a site assessment of the Amarna shoreline. Dr. Stanley invited me to take a look at the vessel he discovered here."

The gunman inched closer. "Where is the tomb?"

Zeibig shook his head. "I know nothing of any tomb."

The gunman looked down his nose at Zeibig. Then in a lightning-quick move, he whipped the gun in a backhand gesture, striking Zeibig in the jaw with its barrel.

Zeibig staggered backward, tumbling into the pit beside the laborers. He landed on his side, feeling a secondary pain as a handheld radio clipped to his belt dug into his hip. He rose to his feet, remaining stooped over, and rested his hand on the radio.

The gunman stared at him a moment, then shook his head and moved on to the others. Zeibig discreetly slipped his hand to the radio's controls and turned off the volume. He then placed a thumb on the transmit button and began tapping it on and off.

The gunman approached Riki, who stood frozen. Stanley stepped forward, placing himself between her and the gunman.

"There's no need for this sort of behavior," Stanley said. "We're on an archeological dig and have simply uncovered a workboat. There's no treasure here, if that's what you're after."

The gunman flung a roundhouse punch, striking him in the midsection. As Stanley doubled over, the assailant jammed his pistol into his throat and forced him back upright. "I don't have time for games or lies. A tomb is here, and I will blow your head off right now if you don't reveal the truth."

Stanley grimaced under the pain of the barrel grinding into his jaw. He blinked rapidly and forced a slight nod. "What is it you want to know?"

20

A stream of air bubbles rose and burst on the Nile's surface, signaling the presence of an underwater diver. A moment later, a woman in a blue Desco Air Hat dive helmet and matching hazmat dive suit bobbed to the surface. She took her bearings, then swam along a safety line to a small boat. She reached out to the dive ladder, removed her fins, and passed them up to a shirtless man with dark hair who waited at the transom.

While Dirk Pitt, Jr., wasn't the spitting image of his father, the resemblance was obvious. They both carried the same tall, lean frame and the same strong facial features cut by an easy smile. The younger Pitt reached out a hand, pulled his twin sister aboard, and helped remove her dive helmet.

Summer Pitt shook a mane of long red hair, then unhooked an underwater camera and passed it to her brother. He shut off a humming air compressor, then turned and held up the camera. "Did you make Ansel Adams proud?"

"Only if he enjoyed taking photos in a blizzard," Summer said. "With the current and murky water, that's what it looks like down there."

"Don't be bad-mouthing the Nile or you're liable to make the river goddess unhappy."

"She needs to goddess up and convince the Egyptians to stop polluting the river."

To avoid burning up under the hot sun, she peeled off the vulcanized dry suit and slipped a T-shirt and shorts over the bikini she was wearing underneath. Tall like her brother, but fair-skinned, she looked at Dirk with piercing gray eyes.

"I think we're in the right spot. I found what could be remnants of stone pilings in an orderly progression from the shore. There are small mounds and undulations on either side, which could be buried artifacts. And I'm pretty sure I bumped up against a hewn block of stone in deeper water. If our estimate of the change in the riverbank is correct, it seems we have all the hallmarks of an ancient commercial dock."

Dirk skimmed through the digital photos on the viewfinder and nodded. "Ansel would indeed be proud. This looks like sufficient evidence to file an excavation plan with the Egyptian Antiquities Ministry. There's the potential for all kinds of cultural debris surviving in the muck next to a commercial dock, even if it's three thousand years old."

"Given the annual floods that used to wash sediment down the river, you may be right. Things probably became buried pretty easily." Summer cocked her head. "What's that sound?"

Dirk listened a moment to a static-filled tapping.

"It's the radio."

He crossed to the wheelhouse and picked up a yellow two-way radio. A repeated clicking came from the receiver. Dirk held the radio to his lips and pressed the transmit button. "Rod, is that you? Come in, please."

No answer, just the continued clicking.

Summer stepped closer. "That sounds like an SOS call."

Dirk listened to the repetitive clicks—three short, three long, then three short again. He tried calling Zeibig once more, but got the same result. He tossed the radio aside and turned to Summer. "Pull the boat ahead while I retrieve the anchor. Our favorite shovel bum may be in trouble."

He pulled on a shirt, climbed onto the bow, and grabbed the anchor line. Summer was already at the wheel, driving the boat against the Nile's current. Dirk gathered in the line as they moved forward until he could hoist up the anchor. Summer spun the boat around and headed downriver, angling closer to the eastern shoreline.

They were located off the ancient city of Amarna in the desert of Middle Egypt, some two hundred miles south of Cairo. Constructed by Pharaoh Akhenaten on a remote, protected plain along the Nile's eastern bank, the city had briefly served as the Egyptian capital over three thousand years ago. Shortly after Akhenaten's death, the capital was moved back to Thebes. The young city was not only abandoned, its stonework and monuments were stripped and salvaged for use at other sites. Still, Amarna represented the only ancient Egyptian city not completely covered by subsequent habitation.

The six-mile-long plain, ringed by high limestone cliffs, contained two small modern villages near the central and southern sections of the old city. But Dirk and Summer were working at the northern end of the plain, near the site of the royal residence known as the North Riverside Palace. Summer drove the boat down the empty river, turning in at a rickety dock. Dirk hopped off the bow and secured the boat, then stepped ashore and waited for Summer to join him.

Even in this remote stretch of desert, the Nile's banks were devoted to agriculture. The twins found themselves in a field of soybeans that stretched along the riverbank like a wide green carpet. Crossing inland, they stopped at a grove of low trees. From a short distance away they could hear shouting voices.

Just beyond the trees lay the site of the ancient palace. Knee-high remnants of a mud wall surrounded the scattered remains of columns, courtyards, and royal buildings that once rose from the grounds. Dr. Stanley's excavation site was a few dozen yards south, marked by several canopy tents, a battered pickup, and a yellow front-end loader.

Summer grabbed Dirk's arm and pointed to a bloody body that lay facedown in the center of the field. "Artifact thieves?" she whispered.

"Probably."

Terrorists at such a remote location seemed unlikely. Given Egypt's long struggle against theft at its many cultural sites, profit seemed a more likely motive. If they were thieves, they were especially brazen to attack an active one. Judging by the body, they were willing to kill to get what they wanted.

Mounds of excavated dirt concealed the terrorists, so Dirk and Summer maneuvered down the line of trees. Crouching behind a poplar tree, they could see three gunmen facing an excavation pit, their backs to a high pile of overburden.

In the pit, Zeibig and a few others stood under the watchful eyes of a heavyset man with a belt of grenades around his waist. As the guard turned into the wind, his scarf briefly dropped from his face, exposing a neatly trimmed black beard. Dirk and Summer watched as Dr. Stanley was pulled from the trench and pistol-whipped by a gunman in a checked headscarf.

"They're going to kill him," Summer whispered. "We've got to find help."

"There's no time. It's a half mile to the nearest village, and the same to the antiquities office up north. Take us too long to get there and back."

"What do you propose we do?"

Dirk stared at the dead antiquities agent, who'd worn a holstered pistol. The three gunmen were now assembled close together above the trench, dust blowing at their feet.

Dirk turned to his sister. "We'll have to move fast. I need to ask you one thing."

"What's that?"

He motioned toward the scene. "Can you drive a front-end loader?"

21

Blood dribbled down Stanley's cheek, but he remained unfazed by the assault. He stood tall and stoic as the interrogator bombarded him with questions.

"I don't know of any tombs. The royal tombs of Amarna are all in the *wadi*, east of here. Any tombs in the city were for commoners and excavated decades, if not centuries, ago."

"What of the tomb hidden here?" The gunman barely concealed his impatience.

"Pure speculation," Stanley said. "We've uncovered a workboat and an offering table, that's all. They might indicate the presence of a tomb. Or they might not. It seems unlikely. If there is a tomb, it could take weeks, or months, to find."

"Where would you look?"

Stanley eyed the offering table, then stared at the ground. Shifting his feet, he waved an arm toward the other side of the excavation.

"Perhaps over there. That area between the boat and the North Riverside Palace. At one time there was probably an important residence there."

The gunman considered the location, then gazed at Riki a moment. He slowly turned back to Stanley. "You deceive me," he hissed. "You will die for this."

As Riki screamed "No!" he raised his weapon to Stanley's forehead.

A mechanical rumble sounded nearby, followed by a puff of black smoke that rose into the air behind them. The gunmen turned toward the noise—and the mountain of dirt suddenly began to cascade onto them.

One man fell, his lower torso buried by the avalanche. He screamed as a giant steel blade burst through the dirt mound just above his head. An accomplice tried to pull him free, but had to jump back as the front-end loader crushed the first man beneath its big, knobby tires.

The third gunman shoved Stanley aside and turned his weapon on the machine, firing into the cab. With its dusty windows, he was unable to see that the vehicle was driverless.

Zeibig realized what was happening and dragged Riki and the two laborers along the trench and away from the collapsing dirt mound. Then, through a cloud of rising dust, another woman dropped into the trench ahead of them.

"Summer?" said Zeibig.

"Quick, this way. Stay in the trench." She motioned along its path.

"Where's Dirk?"

"Hoping to provide us cover. Come on!"

Riki hesitated, but Zeibig pushed her. "Follow Summer. I'll get Harrison."

A few steps back, Zeibig found the archeologist staggering along the edge of the trench. Zeibig grabbed his shirt and pulled him into it. "Come along, Harry, this way."

The two scampered after the others as the front-end loader lumbered behind them, its blade raising a cloud of dust.

The loader's front wheels rolled down the dirt mound into the trench, and the vehicle dropped forward, pinning itself in place. Just a few feet ahead, the two remaining gunmen riddled the cab with gunfire, until they realized it had no driver. They looked about and saw the two archeologists fleeing.

The gunman with the checked headscarf raised his weapon at the two men, then redirected his fire to a tall figure crouched in the center of the field.

While Summer was setting the loader in motion, Dirk had circled the palace ruins and sprinted to the body of the antiquities agent. He ducked beside the dead man and retrieved his sidearm. It was a bulky, antiquated Webley Mk VI revolver, but it still packed a lethal kick with its .455 caliber cartridges.

Dirk had barely gotten his hand around the gun's grip when popping erupted and the sand kicked up in front of him. He dropped flat beside the body, which absorbed a pair of rounds. Targeting the source, Dirk rose and fired two quick shots, then sprinted east across the site.

The gunman recovered to fire another salvo, struck only air, as Dirk dove into the pit that held the offering table. Summer appeared a few seconds later, leading the others through the trench with their heads down.

Summer gave a mirthless grin. "I guess we've got 'em right where we want 'em."

"I've still got a few rounds," Dirk said. "To buy us time to summon help."

"A little tough without cell coverage."

Riki slipped past Summer to the head of the group and poked her head over the side. Dirk eyed the attractive woman.

"You best keep your head down," he said. He popped up for a quick look, leading with the Webley.

The two surviving gunmen had dropped into the trench that ran perpendicularly and were now inching closer. Dirk fired a shot to deter them, the bullet raising dust in front of the trench.

The two men ducked low for a moment, then one sprang up and flung a round object toward the group.

"Grenade!" Dirk shouted. "Everybody down!"

The grenade bounced into the trench near Stanley at the back of the line. It struck the ground a few feet away and detonated.

With its deafening boom, the explosion kicked up a cloud of dirt and more dust. Once the debris began to settle, Dirk moved through the haze to the point of the explosion. He passed the two laborers, who were picking themselves up, appeared unhurt. Zeibig was just beyond, leaning over Stanley.

"How's the professor?" Dirk asked.

His ears ringing, Zeibig couldn't hear the question. He did note Dirk's presence. "Leg," he said.

Zeibig had a smattering of blood on his arm and shoulder, yet he appeared pristine compared to Stanley. The British archeologist was caked in dust and splattered with blood, but his clothes and limbs seemed intact. Zeibig had already torn a strip from Stanley's shredded pants and was using it to bandage a damp red spot near his knee.

His eyes glazed, the archeologist mumbled quietly.

Summer appeared behind Dirk. "We can't take another one of those."

Dirk nodded. He jumped up with the revolver and fired a snap shot at the gunmen's shadowed location in the nearby trench.

He took cover. "We need to move."

"I don't think he can walk," Summer said, motioning at Stanley.

Dirk nodded and climbed past them. He positioned himself with a clear shot down the trench line, raised his weapon, and waited for a gunman to appear.

"Dirk, look at this."

Zeibig was digging at the side of the trench, but his body blocked Dirk's view.

"What is it?"

"An opening."

Dirk rose and fired another shot, then glanced again. Summer had joined Zeibig in tugging a thick chunk of limestone from the trench wall and rolling it aside. Where the stone had been, a black hole beckoned.

"The blast opened a hole in the trench," Zeibig said. "I felt a cool draft on my leg."

The NUMA archeologist pulled his phone from his pocket, activated its light, and stuck it in the hole. He craned his head against the opening, then turned to Summer and nodded.

"It appears to be a passageway."

The Webley barked again. At the far end of the trench, one of the gunmen fell backward, avoiding a bullet by milliseconds.

"Last shot," Dirk said. "Get everyone in there."

Summer and Zeibig had pushed away another stone, opening a three-foot-wide gap in the trench wall. Zeibig waved the two laborers in first, then passed down Stanley before following, with Summer right behind. Dirk turned and looked at Riki.

The young blond woman faced the opposite trench wall and suddenly began scaling it. Dirk lunged over, hooking an arm around her thin waist before she could reach the top and pulling her back down. She turned to him with a wide-eyed look of surprise.

"I'm . . . I'm sorry. I got scared and panicked."

He now noticed her natural beauty. The expressive eyes, full lips, and fair skin that was flawless even under the gritty desert sun.

"We're all scared," Dirk replied, coaxing a grin. "You'll scare me even more trying to go over the top. How about we try this way?" He pointed toward the opening near their feet.

She looked from Dirk to the hole and back again. "My name's Riki," she said, touching his arm. "Thank you." She gazed at him with a nervous smile, then bellied up to the hole and disappeared inside.

Dirk followed, slithering through the opening and dropping onto a stone-paved floor. Zeibig's cell phone light revealed a low, narrow passageway lined with large limestone blocks. The floor angled down to the left, expanding from the low-ceilinged entry point.

"Appears all sealed up this way," Zeibig said, shining his light to the right.

"Then I suggest we go downhill," Dirk said. "With only one light, we'll have to stay together." He reached through the hole and fitted the broken pieces of limestone back into place as best he could. The passageway turned black.

"I've got another light," Stanley said with a weak voice. "It's in my shirt pocket."

Summer knelt beside him and found a penlight in his pocket. She flicked it on and pointed it past the two workmen down the empty passageway.

"Take the lead," Dirk said to her. "Rod and I will help Dr. Stanley."

Summer nodded. She moved past the two Egyptians and stepped cautiously down the corridor. At first she had to duck low to keep from banging her head, but as she moved in deeper, the ceiling height gradually increased. Riki and the laborers tailed close behind, while Zeibig and Dirk struggled to move Stanley.

The passage tracked downhill to a tight bend, which they squeezed through single file. As Dirk finally made the turn, a light gleamed behind him. The gunmen had discovered their escape route and were pulling away the limestone chunks.

"We'd better get a move on," Dirk called out. He supported Stanley's right arm and shoulder through the bend as Zeibig guided the archeologist from the front.

The passageway nearly turned back on itself, then straightened into a long corridor that continued its subtle descent.

"What do you think this is, Rod?" Dirk asked.

Zeibig waved his light at the smooth-carved stone walls, they revealed no markings. "Nothing in the way of inscriptions to tell us."

"Underground passage between buildings," Stanley said. "Or maybe . . ." He was overcome by a fit of coughing from the stale air. Dirk and Zeibig halted until Stanley signaled he was okay, then proceeded.

They reached another bend and again squeezed through sideways. As he pulled Stanley through, Zeibig bumped into Summer and Riki.

Dirk joined them around the corner. "What's the holdup?"

"A burial chamber!" Stanley said.

Dirk could see from Summer's and Zeibig's lights that they were indeed standing in a burial chamber. The room was small, giving the impression of hasty construction. Three of the walls were bare. On the fourth a painted mural showed numerous figures with a river in the background. In front of the mural stood a raised platform with a small wooden coffin. Barely four feet long, its top was carved with the features of its occupant. Unlike the famous tomb of Tutankhamun, the coffin was not gilded, but hand-painted. At the foot of the casket stood an array of clay jars and figures, a model boat, a heavy wooden staff, and a solid gold toy chariot. A faint odor of incense permeated the dank ancient air.

"My word," Summer muttered, "it's a tomb."

The others stood in silence. Zeibig activated the camera on his phone and snapped pictures of the features as Summer illumined them with the penlight.

Their awe was broken by the sound of the gunmen advancing down the passageway.

"This way," Summer whispered. She turned the light on a low-cut doorway in the opposite wall. She hunched down and disappeared into an adjacent room. In silence, the others followed. As he passed the coffin, Dirk reached over and grabbed the wooden staff, then ducked into the room.

Summer had led them into a much smaller chamber, empty of any artifacts or murals. Of greater concern, there was no other way out.

She shone her light around the walls. "End of the line," she whispered.

Dirk helped Stanley to a far corner and set him on the ground. He turned to Zeibig and the two laborers and spoke in a low voice. "Best we can do is try to jump them when they enter." He tapped the staff against his palm. "Everyone else, get down low along the side walls."

He and Zeibig took position on opposite sides of the entrance as the others hugged the ground. They extinguished the lights, and the room fell as black as the bottom of a well.

In the eerie darkness, the seven heard only the beating of his or her pounding heart. The spirit of the tomb's three-thousand-year-old occupant seemed to permeate the interior, chilling the air with a deathly silence.

Then the gunmen entered the burial chamber.

22

Despite the cool underground air, Dirk felt a film of sweat around the ancient staff in his grip. He stood poised by the anteroom's low doorway, arms raised to strike the first gunman to enter. He suddenly felt a presence next to him and scraped his elbow against a female form. Too short to be Summer, he realized it was Riki. She leaned against him lightly, placing a trembling hand on his shoulder for support.

A light flickered beyond the opening as the two gunmen surveyed the burial chamber. Several times it flicked toward the doorway, but they showed no interest in its interior.

Inside the anteroom, the occupants remained silent, barely breathing.

Then the burial chamber erupted in gunfire. The bursts echoed off the limestone walls and into the anteroom, yet no bullets came with it. After multiple shots, the chamber fell quiet.

Dirk and Zeibig held their position at the doorway. The only thing to enter was gun smoke. The cell light moved again, followed by rustling across the stone floor. The chamber then fell dark and silent.

Dirk and the others remained frozen, their senses heightened, no one saying a word. Dirk finally rose, giving a half hug to Riki, standing next to him. “Stay here,” he whispered to all in the room.

He felt along the top of the doorway and ducked into the burial chamber. Even on dives to the bottom of the ocean, he could not remember being exposed to such total, suffocating blackness. Groping blindly, he stretched his arms in front of him and shuffled across the floor. Shell casings crunched beneath his feet as he moved toward the opposite entrance. Though he couldn’t see it, his lungs felt the heavy smoke.

His hands eventually found the opposite hall and the entrance to the burial chamber. He felt his way through it, catching a faint light to his right. The gunmen had cleared the first corridor and were now in the outer passage, their light reflected around the far bend.

Dirk returned to the chamber and called softly, “It’s safe to come out.”

The cell phone and penlight turned on. Summer guided the group out, with the two Egyptian laborers supporting a semiconscious Stanley.

“You sure they’re gone?” she whispered.

“Yes.” Dirk took his sister’s wrist and aimed the penlight toward the front wall. The pedestal table was now empty of the coffin. “They got what they wanted,” he said.

Riki sighed. “They were indeed tomb robbers.”

"What was all the gunfire about?" Summer asked.

"I guess they didn't care for the mural." Zeibig pointed his phone light at the wall. A small section of the lower corner had been targeted, obliterating the image painted there.

"That's strange," Summer said. "Why would they shoot up a mural?"

"Here's something else that's strange." Zeibig stepped to the foot of the pedestal, where the clay figurines still stood. The jars and figures, the model boat, and the little gold chariot had been left untouched. "It doesn't make much sense that grave robbers would steal a plain wooden casket and leave behind a gold artifact."

Summer shook her head. "Perhaps they didn't see it."

"One other thing is odd," Zeibig said. "I caught a glimpse of one of the men while we were in the anteroom. It appeared he had put on a surgical mask and rubber gloves."

"I can see protecting the artifacts by wearing gloves," Summer said, "but the mask is extreme."

Riki brushed against Dirk's side. "Is it safe to leave now? We need to get medical assistance for Dr. Stanley."

"Of course. Summer, can you take the point again?"

Dirk and Zeibig took hold of Stanley while Summer led the others out of the chamber and into the inner corridor. A faint rumble sounded as she moved slowly down the passage, stopping and turning off her light every few steps in case the gunmen were waiting. Eventually she reached the first bend and peeked around the corner.

The outer corridor was dark and silent. She moved forward again until a mound of dirt blocked her path near where they'd entered the passageway. She looked up, expecting to see pin-pricks of daylight through the broken limestone ceiling.

Instead, it was completely dark. She raised her light and saw why.

The front-end loader's steel blade was wedged against the opening, sealing them underground with the ghosts of the an-cient dead.

23

Dirk used the burial staff to pry at the cracked sections of limestone around the original entry hole. A few small pieces fell away. It was in vain. The front-end loader's blade overlapped heavy slabs of limestone on either side of the opening, and there was no breaching those.

"My kingdom for a pickax," he muttered, banging the staff against the wall. "Those other sections of stone aren't going to be budged with a wooden stick."

Zeibig flashed his cell light around the walls. "Solid construction, I'll give them that. Thick limestone slabs for the walls, floor, and ceiling. Easy to see why it's lain undisturbed for three thousand years."

"That's well and good for the Egyptian who was buried here," Summer said, "but how do we get out?"

"Somebody will come to check on the dead antiquities agent, as well as the families of the two workers." Riki motioned toward the laborers. "They'll notice the loader is not where it should be."

"True." Summer nodded. "How long will that take?"

The corridor fell quiet. Then Dirk approached Stanley. "Professor, we fell into this place through the ceiling. How would one have originally entered the tomb?"

Stanley sat on the floor with his back to the wall, his skin as pale as the stone behind him. He teetered on the brink of unconsciousness, wrestling with the pain from his leg wound.

He looked at Dirk with glassy eyes and forced a smile. "Steps," he said softly. "Look for steps that would lead to the surface, perhaps in a concealed entry."

"Of course. Thanks, Professor." Dirk looked to Zeibig. "Why don't you stay here with Dr. Stanley and the others while Summer and I have a look around."

Zeibig nodded. Dirk groped for the wooden staff, then rose and approached Summer. She guided him with the penlight to the pile of dirt at the end of the passage. They had to crouch as Summer moved her light about.

"We can't get past this mess," she said, "without some serious excavation."

"There was just a block wall beyond," Dirk said. "I think we can assume the entrance wasn't there."

"Let's backtrack to the chamber."

Summer turned and led them down the corridor, squeezing past the others. Dirk lingered a moment as he moved past Riki, inhaling the scent of her perfume as she gave him a light smile. He joined Summer as she ran the penlight up and down the side walls, stopping now and again to study the seams between stones. There was no hint of an unusual cut or a hidden door. The ancient Egyptian masons had fitted the stones with expert craftsmanship.

They reached the first hairpin bend and made their way through the smooth, curved walls into the inner corridor. Dirk ran his hands along both sides until they reached the burial chamber. Inside the chamber and the anteroom, they examined every inch of the walls and floor. Nowhere could they find evidence of a step or a hidden entry. They made their way back through the passageway.

"There must be another way in," Summer said.

Dirk tapped the floor with his staff, producing a dull thud. "Seems to be solid limestone in every direction we turn."

At the outer bend, Summer squeezed through ahead of Dirk. As he followed her, the top of his staff brushed the wall.

Summer stopped. "Hey, do that again."

"Do what?"

"Tap the wall. It sounded different."

Dirk rapped the staff against the side wall. It produced the familiar deep thud.

"No, back where the bend is."

Dirk backed halfway around the bend, then gave the curved wall a sharp rap. The sound was notably lighter. Dirk rubbed his hand against the curve and rapped his knuckles against it.

"It's a softer material. Almost feels like plaster. It makes sense. There's a lot more work involved in carving a curved wall from a slab of stone. And there are no seams. We should have noticed it."

"Easy to miss in this light." Summer rubbed the wall as well.

"Maybe plaster mixed with sand. It has nearly the same texture as the limestone. Do you think we can break through it?"

"We can try. Stay here, I'll be right back."

Dirk took the penlight, leaving Summer in the dark for a minute as he hiked up to the others. He returned with two jagged chunks of limestone that had fallen into the passageway. He passed one chunk and the penlight to his sister. Taking the other chunk, he held it on edge and struck it against the wall.

The stone sliced a deep gouge into the plaster, kicking up a cloud of white dust. Dirk turned and smiled at his sister. "Crude, but effective."

Summer held the penlight with her teeth and joined in chipping away at the plaster wall. As it fell away, they could see the plaster was about two inches thick. Beyond it lay packed sand.

Starting at shoulder height, they each cut a slim vertical seam toward the floor. Dirk reached the ground first.

As he cleared the debris, Summer called him aside. "Look at this."

She had knocked away a chunk of plaster at knee level, exposing a slight gap. She dug out some of the sand behind it and exposed the lip of a horizontal limestone slab.

"A step," Dirk said as she aimed her light. "That has to be it."

He attacked the plaster above the slab with renewed fervor. Together they carved a two-foot-wide opening in the plaster, then began digging at the sand behind it, exposing two more steps.

Soon there was room for only one, so they took turns digging out the sand while the other scooped it to the side. They dug a tight tunnel following the steps upward until they reached a ceiling of limestone pavers smaller than the slabs over the passageway. Dirk easily broke the light mortar that held them together and pulled away the pieces.

The sand above them gave way easily, but he still had to scrape through an additional foot with his rock before a sharp jab poked a small hole that let in some daylight. He took a sandy shower as he carved away a larger opening, then poked his head aboveground.

There was no sign of the tomb robbers. The body of the antiquities agent had vanished, as had, he supposed, that of the third gunman.

He dropped back into the hole. "Looks safe up top."

Summer grinned. "I'll go tell the others we found the front door."

Stanley was the first to appear at the base of the steps, aided by Zeibig and one of the laborers. Dirk helped hoist the archeologist through the opening, then stretched him out on the desert sand.

"Still hot out," Stanley whispered with a pained smile. He looked back at the opening. "You did it."

"Your clue to look for the steps was the key," Dirk said.

"Likely the entrance to a family necropolis. But only a child was buried there. After Akhenaten died, the family must have abandoned the home, like everyone else in Amarna."

"I wonder why they didn't relocate the casket."

"We'll never know the answer." His eyelids drooped heavily.

Dirk turned and helped Riki and Summer through the entrance, then looked toward the village to the north.

One of the laborers climbed out and approached him. "There's a doctor in the village. I will go and find him."

Before Dirk could reply, the man turned and sprinted across the desert.

Summer rummaged in the archeologist's camp and returned with a small medical kit. Stanley's wounds were bandaged by the time an SUV roared up with the doctor, a policeman, and the director of the local antiquities authority. Finding Stanley's pulse weak, the doctor called for a medical evacuation. In fifty minutes, an air ambulance from Assiut arrived and whisked him away.

As the sand kicked up by the helicopter settled, the remaining group made their report to the authorities. The young policeman seemed overwhelmed, but took abundant notes. Dirk suspected that in this remote part of Egypt, there would be little capacity to investigate the attack.

With Zeibig's help, he found a tarp, and they used it to cover the new entrance to the tomb.

"The site will remain under twenty-four-hour surveillance until archeological and security teams can be summoned from Cairo," the antiquities man promised. "We will do everything in our power to recover the lost artifacts."

"I hope you also recover the thugs who killed your man," Dirk said.

At the campsite, Riki was gathering her belongings. Dirk approached and offered a hand. "Can I give you a lift somewhere?"

She looked into his eyes and answered with a hopeful smile. "That would be really nice. I was due to head back to Cairo in two days with Dr. Stanley and catch a flight home. Where are you headed?"

"Upriver to Assiut, where they took the professor. We borrowed a survey boat from the university there."

"That would work great for me. They have a sizable airport, from which I could catch a flight to Cairo. And it would be great to see how Dr. Stanley is doing. You sure you have room aboard?"

"It's not a royal barge, but we'll make it work," Dirk promised. "Even if I have to sleep on the roof."

24

It was nearly dusk when Riki boarded the survey boat with Dirk, Summer, and Zeibig. They sailed a short distance up the Nile, then anchored for the night in a protected cove. Dirk fired up a grill on the deck and cooked lamb kabobs while Summer helped Zeibig prepare falafels in the galley.

"I was expecting tinned stew," Riki said as she joined the others at the stern deck workbench that served as a dinner table.

Dirk popped the cork on a bottle of Italian white wine and filled everyone's glass. "We try not to suffer too much when we're in the field." He raised his glass in a toast. "To a beguiling day in the desert."

Hungry from their ordeal, the four devoured the meal.

"So what exactly is NUMA doing here in Amarna?" Riki asked, filling her plate with seconds.

"We're supporting a joint project with the Egyptian Antiquities Ministry and the University of Assiut," Dirk said, "to survey the shorelines of the ancient cities of Amarna and Akoris. Summer conducted a marine life survey off Amarna last year and spotted some submerged cultural remains just south of here. Rod and I joined her to conduct sonar and sub-bottom profiles of the sites."

Summer laughed. "I was lonely, not having anyone to share the one-hundred-ten-degree temperatures with."

"Been here long?" Riki asked.

"Long enough," Summer replied, placing another kabob skewer onto her plate. "A month for me, about two weeks for the guys. We were scheduled to wrap things up tomorrow."

"I'm glad you were around," Riki said. "I can't imagine what would have happened if you hadn't arrived."

"You have Rod to thank for that," Summer said. "He was clicking away on his radio, and we finally realized it was a distress call."

"Nervous fingers," Zeibig said.

"What's your involvement with Dr. Stanley and the excavation?" Dirk asked.

"The company I work for has been a major sponsor of Dr. Stanley's work in Egypt for many years. I handle public relations for the firm, which enables me to spend time firsthand with Dr. Stanley. The company's founder was an amateur Egyptologist who befriended him many years ago. He's no longer with us, yet the firm has continued the sponsorship as a legacy to his passion for all things Egyptian."

"A worthy cause," Zeibig said. "But you mentioned this wasn't your first foray into the Egyptian wilds?"

"Not at all. I have worked with Dr. Stanley on several digs in

Egypt." She gave a sheepish grin. "My thesis was on the archeological record of Nefertiti."

"You have a background in archeology?" Dirk chided.

As Riki nodded, Zeibig laughed. "I knew there was something about you I liked."

"Maybe you can shed some light on the artifact Summer found yesterday." Dirk rose and disappeared into the pilothouse.

"It's a small stone with an inscription. I found it underwater, where we believe a merchant dock may have been located," Summer said. "I was hoping to have Dr. Stanley examine it."

"Perhaps he can see it in Assiut," Riki said. She looked up as Dirk appeared, holding a jagged piece of flat stone. Summer cleared some dishes so he could set it on the table.

"We aren't supposed to remove artifacts," Dirk said. "Summer uncovered this accidentally and received authorization to bring it up."

Nearly two feet wide and the color of alabaster, the stone had a worn panel of hieroglyphics across the top and the fragment of a carved image below.

"I'd venture it came off some sort of monument," Zeibig said.

"It was buried almost a foot beneath the river sediment," Summer said. "I discovered it when I moved our anchor line. I probed the vicinity, didn't locate any other fragments."

Riki leaned over the stone and studied the markings and image.

"Can you read hieroglyphics?" Summer asked.

Riki's eyes remained locked on the stone as she shook her head. "Just a few symbols here and there. I can see a notation for the Nile and the god Osiris. It most likely represents an homage to the Nile, a common theme."

"How about the carved image?" Dirk asked. "We all decided it depicted a woman in a boat, followed by another boat with archers."

"I would suggest it represents a ceremonial voyage, perhaps the queen or a princess, with a royal escort," Riki said. "It could be just a dignitary taking a voyage downriver to Memphis, with good wishes offered to the Nile and its goddess."

"Makes sense," Summer said. "Anything of interest about the boats, Rod?"

"Standard reed craft, typical Nile transport. No ornamentation is depicted, as is normally found on royal or ceremonial boats."

"I know some experts in Cairo who might shed some light on it," Riki said. "Do you think I could borrow it for them to examine?"

"We'll need to turn it over to the archeology department at Assiut University first," Summer said, "but I'm sure they'd have no problem in loaning it or providing a duplicate casting."

"That would be fine. Did you make any other discoveries?"

"Just the piling remnants—or what we think are piling remnants. My task before bedtime is to organize our sub-bottom sonar records into a coherent map of targets and see how they line up."

"Which reminds me," Zeibig said, "I have some notes to take on Dr. Stanley's barge while things are still relatively fresh in my head." He stood and cleared the remaining plates off the table. The others joined in, putting away the food and dishes. Summer and Zeibig retreated to the cramped galley table below to work on their assignments.

"How about you?" Riki asked. "No homework?"

Dirk shook his head with a smile. "Not when there's a desert sunset to watch. Join me on the skyline terrace?" He pointed to a ladder that led to the wheelhouse roof.

Riki gave him a bemused look, then climbed the ladder. Dirk grabbed the rest of the wine and a pair of glasses and followed her. The small roof held only a high-backed cushioned bench secured to the forward rail. Dirk untied the lashings and dragged the bench until it faced west, across the river. The sun was already dipping beneath the horizon, casting an explosion of orange across the sky.

"The best part of the day in Egypt," Dirk said, pouring two glasses of wine and joining Riki on the bench.

"At last, the heat is vanquished." She watched an antiquated *dhow* sail upriver with a light breeze at its back. "I don't know how the locals survive it."

"A few thousand years of genetic acclimation probably helps."

"I don't think I could get used to it, even in a few thousand years." She looked at Dirk. "Must seem like a long ways from the ocean."

"Yes, but I'm partial to warmer climates. Summer and I grew up in Hawaii."

"How did you both end up at NUMA?"

"We were always around the water. She studied oceanography, while I went into marine engineering. Eventually we united with our father at NUMA, and now we work on underwater projects around the world."

She could see the joy in his face. "You're lucky to do what you love."

"Digging up ancient mummies between press conferences doesn't sound so bad either," he said.

Riki nodded. "I enjoy the work . . . Some elements of the job can be difficult," she replied vaguely.

Dirk waited for her to go on. She said no more. He could see there was a fragility in her eyes. He had seen it earlier, during the attack in the trench, some distant sense of vulnerability. It was a trait he found highly alluring.

The sun vanished, and the sky turned a ruddy gray. An uptick in the breeze off the Nile lent a sudden briskness to the air, and Riki nudged closer to Dirk.

"Do you ever make it to Great Britain?" she asked.

"On occasion. Summer and I were in London just a few months ago."

"You should come back," she said softly.

"I'd like that."

The conversation fell silent. A cool gust drove her to burrow close, and he slipped an arm around her. They were still huddled in the same position when the sun appeared in the eastern sky the following morning.

25

Three hours after the NUMA research boat resumed its journey up the Nile, the modern buildings of Assiut appeared on the western bank. One of the world's oldest cities, Assiut maintained its relevance as a university town, an important agricultural center, and the largest city in Upper Egypt.

At the helm, Summer navigated through a lock alongside a pair of dams known as the Assiut Barrages before reaching a riverfront dock. Dirk tied up the boat and hopped back aboard to find Summer and Riki crowding around Zeibig and his cell phone.

"We finally have cell coverage?" Dirk asked.

Zeibig nodded. "For about the past ten minutes."

"Then what's all the excitement? Did you finally get a selfie with a camel?"

"Rod snapped some pictures inside the tomb," Summer said. "Including the mural before it was shot up."

"I managed a good shot of the corner that was defaced." Zeibig held up the screen for Dirk to see. It showed a woman extending a hand to a man standing with a staff. Behind him a small group of people huddled in the distance.

"Nothing dramatic about that," Dirk said. "You sure this was the section that was shot up?"

Zeibig nodded. "I snapped a few more on the way out." He flipped ahead to a wide view of the mural, showing the damaged lower-right corner. "It is rather curious."

"Maybe it was random gunfire to keep us hiding in the anteroom while they made their escape with the coffin," Riki said. "And the lower corner offered less chance of ricocheting bullets."

"Could have been," Dirk said. "Either way, I think the police and antiquities authorities should see a copy."

"Yes," Zeibig said. "Perhaps it can be restored. I'll see that Dr. Stanley gets a copy."

"Speaking of which," Riki said, "I think I'll call the hospital and see how the professor is doing." She hopped onto the dock and pulled out her phone.

"We should go check on him," Summer said. "We can unload the boat later."

"If lunch is thrown in somewhere, I'll go along with that," Dirk said.

Riki returned a minute later. "The duty nurse said he's doing well and available for visitation. I'd like to go see him straight away."

"Just what we were thinking," Summer said.

They flagged down a taxi and squeezed inside, taking a short ride to the Assiut University Hospital. A huge, modern complex, the hospital stood on the open-landscaped grounds of Egypt's third-largest university. They obtained Stanley's room number at the admissions desk and rode an elevator to the fourth floor.

They found Stanley in a private room overlooking a courtyard. The professor was propped up in his bed reading an English version of the *Al-Ahram Weekly*. His left leg was heavily bandaged, but he otherwise looked the picture of health.

Riki rushed over and gave him a hug. "How are you feeling, Professor?"

"Pretty fair, actually." He perked up at her appearance. "The leg's a little sore, and I'm still a bit tired. Otherwise, I feel good."

"We were worried when you lost consciousness coming out of the tomb," Zeibig said.

"I slept through a nice helicopter ride, or so I'm told. Guess I was a pint low when I got here. The good doctors gave me a transfusion. Pharaoh Akhenaten should be pleased . . . I now have Egyptian blood running through my veins."

Zeibig smiled. "Next thing you know, you'll want to start building a pyramid."

"Only because of you." He turned to Dirk and Summer. "I didn't get a chance to thank you for saving my life. And those of my workers."

Dirk shook his head. "We didn't save the antiquities agent's life, I'm afraid."

"A tragedy these thieves are still at work. It's the second time I've been hit by a tomb robber. You remember, Riki, we got nicked for a child's sarcophagus near Thebes a few years ago."

"I remember," she said. "At least no one got hurt there."

"Occupational hazard in these parts, I suppose."

"When do they cut you loose?" Summer asked.

"Another day or two. I'm chafing to get back to Amarna and have a look at that tomb with some proper lighting. It's quite a marvelous discovery. I guess we have the thieves to thank for that."

"You would have found it eventually," Riki said. "You knew the offering table was a likely indicator of something more."

"I did at that. I just wish I could remember what we saw inside."

"I can help you there." Zeibig pulled out his phone and showed Stanley his photos of the tomb. "Both before and after images. I'll be sure and send these to you."

Stanley admired the photos of the coffin, then focused on the mural, trying to interpret the image. Similar to those in other Egyptian tombs, it combined hieroglyphic panels and larger illustrations, segmented into three sections.

The left side featured several people kneeling, their arms raised in apparent worship to the sun. Behind them was a small sarcophagus. The center panel showed a man and woman at the top, seated on thrones and wearing tall hats. The rays from the sun shone only on them. The right panel displayed a narrow band of blue with small groupings of figures on either side. The illustrations were split by two vertical blocks of hieroglyphics.

Stanley smiled. "A bit dark in there, but some wonderful images nevertheless. Note the bright colors. Nearly as impressive as the murals in the tomb of Nefertari."

"Can you tell us what it represents?" Summer asked.

"I can with a few of the elements. The image on the left is an homage to Aten, similar to inscriptions uncovered elsewhere in

Amarna." He sat up straighter. "As you may know, when the Pharaoh Akhenaten came to power, he built the city of Amarna from scratch. Part of his incentive came from his decision to abolish the polytheistic worship system that all previous dynasties had supported. He later became known as the Heretic Pharaoh for brushing away the many gods and establishing a monotheistic religion based on worship of the Aten, or sun disk."

Stanley took a sip of water. "Unfortunately for the Pharaoh, his son Tutankhamun would reverse things after his death. Akhenaten's entire reign was purged from the Egyptians' historical records. But for a few years, Akhenaten led a simpler devotion in a capital city of his own making. His power is represented by the seated image of the pharaoh and his wife, Nefertiti, at the mural's top center."

"Are the figures in the left mourning the loss of their child?" Summer asked.

"I believe the parents of the deceased are asking Akhenaten and Nefertiti for solace from the Aten. Notice the sun's rays are striking only the seated couple." He held up the photo to the others. "That indicates it's the Pharaoh and his wife, as they were the only ones who could communicate directly with the Aten. Let me see if I can make out anything with the hieroglyphics."

He enlarged the photo and focused on the left block of symbols.

"It says 'The parents of the King's nephew mourn the loss of their son to the Great Illness. They ask for the Aten to stem further suffering.'"

"Pharaoh Akhenaten's sister was mentioned on the offering table," Riki said.

"Yes, that's right. It would seem our assumption has proven correct about the tomb being for Akhenaten's nephew. Our excavation is adjacent to the North Riverside Palace and likely the family's residence. Although a member of the royal family, the Pharaoh's sister apparently didn't have the clout to have a tomb with the other royals in the cliffs east of Amarna. Nevertheless, the tomb's layout is still elaborate. It would no doubt be intended as a family tomb and was pressed into service early when the boy died."

"The cause of death seems to relate to the third panel," Zeibig said. "At least in the upper section, where it appears there are dead people along the river."

Stanley browsed the next photos, enlarging one of the mural's right portion.

"I see what you mean. It appears to show several figures holding limp children." He looked up from the phone. "There is historical evidence of a widespread plague striking during Akhenaten's rule. Perhaps that felled our tomb's resident."

Zeibig pointed to the lower corner. "This portion, here, was the section shot up by the thieves."

Stanley enlarged the photo. "We have a woman in fine attire standing in a boat. She's waving or passing something to a man on the opposite shore. I'm not sure what that signifies."

"Any light shed by the hieroglyphics?" Summer asked.

Stanley studied the second panel of symbols. "'The royal daughter imparting the Apium of Faras prior to fleeing Egypt.'"

"Why would a royal daughter be fleeing Egypt?" Zeibig asked.

"Good question," Stanley said. "Akhenaten had six daughters that we know of, plus his young son Tutankhamun. It would have been unusual for a royal to flee the country. Perhaps it was due to turmoil after his death." He rubbed his chin. "His cult of the Aten was controversial, especially with the high priests. There was likely a power struggle after his death, which may have affected the royal family. Akhenaten's successor was a shadowy figure who may have come from the priesthood. He served as pharaoh only briefly, until Tutankhamun took the throne. Of course, Tut was just a young boy under the guidance of elder advisors, and promptly abolished the worship of the Aten."

"Political skullduggery at its finest," Zeibig said.

"What does the Apium of Faras mean?" Summer asked.

"That's rather interesting, if my interpretation is correct. Faras was a well-known ancient city and fortress. I'm not aware of an associated apium—or cure, if you will—which may have been a remedy for the illness."

"Perhaps," she said, "the meaning exists in Faras."

"A good bet," Stanley said, "but I'm afraid we'll never know."

"Why's that?"

"Because the city of Faras, or what's left of it, sits at the bottom of Lake Nasser."

A nurse entered the room with the professor's lunch, compelling the group to say their good-byes. Zeibig promised to send Stanley the photos, and Riki committed to meet him in Amarna in a few weeks.

Outside the hospital, the group was greeted by a blast of hot, dry air.

Dirk turned to Riki. "Do you have time for lunch before your flight?"

She nodded. "I have an hour or two before I should make my way to the airport."

"Since we're on a college campus," Summer said, "there should be plenty of cafés nearby."

They followed a sidewalk that fronted the main boulevard along campus. As they approached a side street, a white sedan cut across traffic and screeched to a stop beside them. With their attention drawn to the car, no one noticed a man wearing a ball cap and sunglasses rush up behind them. He jammed a pistol in the small of Zeibig's back. "You, in the car." He shoved Zeibig toward the vehicle, then spun around and waved the gun at the others, motioning them to back away.

Dirk glanced at the car. The driver held a gun in the crook of his left elbow, aimed in his direction. It wasn't the gun that dismayed him, but the man's neatly trimmed black beard. He was the same heavyset man who'd tossed a grenade at him in Amarna.

Summer recognized him, too. "Rod, do as he says."

Zeibig fumbled to open the door, then slid into the backseat. The sidewalk gunman jumped in and slammed the door.

As the car screeched away, Dirk and Summer turned to each other with the same look of dread. And the same question in their head.

Why had the gunmen followed them to Assiut and kidnapped Zeibig?

26

Call the police," Dirk yelled. "I'll see if I can follow them."

He took off at a sprint, chasing the car as it sped down the block. He hoped he could flag a passing car, but saw only a dilapidated produce truck traveling the opposite direction. Ahead on the sidewalk, he spotted a female student wearing a hijab parking a red scooter at a bike rack.

The girl was startled when Dirk ran up and grabbed the handlebars, yanking the machine toward the street.

"Sorry . . . need to borrow it," he said. "Police coming." He pointed back at Summer and Riki, then searched for the starter.

The girl stormed after him, demanding in Arabic that he give it back. Dirk turned the key, twisted the throttle, and zipped away before she could get close enough to hurl more than an insult.

The scooter, a twenty-year-old faded red Vespa, looked like

it had weathered a hundred sandstorms. Dirk was relieved that despite its appearance, the old thing ran strong and true.

A full block ahead, the white sedan was forced to slow as it followed a bus into a traffic circle. Dirk kept the throttle pegged, racing through the light traffic. The sedan entered the traffic circle, passed the first two exits, and turned onto a side street that ran through the center of the university.

Dirk bypassed the circle, swerving around an oncoming car and cutting the corner with a sharp left turn. The move shaved several seconds off the sedan's head start, and Dirk closed to within twenty yards.

Unaware of Dirk's pursuit, the driver motored at a leisurely pace down the tree-lined road. Hearing the oncoming wail of the Vespa, he glanced in his mirror and saw Dirk approaching fast. Rather than step on the gas, he stomped on the brakes, then threw the car into reverse.

Dirk saw the backup lights, released the Vespa's throttle, and braked hard. He was too close. As the car's trunk came barreling toward him, he swerved hard to the right. The bumper just nicked his rear wheel, sending him sliding across the road toward a large sycamore tree.

Dirk goosed the throttle and pulled up on the handlebars. The Vespa pitched forward, hopping a curb and lurching past the tree. Dirk then locked up the brakes, but had to swerve again to miss a student on a bicycle. With nowhere to go, he bounded across a sidewalk and skidded into a bougainvillea bush. Sharp thorns pricked him in a dozen spots. He was otherwise unhurt. The Vespa, with a few more scratches added to its battle-scarred surface, signaled its durability with a *putt-putt* idle.

A pair of students helped pull Dirk from the bush.

"Are you hurt?" one asked.

"Only my ego," he said. "Thanks all the same."

He gave the scooter a quick once-over, hopped aboard, and twisted the throttle. The sedan had already sped off down the road. Dirk drove across the sidewalk and off the curb, resuming the chase a block behind. This time the Vespa was less cooperative, thumping from a bent rear wheel that rubbed against the frame.

Dirk coaxed as much speed as he could from the scooter while trying to keep the car in sight. The sedan had reached the far side of the campus, where the road ended at a cross street fronting a waterway called the Ibrahimiya Canal. The car turned right at the canal road and disappeared, heading toward the Nile.

Somewhere in the distance a siren wailed. Dirk hoped Summer and Riki had given the police an accurate description of the car. As he reached the crossroad, he was forced to slow for a flatbed truck, then turned right. He zipped around the truck and looked for the fleeing car.

It wasn't there.

He held the throttle down and desperately scanned the surroundings. Then the car appeared, passing above him. Ahead, a circular exit ramp looped over and around to a bridge that crossed the Ibrahimiya.

Dirk steered onto the ramp. As he circled onto the bridge, he saw a wisp of smoke. The white sedan had locked up its tires and was skidding to a stop along the curb. The back door sprang open, and Zeibig was shoved out. The backseat gunman followed, one hand grasping Zeibig's shirt, the other a pistol. They staggered onto a pedestrian walkway. The gunman gave Zeibig a hard push that sent him sprawling against the side bridge rail.

As Dirk closed fast, the gunman regained his footing and angled his pistol toward Zeibig. Approaching a drainage cut in the curb, Dirk nudged the Vespa onto the walkway and steered toward the men.

The gunman wheeled around to see Dirk barreling down at full speed. He raised the gun to fire. Then self-preservation took over, and he dove for the safety of the car.

He was a hair late.

The scooter's nose clipped the gunman in the shoulder, knocking free the gun—and very nearly the gunman's arm.

The collision threw the scooter into a high hop and a skid. Dirk bounced into the air, barely hanging on as the Vespa slammed into the bridge rail. He could do only one thing to save himself—push off the scooter at impact.

As the Vespa came to an abrupt halt, he shoved off with his arms. The momentum sent Dirk flying over the bridge rail. He tried to compress his body into a tuck as he braced for impact. It didn't come. At least not right away.

It was a twenty-foot drop to the canal below, where he splashed hard into the water.

The cool canal eased any sense of physical shock, and he stroked to the surface. He swam to a concrete abutment, grasped the corner, and caught his breath. Once he'd regained his bearings, he shook off a pain in his knee and elbow and swam for the nearest shore.

At the canal bank, Zeibig rushed down and pulled him ashore. "Are you all right?"

Dirk nodded. "I had a nice rotation, but could have made a cleaner entry."

"I'd rate it a ten. That was quite the kamikaze move."

"I thought he was going to shoot you." He looked up to the bridge. "Are they gone?"

"After you nearly took the guy's arm off, he was in no mood to stick around. Crawled into the back of the car, and away they went. I think the sirens did the trick, though it came from a wayward fire truck."

"Good riddance all the same," Dirk said. They made their way up to the road. "I recognized the driver. He was at Amarna yesterday, the one with the grenades. What did they want from you?"

"I don't know. They took my phone and demanded its passcode. That was it. I still have my wallet. And my hide."

Back at the bridge, Dirk gazed at the remains of the Vespa and shook his head. "Let's see if we can find the girls."

They hiked back across campus and found Summer and Riki still outside the hospital, speaking with an Egyptian police officer who'd just arrived. Summer did a double take when she saw Dirk's soggy clothes.

The student in the hijab had a different reaction. "That's him. He's the one. He's the man who stole my scooter." She lunged at him.

Dirk jumped back, bumping into Riki.

She laughed. "Are you always so magnetic to the opposite sex?"

Dirk walked over to the officer, holding his palms up. "Yes, I borrowed her scooter to rescue my friend. I'm sorry, it's now wrecked. I promise I will buy her a new one."

The skeptical officer oversaw an exchange of information. The young woman was finally pacified when Dirk and the others pooled some cash and handed it to her. The officer then interviewed Zeibig about his abduction. He took note of the information as if it was a daily occurrence, then asked Zeibig where he was staying.

"On a boat, but departing for the U.S. tomorrow."

The officer made another note and left.

"I'm not going to hold my breath that we'll hear from him again," Summer said.

"It's not that big a city," Zeibig said. "They might track down the owner or encounter the car elsewhere."

"Hopefully, *we* won't . . . Everyone still up for lunch?"

Dirk patted his damp clothes. "As long as there's no dress code."

They had lunch at a sidewalk café a few blocks away, then made their way back to the boat. Summer was the first to board. She stopped when she saw the wheelhouse. She turned to the others with a glare in her eyes. "We've had visitors."

The wheelhouse and galley looked like a tornado had passed through. Papers, stores, and furniture were strewn about. The carnage carried over to the three forward cabins. Each had been tossed. Oddly, their laptops were still there.

"Wonder what they were after," Dirk said.

"I don't see anything missing," Summer said. "Not that we had a great deal worth stealing."

"I know what they took," Zeibig said a short time later. "The stone carving from Amarna."

A thorough search revealed it was the only item missing.

"They must have tracked us here." Dirk picked some survey records off the floor and tossed them onto the galley table.

"Maybe looking for more items from the tomb," Riki said. "That carving would fetch an attractive price from a private collector."

"That's just great," Summer said, rolling her eyes. "We get to file another report with the local police."

Zeibig sighed. "Going to have to use your own phone."

"Probably not worth the trouble," Dirk said. "They've gotten everything they wanted out of us. But it might be worth calling the hospital to request security for Dr. Stanley."

Riki checked her watch.

"Time to go?" Dirk said.

"I'm afraid so."

While Dirk took her bags ashore, she said her good-byes to Summer and Zeibig.

"I'm sorry for all the trouble," she said. "Egypt is never the safest place in the world. The professor and I can't thank you enough for your help."

"Just make sure he keeps shoveling dirt, will you?" Zeibig said. "It's the best thing for him. Have a safe flight."

She met Dirk waiting on the dock, and they walked slowly to the riverfront street above the marina.

"Will you be back to Egypt soon?" he asked.

"I'm afraid I have plenty of work waiting for me in the UK. How about you?"

"We're about wrapped up here, but we have some down time before our next project. Perhaps I can finagle a detour on the way home." He paused to gauge her reaction.

"I'd like that."

When the cab approached Dirk opened the door, tossed in her bags, and gave Riki a hug. "See you soon."

"I hope so." She reached up and kissed him, then slipped into the cab. As it pulled away, she looked back at Dirk as he waved.

"Airport?" the driver asked.

She waited until the boat and dock fell out of sight.

"No," she said in a sober tone. "Take me to the Ramses Hotel."

27

Pitt stepped past his collection of antique cars and climbed the spiral staircase at the back of the airport hangar. The stairs led to a second-floor apartment that overlooked the vehicles parked below. Entering the apartment, he was surprised to find the dining table elegantly set for dinner. A pair of tall candles burned between the two place settings, next to an open bottle of red wine.

Loren stepped out of the kitchen, carrying a steaming pot to the table. She removed a pair of oven mitts, wrapped her arms around Pitt, and gave him a lingering kiss.

"You're right on time," she said with a glimmer in her eye.

"What's the special occasion?"

"I depart for Scotland tomorrow. I feel bad for leaving, as I'd expected you'd still be working in Detroit. Plus, after your escapade in College Park, I thought you could use a relaxing meal."

"You get no argument from me. What's for dinner?"

"Bouillabaisse. I used St. Julian Perlmutter's recipe."

"Then it must be good." Pitt poured the wine, a bottle of Châteauneuf-du-Pape, as she dished up the Mediterranean seafood stew.

"I don't know if this trip is even a good idea," Loren said as they started to eat. "I felt obliged when Evanna McKee phoned to invite me. She practically begged me to attend."

"She's certainly forceful. It could be a good networking opportunity, if nothing else."

"True, but that doesn't mean much to me. There's something strange about that woman. I can't quite put my finger on it. She was quite inquisitive, playing Twenty Questions with me."

"What did she want to know?"

"She asked about the committees I serve on and my interaction with Senator Bradshaw and other key legislators. She also inquired about my political aspirations."

"Your political aspirations?"

"I laughed and told her I had none. McKee seemed more interested in my career than I am. Do you know what else she wanted to know? She asked if I wanted to be president!"

"What did you tell her?"

"I said I'd be honored to serve in the job, but I'd never be willing to go through the election gristmill required to win it."

"Smart girl."

"She proceeded to name-drop all over the place and expressed a willingness to help me advance my stature. What do you think of that?"

"Promoting women to positions of leadership is apparently important to her," Pitt said. "She may be looking for help in getting her company's products into the U.S. Or she may see that you have considerable influence in Washington and wants you as a member of her club."

"You're probably right. She also seemed to be knowledgeable about NUMA's work and peppered me with questions about you."

"What did she want to know?"

"She asked about the Detroit project and other underwater jobs you've been involved with. Oh, and she asked about El Salvador and if you were going back there."

"Go back to El Salvador?" Pitt sat back in his chair, contemplating the question. "One of the water samples from Cerrón Grande Reservoir was to have been sent to a research scientist at one of her companies."

"That's curious," Loren said. "A friend who's an environmental lobbyist told me a couple of interesting things. While she doesn't know McKee personally, she does know some people who work for the company. They'd told her about one of their cleanup projects in the Middle East a while ago. They claimed some of the people deploying their product became very sick, and a few even died. It was all covered up under the guise of a flu outbreak."

"The sample bioremediation product they provided to NUMA tested out perfectly safe," Pitt said, "but who knows what's been deployed in other parts of the world."

"The EPA gave them a green light in Detroit as well," Loren said. "The other thing my friend mentioned was the untimely death of a high-level researcher who worked for BioRem Global. Apparently, he recently died in an auto accident."

"Sad," Pitt said, "yet not uncommon."

"Yes, but my friend said there were rumors it was no accident."

"Killed? Why?"

"That's what I asked. She thought it might have had something to do with a secret area of research they've delved into."

Pitt considered the comments, swirling the wine in his glass.

Later, when their meal was finished, they cleaned up the dishes and retired to the living room.

"I guess I should get packing," Loren said a few minutes later. "Can you pull out a suitcase for me?"

Pitt returned a moment later carrying two large suitcases.

"I only need one," Loren said.

"The other one's for me."

"Where are you going?"

"Scotland," Pitt said with a crooked smile. "I think I'd like to pay a personal visit to the BioRem Global research headquarters and its inquisitive chief executive."

28

She seems like a nice girl, if a little quiet," Summer said as Dirk stepped back onto the boat.

"Yes, Riki's got a good head on her shoulders."

"As if that's all you're interested in."

"I'm sure I don't know what you're talking about."

Zeibig emerged from the galley with an armload of sonar records. "If Riki had seen the end of Evel Knievel's mad scooter ride, she'd probably have left him a lot earlier."

Dirk shook his head. "Like I said, I'm sure I don't know what you're talking about."

"The university wants their boat back tomorrow, presumably without the scattered mess," Zeibig said. "Perhaps you can help organize our equipment while I clean up the records."

"Only too glad to help." Dirk fled his sister's gaze.

By early evening they had organized the boat and packed their sonar equipment for shipment home. A refreshing breeze off the river filled the galley as Zeibig plopped onto the bench with a chilled bottle of water. Summer sat nearby with her laptop as Dirk joined them.

"I think that about does it," Dirk said, stretching his arms. "Just need to pack our personal gear and we're off in the morning."

Summer looked up from her computer. "I was able to contact the Egyptian police officer we spoke with. I told him about the boat and the missing stone. He said he'd add it to the report, but there's not much he can do without a picture."

"Gone with Rod's phone now," Dirk said.

Zeibig contemplated the bottle of water in his hand. "Perhaps not."

"What do you mean?" Summer asked.

"Before we left Amarna, I tried to email some photos of the tomb to the NUMA archeology database. I forgot we didn't have a phone signal, so it didn't send."

"But it may have sent," Dirk said, "when we reached Assiut this morning and got a signal."

"That's what I'm thinking. I'm pretty sure I included some pictures of Summer's stone."

"If it's out there," Summer said, "then Hiram can find it." She looked at her watch. "It's just after eleven a.m. in Washington. Let's give him a try."

She tapped her keyboard and initiated a video call to NUMA headquarters. After several rings, an image appeared—a lean, fit man with a long ponytail, wearing a Derek and the Dominos T-shirt. He sat at a curved table backed by a massive video board.

"Livingston, I presume?" he asked.

"No, it's Pitt, Pitt, and Zeibig, I'm afraid." Summer pivoted the laptop so he could see the others. "You do have the right continent."

"How's our wandering band of river nomads?"

"Hot, dusty, and in need of a cold beer."

"Afraid I can't help you there."

"We're actually looking for some ethereal support as well." She described the stone and tomb discovery and resulting incidents, and Zeibig's phantom photo upload.

Hiram Yaeger looked at Summer and nodded. "I'm glad everybody is safe now. As for the download, that's pure child's play." He turned to a computer console and began tapping its keys.

Yaeger served as the head of NUMA's Computer Resource Center. Despite his hippie appearance, Yaeger was no slacker. He had single-handedly built up the agency's computing resources to rival those of the major intelligence organizations. A top-of-the-line supercomputer helped drive the horsepower that collected, sorted, and analyzed ocean currents, water temperatures, marine life, and weather conditions from thousands of points around the globe. Before Summer knew it, Yaeger flashed onto the large video board a photo of Amarna from the Nile.

"Is this the one?" he asked. "I located a file on one of the servers that hit Rod's archeological database about ten hours ago. It contains nothing but JPEG images."

"That's the one," Zeibig said, slapping the table. "Nice work, Hiram. Can you run through the files in order? There should be an early photo or two of a white stone tablet that Summer pulled from the river."

Yaeger flipped through a dozen photos of the survey boat, the Nile shoreline, and some sonar records, then found a photo of Summer passing up an object from the water. The next showed a close-up of the tablet, still wet from the river.

"That's it," Summer said.

More typing came from Yaeger. "I just emailed it back to the three of you."

"Hiram, while you have it up," Dirk said, "could you have Max tell us what she thinks of it?"

"Sure," Yaeger said. "Let me wake up the beast."

In front of the video board, a striking woman suddenly appeared, dressed in a tight blouse and short skirt. A holographic image modeled after his wife, Max had been created by Yaeger as a user-friendly interface to the complex computer network.

"Good morning, Hiram," the image said in a seductive voice. "You have company today?"

"Yes, Max, friends in Egypt." He identified the group on the video call.

"Always a delight to have someone intelligent to talk to." She turned to her creator and winked. "How may I serve you?"

"Take a look at this photo of a stone tablet that Summer recovered from the Nile off the ancient city of Amarna," Yaeger said. "What can you tell us about it?"

Max looked at the photo while the computer scanned the image and compared it to an internal archive, followed by a search of dozens of academic and private research databases around the world. In seconds, she displayed a beaming smile.

"Congratulations, Summer," she said. "You've made what appears to be a very ancient and most unique discovery."

"Except for the fact it has since been stolen," Summer said. "What can you tell us about it?"

"While not definitive, the slab appears to be made of alabaster, which can be found in numerous desert regions of Upper Egypt, and was used by the ancients in many of their structures and monuments. Though damaged, there is a clear representation of the sun in the manner used to depict the god Aten during the reign of Pharaoh Akhenaten. So it was likely carved during the Eighteenth Dynasty in the New Kingdom era, dating to approximately 1350 B.C.E."

"Just what we hoped for, having found it at Amarna. Can you decipher the hieroglyphics?"

Max wrinkled her nose. "It appears to be a fragmentary piece from a larger slab or monument. Absent the full text, I can translate only the visible glyphs, which are somewhat inconclusive. As you can see, there are two sections of hieroglyphics. On the left, we have symbols in an upright oval. This is a standard cartouche, which typically signifies a royal name. In this instance, we have Princess Meritaten, the eldest daughter of Pharaoh Akhenaten and his wife, Nefertiti."

"Was she buried at Amarna?" Zeibig asked.

"No. A surviving boundary stela—or marker—in Amarna describes tombs having been prepared for Akhenaten, Nefertiti, and Meritaten, but they were never used. The mummy of Akhenaten has only recently been identified as the likely occupant of tomb KV55 in the Valley of the Kings near Thebes. No tomb or mummy has been found of Meritaten," Max said, "which may be explained by the stone's other inscription."

"Go on," Hiram said.

"The second section indicates it's an homage or appeasement to the god Aten, in memory of the Pharaoh and others who died in Amarna from the tainted waters of the Nile. Princess Meritaten, absent from her father at his death, is condemned for providing aid to someone named Osa. Or at least that is the first part of his name, as the stone is fractured there. That's all I can decipher from the visible glyphs."

"That's pretty dramatic," Summer said. "I was expecting something more on the order of 'King Tut Slept Here.'"

"That is an important note about Akhenaten dying from a river illness," Zeibig said.

"It seems to relate to the mural and what Dr. Stanley said about a plague," Dirk said. "Let's see what Max can make of the tomb mural. Hiram, can you flip through a few more of Rod's photos?"

Several dark photos appeared on the screen.

"There, stop at that one," Zeibig said. "That's the best shot of the entire mural before it was shot up. Max, what can you tell us about this image?"

Max seemed to squint at the video board as the computers in the back room processed the image with silent efficiency.

"Based on a comparison with other Egyptian burial sites, it relates to the tomb itself," Max said. "There is a depiction of the deceased, a young boy, on a journey to the afterlife. A request is made, through the Pharaoh, that the Aten watch over the child on his journey to the afterlife."

"That was Dr. Harrison Stanley's interpretation," Summer said. "He indicated that the image on the right depicts a royal daughter imparting something called the Apium of Faras before fleeing Egypt."

"Yes, that is my translation of the hieroglyphic panel as well. The image appears to show dying children along the Nile, behind the royal daughter."

"Is any other information apparent?" Dirk asked.

The portion of the mural was instantly enlarged on the video board behind Max. Though her back was to the screen, she relayed the information as if she had studied the image.

"There are two small inscriptions faintly visible under enlargement," she said. "The woman on the boat passing the bag ashore has a cartouche on her bracelet." She hesitated as the photo enlarged again and focused on her wrist. "The hieroglyphics on the cartouche read 'Meritaten.'"

"Meritaten again, as on the tablet," Summer said, surprise in her voice. "Is there any identification on the two men near her?"

"None that can be seen. Their attire is that commonly depicted on laborers."

"This Princess Meritaten seems to have had a notable presence in Amarna," Zeibig said.

"Max," Hiram said, "you indicated you found two small inscriptions. What was the second?"

"It is a marking on the bag carried by Meritaten," Max said. "It is labeled 'Faras.'"

"The Apium of Faras," Dirk said. "Does that mean anything to you, Max?"

"There are references to it as a powerful curative. Faras was an administrative center in the Nubian region of Upper Egypt.

An important temple existed in the city, contained within a walled fortress. The priests of Faras were known for their medicinal powers. King Tutankhamun dedicated a shrine to them and their famed herbal medicine. In later centuries, an important Christian cathedral was built in the city, which was excavated in the 1960s before the area was flooded by the construction of the Aswan High Dam."

"Was the Tutankhamun shrine removed before the flooding, like some of the other Egyptian monuments?"

"No, the temple and its shrine were not recovered ahead of the flooding, presumably due to their deteriorated condition."

"Max, would you have a precise location of the temple?" he asked.

"Yes, I can interpolate from the report of a British excavation performed there in 1903." She provided a GPS coordinate. "Just watch out for crocodiles."

"Thanks. And thanks again, Hiram. You preserved some valuable information for Egyptian archeologists everywhere."

"No problem. I'm here if you need me."

Max and Yaeger disappeared from the screen as Summer disconnected the call. She opened her email and pulled up Zeibig's photo of the undamaged mural.

"It's a remarkable image," she said, "of an interesting woman."

"I'd like to know her full story," Zeibig said.

"Something just doesn't make sense," Dirk said. "I can understand the interest by antiquities thieves in the Amarna tomb, and also tossing our boat for more artifacts. But why risk additional exposure by stealing Rod's phone?"

"Maybe it was exposure that they feared," Zeibig said. "Perhaps they thought I had taken pictures of them at some point."

"Could be," Summer said. "I think it was the unaltered mural they were really worried about."

"Maybe so," Dirk said. "What self-respecting tomb raider would leave behind a solid gold chariot?"

"Then the question is, what's so important about this image of Princess Meritaten in the mural?" Summer enlarged the photo's lower corner, highlighting the princess on the boat.

"Maybe it's not the princess," Dirk said. "Maybe it's what she's holding."

"The Apium of Faras?"

Dirk nodded.

"It just looks like an herb of some sort," Zeibig said. "What could it possibly represent?"

"Maybe nothing," Dirk said. "There's one way to find out."

Summer frowned. "Max said the temple is buried at the bottom of Lake Nasser."

Dirk gave his sister a smile. "Since when are you afraid of a little water?"

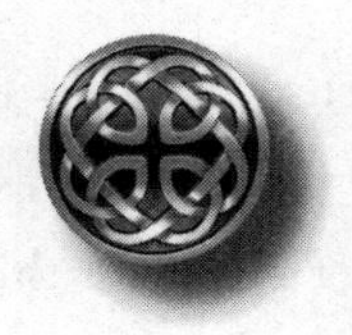

29

A little water, in the case of Lake Nasser, amounted to nearly thirty cubic miles' worth. Created by the construction of the Aswan Dam in 1902, and supplemented by the Aswan High Dam in 1971, Lake Nasser is one of the world's largest man-made bodies of water, extending over three hundred miles, from the Upper Egypt city of Aswan to the northern Sudan desert.

Summer glanced out the window of a propeller-driven commuter plane and studied the expanse of dark water. The lake's shoreline was a jagged line of capillary-like intrusions into the desert sands. The harsh and empty wasteland that surrounded the lake offered few signs of life.

She leaned over to Dirk. "This lake is huge. We've been flying over it for half an hour."

"I'm more concerned about its depth." Dirk's nose was buried in a report on Nubian archeological excavations before the completion of the Aswan High Dam. "Some areas reach six hundred feet deep."

"If that's the case around Faras, we should have followed Rod to Cairo and flown back to D.C."

"The good news is that Faras is a long way from the dam. It's near the Sudanese portion of the reservoir they call Lake Nubia. The maximum depth there is four hundred twenty-five feet, with an average around eighty."

"I'll take the average. Where does Max put it on the lake?"

"Near the center corridor, unfortunately, a dozen miles south of Abu Simbel. The water level changes constantly, so we won't know the depth until we get there."

The plane touched down a short time later at Abu Simbel Airport, and Dirk and Summer followed a throng of tourists onto the baking tarmac. They collected their bags, made their way past a pair of tour buses, and hailed a weather-beaten cab. It was less than a five-minute ride through the dusty village to a cracked concrete dock aside the lake. A smiling, mustachioed man dressed in white waited for them beside an open-topped runabout.

"Ms. Pitt? I am Ozzie Ackmadan, proprietor of the Abu Simbel Inn." He rushed over and shook Summer's hand. "I have the boat you called about all ready. It is full of gas and has two dive tanks that were delivered this morning."

"Very kind of you to meet us here."

"Enjoy your day on the lake. You can return the boat right here. The hotel is just two blocks over." He pointed up the road. "I have two rooms reserved for you tonight. Let me take your luggage, I have a vehicle right off the dock."

"Thank you," she said. "We'll look forward to seeing you later."

Dirk loaded their dive bags into the boat and cranked on the outboard motor. Summer released the dock lines and hopped aboard, taking a seat on the bow as Dirk guided the boat out of the small cove.

He briefly turned the boat north, hugging the eastern shore to take in the view of one of Egypt's most iconic sites. Facing the water was the Temple of Abu Simbel, featuring four colossal statues of the seated Pharaoh Ramses II.

"It's quite impressive in person," Summer said, admiring the scale of the statues compared to the tourists milling about their base like ants.

"Equally impressive," Dirk said, "is that they were relocated here in the 1960s from their original site, along with twenty-three other important temples and monuments that would otherwise have been flooded by the Aswan High Dam."

"Too bad our Faras temple was one of the victims."

Dirk looped the boat around to the south and opened the throttle. Leaving Abu Simbel, they motored into a barren stretch of the lake that stretched for fifty miles to Sudan.

Dirk reached into his dive bag and powered on a GPS unit he had purchased in Assiut. He'd already entered the coordinates of the Faras temple provided by Max and steered toward the point a dozen miles away. As the boat bounced through the waves, Summer assembled their dive kits and confirmed the borrowed air tanks were topped off.

Reaching the designated location a half hour later, Dirk positioned the boat over the coordinates, and Summer released an anchor off the bow. She let the rope slip through her hands, measuring the line as it went. When the line went slack, she tied it off to a cleat and turned to Dirk. "Looks to be about seventy-five feet. We got lucky."

"Our real luck will be if we can find any remains of the temple."

Despite a surface water temperature of eighty-five degrees, they slipped on lightweight wetsuits since it would be considerably cooler at the bottom. Before they donned their tanks, Dirk pulled a sheet of paper from his dive bag and showed it to Summer.

"Hiram found a hand-drawn image of Faras from the 1890s. It identifies the layout of the temple. Much of the building materials had been dismantled for reuse, but there were still remnants of the temple and a notable shrine wall. The fortress around it was quite a large structure. The remains look significant, so we should be able to see those. The temple was at the northernmost end of the fortress and contained a small sanctuary."

Summer studied the drawing and nodded. "That gives us something more than a needle in a haystack. If we can locate the temple and sanctuary, then we have a shot at finding the Tutankhamun shrine and its description of the Faras apium."

"The early British archeologists placed it in the sanctuary. Let's see if Max put us close."

Dirk grabbed a large flashlight while Summer clipped an underwater camera to her buoyancy compensator, then they both plunged over the side. After sweating in their wetsuits on the boat, the warm water brought welcome relief. They met at the anchor line and began their descent to the lakebed.

The freshwater lake had good visibility. As expected, the

water turned colder as they passed a thermocline on their way down. Dirk found the anchor buried in soft silt. He hovered above it and scanned the surroundings as Summer joined him.

The lake bottom was nearly as barren as the surrounding desert. There was just enough vegetation to attract a trio of meandering perch that nibbled on some moss-covered rocks.

The brown lakebed's surface was broken in places by rock outcroppings that reached skyward in jagged shapes. To Dirk's disappointment, nothing within their immediate range looked man-made.

Summer tapped him on the arm and pointed to one of the outcroppings. At first glance, it seemed a random collection of boulders like all the others. As he swam closer, Dirk saw Summer wasn't pointing at the rocks. She was pointing at a protrusion from the lakebed just beyond.

It rose only a foot or two, but extended linearly for nearly twenty feet. Dirk brushed a hand across the top, sweeping away a thick layer of silt. As the water cleared, he could see a layer of baked mud bricks beneath. It matched the description of the fortress walls. Dirk gave Summer a thumbs-up.

He turned back to the wall and drove his hand down the face of the bricks, working his way up to his elbow. Even at this distance from the Aswan Dam, silt had been building up, covering the ancient city's remains. It would make their search much more difficult.

They tracked the remnants of the wall west for a few yards to a corner mound and a faint ridge running north. They followed the ridge as it turned east. Both divers ascended a few feet to get a wider view of the fortress walls. Once again, Summer spotted their objective.

A short distance to the north, a round object poked from the sediment, the remnant of a column. Summer swam closer, brushed away a few inches of sediment, and exposed its fluted exterior. While the fortress would have been constructed functionally, ornate columns would more likely have been part of the temple.

The excavation records showed the temple's dimensions as fifty-six by twenty-six meters. Unlike the fortress, no clearly defined border walls had survived. As they swam north, several more stumps of columns became visible, part of the temple's central courtyard. Following the stumps, they came to a low section of stone wall. Beyond it lay a tightly packed congregation of additional column bases.

There was no longer any doubt. The packed section of columns, broken and embedded in silt, matched the drawing of the temple's main hall. They slowly swam over the column pieces, which rose from the silt like the teeth of a dinosaur. Just beyond was the ancient temple's sanctuary.

They swam past the hall, hoping to discover the temple monument beyond. Instead, a chunky stone wall a few yards away marked the back of the sanctuary. Inside, where the monument should have been, was only sand and rock.

The historical account had said much of the temple's stonework had been carried off to build later monuments. Still, the drawings indicated a small niche and wall face had survived to the 1890s. At that time, the heart of the sanctuary had still been there.

With their time at the bottom limited, Summer skimmed over the enclosure, scouring every rock and protrusion. Dirk focused his attention on the sanctuary's southeast corner. No obvious structures rose from the sediment, but he hesitated at a flat protrusion next to the hypostyle hall.

He slipped a hand into the muck and felt a smooth slab of stone down several inches. He scooped his arm across the stone, pulling away the sediment and kicking up a dirty cloud. He held still, listening to his breathing through the regulator, while the water cleared. He leaned closer, stared at the exposed stone, and smiled.

A deeply etched row of hieroglyphics stretched along the slab's jagged bottom.

Dirk waved Summer over, then attacked the heavy silt in earnest. Summer joined in at the opposite end. A cloud of murky water enveloped them. Then, as the current carried it away, they could see their discovery.

Six inches thick and made of red marble, the rectangular slab was ten feet long with a rounded top. Carved in the traditional Egyptian style of memorial stelae, it was shaped much like a modern tombstone. Its jagged base matched a nearby footing, indicating it had toppled from the sanctuary's niche. When it had fallen, the slab had cracked in multiple places, making it useless to those who cannibalized the temple's other stonework.

The hieroglyphics covering the still highly polished surface of the slab meant nothing to Dirk and Summer, yet it sparked in them the thrill of uncovering such a record of antiquity. Dirk rubbed his hand along the inscriptions, which were still crisp. Summer retrieved her camera and hovered over the monument, gazing at it in wonder. As she began snapping photos, they heard a muffled boom and felt a vibration.

They looked at each other, then scanned the lakebed. The source was too far away to determine the direction. But it had sounded man-made.

Then Dirk looked south and noticed a small glimmer high in the water, a bright object descending from the surface. As it fluttered to the bottom, landing just beyond the colonnaded courtyard, he identified the object with both dread and certainty.

It was their anchored boat.

30

A grenade had caused the boat to sink.

At least that's what it looked like to Dirk. The small hull showed a fist-sized puncture near the bow, with wide cracks streaming from its center. Black singe marks and smaller shrapnel scars peppered the area around it. The forward seat bench had been blown off, and it dangled from the gunnel by a single metal pin.

Summer pointed to the outboard motor and gas can tied to the transom. Both were intact, indicating the explosion was no accident.

Their bottom time had expired, so they had no choice but to ascend. Dirk pointed to the surface and held up three fingers, which he collapsed to a zero, then motioned flat with his whole hand. Summer nodded and kicked her fins gently to rise.

At forty feet, she released a burst of air from her buoyancy compensator to slow her ascent, and leveled off ten feet later. Dirk appeared alongside.

They were deep enough to avoid detection from the surface, yet close enough to spot any waiting vessels. One floated directly above them.

Aside from its white hull, Dirk could surmise little from beneath. Whoever stood on the boat wasn't there to welcome them with cocktails and hors d'oeuvres. As he studied the vessel's underside, he made out a pair of shadows over the near side.

It was their air bubbles. The visitors had spotted their exhaling air and were waiting for them to surface.

Dirk turned toward Summer, motioning for her to stay where she was. He released some more air from his buoyancy compensator, slipped out of its harness, and passed it with his tank to Summer. He signaled instructions and waited until she nodded. Dirk could see concern in her gray eyes, so he winked at her. He unbuckled his weight belt, let it drop to the bottom, and took a final breath from his regulator. He pulled it from his mouth, eased away from Summer, and swam for the surface.

Rather than ascend straight up, Dirk angled toward the center of the boat and its shielding cover. He exhaled as he swam, but slowly, releasing a minimum of bubbles. As the boat's shadow loomed over him, he reached up to touch the hull, staying well clear of the idling motors. He eased himself to the opposite side and poked his head just above the water to catch his breath. Low voices sounded across the deck, followed by a shout.

Summer was right on time. Having counted to thirty, she

released a jolt of air from Dirk's regulator, sending a flurry of bubbles upward. Then she topped up his buoyancy compensator and let it go, watching it ascend behind the bubbles.

Dirk tore off his mask and fins and pulled himself up the side of the boat for a quick peek. Two men at the opposite rail were peering over the side. One held a compact assault rifle, the other pointed at the water. As the buoyancy compensator broke the surface, the gunman let loose a long burst.

Using the clatter for cover, Dirk heaved himself onto the cabin cruiser and sprinted the few steps across the deck. He threw out his elbows and charged. The gunman detected movement. Before he could turn, Dirk's elbows struck him high in the back, knocking him forward. Cradling his gun, the man had no chance to catch his balance. His knees jammed against the rail, and he toppled over the side.

Dirk bounced back and tried to regain his footing, then felt a glancing blow to his chest. He looked up and grinned at the second man, whose punch had slid across his slick wetsuit. Dirk recognized his opponent. It was the same man he'd crashed into with the Vespa in Assiut. The gunman now wore a sling on his right arm, but cast it aside to throw a cross punch.

Dirk sidestepped the jab, the man leaped forward. He clasped Dirk, pinning his arms and trying to shove him overboard.

Inches away, the boat's twin outboards let out a wail. The unseen pilot in the wheelhouse had thrown the throttles forward.

The deck rose beneath their feet as the props dug in. Clinched together and unable to grab for balance, both men tumbled backward onto one of the engines' housings. Dirk landed alongside the other man and could feel them both sliding off the cowl.

Dirk reached out with a foot and caught the lip of the transom, holding himself for just a second. The other man kept sliding and grabbed for Dirk. Their combined weight was too much, and Dirk lost his hold. The delay allowed him to twist atop the other man as they slid off the motor housing.

The twin propellers were spinning at better than 6000 rpm when they fell into the water and the gunman's back struck the blades. Dirk felt a slight bounce, then the man's grip went limp as they submerged into red-tinted water. When the engines' roar receded, he pushed the lifeless body away and surfaced.

A few yards away, the other gunman struggled to tread water. He'd lost his rifle and seemed less concerned with Dirk than with staying afloat.

In the distance, the cabin cruiser turned a tight arc and looped back toward them. Dirk watched for it to slow and pick up the other man, who began yelling and waving his arms. Instead, it kept its speed and barreled directly toward Dirk.

As the boat's sharp prow approached, Dirk bent his torso and tried to dive. But his buoyant wetsuit interfered. Without his fins, he struggled to stay underwater. As the hull drew near, Dirk turned and swam toward the gunman, kicking and flailing as hard as he could.

The boat's pilot briefly lost sight of him, then tried to correct course a fraction too late. The boat roared past Dirk, missing his legs by inches. Dirk stopped and surfaced, tracking the boat as it ran out a short distance and began to turn.

A hand clasped his shoulder, and he turned to find the floundering gunman grasping for support. It was the bearded driver from Assiut.

"Help me," he gasped. "I'm drowning."

The man was in a full panic, thrashing and kicking while he clung to Dirk's back.

As Dirk struggled to free himself, he kept one eye on the cabin cruiser. It had completed its turn and was barreling back toward them.

Entangled with the gunman, Dirk had no chance to dive clear. He needed to break free. He flung an elbow backward and struck the man hard in the ribs. Desperation raged in the gunman's eyes. Dirk thrust his arms skyward to break the man's grip, but the gunman's fingers were embedded in his wetsuit like a vulture's claws. The roar of the boat thundered in Dirk's ears. He braced for impact as something clasped his ankle.

An instant before the boat struck, he was yanked underwater. The gunman clung to him as he was pulled downward. The boat struck. The hull rammed into the gunman's body.

The man's hands fell loose, allowing Dirk to separate and descend another foot. The white hull raced by, the deadly props buzzing just inches from his head.

As the maelstrom subsided, Dirk felt a fin brush past his face. Summer, with an elbow hooked around his ankle, swam for the bottom like a demon. She pulled him down to her and passed him her regulator. As he drew a deep breath, she purged air from her B.C., attaining neutral buoyancy. She maintained an inverted position, kicking her fins lightly as he clutched her vest. Together they swam horizontally, maintaining their depth while exchanging the regulator. Above, the cabin cruiser made several more high-speed passes.

Dirk and Summer waited until the boat roared away and its motors faded to silence. They remained underwater until Summer's tank was nearly empty, then they surfaced.

Dirk scanned the lake. Far to the north, he spotted the boat. He turned to Summer, who floated alongside, clearing her mask.

"Are they gone for good?" she asked.

"I think so. Thanks for the undertow. That was the closest haircut I've had in a while." He rubbed a hand over his scalp.

"Quite the hit-and-run driver. I had a pretty good view of events from downstairs. Whoever was driving that boat had little regard for his own men." She nodded toward the second gunman's body, which drifted a short distance away.

"I didn't see who was driving," Dirk said. "The other two were our armed friends from Amarna and Assiut."

"Hard to believe they tracked us all the way here."

Dirk gazed at the vast expanse of empty water and the arid wasteland around the lake. "A good place to kill someone without eyewitnesses."

"But not a great place to be abandoned without a boat. Do you think they were trying to kill us for what we already know?"

"That, or what we might find at Faras." Dirk pointed to the camera attached to Summer's B.C. "You got the pictures?"

"I got them. Whether they have any bearing on what we've already found remains to be seen."

"Speaking of bearings, do you prefer to swim west or east?"

They were nearly dead center in the lake, with a two-and-a-half-mile swim in either direction to reach shore.

Summer glanced west, then turned east. She tensed, her eyes large with fear. "I don't think we want to go east," she said in a bare whisper.

Dirk turned toward her gaze.

Barely thirty feet away, a pair of cold yellow eyes protruded just above the surface, eyeing the two with lethal desire.

31

The Nile crocodile was a beast long worshipped by the ancient Egyptians. A favored god named Sobek took the form of a crocodile. Depicted with a man's body and a crocodile head, he was believed to have created the Nile and provided strength and power to the pharaohs. Yet Sobek was also considered a dark god who required appeasement to protect the people from his river-dwelling manifestation. As an homage, live crocodiles were often kept in temple pools, and mummified crocs have been found in numerous ancient tombs. Yet the deadly reptile was rightfully feared as well.

Brother and sister cared little about the ancient treatment of the animal that had roamed the region for thousands of years. All they knew was that Nile crocodiles in Africa inflicted twenty times more fatalities a year than all of the combined shark attacks around the world. That, and the fact that the fifteen-foot behemoth in front of them appeared more than a little curious.

"Give me your fins," Dirk whispered, "then get behind me and slowly back away."

Summer slipped off her fins and passed them underwater to Dirk. She moved with desperate slowness, despite her heart's pounding. She tried not to look at the croc as she pushed away and stroked backward.

Dirk treaded water until Summer gained a healthy distance, then he eased to his left. The croc eyed him for a minute, then its powerful tail whipped the surface, and the reptile cut through the water like a green torpedo.

Dirk turned and stroked as fast as he could. He swam on the surface, intentionally splashing his strokes and kicks to draw the croc toward him. He didn't hesitate to see if the animal was following, he just swam like he was on fire. He needn't have worried. The croc took an immediate bead on him.

It was a race Dirk had no chance to win. Propelled by its massive tail, the Nile crocodile could swim in bursts of up to twenty miles per hour.

Dirk wasn't trying to outrace it, only lead it to an easier target. The second gunman's body had started to drift downstream, but still bobbed a short distance away.

As Dirk raced for the bearded man's body, he could sense the croc closing. Nearly to the gunman, he heard a loud snap and felt a tug on his swim fin. He kept swimming, up to and past the bloody body, then he stopped and held his breath.

The croc's open jaws surged out of the water and clamped down on bone and flesh. With a whip of its tail, it pulled the gunman beneath the surface. Descending into the lake, the croc followed its preferred method of killing—by drowning prey while locked in its powerful jaws—not knowing that in this instance the prey was already dead.

Dirk kept still as the croc descended beneath him. Once it was out of sight, he swiftly swam away, this time taking smooth, quiet strokes.

"He may return for seconds," Summer said when he reached her side.

Dirk resumed his stroke. "Let's not stick around to find out."

Summer jettisoned her tank, and together they raced twenty yards up current. Angling toward the west, they slowed and continued at a measured pace.

"I hope he doesn't have any friends." Summer looked ahead and over her shoulder. When Dirk didn't reply, she gave him a nudge. "What do you know that I don't?"

"They say there are ten thousand Nile crocs in Lake Nasser."

"Ten thousand! You were crazy for letting us dive here."

"I liked our odds in the middle of the lake."

"Yeah, I did, too . . . when we had a boat!"

"At least you don't have to worry," Dirk said, grinning between breaths. "They don't attack their own kind."

Summer shook her head and kept swimming, though she knew the concentration of crocs would be higher in the shallows. For now, the lakeshore was still over a mile away. With every stroke, she wondered if they'd make it that far.

They didn't.

Ten minutes later, Dirk heard a chugging sound and stopped to look. A small ferry appeared, crossing the lake from the

Sudanese town of Wadi Halfa north to Abu Simbel. Dirk and Summer swam toward its path, waving and yelling when the vessel drew near.

The ferry was little more than an open-decked motorized barge, with a small pilothouse at the stern and a canvas canopy over the main deck. A short, wrinkled man steered alongside and cut the engine as a teenage deckhand helped pull them aboard.

"Far from land," the teen said in broken English. He stepped aside after they were on deck and began coiling a long rope as if a lake rescue happened every day.

Summer spied a handful of passengers on a bench beneath the awning and headed for an empty spot. Dirk followed, gazing at a pair of camels hitched to the rail near the bow. Leaving a damp trail of footprints, he sat down beside Summer. On his other side, an old man in faded khakis napped, his face and head tucked under a straw fedora. At his feet, a small dachshund shared in the slumber, curled against a canvas knapsack with the initials C.C. stenciled on the side.

The man stirred at the squishing sound as the twins sat down in their soggy wetsuits. He raised the brim of his hat, studied the pair through clear gray eyes, and smiled. "Interesting place to be taking a dip," he said in perfect English. "Did you know the lake is teeming with crocodiles?"

"You don't say?" Dirk held up his two fins, one of which showed a large bite mark, and handed them to Summer. He glanced again at the camels. They were loaded with picks, shovels, and modern camping gear. "Are those your camels?"

"Good ol' Margy and Bess." The old man pointed toward

the animals with an arm that was brown and leathery from years in the sun. "At their age, they're no longer ships of the desert. More like leaky tow barges."

"May I ask," Dirk said, "what you're doing way out here?"

"Just a bit of archeological prospecting."

"Aren't all of the rich royal tombs far north, in the Valley of the Kings?"

"Most of the pharaohs of the New Kingdom were buried near there," he said. "It just so happens the tomb I'm searching for isn't Egyptian, but Macedonian."

"You don't mean Alexander the Great?"

"Very good, my boy. You know your history."

Dirk shook his head. "Isn't he believed to be buried somewhere under the streets of Alexandria?"

"Could be. Some think he's buried at Siwa Oasis out in the desert. Others think he might be somewhere else." The old man raised an arched brow in knowing insightfulness.

Dirk nodded. "I hope you find it."

"Someone will eventually. Might as well be Margy, Bess, Mauser, and me." He motioned toward the sleeping dachshund. "What are you kids doing on this part of Nasser?"

"Diving on the city of Faras." Dirk explained their quest for the Tutankhamun memorial. He left out the attack on their boat.

"I guess there are a few ancient mysteries still hidden under these waters on account of the Aswan Dam. What interests you in the Tut memorial?"

"The reference to a curative called the Apium of Faras."

The old man shook his head. "Never heard of it. Scientists

are finding cures for disease in all kinds of odd plants and marine life these days. I suppose someone might see riches in discovering an ancient remedy, or in keeping it out of someone else's hands. It seems a lot of folks, for one reason or another, are searching for the secrets of the ancient Egyptians."

"We're not fully sure of its significance ourselves," Summer said.

"History has a way of offering clues if you look hard enough. Sometimes, they're even right in front of you."

He rose and stretched his legs as the ferry began to slow. The dachshund also woke and stretched, following at the man's heels.

"I guess we'll be off," the man said. "Good luck with your quest."

"And you as well," Dirk said.

The ferry pulled into Abu Simbel, bumping to a stop against the same concrete dock Dirk and Summer had departed from a few hours earlier. The old man gathered his camels and led them off the boat, then trudged across town with the dachshund following right behind.

"Crazy old coot," Summer said.

"Crazy like a fox," Dirk said. "He had some interesting insights."

"And we've got potentially more." She held up her camera. But her face turned to a grimace as she glanced across the inlet. The cabin cruiser that had tried to run them down sat beached on the far shore.

She turned to Dirk. "You think they're waiting for us?"

He looked at the boat. There was no mooring line to shore.

"Looks like a rushed landing. I suspect they're long gone. Maybe Ozzie can tell us who they were."

"He said the hotel was this way." Summer stepped off the dock and up a dirt road.

Dirk caught up with her, shaking his head. "This is going to be a costly night's lodging," he muttered.

"How so?"

"Two rooms, dinner, and a speedboat. All on top of a brand-new Vespa."

Summer laughed. "Remind me never to let you borrow my car."

The wide grin on Ozzie Ackmadan's face faded at the news of his lost boat. His joviality returned once Dirk offered to buy him a new replacement.

"I'm not sure what happened," Dirk said. "I think the small white cabin cruiser at the dock may have accidentally rammed it while we were diving."

"That is my cousin's boat," Ackmadan said. He was on the phone an instant later. After a brief yet animated conversation, he held the phone aside. "My cousin says he rented the boat this morning to two Cairo men who paid cash. He doesn't recall their names. He's waiting for them to return the boat and keys."

"Did one of the men," Dirk asked, "have his arm in a sling?"

Ackmadan relayed the question. "Yes," he said.

"Tell your cousin they ditched the boat by the inlet, and it is not secured. I'll bet the keys are still in it."

Ackmadan hung up the phone a minute later. "My cousin is very angry. He said he was calling the police to report the men."

"I doubt they'll find them," Dirk said with a glance at Summer. "I think his boat is okay."

They were shown to their rooms, where they cleaned up for dinner. Summer retrieved a laptop from her luggage and waited for Dirk at a patio lounge that overlooked the lake. A leaky maze of overhead misters cut the baking temperature as the sun faded in the west.

"Is it safe to be seen in public?" Summer asked as he took a seat at her side.

"After all that swimming, I'm too tired to care." He passed her a gin and tonic he'd collected at the bar.

"I'd like to know," Summer said, "who these people are."

"Tomb raiders of some sort." He noticed an underwater photo appear on Summer's computer and leaned in for a closer look. "Faras?"

"Just downloaded from my camera." She scrolled through a dozen underwater images showing the temple courtyard and shrine, then stopped at a distant photo of the Tutankhamun marker.

"Nice image," Dirk said, "but difficult to make out the hieroglyphics."

"I snapped a few close-ups before we left." She scrolled to the next three photos, each of which featured detailed views.

"Nicely done," Dirk said. "Those should enable translation."

Summer tapped at the keyboard, then closed the screen. "I just sent the photos to Hiram and asked him to have Max translate the inscription." She took a sip of her G and T. "If the WiFi here isn't as weak as the drinks, we should have a response after dinner."

Dirk waved over a waiter, and they ordered grilled perch,

fresh from the lake. Hungry from their ordeal, they both cleaned their plates. After they split a dried fruit and date compote called *khushaf* for dessert, Summer checked her email.

"Hiram came through." Her eyes beamed.

"What does the stela say?"

"Here's Max's translation. 'The King of Upper and Lower Egypt, Nebkheperure, gifts this sanctuary to the priests of Faras. His Majesty reflects on the good of the Faras priests and their curative powers with the plant of Shahat. The sacred apium, taken by Princess Meritaten and thence distributed to the relief of the Habiru slaves, is recognized for its bountiful power. His Majesty directs the priests, in thanks, to pursue all avenues to restore the apium for the health of the Royal Family, in beloved veneration of Amun.'"

"Well," Dirk said, leaning forward. "That was revealing."

Summer read it again with eyes wide. "I can't believe it, another reference to Princess Meritaten."

"It confirms what we saw in the mural. The apium was indeed acquired by Meritaten—and apparently led to her exile."

"It also gives us a clue about the plant, evidently from a place called Shahat. Perhaps we can now solve the mystery. But who is this King Nebkheperure?"

Summer shrugged and tried an internet search. She nodded at the result. "I should have guessed. It was the throne name for Tutankhamun. He was, of course, the younger brother of Meritaten, as well as the son and successor of Akhenaten."

"There was a family that left their mark," Dirk said, shaking his head. "It sounds like they didn't realize what they had with this apium until Meritaten came along."

"She seems to have provided the slaves with the apium against the epidemic. Maybe there was a shortage, and that caused the strife."

Dirk looked out on the lake. "The tablet you found indicated that Akhenaten himself may have died of the epidemic. Maybe Meritaten took the blame—or was resented for helping others when her father died."

"Tutankhamun seems to indicate," Summer said, "they hadn't realized the power of the apium. Perhaps the Pharaoh shunned it against Meritaten's better judgment, then she was caught up in a power struggle after his death. Maybe there is something real to this apium. It could be it's what the gunmen are after." She took another sip of her drink. "One thing still bothers me. The gunmen at Amarna who stole the mummy."

"I've been wondering about that, too," Dirk said. "Why didn't they kill us in the tomb when they had the chance?"

"Maybe they didn't realize what we knew, or were to find out," she said. "That's not what's bothering me. When they came into the tomb, Rod said he glimpsed one of them wearing a surgical mask and rubber gloves."

"Both the mural and the stela mention an epidemic."

"Yes, but the gunmen hadn't seen either one. It's no secret that an epidemic had struck Amarna, yet those precautions seem odd for some ordinary grave robbers."

"Unless," Dirk said, "they were specifically aware of the disease and had targeted the tomb for that reason."

"Exactly my point."

"You know, Riki told me something interesting. A few years ago they discovered another child's tomb in Thebes. She said how furious Dr. Stanley had been when they returned to the site and found it had been ransacked."

"Strange he's had two mummies of children stolen from under him. Someone's been watching his fieldwork with a close eye."

"There are no mummies to be had in Faras."

"True. Only the stela"—Summer tapped the screen—"and the Apium of Faras."

"Both relate to Meritaten," Dirk said. "Maybe someone doesn't want her, or the apium, to be discovered."

"The Egyptians didn't exactly leave us the recipe. But, we do know Meritaten took it with her when she fled."

"Then there's only one way to discover the apium," Dirk said. He finished his drink in a gulp and gave his sister a willful smile. "We find Meritaten's grave."

PART III

SECRETS OF THE LOCH

The Sea Nymph on Loch Ness

32

The shoes," said a voice on the phone in the measured tone of a robot. "Where did you say they came from?"

"A reservoir called Cerrón Grande in El Salvador," Rudi Gunn replied. "A U.S. aid worker named Elise Aguilar wore them into the water there."

The voice on the phone paused. "Wasn't that where that dam broke?"

Dr. Susan Montgomery's methodical nature suited her occupation as a research epidemiologist with the Centers for Disease Control in Atlanta.

"Yes," Gunn said. "That's what made acquiring a sample so difficult."

"I never did receive the samples from Dr. Nakamura. I can't believe he's gone."

"His water samples were destroyed, that's why we sent the

shoes. We have reason to believe the samples may have had something to do with his death."

"How is the health of Miss Aguilar?"

"I saw her yesterday, and spoke with her again this morning," Gunn said. "Aside from an unrelated injury to her arm, she appears to be doing fine."

"Are you aware of any reported illnesses in the vicinity of the water sample?"

"Elise believes there may be a pattern of child deaths in some of the villages surrounding the reservoir."

"Can you put me in touch with Miss Aguilar? I'd like to send a CDC team down to Cerrón Grande to investigate."

"I'll have her give you a call. What have you found?"

"I can't say for certain at this point, as we just extracted a sample," Montgomery said. "It does appear to contain a waterborne bacterium that resembles cholera."

"Cholera usually results from poor water sanitation, doesn't it?" Gunn asked. "Could the reservoir water just be tainted from an unhealthy runoff?"

"Possibly." Montgomery paused. "But it's curious, since there have been no reported incidences of cholera in El Salvador in more than a decade. More worrisome are the potential deaths you mentioned."

"The circumstances do seem strange," Gunn said.

"Still, I don't wish to be premature," Montgomery cautioned. "We'll know more shortly. Biochemical and DNA testing will confirm exactly what's in the water. In the meantime, I would check the health of all parties who have been in or around the reservoir."

"Thank you, Doctor. I'd appreciate it if you can keep me apprised of your findings."

"I certainly will. I'm glad you and Miss Aguilar turned to us for help."

Gunn made two more calls. Though it was after five p.m., he had one more task for the day. He took the stairs to the fifth floor and found Hiram Yaeger at his usual post, the curved table in front of the huge video board. He was reviewing code with a pair of young software engineers, and Gunn waited until they returned to nearby cubicles before sitting beside Yaeger.

"Hope I'm not interrupting," Gunn said.

Yaeger shook his head. "A minor software glitch with our North Atlantic iceberg-tracking satellite system uplink."

"I just got off the phone with Dr. Susan Montgomery of the CDC in Atlanta. It seems that there *is* something in the waters of Cerrón Grande Reservoir."

"Is Pitt in any danger?"

"Doubtful. He'd have exhibited ill effects by now. I left him a message, but he just departed on an overseas flight. I also spoke with the young woman he rescued, Elise Aguilar, and she's fine. She agreed to see her doctor, just to be sure."

"What's in the water?" Yaeger asked.

"Montgomery thinks it could be cholera. She's waiting for test results."

"Dirk and Elise would have felt that pretty quick."

"Agreed."

"You think it's something more than that?"

"To be honest, I don't know what to think. Montgomery indicated there'd been no reported cases of cholera in El Salvador in years. Can you check if there've been any other cholera-type outbreaks recently?"

Yaeger was tapping a keyboard before Gunn finished his sentence. The video board displayed a glowing map of the world's oceans, save for an upper-corner table of Egyptian hieroglyphics. At Yaeger's instruction, the table disappeared, replaced by the search page.

"What was that?" Gunn asked.

"The inscription on a monument Dirk and Summer found on the bottom of Lake Nasser."

"I thought they were on their way home," Gunn said. "I canceled their remaining project work until the Egyptian authorities agreed to provide better security. They and Zeibig were lucky not to have been killed by those tomb robbers."

"They seem to think there's something at play beyond artifact theft."

Gunn shook his head. "Whatever it is, it's not worth the risk."

The corner video screen came alive with a list of worldwide cholera outbreaks over the past two years. The deadliest incidences were in Africa, Yemen, Haiti, and India.

"Global cholera numbers have generally been receding, but it looks like there's been a recent uptick. Sub-Saharan Africa has long wrestled with the disease," Yaeger said. "With the ongoing war, Yemen has had a severe disruption of health and sanitation services. Haiti is still recuperating from its earthquake, while India continues to upgrade its weak infrastructure."

"Its occurrence in those locations is understandable. Are there any other significant outbreaks of the disease?"

Yaeger tapped his keyboard again. "A number of places have indeed seen an increase in reported cases within the past year. Mumbai, Cairo, Karachi, and Shanghai top the list. I recall a large outbreak in Mumbai hitting the news recently, which was apparently widespread throughout the city."

"I'm surprised to see Shanghai on the list," Gunn said.

Yaeger initiated a side search. "According to news reports, it was due to suspected pollutants that weren't properly treated at a wastewater facility. Fatalities have been ongoing."

Gunn shook his head. "I guess we'll have to wait and see if the CDC and the FBI come up with anything in El Salvador."

He stood to leave, but Yaeger raised his hand. "Hang on, Rudi. I've got some additional research you asked for." He reached for a thin folder and passed it to Gunn.

Gunn glanced at the title page, retook his seat. "BioRem Global Limited, our partner in Detroit. What did you find of interest?"

"Not much, I'm afraid. It's a privately held company, so the public record is slim. It was founded in the late 1990s by Dr. Frasier Smyth McKee, who was by all accounts a genius biochemist. He left a research post at Edinburgh University to start the firm. He originally focused on cleaning up oil spills in the North Sea using microorganisms." Yaeger nodded toward the file. "The firm has since expanded its product portfolio to treat a variety of hazardous wastes with genetically engineered microbes."

"Is McKee still around?"

"He was killed in a boating accident five years ago. His wife, Evanna McKee, inherited the company, and runs it today."

"Yes, I've spoken with her."

"She's a major figure in the world of business and politics, though the company itself is nearly invisible."

"What's the scope of their work?"

"Difficult to say. Many of their jobs are contracted privately. No one likes to advertise they have a toxic spill. The file lists a handful of high-profile jobs that made the press."

Gunn flipped through the report. "They're certainly Johnny-on-the-spot when it comes to international accidents," he said. "A fertilizer plant fire on the Yangtze River, a chemical spill on the Seine near Paris, and a ruptured oil tank in Karachi. And that's all in the past six months."

"Their global presence is much more notable over the past two years."

Gunn turned the page and stiffened in his chair. The sheet listed three additional projects.

"A petroleum pipeline rupture near Mumbai, a leaking cyanide leaching pit at an El Salvador gold mine, and a chemical spill in Cairo." He glanced at the video wall, which still displayed the table of cholera outbreaks.

"Mumbai and Cairo are on the list, along with Karachi. The Yangtze River site could be Shanghai. And that's in addition to El Salvador."

"Does seem like some common ground," Yaeger said. "Let's see what we can find out about the gold mine cleanup."

He retrieved a handful of local news articles from the Salvadoran media and had them translated from Spanish. The two skimmed the articles on the big screen.

"A cyanide leaching pit at the former Potonico gold mine was breached in an apparent landslide," Yaeger said. "Authorities questioned whether environmental protestors may have triggered the slide to generate support for a countrywide ban on mining."

"Where is it located?" Gunn asked.

Yaeger displayed a map of El Salvador. "Northeast part of the country. Thirty miles from San Salvador, on the shores of Cerrón Grande Reservoir."

"Bingo! There's a connection."

"Sounds like the BioRem product for cleaning up the gold mine mess," Yaeger said, "may have had some unpleasant side effects."

"Fatal side effects that may have spread through the reservoir—and that, possibly, were sufficient motivation to blow up the dam and kill the U.S. aid team. What can you find on their Cairo project?"

Yaeger retrieved and translated local Egyptian news accounts. "Looks like a tanker spill in the Nile, at the head of the Ismailia Canal. Another collision, this one accompanied by a large fire."

"Any correlation with the cholera outbreak?"

Yaeger skimmed the results. "It appears there was a brief yet widely dispersed outbreak in Cairo's northeastern suburbs. Two hundred fatalities were recorded, but the actual number is believed much higher on account of unreported deaths. Authorities believe the source was tap water that was improperly treated. The outbreak occurred several days after the tanker accident."

"Another hit," Gunn said.

"Take a look at this article from the *Cairo News*."

A news snippet appeared with a side box translation titled "No bodies of crew recovered in fiery late night collision on Nile."

"Sounds just like Detroit," Yaeger said.

Gunn leaned forward as he read the article. Then he slumped into his seat and loosened his tie. "Hiram," he said. "I think we're going to need some coffee."

33

St. Julian Perlmutter was seated at his kitchen table, wearing his favorite paisley robe, when the phone rang. He reached past a stack of open books and a plate of half-eaten Danish, to answer a brass telephone salvaged from a 1940s luxury liner.

"Perlmutter," he said in a gruff baritone that originated deep in his massive frame.

"Hi, Julian. It's Summer."

"Well, hello, Miss Pitt." His voice melted to jocularity. "How are things in the Nile Valley?"

"Insufferably hot, and as dry as a naked martini. I hope I didn't wake you."

Perlmutter glanced at an antique clock mounted above the stove, which read eight-fifteen a.m. "Not at all. Been up since five, poking around with your inquiry."

"So you received my email?"

"Indeed. It's quite a tale you two have cooked up. Egyptian princesses and ancient plagues."

"It does sound rather unbelievable," she said. "That's why we wanted to run it by your learned eye, as well as to ask if you had any research on Princess Meritaten fleeing Egypt by sea."

Perlmutter, a longtime friend of the Pitt family, was perhaps the world's foremost marine historian. His Georgetown house outside of Washington was packed to the rafters with ship logbooks, sailing narratives, and maritime history books. The heavily built historian, known for his fondness of gourmet dining, had an encyclopedic knowledge of sea vessels, from the first dugout canoes to the latest cruise ships.

He chuckled into the phone. "I'm no Egyptologist, but I know a good one, Bob Samuelson out of Columbia. We had a nice chat about your discoveries. He confirmed your findings about the Habiru and their connection to Meritaten are quite stunning, particularly the Amarna mural that may depict a plague.

"As your British archeologist noted," Perlmutter said, "there's evidence of a widespread epidemic during the reign of Akhenaten that may have killed members of the royal family. Dr. Samuelson noted an interesting fact. After Akhenaten, no pharaoh sired a male heir for nearly fifty years. At least in his lineage, there was a long-term absence of male offspring."

"That's curious," Summer said. "Whatever the plague, Meritaten may have had some sort of cure in the form of the Apium of Faras."

"Our interpretation as well. Do we know if the child in the Amarna tomb died from this plague?"

"The tomb mural seems to indicate that, but with the mummy stolen, we'll never know."

"Of course. It seems as if someone is going to quite a bit of trouble to conceal the young princess and her connection to the Habiru. Or perhaps the curative."

"That's our conclusion as well," Summer said. "We have Hiram Yaeger on the hunt for what the Apium of Faras might actually be. We hoped you might shed some light on where Meritaten may have sailed in her bid to escape."

"I do have information on the the travels of an Egyptian princess," he said. "You see, the ancient Egyptians were in fact excellent sailors and shipbuilders. The first use of a sail may well have been on a reed boat in the Nile, and later they constructed huge barges to transport stone for their construction projects. In the New Kingdom period, when Akhenaten ruled, Egypt was known to trade with mainland Greece and as far away as the Horn of Africa. So there's no doubt our Princess Meritaten had the means to travel a great distance in a sailing vessel, or perhaps a fleet. And apparently she did."

"You found evidence of her voyage?"

"And quite a bit more. The archeologists tell us there's been no discovery of her burial in Egypt, so it's safe to look beyond. There we find circumstantial evidence she may have traveled to the Iberian Peninsula and established a settlement near Amposta, Spain, south of Barcelona."

"That sounds logical," Summer said. "Just across the Mediterranean, yet beyond the reach of Egyptian authorities. That's a marvelous discovery, Julian. Are there ruins in Spain that Dirk and I should examine?"

"You won't want to waste your time there, as she didn't stay in Spain long. In fact, you'll want to look quite a bit farther north," Perlmutter said. "It seems our Egyptian princess was well traveled—and she had a more profound impact on history than you could have imagined."

"What could that be?"

Perlmutter let out a chuckle. "Would you believe, my dear, nothing short of founding a Celtic empire?"

34

Loren shook her head, then closed the window. "Slow down! I agreed to the car. I didn't say you could drive like a madman."

Pitt shrugged. "It's the car's fault. It just wants to swallow the road."

He couldn't help himself at the Edinburgh car rental office, after their flight from Washington landed. Amid the rows of Euro sedans and coupes, he spotted a black MINI John Cooper Works. Pitt couldn't resist the 2.0 liter, four-cylinder Twin Power Turbo, sixty-two miles per hour in a little over six seconds. He made the upgrade while Loren was in the ladies' room.

"Last car they had left," he said as he compressed their bags into the microscopic backseat.

"Oh, right," Loren said smiling. She had seen the poster advertising the promotion with Mini Cooper and knew it was a done deal. Once outside the city they traveled north from

Edinburgh into the Scottish Highlands. Loren settled into her seat and enjoyed watching Pitt and the car work as one as he shifted through the curves and around the hilly terrain. She laughed to herself. She did know her husband.

Occasionally they pulled off so they could admire the rugged landscape's sweeping vistas. Slowly the deep blue lakes that dotted the low, rolling mountains grew darker and more foreboding the farther north they traveled.

The road ultimately descended through a patchwork of lush farm fields before entering the town of Inverness. At the confluence of the River Ness and Moray Firth, the bustling harborfront city was known as the capital of the Highlands. Pitt drove through the city, crossed the River Ness, then followed its westerly course until it was swallowed by the famous loch.

Loren gazed down the length of Loch Ness, which extended to the horizon. "It's much bigger than I thought."

"Offering plenty of places for Nessie to hide," Pitt said.

"It's beautiful, monster or no."

They followed the north shoreline for several miles, passing the village of Drumnadrochit and the ruins of Urquhart Castle. The thirteenth-century fortress, on a promontory overlooking the lake, became famous in the 1930s when an object photographed in the nearby waters was alleged to be the Loch Ness Monster.

Pitt passed a busload of tourists and continued down the road, cruising through a handful of tiny villages. Near the lake's midpoint, Pitt tapped on the brakes at a heavy iron gate flanked by stone columns and a massive header. Inscribed on the keystone were McKEE and the image of a hawk in flight.

"I believe this is the place," Pitt said.

"Modest residence." Loren gazed down the drive at an imposing stone manor.

A uniformed female guard checked their names on an iPad, then directed them through the gate to a side parking lot. Pitt pulled to a stop alongside a Mercedes-Maybach sedan that was dropping off several smartly dressed women.

Loren looked at Pitt and cringed. "We couldn't have arrived in something more dignified?"

Pitt leaned over and kissed her. "It wouldn't have been nearly as much fun."

He unloaded their bags, and accompanied Loren to the manor's portico. The front façade included a mix of old and new stone, as though someone had taken the ruins of an old castle like Urquhart and rebuilt it into a modern mansion.

The layout was of a classic medieval castle, but on a much smaller scale. High battlement walls stretched to the water's edge, with round turrets at each corner. An open courtyard was at the center, with rooms built along each of the surrounding corridors.

Loren and Pitt handed their bags to a porter and climbed the steps. They passed a second layer of security and stepped through a pair of towering carved wooden doors into a warmly lit open rotunda filled with high-powered women sampling champagne and hors d'oeuvres. A loud murmur of conversation echoed off the marble floor. They'd taken only a few steps before they were greeted by Audrey McKee.

She introduced herself to Loren and shook her hand, then

turned to Pitt. "So nice to see you again. I was pleasantly surprised to see your name on the guest list."

At first, Pitt didn't recognize Audrey as the woman he'd met in Detroit. Instead of a work jumpsuit, she now wore a magenta business suit with a silk blouse. Her dark red hair flowed loose, and she had a trace of makeup on that highlighted her searching eyes.

"The pleasure is all mine," Pitt said. "I also wasn't expecting to see you here."

"This is a highlight event for both the company and my family. It's a great honor to have you both with us." She glanced about the rotunda. "We have some important dignitaries from the world of business and politics I'd love you to meet."

Loren had already eyed a European prime minister, a fashion company magnate, and the CEO of a media conglomerate. "It would appear," she said, "to be quite an international gathering."

"Very much so. We invite leading women from around the globe and always have an impressive attendance." She looked at Pitt with a mock frown. "I'm afraid this afternoon's events are reserved for the ladies. I'd be happy to arrange a tee time for you, if you like. There's a wonderful golf course in Inverness. Or the loch is always a challenge if you prefer to try your hand at fishing."

"Actually," Pitt said, "I have an appointment with a scientist at your affiliate company, Inverness Research Laboratory, later today. Perhaps you know him. Dr. Miles Perkins?"

Audrey gave a slight nod. "Dr. Perkins has performed some

key developmental research on our environmental products. May I ask why you are seeing him?"

"A mutual acquaintance at the University of Maryland recommended his expertise. I'm looking for an analysis of a water sample from a lake in El Salvador."

"I see. I'm sure he'll be able to help you. In the meantime, let me have someone show you to your room. You must be tired from your travels. Loren, we'll convene in the grand dining hall in about an hour, if you'd like to freshen up first." With a subtle nod a uniformed doorman appeared.

"That would be nice," Loren said. "Thank you for the invitation and for allowing us to stay here. I wasn't expecting a castle."

"It's only a fraction of its original size," Audrey said. "It was originally built by the Jacobites in the 1600s, then fell to ruins. My father purchased it from a private owner and rebuilt it to his own design. It's rather small, as far as Scottish castles go, but it does have a rich, local charm. I hope you enjoy your stay."

The doorman escorted Pitt and Loren down a side corridor to their room at the end. Audrey watched them depart, then mingled with a few of the guests. She worked her way across the rotunda to an ornate stairway and climbed to the top landing. She retrieved a key card and entered a door to the side.

Inside was a long, narrow room with a one-way mirror overlooking the rotunda. Evanna McKee was sitting in an embroidered chair, studying a typewritten speech. Rachel, the tall black woman and ever-present watchdog, was sitting in the far corner.

"The guests are anxious to see you," Audrey said.

McKee didn't look up. Audrey noticed a sense of heaviness about her.

"They'll be more attentive if I make a dramatic entrance in the dining hall," McKee said softly. "Are all of the effects ready?"

"Everything is prepared. Lights, music, aromatherapy—and of course the drinks. You will have the most receptive audience on the planet. The UN Environmental Program director will introduce you, and she is suitably energized for the task."

"Very good. It's our most impressive crowd yet."

"There is one problem." Audrey cleared her throat. McKee looked up with a studious gaze.

"The NUMA Director, Dirk Pitt, has accompanied his wife."

"So I saw." McKee raised a slender finger toward the one-way glass.

"He confirmed his appointment with Dr. Perkins this afternoon. He says he brought a water sample from El Salvador that he wants tested."

McKee barely moved, her features still, as if cut from an iceberg. "I was aware of the appointment. Our good Dr. Perkins is prepared to meet him. But I didn't know about the water sample."

"Our people claim they recovered them all in Washington."

"Then, it will be an opportunity to determine if more exist. Monitor what Pitt knows. If it is too much, you must be prepared to eliminate him."

She gave her mother a knowing smile. "That is a task for which I am quite prepared."

"Very well. You best go attend to the guests. I'll be down shortly."

Audrey gave her mother a kiss on the cheek, then left the room followed by Rachel. McKee sat alone and stared at the one-way mirror. Her focus was not on the guests below, but at her own reflection. The face in the glass stared back at her with a familiar look of worthlessness. An emotional wave of self-loathing fell over her, as the grasping talons of depression clawed at her mind.

The battle with her demons was everlasting, one she had waged for most of her life. It had originated at an early age, when her father had abandoned the five-year-old Evanna and her mother without saying a word. One day he was there, the next he was gone. Rumors told of him moving to Dundee and starting a new family. The young Evanna felt responsible, carrying the guilt of the separation and the grief it imposed on her mother. The guilt only exploded when her mother, unable to cope with the emotional and economic strain, took her own life.

Evanna's world spun out of control. Raised by a senile aunt and an abusive uncle, her guilt burgeoned into rage. Rage against her father, her uncle, and most all men. A cloud of despair, along with her own suicidal thoughts, followed her like a shadow.

She found temporary escape from her ills by marrying a young soldier named Sadler. A daughter arrived, bringing new joy to her world, then her husband was taken from her to serve in the Middle East. The gloom and depression returned, along with a failed suicide attempt. Things turned up when Frasier McKee entered her life. His bright, enthusiastic, fun-loving personality swept her away, promising a happy life. That, too, came to a bitter end.

McKee put her hands to her face and peered at her reflection. As she had done so many times before, she willed away her doubts and depression with anger. Clenching her hands into fists, she squeezed until her knuckles turned white, and took a deep breath. Rising from her chair, she extended her body erect, then strode from the room with vengeance on her mind.

35

Dr. Susan Montgomery inserted a slide into the chamber of the electron microscope and activated its power controls. Once the machine created a vacuum and scanned a beam of electrons over the inserted specimen, a dark, blurry object appeared on the attached desktop monitor. She adjusted the magnification until a trio of oblong shapes appeared on the screen. They were blackish in color with a fuzzy perimeter, and resembled a handful of licorice jelly beans.

The epidemiologist for the CDC Surveillance and Data Branch compared the image to a stock photograph of *Vibrio cholerae* stored on the computer. Visually, at least, the bacteria sample on her glass slide was a dead ringer for the cholera-inducing bacteria. But a battery of other biochemical tests had told her that it was not the same.

Montgomery knew that not all forms of the cholera bacteria were toxic. The bacteria in the water sample from Cerrón

Grande, however, showed clear evidence of toxin production. And it passed most of the biochemical tests for *V. cholerae* O1, the classic subset, or serogroup, most commonly found in lethal outbreaks of the disease. Yet several of the test results were inconsistent, leading her to believe she had something different on her hands.

She was well aware that cholera, as a disease, had been a scourge of mankind for centuries, if not millennia. No less than seven worldwide pandemics had been attributed to cholera since 1817 alone, killing millions in the process. The disease, still common in developing countries, was normally spread by water supplies or food contaminated with fecal matter. Children are most harmed by the disease, often succumbing to rapid dehydration.

Cholera as a modern danger was exhibited in Haiti after the 2010 earthquake. Aid workers from Nepal inadvertently contaminated the Artibonite River, Haiti's largest waterway and a major source of drinking water. The outbreak has led to over ten thousand deaths in the devastated country in the intervening years.

Montgomery stared again at the magnified image on her monitor, when the door to the lab swung open and a bushy-haired man in a green lab coat entered. He carried a binder under his arm and a grimace on his face. Montgomery knew the division's Lab Research director to be an ebullient jokester, and she immediately noted the change in his demeanor.

"Hi, Byron," she said. "Are those my DNA homology reports?"

"Yes. You might want to remain seated while you read them." He pulled up a chair and passed her the binder.

"Troubling results?"

"I'll say. Preliminary analysis shows exactly what you suspected. The El Salvador sample bacterium does indeed have a different genetic makeup than *Vibrio cholerae* O1. DNA analysis shows an additional seventeen gene clusters in the genome structure. At this point, we're not sure of the significance."

"Seventeen?" Montgomery said. "That is a notable difference. Likely an isolated mutation, which has reproduced in the El Salvador reservoir."

Byron gave her a sober stare, then shook his head. "I'm afraid not. The computer found the same, or similar, bacteria in two of the three other water samples you sent down for analysis. In addition, we made a hit on five additional baseline control samples in our database."

Montgomery nearly popped out of her chair. "What did you say?"

"You gave us suspected pathogen water samples from Cairo, Mumbai, and Haiti. Both Cairo and Mumbai resulted in virtually the same results as your El Salvador specimen. In addition, we found evidence of similar pathogens in water samples we were testing from Karachi, Rio, Paris, Shanghai, and Sydney. Only the sample from Haiti came back different. It contained the classic *V. cholerae* O1."

"The rest were the same?" Montgomery asked. "You're sure about that?"

"Yes. Well, they all have the same structure as the El Salvador sample, except for Paris, Rio, and Sydney. Those samples each showed an additional genetic cluster. Between the samples, it appears to be two totally new serogroups we've never seen before."

"Not one, but two? It can't be." Montgomery shook her head. "A new pathogen takes time to spread. Simultaneous appearances across the globe are unheard of, even today."

"True, but the Cairo, Haiti, and Shanghai water samples are several weeks old."

Montgomery flipped through the binder, studying the analysis. "I'm not aware of any cholera outbreaks in Paris or Sydney—nor Rio, for that matter."

Byron shook his head. "Perhaps the added genetic structure has reduced the toxicity."

"Thank heavens, if so. Still, how did it appear in the public water supplies of Paris and Sydney? Those were treated water samples, weren't they?"

"Yes, the samples are from the public water system. And your guess is as good as mine."

Montgomery couldn't believe what she was hearing. A mutated form of the cholera bacteria seemed to be spreading like a global pandemic, yet without a massive death rate. At least for now. How had the same pathogen spread so quickly? She gazed at Byron and saw from the look on his face that he had more bad news.

"Something else?"

Byron nodded. "Each of the samples, except for Haiti, contained a significant portion of bacterium in a transient hypermutation state."

Montgomery cringed. All bacteria were capable of mutating into potentially more dangerous forms. Typically, signs of mutation occurred in a very tiny percentage of a bacterium colony. Bacteria in a hypermutation state, however, had upward of a thousand times higher likelihood of successfully mutating.

Montgomery felt like she had taken a blow to the stomach. She gazed at the computer monitor with the image of the fuzzy jelly beans.

"You know what this means?" she said in a low voice.

When Byron didn't respond, Montgomery answered her own question.

"It means we could be facing an entirely unknown catastrophic killer. And we have no clue how to stop it."

36

What a beautiful view of the lake."

Loren pulled open a heavy panel of curtains, exposing a southwesterly view down the length of Loch Ness. A group of people paddled kayaks along the near shore, but otherwise the calm surface was empty of boats.

Pitt lifted their luggage onto the porter stands. "This is quite a room. You must rate high on the guest list."

Though not large, their room was exquisitely decorated with Edwardian antiques. Wood-paneled walls supported oil paintings of hunting scenes and two large beveled mirrors. Across from the picture window and sitting area was an ornate four-poster bed.

"I hardly think that's the case." Loren crossed the room and opened her suitcase. "There was no shortage of movers and shakers in the lobby. Even the Spanish prime minister is here. Evanna McKee must have quite the network."

"Be sure and find out what she's selling."

Loren shook off the comment and pulled out a wrinkled dress. "Customs really went through our luggage."

Pitt opened his bag and found similar evidence of turmoil.

"How long will you be gone?" Loren asked, moving to the bathroom to brush her hair and reapply makeup.

"My meeting is in town, it shouldn't last long. Sounds like they may not let me back in for a bit. I may be forced to while away the time at a local pub."

Loren stepped back into the room and embraced him. "Don't be gone long. And if they lock the front door, I'll dangle a bedsheet out the window."

Pitt escorted her back to the rotunda, which was beginning to clear out as the guests moved to the dining hall. Pitt kissed Loren good-bye, then exited the manor. He hopped into the Mini and retraced his route back to Inverness.

Just before reaching the city, he spotted a park near the river and pulled in. At the riverside he retrieved a glass vial from his pocket and filled it with water from the River Ness. Ten minutes later, he drove into the parking lot of a nondescript building at the opposite end of town. The structure had dark-tinted windows facing the street and a fenced warehouse yard in back. The only identification was a small sign by the door marked INVERNESS RESEARCH/BIOREM GLOBAL LTD.

Inside, Pitt found an empty waiting area and a middle-aged receptionist seated at an enclosed desk.

"May I help you?" she said in a brusque voice. Black bangs hung over a pair of dark eyes that regarded Pitt with the enthusiasm normally reserved for an encounter with the undertaker.

Pitt introduced himself and cited his appointment with Perkins.

"Dr. Perkins is expecting you," she said. "Would you please sign in while I call him?" She handed him a sign-in sheet and a clip-on visitor badge, then picked up the phone. "He'll be right out," she said.

A heavyset bald man about forty emerged from the corridor, wearing a white shirt and tie and an ill-fitting sport coat. He was younger than Pitt expected and strode with the forceful gait of a rugby player.

"Mr. Pitt?" He extended a hand that was as hard as granite.

"A pleasure to meet you." Pitt shook hands with an equally firm grip. "Thank you for seeing me on short notice."

"It's not every day I get a visitor from America. Come join me in my office."

He led Pitt into the first open office down the hall. It was a bare-bones affair, with a plain wooden desk and a pair of guest chairs. A bookshelf behind the desk housed a handful of scientific journals and texts, while the desk held only a phone and a family portrait.

"Please, take a seat." Perkins parked his wide frame behind the desk. "Did you just arrive in Scotland?"

"This morning. My wife is attending a conference at McKee Manor."

"Ah, the Women's Governance League," he stated. "So, what can I do for you?"

Pitt reached into his coat pocket, retrieved the small vial, and set in on the desk. Perkins locked eyes on it, then reached over and grasped it.

"It's a water sample taken in El Salvador," Pitt said. "El Cerrón Reservoir, to be precise."

He looked for a reaction. Perkins had none.

"Why El Salvador?" he asked.

"It was one of four water samples given to Dr. Stephen Nakamura at the University of Maryland to analyze. Unfortunately, the other three were lost with Dr. Nakamura's passing."

"I heard about the fire in his lab," Perkins said. "A tragic loss."

"Did you know him well?"

"We met at a seminar a few years ago. It was a professional relationship. He gave you this sample?"

"It was from the same source as the others in his possession. I understand he was sending you one to analyze."

"Yes, he had emailed me about it. Thank you for bringing it." The tension in Perkins's voice indicated annoyance rather than gratitude. "Can you tell me the sample's significance?"

"A U.S. agricultural aid team believes there may be a connection between the water and some mysterious deaths in villages along the reservoir."

"I see. Well, we can certainly take a look at it."

"Perhaps you can answer a question," Pitt said. "Why would Dr. Nakamura send a water sample to you here in Scotland?"

"Our firm is at the forefront of bioremediation research," Perkins said. "We have the resources to analyze and identify biological impurities that other facilities may lack. Plus, Dr. Nakamura was a friend of our company's late founder, Frasier McKee."

As Perkins held the vial to the light and swirled it around, Pitt glanced at the family photo on the desk. It showed Perkins outside a soccer field with his wife and two small boys. Several older cars were parked next to the field. Pitt noticed that Perkins was wearing the same clothes now as in the photo.

"Did Dr. Nakamura indicate," Pitt asked, "what he thought the water sample might contain?"

"No. But I will be happy to share our analysis with you. It should only take a day or two."

As if on cue, the desk phone rang. Perkins listened briefly, then hung up. "I'm sorry, Mr. Pitt, I'm needed in the lab. It was very nice meeting you." He rose from behind the desk.

"Thank you for your time." As Pitt rose, he pointed at the photo. "You have an attractive family. What are your boys' names?"

Perkins glanced at the photo. The hesitation in his voice was minuscule, but unmistakable. "Finn and Liam."

With no further comment, he escorted Pitt to the lobby. "Enjoy your stay in Scotland," he said. He shook Pitt's hand and vanished down the corridor.

Pitt drove a few blocks into the city, then turned around. He circled back to the building, approached from a side street, and parked a block away.

While the Mini was concealed from the road, he had a clear view of the front of BioRem. Keeping one eye on the building, he pulled out his phone and called Hiram Yaeger at NUMA headquarters.

"Calling to get my order of Scotch whisky?" Yaeger asked.

"I thought you were a confirmed wino," Pitt said.

"Certain days require something a little stronger than grape juice. What can I do for you?"

"How about a quick and dirty biography of one Dr. Miles S. Perkins of Inverness, Scotland."

Yaeger's fingers flew over a keyboard. Pitt had a response in seconds.

"Dr. Miles S. Perkins, Ph.D. in biology from Aberdeen University?"

"Sounds like our man."

"Born in Kirkcaldy, Scotland, age fifty-five. Background in chemistry and microbiology. Taught at the University of Edinburgh for many years. Was a disciple of Dr. Frasier McKee. Joined his company, BioRem Global Limited, in 2010 as Chief Science Officer. He's published many papers on microbiology and the use of bacteria for industrial benefit. Has been married twenty-seven years to one Margaret Anne Perkins. No children."

"No children?" Pitt said.

"None that I show."

"Do you have any photos of him?"

"A few from his days at the university. Slight man with glasses, wavy dark hair. I'll email you the best ones. Did you meet him?"

"Allegedly," Pitt said. "Thanks, Hiram. I'll get you that whisky."

"Bowmore's, if you please. Thanks, boss."

Pitt's suspicions were confirmed. The man wasn't Perkins, or even a good imitation. If he had to guess, he'd say the imposter was a security man pressed into service. His speech and mannerisms didn't fit a respected scientist. The family photo looked like it had just been produced, with the fake Dr. Perkins Photoshopped in with another family. Then there was the sterile office and the semivacant building. The looming question was, why?

The answer, he hoped, was forthcoming when a gray Volkswagen appeared from behind the building. When the car turned onto the frontage street that led out of town, Pitt saw that the driver was bald. Pitt started the Mini and followed at a distance, motoring past the BioRem building.

Inside, the receptionist stood at the window and watched Pitt drive by. She hurried to her desk and dialed a number, cursing when the phone at the other end went to voicemail. She dialed a second number, which was answered on the first ring.

"A problem with the meeting?"

"No, it went well," the receptionist said. "He claimed to have a water sample from El Salvador, which we obtained. I'll send you the video straight away. The problem is Richards. He just departed with the sample to take it to the lab. I think Pitt is following him."

"Did you try calling Richards?"

"Yes, but he didn't answer."

"I see. He should have shown more caution." A pause. "Position one of the lorries on the lab road from Foyers. Meet him on the way back. And make it look like an accident."

The receptionist had no opportunity for debate. With a click, the line fell dead.

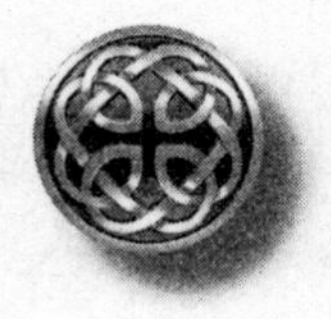

37

The Volkswagen drove south from Inverness, following Dores Road along the River Ness to the town of the same name. The car passed through the village, then turned onto a smaller road that hugged Loch Ness's southeastern shore.

Pitt hung back, staying just within sight. He followed the Volkswagen for ten miles, falling in and out of view, until they reached Foyers, a village known for its nearby waterfalls. The paved road turned south past the town and away from the loch. The VW disappeared around a bend, but when Pitt accelerated through the curve, the vehicle had vanished. He noticed a light spray of dust to his right, braked hard, and whipped the Mini onto a one-lane dirt road that snaked into the trees. The Volkswagen appeared for an instant ahead, then was swallowed by a dip.

Pitt slowed, keeping well out of view, as the road passed a pair of quaint Victorian houses, then crossed a narrow wooden bridge across the River Foyers. The road zigzagged through a forested ridge near the lake. The loch's blue waters flickered through the trees on Pitt's right as the road paralleled the shoreline. He continued along, noting there was no place the VW could have turned off.

A mile on, Pitt noticed a marker to the side, the first he'd seen on the narrow lane. He pressed the accelerator when he drew closer and saw it was not a marker. It was a camera on a post. After he sped past it, the road curved and dipped down a short hill, then ended at an open arched steel gate. A quick glance revealed a high metal fence ran from the gate to the upper woods on the left, and downhill to the loch on the right.

Pitt hit the brakes and skidded to a stop at the crest of the hill. The thick steel gate slid closed, and the gray Volkswagen pulled into a parking lot, partially concealed by a thick hedge, just beyond. The man posing as Perkins exited the car and disappeared down the paved walkway.

Pitt backed the Mini up and over the hill and turned around in a small clearing behind the roadside camera. There were more cameras mounted above the entry gate. If anybody was watching, someone would soon be sent to investigate.

Pitt didn't wait for a welcome. He jumped out of the car, sprinted into the trees to his left, then turned and angled his way toward the compound. He approached the fence, a ten-foot-high steel structure topped with concertina wire. Just beyond it were electronic sensors mounted on short poles every few yards. Extreme security, Pitt thought, for an environmental research lab.

He edged toward the fence, remaining concealed, until he had a clear view of the compound. It was dominated by a low-roofed building partially sunk into the ground, like a bunker. It appeared drab and functional, built of concrete, with no apparent windows. Concealed along the lakeside by thick foliage, the entire structure blended with the surroundings.

Pitt ducked back into the trees and retraced his steps so he could approach the complex from the waterfront. The high fence extended to the water's edge, concealed and anchored by large boulders on the inner side. Past the rocks, a vessel lay moored just off the shore.

It was a small tank barge, similar to ones Pitt had seen on the Mississippi River and in the Gulf of Mexico, used to transport chemicals or fuels, usually along inland waterways. Painted dark gray, the tanker was laced with tire bumpers along its flank that looked like a string of black donuts. No deckhands were visible, as the vessel sat a short distance from shore.

Pitt's focus was jarred by the hostile barking of a large dog. A brown blur raced from the dock, and he backpedaled away from the fence. By the time the Rottweiler reached the barrier, Pitt was already lost in the trees, returning to his car. He'd seen enough for one day.

Back in the Mini, he accelerated away briskly. He had driven less than a quarter mile when a slow-moving vehicle approached from the opposite direction. It was a large commercial truck with a high cab and a wide, raised bumper that dominated the narrow road. Pitt slowed and pulled to the left, easing the wheels onto the shoulder. Though a tight squeeze, there was enough clearance for the truck to pass.

But the truck had no intention of squeezing past.

Rather than slow and pull to the opposite side, the truck

driver upshifted to gain speed. The truck's prow eased toward the side of the road—Pitt's side of the road.

With nowhere to go, Pitt jammed the Mini into reverse and stomped on the gas. The little car leaped backward amid a spray of gravel and mud.

Pitt turned the wheel to center the car on the road as the truck loomed through the windshield.

There was no avoiding it. The truck was just too close, Pitt's acceleration a touch too late. The truck's grille and bumper engulfed his view as it bashed into the Mini. It wasn't a crushing blow. By luck, it had struck evenly, pushing the Mini straight back. Pitt maintained his grip on the wheel and kept the accelerator floored.

Pitt shook off the impact, controlling the Mini's trajectory as its tires regained traction. Holding to the crown of the road, the car continued its rearward acceleration.

The truck's grille still filled Pitt's windshield, and it closed once more. This time, it struck only a glancing nudge. The Mini finally reached a higher speed and began to outdistance the truck. As the small car pulled away, Pitt glanced up at the truck's cab and saw a familiar face behind the wheel.

It was the dark-haired receptionist from the BioRem building, and she tried to bear down on Pitt a third time.

Driving backward at speed, Pitt kept the Mini on the road. There was no room for error—or escape. A tight corridor of trees lined the road all the way to the gate.

The Mini's engine screamed. The tachometer neared the red line. He couldn't drive any faster. The pursuing truck quickly approached.

In the rearview mirror, Pitt saw the camera pole fast approaching. Behind it lay a small clearing where he had turned the car around. Ahead, the truck was closing the small gap, its driver looking determined. If she didn't catch him before the front gate, she would flatten him against it at the end of the lane.

He looked again in the mirror. He had only one chance.

He held steady until he was less than a hundred feet from the camera pole, then mashed the brakes. The Mini shuddered and skidded under the grip of its antilock brakes, but held a true line as it quickly slowed. Pitt kept one eye on the fast-approaching truck and the other on the camera pole. The pole arrived first.

As it appeared out the side window, Pitt let off the brakes and turned the wheel to the left. The rear end whipped around in the same direction. Pitt instantly returned to the brakes as the Mini slid backward off the road.

The truck arrived a second later, traveling too fast to do anything but veer in Pitt's direction.

Pitt slid off the road, the truck kissing the front end of the Mini as it passed, ripping off its bumper and sending it into a three-hundred-sixty-degree spin. The blow saved Pitt's life. Rather than slam backward into the trees, the Mini expended its momentum in the spin, bounding against the side of the truck before sliding to a halt along the road's shoulder.

As the receptionist tried to bring the truck to a rapid stop, Pitt took stock of his situation. He was uninjured, the car was mostly intact, and the engine was still idling. He shoved the gearshift into drive and floored the gas. The tires spun on the loose soil, and the Mini darted ahead. In his rearview mirror, he saw only the truck's brake lights as it disappeared over the hill.

Pitt drove with a heavy foot down the dirt road until he reached the paved, lakeside road at Foyers. As he drove slowly through the village in the growing dusk, he eyed a small stone church near the waterfront. He turned down its tiny track and parked behind it. Stepping to a bank of high shrubs along the side of the church, he crouched and watched the road. After ten minutes without sign of pursuing traffic, he returned to his battered Mini.

The shore was just down a short hill, and Pitt noticed a small dock with a skiff tied to it. He studied the opposite shore and located the McKee Manor a short distance to the west. It lay almost directly across the loch from the hidden facility.

He leaned against the Mini's fender, pulled out a cell phone, and dialed a Washington, D.C., phone number. Al Giordino grunted hello at the other end.

"Al, do we have any NUMA submersibles available in UK waters?"

"Let me check." Giordino consulted a computer in the NUMA technology lab. "You're in luck," he said a minute later. "The *Sea Nymph*, one of our smaller submersibles, is collecting dust on the deck of the Arctic research ship *Norse*. The *Norse* is laid up in a Liverpool dry dock for the next few days to repair her thrusters."

"How'd you like to hop a plane to Liverpool, load it on a truck, and drive it up to Scotland?"

"It just so happens I have a thing for women in tartan berets, so the answer would be yes. What's wrong? Your hosts not treating you to a good time?"

"They've been very entertaining." Pitt tapped the Mini's mangled front end with his foot.

"I should be able to get there in twenty-four hours, give or take."

"Meet me at a village called Foyers. There's a small dock behind the local church near the waterfront. It's on Loch Ness."

"Are we hunting a monster?"

Pitt gazed across the water at the manor. Yellow ground lights illumined the exterior, casting the residence as a disquieting beacon against the growing dark.

"We may be at that."

38

Loren felt nauseated, relaxed, and giddy—all at the same time. Must be jet lag mixed with alcohol, she thought, as she swirled a glass of champagne that had been thrust into her hand upon entering the banquet hall.

The largest room in McKee Manor, the high-ceilinged hall was decorated in medieval splendor. Thick marble columns jutted from each corner, dividing walls that were graced with massive paintings of the Scottish Highlands. Far above a rich parquet floor was a ceiling fresco of the Annunciation worthy of Michelangelo. Loren couldn't help notice that the image of Mary bore a striking resemblance to her host, Evanna McKee.

The hall's usual banquet tables had been replaced with small high tops, where the governance league's women congregated with their drinks. Color-changing mood lights flashed from above while relaxing spa music wafted from hidden speakers.

Loren detected the scent of lavender as she waded through the energetic crowd toward a small stage in the center of the room.

"Congresswoman Smith?"

A familiar-looking woman with short brown hair waved her to a nearby table.

"I thought that was you." She spoke with an Australian accent and extended a hand in greeting. "Abigail Brown from the World Bank."

"Of course, Madame Prime Minister. We met at the International Disaster Relief conference at the UN last year." Loren felt slightly embarrassed for not recognizing the former Australian prime minister, who now served as CEO of the World Bank.

"Please, call me Abby. You did a splendid job in raising aid for the displaced in Bangladesh after that terrible monsoon flooding."

"It's never enough. And there's always another disaster waiting in the wings, it seems." Loren motioned toward the stage. "Have you attended the seminar here before?"

"This is my first time, but I've been looking forward to it."

"I met Mrs. McKee just a few weeks ago," Loren said. "I wasn't aware she was so well connected."

"Quite so. Her husband's environmental products have been put to good use around the world, and she has been an integral part of the success. And she works tirelessly to promote women into positions of leadership. I heard through the grapevine she even lobbied for my nomination to the World Bank, yet I barely know her."

"Did you know her husband?"

"I'm afraid not. Frasier McKee died several years ago. He was apparently quite a brilliant man." Brown looked across the room, then held a hand in front of her mouth. "He was also a notorious womanizer. Rumors are, he was about to divorce Evanna to marry his Colombian mistress just before he died."

"Is that why men aren't welcomed to the conference?" Loren grinned.

Brown nodded, then rubbed her temples and squinted. "I do wish they would tone down the light show. It's making me dizzy."

"I feel the same way," Loren said. "I thought it was the champagne."

Unknown to the guests, the flickering colored lights were more than just ambiance. Special bulbs emitted pure shades of violet, pink, and magenta, frequencies known to have a calming and submissive effect. Near the light fixtures, aerosol jets dispersed a fine mist containing chamomile, patchouli, and lavender oils that added to the effect.

The psychological inducements didn't end there. The champagne and water glasses offered to each guest were laced with trace amounts of mescaline and scopolamine. The combined effects were designed to create an altered state in the guests, maximizing their sense of receptiveness and suggestibility. It was the groundwork for something approaching mass hypnosis.

The lights dimmed as an orchestral march was piped through the hall. The women fell silent as a spotlight illumined the stage and Evanna McKee strode into its beam. She wore a tailored white linen business suit accented by a heavy gold necklace and earrings. With her hair pulled back into a bun, and a perfect application of makeup giving her face a flawless glow, she appeared equal parts CEO and aged beauty queen.

The crowd erupted in a fury of applause.

"Ladies, friends, leaders of the world," she said, "I welcome you to McKee Manor. We meet again in the cause of sisterhood and the fight for a new global order. I stand before you with the promise that with your help, we will bring meaningful and lasting change to the world, a world in which women will take their rightful place at the forefront of power."

She spoke with the confident, authoritative voice of a practiced politician. And as with a charismatic politician at a rally, the crowd cheered her every phrase.

"Today," she said, "we are facing a crisis of global leadership. For decades, for centuries, and for millennia, we have seen nothing on this earth but wars, conflict, famine, and disease. Despite the advances in knowledge and technology, we are still burdened by the same calamities. The world today is more corrupt and dangerous than ever. This has been brought about by a crisis in leadership—a crisis of male leadership."

Shouts of support pierced the room, and McKee smiled.

"It is our role, our responsibility, dare I say our destiny, to take control of the failed institutions we hold dear, and to lead them to a better place. As women, we have been oppressed and devalued too long. It is our turn to right the wrongs of the past. It is our turn to banish mistrust, arrogance, and the provincial thinking that has shackled our society. It is our turn to lead the world to a place not of pain and suffering, but of hope, optimism, and betterment for all."

The room erupted in cheers. Even Loren felt an odd sense of

elation and an urge to support McKee. Once the applause quieted, McKee continued with a rising intensity.

"We cannot succeed in our quest alone. We must work together. Each and every one of you must lend a hand to your sisters. Grab hold, support one another every step of the way, and help each ascend to the top. Only by standing together can we reach the pinnacles of power necessary to make real and lasting change."

Her voice grew soft, and her eyes took on a distant look.

"The world will soon be changing in our favor. For the next generation and beyond, the road will grow less arduous. But there must be no pause in our fight, no relaxing over gains made along the way. We must all keep climbing the ladder, shatter the ceiling, and take our rightful place at the top of the mountain. Together, we—the Sisterhood of Boudicca—will achieve the victory that awaits us. Thank you."

As the spotlight faded to black, deafening applause filled the hall. Some women cheered, others swayed as if in a daze.

The hall lights were gradually turned up, and Loren glanced at Brown. The Australian woman had mascara streaks beneath her eyes as she openly cried with emotion.

Loren reached up a hand and felt her face. Without really knowing why, she found a stream of tears was flowing down her own cheeks.

39

The jetliner broke through a low layer of nimbus clouds on its final descent, exposing the earth to view. A patchwork quilt of green pastures and farm fields extended as far as the eye could see. Dirk glanced out a window at the verdant expanse and saw why Ireland was dubbed the Emerald Isle.

"Who would have thought we would be chasing an Egyptian princess to Ireland?" he said to Summer, seated next to him.

"Julian said we might be surprised at what we find here."

The plane touched down a short time later at Shannon Airport in southwestern County Clare. Clearing customs and collecting their bags, Dirk and Summer picked up a rental car and drove to the cargo terminal.

"Package for NUMA?" Summer asked at the desk as Dirk made a phone call.

She signed for two boxes and wedged them into the trunk

while Dirk completed his call. As she slammed the trunk closed, she noticed her brother was grinning.

"Don't tell me. Riki Sadler?"

Dirk nodded. "Sounded surprised to hear from me, but she has some pending business in Dublin she thinks she can move up. She'll try to hop a flight from Edinburgh and meet up with us in the next day or two. She said she looks forward to seeing us again."

"Us?" Summer arched her brow and tossed Dirk the keys. "Since you're so happy, you can handle the driving here."

Dirk climbed into the right-hand seat and started the car. Keeping glued to the left shoulder, he navigated through the city of Limerick, then southeast across sixty miles of open country to the town of Tralee. A charming Irish country town founded by the Normans in 1216, it was best known for its annual beauty pageant, where the "loveliest and fairest" woman from across the country was crowned the Rose of Tralee.

Dirk followed Summer's directions, locating their hotel between the city hall and a large town park. After checking in, they walked several blocks to a large mustard-colored building labeled KIRBY'S BROGUE INN. Inside, they found a warm and inviting pub just beginning to fill up with the early-evening drinking crowd.

They no sooner entered when a slight man approached from the back. He had salt-and-pepper hair with a matching mustache and wore a wrinkled oxford shirt beneath a herringbone tweed jacket.

"Be you the Yanks from NUMA?" he asked in a heavy brogue.

"One and the same." Dirk introduced himself and Summer. "You must be Dr. Brophy."

"Eamon Brophy, at your service. Brophy to my friends. Come along." He turned on his heels. "I've got a quiet table in back. Any opposition to joining me in a stout or two?"

"I'm a stouthearted man," Dirk said with a nod.

Brophy slapped a hand on the pub's main bar and called to a raven-haired barmaid. "Noreen, a triplet of Guinness, if you please."

He continued to a small corner table sided by framed posters of old whisky advertisements. As they took a seat, Dirk noted an empty beer glass on the table next to an antique clay pipe.

"This is just what I would have imagined," Summer said.

"Aside from the beer," Brophy said with a wink, "they've got the best pub food in all of Kerry."

"Do you live in Tralee?" she asked.

He shook his head. "After I retired as archeology department head at Dublin University, my wife and I bought a small farm near Annascaul, overlooking Dingle Bay. It's about thirty kilometers to the west."

Noreen arrived with the beers and cleared away Brophy's empty glass.

"Thank you, lass." He raised his glass and tilted it toward Dirk and Summer. "To my new friends. May misfortune follow you the rest of your lives, but never catch up."

He downed a healthy swallow, then set the glass on the table. "Now then, my old mate St. Julian Perlmutter tells me you're on something of a thirty-five-hundred-year-old scavenger hunt originating in North Africa."

"We're pursuing the tale of Princess Meritaten." Summer explained their discoveries in Egypt. "We found evidence that a plague struck Egypt in the reign of Pharaoh Akhenaten, yet a group of slaves were spared on account of the Pharaoh's daughter."

"The evidence *is* intriguing," Dirk said.

"Meritaten seemed to help the slaves, known as the Habiru," Summer continued. "They survived the plague because Meritaten gave them something called the Apium of Faras—an ancient remedy based on a plant called silphium."

"Never heard of it," Brophy said.

"That's because it's extinct," Dirk said. "We found a reference on a shrine in Faras, Egypt, that the apium came from a plant grown in a place called Shahat. Our research found only one matching ancient place-name—in Libya."

"It's a place high in the forested uplands of northeast Libya," Summer said, "and was the only region where silphium was known to grow. The locals harvested it after it gained widespread use as a seasoning and a medicine. The Egyptians even had a glyph that represented the plant."

Brophy took another drink and kept listening.

"The Greeks and Romans valued silphium highly," Dirk said. "Hippocrates and Pliny the Elder wrote of its power over a wide range of ailments. In fact, silphium may have gone extinct on account of Roman demand. The plant couldn't be cultivated, so its wild growth was likely overharvested. It was so valuable that Caesar stored some in the Roman treasury, and legend has it that the last stalk was presented to Nero. Today, we can only speculate about the plant's characteristics. Some botanists think it was related to fennel."

"I see." Brophy rubbed his chin. "So this silphium—or Apium of Faras—protected the slaves Habiru from the plague. And if you find the grave of Meritaten, you find the apium."

"It's possible," Summer said. "There seem to be other parties also interested in the discovery."

"We know it sounds improbable," Dirk said, "but can you tell us of any links between Princess Meritaten and Ireland? Julian said there was something in the historical record."

Brophy smiled. "Have you ever considered the origins of Scotland?"

Dirk and Summer looked at each other with raised brows. "Not specifically," Summer said.

"The name Scot is the Latin word for 'Gaels.' *Scotia* means 'land of the Scots.' It came into common use in the Middle Ages to refer to the Gaelic-speaking region of northern Britain."

Dirk looked at his sister again. Had the archeologist enjoyed too much stout before they'd arrived?

"But centuries earlier," Brophy said, "the name Scot referred to Ireland. There are references to Ireland as *Scotia major*, and to Scotland as *Scotia minor*."

"I thought Ireland was called Hibernia?" Summer admired a shamrock the barmaid had formed in the foamy head of her Guinness, then took a sip.

"Indeed," Brophy said. "That was its classical Latin name, derived from a Celtic word, *Iveriu*, by which Ireland ultimately took its name."

Summer set down her pint. "Who were the Gaels?"

"Aye, the Gaels were the first peoples to settle Ireland in the Neolithic Age. Gaelic as a language comes from one of the later

Celtic tribes that roamed the land. It evolved into our current Irish language, while Scotland developed its own form of Gaelic. What I think you'd be more interested in knowing is the origin of the word *Gael* itself."

He reached for his beer, drained half the glass, and wiped the foam from his mustache. "The name Gael derives from the Old Irish word *Goídel*, which some say means 'wild men' or 'warriors.' Yet Irish legend says Gaels originates from one Goídel Glas."

"Sounds like a fragile character," Summer joked. "What's his story?"

"For that, we must go to the *Chronica Gentis Scotorum*, the first written history of Scotland, which dates to around 1360. In the *Chronica*," Brophy said, "our friend Goídel Glas is known by the name of Gaytheus or Gaythelos. He is described as a young Greek prince who was cast out of his homeland. He traveled to Egypt, moved to Spain for a period, then sailed to Britain."

"He was in Egypt?" Summer asked. She and Dirk leaned closer.

Brophy took another sip of his beer and nodded. "He was. And while there, he took a bride. The daughter of a pharaoh, no less. She was later called Queen Scota, in the Irish history books."

Dirk and Summer looked at each other.

"Could she have been Princess Meritaten?" Dirk asked.

"The name of her pharaoh father isn't identified, and Scota is obviously not an Egyptian name. Other contemporary accounts refer to a pharaoh named Achencres. It turns out," Brophy said, "that is a Greek rendering of Akhenaten. So if the early accounts are true, it's likely that Princess Meritaten and Queen Scota are one and the same."

"We discovered evidence," Summer said, "that Meritaten fled Egypt at great risk to her life."

"The Irish accounts say Scota—or Meritaten—and her husband, Gaythelos, fled Egypt on account of certain plagues. They sailed to Spain, then took to the seas again and ultimately landed in Ireland."

Summer shook her head. "It seems remarkable they could have sailed this far."

"Aye, there's much we don't know about that age of seafaring. What evidence we do have suggests that even back then, trading occurred between our isles and the Mediterranean. Once our good princess arrived, she appeared in multiple historical accounts, but, mind you, they vary in detail. If we look at a sixth-century rendition known as the *Book of Invasions*, the story says that she and her tribe of warriors arrived in Ireland with a fleet."

Brophy tried to catch the barmaid's attention. "The third day after landing, they engaged in battle with the indigenous people. Here, at the Battle of Slieve Mish, Queen Scota died. Her forces continued the fight, and were victorious. It is said the rule of the country was split between her two sons, and that the people became known as the Scottis. Their descendants later migrated to Scotland, but only after building, in the following centuries, something of a Celtic empire."

"It seems almost unbelievable that an Egyptian princess and her heirs could have ruled Ireland and Scotland in the Bronze Age," Summer said. "Any chance it's more than a myth?"

Brophy placed his elbows on the table and leaned forward. "There's usually a kernel of truth behind every myth.

Unfortunately, we don't have records in Ireland that go back thirty-five hundred years." He smiled. "There's no denying, though, that she's a part of the earliest histories of Ireland and Scotland."

"What about the archeological record?" Dirk asked. "Are there any physical clues that suggest contact with Egypt?"

Brophy nodded. "There are some intriguing links. A trio of Bronze Age ships were discovered years ago in Yorkshire, and another in Dover, that some believe are of Egyptian design. Language experts find some similarities between ancient Gaelic and the Phoenician tongue. And recent DNA studies have shown a proportion of Irish Celtic blood originated from Iberia and North Africa." Brophy leaned closer. "The most interesting connection is probably at Tara."

"The home of Scarlett O'Hara?" Summer said.

"Frankly, my dear, no," Brophy said in his best Clark Gable voice. "The Hill of Tara, north of Dublin, is an ancient site regarded as the most sacred venue of the early Irish kingdoms. In the 1950s, a burial site was discovered there containing a Bronze Age skeleton that was carbon dated to around 1350 B.C.E."

"That's the same era as Meritaten," Summer said.

"The body was adorned with a bronze necklace that contained turquoise-colored beads. Faience beads, they call them. They are believed to have originated in Egypt. They are, in fact, identical to faience beads in the gold collar piece worn by Tutankhamun."

"Could the skeleton," Summer asked, "have been Meritaten?"

"No, it was a young male. They refer to the lad as the Prince of Tara."

"If his remains have survived," Dirk said, "then so could Meritaten's."

"Where could she be buried?" Summer asked. "You said that she died at Slieve Mish. Is that a specific battlefield?"

Brophy shook his head. "It's a mountain range extending along the Dingle Peninsula. The battle likely occurred over a long front and lasted for weeks, possibly months. The historical accounts suggest she was buried between Slieve Mish and the sea."

"How big an area would that be?"

"Nearly twenty kilometers long. But we don't have to search that much ground. Our task is a bit easier." He smiled. "It's why I had you meet me in Tralee. Just five kilometers south of here is where we need to be."

"Not in the mountains?"

"No, just a picturesque glen. Glenscota, it's called. The historic burial place of Queen Scota."

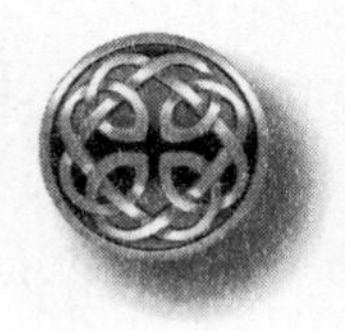

40

Pitt returned to the manor well after dark. He nosed the battered Mini against a stone wall to conceal the front-end damage, then strode to the estate's entrance. McKee's guardian, Rachel, stood just inside the door and gave Pitt an unfriendly nod. The rotunda was otherwise empty. Pitt made his way to his room, which was dimly lit by a small table lamp. He found Loren in bed, asleep.

He sat on the edge of the bed and brushed Loren's hair from her face. Her eyes nudged open with a struggle.

"There you are," she whispered. "I couldn't stay awake. Must be the jet lag. I had some dinner brought to the room, if you're hungry." She motioned toward a covered platter on a side table.

Pitt kissed her on the cheek. "Get some rest. I'll join you shortly."

She smiled, closed her eyes, and drifted back to sleep.

Pitt stepped to the tray and lifted the cover, revealing a plate of grilled salmon and potatoes. He took a few bites, poured a glass of wine from an open bottle, and sat by the picture window.

The loch appeared as a black ribbon unfurled across the landscape. A handful of yellow lights twinkled from the low gray hills on the opposite shore. To the south, Pitt found a dark smudge on the water, the outline of the tanker. Sipping his wine, he stared for a long time at the tanker and the invisible facility behind it.

IN A LOW-LIT ROOM on the second floor, Evanna McKee watched his every move on a color video monitor. An entire wall of monitors captured the live feed from a dozen security cameras around the manor, including a handful concealed in select guest rooms. She watched as Pitt finished his meal, undressed, and climbed into bed.

"He doesn't appear to be a ghost," she said in a hard voice.

At a desk across the room, Audrey looked at her mother and shook her head. "Irene reported that while she tried to run him over outside the lab, he slipped by her and escaped."

"Did he penetrate the facility?"

"He got no farther than the front gate."

McKee came over and sat across from her. Heavy makeup she wore for her earlier speech made her face look thick and pasty under the fluorescent lights.

"I watched the video of his interview with Richards." She frowned. "I think Pitt knew he was not speaking to the real Perkins. Why did the fool rush back to the lab so quickly? He should have known better."

"He was anxious to test the water sample Pitt gave him."

"And?" McKee leaned forward, her face a tightly wound spring.

"There's no reason to worry, Mother. There were zero concentrations of our biological products. Richards thinks Pitt just took some water from the loch."

"He knows something, or else he wouldn't be here."

"Professor Nakamura indicated that he'd received all the El Salvador water samples taken by the agriculture scientist. They were recovered from his office. Pitt is only guessing—but, I agree, he is dangerous."

"How long are they staying?"

"Even though the seminar ends tomorrow, I extended Loren's invitation for an extra day, along with the World Bank director. Both are new this year, and represent very influential positions. I thought we could work the two of them together."

"Very well," McKee said. "But keep a close eye on Mr. Pitt. If he approaches the lab again, kill him on the spot."

"That may jeopardize our influence with his wife."

McKee's eyes burned with malice. "Then we'll just have to amplify the treatment."

The door opened, and Riki Sadler stepped in holding a cup of tea, which she presented to McKee. She sat down beside her.

"Mother, I just received a call from the NUMA pair that disrupted our tomb recovery operation in Amarna." Riki spoke slowly and with reverence, not wishing to stir her mother's temper.

"I thought they were dead."

"I did as well. There was no sign of them when I left the dive site in Lake Nasser. I don't know how they survived."

"They proved to be quite an annoyance in Egypt."

"When I arrived in Amarna, I didn't realize Dr. Stanley was so close to uncovering the tomb. Their presence was unexpected."

"Do they know anything?" McKee asked.

"They've uncovered the link between the Egyptian princess Meritaten and the Apium of Faras."

McKee leaned forward with a furrowed brow. "So they know the power of the apium. I saw a photo of the tomb mural. It seemed to confirm its use as a remedy for the plague."

"Father knew of it when he found a reference on a monument in Thebes, yet he was never able to verify its existence."

"If this apium was a cure for the plague, then it would act as a cure for our developed agent," Audrey said.

"The NUMA people, they must also know it's extinct?" McKee asked.

"I think so. I just learned they believe Meritaten is buried in Ireland, in the person of Queen Scota. And they think she may have the apium in her tomb."

"Queen Scota?" McKee said. "Is there evidence of her grave?"

"Apparently, there is a gravesite in County Kerry that has never been properly investigated."

"You must go there and ensure nothing comes of it. Take the company jet. Leave as soon as you can, and take Gavin and Ainsley with you." She stroked her daughter's hair. "We are on the verge of great things. Let us be strong at this critical hour."

"Yes, Mother." Riki rose and left the room.

McKee watched her leave, then gazed at Audrey. They were so different, her two daughters. Riki was innately kind and naïve in the ways of the world, while Audrey suffered no such afflictions. It was Frasier's doing, she knew.

Arriving home drunk late one night, he had staggered into one of his daughter's bedrooms in the dark. Perhaps he was seeking Evanna, or more likely his stepdaughter, Riki, yet he fell in with Audrey. Never a word was said, but the damage was done. Audrey became a bitter shell of her former self, while Evanna rekindled the anger she had suppressed for years. No more, she had told herself, and she acted to ensure it.

McKee spoke to Audrey with worry. "Your stepsister shows uneasiness."

"She was feigning interest in Pitt's son to determine what he knew. Maybe she is reluctant to kill him."

McKee nodded. "She's not strong like you. She never has been. Perhaps we shouldn't have protected her from the truth."

"There is no need to relive the past now," Audrey replied stoically.

"If only she were as strong as you. Perhaps she can still learn. Call Gavin and tell him to kill the son in Ireland at the first opportunity."

She turned back and gazed at the monitor of Pitt's room, wondering if she should do the same with Dirk's father.

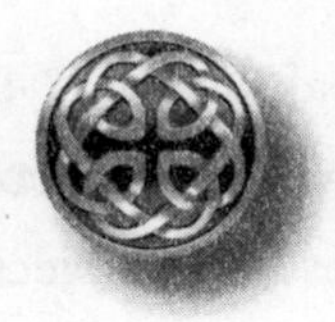

41

Winding down a narrow country road five kilometers south of Tralee, Summer was shocked to see a roadside marker proclaiming FEART SCOITHIN.

"Scota's grave?"

"Aye," Brophy said from the backseat. "Vale of the Little Flower, as the spot is called. Pull off here. We'll have just a short hike."

Dirk found a clearing beside the road and eased the rental car to a stop. He opened the trunk and removed the crate they'd picked up at Shannon Airport. Inside he found a rectangular box, an LED panel, four wheels, a frame, and a wrench. He assembled the pieces into the shape of a lawn mower, with the screen mounted on the handlebars.

Brophy shook his head. "You going to mow the grass with that thing?"

"In a manner of speaking, yes," Dirk said. "It's a ground-penetrating radar system. If the soil conditions cooperate, it will give us a peek at any subsurface objects."

"Like a sarcophagus?"

"Like a sarcophagus."

"Then let's go cut some grass." Brophy grabbed a shovel from the trunk and turned from the car.

He led them through a gate that fronted a small groomed trail. Grassy hills rose in an arc before them, but the path angled through a narrow valley lined with birch trees and heather. Dirk flipped over the radar system so he could tow it across the trail on two wheels.

Brophy pointed to his right. "The high hill over there, that's Knockmichael Mountain. We're at the eastern end of the Slieve Mish Mountains. And it was somewhere near here, in this glen above Tralee," Brophy continued, "that the great battle took place. Meritaten and her forces fought the ruling tribe and defeated them, taking control of the land. But she died during the engagement."

The scenic glen, with a babbling brook called Fingal's Stream meandering through it, looked peaceful. Summer found it hard to imagine the battle between Bronze Age warriors armed with axes, swords, and spears, fighting hand to hand across the sedate countryside. A growing black cloud, threatening a rain shower, darkened the skies.

They climbed the trail for thirty minutes, crossing a small bridge over the stream. The trail ended in a wide clearing dotted with stones and surrounded by young oak trees. At the far end, boulders covered a small hillside capped by a concrete cylinder grave marker.

Brophy waved toward the marker. "Bloody hideous thing. Don't pay it any heed for the location. We should search the whole clearing."

Dirk lowered the radar system's rectangular antenna until it grazed the ground, then powered the unit on. He adjusted the gain until a cluster of wavy gray lines filled the top half of the screen. Similar to airborne radar, the device sent microwave pulses into the earth, which were reflected in the form of a two-dimensional image.

Brophy leaned over Dirk's shoulder. "How's it looking?"

"While the system's designed to reach a twenty-foot depth, we'll be lucky to scan a third of that. The soil is probably clay-based and moist, which is not friendly to ground-penetrating radar."

"Or lost artifacts," Summer said.

Brophy smiled. "Makes it harder to dig, too. Someone burying something wouldn't likely go too deep."

Brophy followed with Summer as Dirk pushed the GPR unit across the clearing. Dirk made orderly passes back and forth, snaking around upraised stones as necessary. He stopped at one point and had Brophy dig down a few inches until he struck a rock.

"Just testing." Dirk smiled. "I had a dark spot that looked like a stone."

Brophy scowled and leaned on the shovel. "I'm not here for the testing, I'm here for the finding."

Dirk laughed and pushed the unit ahead to escape the Irishman's wrath. He bypassed a few small targets as he worked his way to the rock-strewn monument. From there he enlisted

Summer's help to muscle the device up the hillside, maneuvering it between and around the stones that surrounded the marker.

Brophy sat on a rock watching, waiting for a cry of "Eureka!" It never came. They carried the unit back down the hill and joined Brophy on two nearby stones.

"Either she's not here," Dirk said, "or she's buried deeper than we can see."

Summer gazed at the valley that cut through the hills above them. "Could she be farther up the glen?"

"Possibly." Brophy pulled out his clay pipe and lit a bowl of cherry tobacco. Its sweet aroma drifted over the clearing. "She could be anywhere in the Slieve Mish Mountains, I suppose. One could spend a lifetime kicking over stones and never find her." He waved his pipe across the site. "One thing bothers me a wee bit. Our major Bronze and Iron Age burial sites are elevated spots, at strategic positions. This site is neither." He waved his pipe toward the highest hill to the north.

"If it was me, I'd have buried her there, atop Knockmichael. But then, I wasn't standing here, weary from a fight, thirty-five hundred years ago."

"I agree." Dirk rose to his feet. "Unless they buried her here in the heat of battle and never came back for her." He began pushing the GPR across the clearing again. As he weaved around a large rock, a small blur appeared on the screen. It was one of the targets he'd ignored earlier, appearing small and indistinct next to the protruding stone. As he walked perpendicular to the earlier survey, it showed a thin, linear shape. He circled over the object a third time, stopped, and asked Brophy for the shovel.

He passed it to Dirk. "Another stone?"

"Something small, whatever it is."

He slid the blade against the face of the exposed stone and scooped out a mound of dark, compact soil. "Surprised we saw much of anything through this," he said. He expanded the hole, knowing the object was roughly a foot deep. The dense soil came out surprisingly easy, and he dug until the shovel clinked against a hard object.

He gently moved away the covering dirt. Summer dropped to her knees and reached into the hole, brushing away the loose soil with her hands.

"It's a statue." She waved away Dirk's shovel. She clawed at the ground, pulling away small clumps of dirt until she exposed the object.

It was indeed a carved statuette, made of heavy gray stone, and nearly a foot long.

"Go ahead, take it out." Brophy stood at the edge of the hole, leaning over her shoulder.

Summer pulled away more dirt until the statue came free. She gently lifted it from the hole and raised it in the air, like an actor winning an Oscar, holding it for the others to see.

It was a roughly hewn figure of a barefoot woman wearing a robe. Only, it featured the head of a lioness.

"Look at the headdress!" Summer said.

The figure wore a striped *nemes* headdress, commonly depicted on the images and funerary masks of Egyptian pharaohs.

"I believe that's Sekhmet." Brophy's voice rose an octave. "If my memory serves, she was considered an Egyptian warrior goddess, feared as the 'lady of terror.'" He raised a brow at

Summer. "She was also a healer who could avert plague and cure illness."

"I thought you were a Celtic historian?" Dirk said.

"I interned at the British Museum for a year in their Department of Ancient Egypt," he said with pride.

Summer turned it over in her hands. "There's no doubt it's Egyptian?"

"Not unless someone planted a tourist souvenir for a hoax." Brophy ran a finger over the statue. "Certainly looks like the real thing."

"While it appears to be a genuine artifact," she said, "there's no evidence of a grave. Do you think it's deeper than the GPR can read?"

"Perhaps, since this was only a foot deep." Dirk kicked a clod of dirt back into the hole. He bent and pointed at the large stone.

"There's something." He brushed away a layer of soil that clung to the now exposed rock face. The dirt fell away, revealing a line of symbols carved into the rock.

"Hieroglyphics?" Summer asked. It was her turn for her voice to rise in pitch.

"Professor," Dirk said, "hand me that shovel again."

He dug down several more inches, exposing a flat section of stone. Faintly carved on its face was the image of a boat, with a clear line of hieroglyphics inscribed beneath.

Summer squeezed next to Dirk to take a closer look.

"It is! The markings are Egyptian hieroglyphics."

"Well, I'll be," Brophy said, eyeing the inscription over her shoulder.

"This would make for a nice tomb marker." Summer pulled

out her phone and snapped several pictures. "I'll see if Max can translate it."

Dirk pointed to the image of the boat. "Looks similar to an Egyptian barque or Byblos boat." He ran the GPR in expanding circles around the stone, then chased Summer out of the hole and dropped the unit into the pit. He studied the screen and shook his head. "Not seeing anything else in the vicinity."

The clouds overhead began to open up, delivering a handful of sprinkles that grew into a downpour.

Brophy gazed skyward. "Perhaps the gods are telling us that's all to be found here."

"Or all that we're meant to find." Dirk pulled the GPR from the hole. Summer passed the statue to Brophy and grabbed the shovel. She refilled the pit, burying all signs of the carvings on the rock.

"I'll notify the university," Brophy said. "This should incite the archeology department to perform a thorough study."

Dirk dragged the GPR back to the car and tossed it into the trunk as the others climbed inside. As he hopped into the driver's seat, Summer checked her phone.

"I guess I had a phone signal on the way back. Hiram just responded." She smiled. "Max came through, again."

"Pray tell," Brophy said. "What does the inscription say?"

"'At this place, the Princess from Amarna died in victorious battle,'" Summer said. "'She now rests at Falcon Rock by the sea, for her journey to the Underworld.'"

"The Princess from Amarna," Dirk said.

"She died here." Summer nodded. "The legend is true. But she was taken away . . ."

Dirk wiped a bead of rain off his brow. "Professor, any idea about this Falcon Rock?"

Brophy shrugged. "It's not a landmark I'm familiar with. Must be somewhere along the coast." He thought a moment. "We need to get to Killarney."

"Is that a potential location of Falcon Rock?" Summer asked.

"It's the home of the Franciscan Friary. Their library has a rich collection of early Irish manuscripts and geological records. I'll bet my buttons they have a historical place-names reference or two that will give us the answer."

Dirk started the car. "Which way to Killarney?"

"Head on down the road a spell. We'll eventually turn east, leaving the Slieve Mish at our back. It's about fifty kilometers, through a beautiful stretch of County Kerry."

As Dirk pulled onto the narrow lane, he failed to notice a silver Audi parked behind a thick hedge. The concealed sedan had followed them unseen from Tralee. The Audi's driver started the vehicle and entered the road, following just out of view of Dirk's rental car.

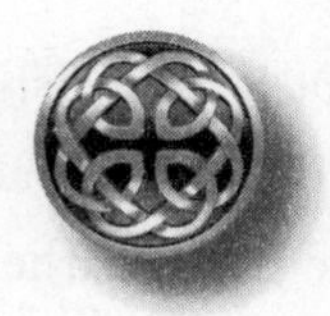

42

A casual buffet breakfast was set up in the manor's rotunda, teeming with Evanna McKee's rich and powerful guests. Pitt and Loren found a quiet side table, where they sampled smoked salmon from the loch with bagels and coffee.

Audrey McKee flitted about, making the social rounds, and made a point to stop at their table. "Good morning," she said with a plastered smile. "Did you sleep well last night?"

"Like the dead," Loren said. "I'm afraid I'm still feeling a bit groggy and out of sorts."

"A good breakfast should cure that. At least I hope so. We have a busy day filled with seminars and speakers." She leaned forward and whispered. "You won't want to miss the Spanish prime minister's talk. It will be very motivating."

"I look forward to it."

"And Mr. Pitt," she asked, "what's on your agenda today?"

"I'm going to attempt a little fishing on the loch. I understand a boat can be had down the road at Drumnadrochit."

"Indeed. It should be fine weather for a day on the water. Perhaps you can bring back some fresh fish for the kitchen."

"I'll certainly try."

"Well, good luck. Loren, we'll look for you to join us in the dining hall shortly."

As Audrey moved off to mingle with the other guests, Loren leaned across the table and spoke in a low voice. "I've never known you to have the patience for fishing, even on vacation."

Pitt glanced around the room, wondering if there were eavesdropping devices. "It all depends on the quarry. I'm of the opinion there's a large catch to be had in these waters."

Loren shook her head. "Well, just don't bring back any monsters." She rose stiffly and turned her back on him, joining the other women migrating to the hall. Uncharacteristically, she neglected to kiss him good-bye.

Pitt watched her leave with growing concern. Loren was turning more distant by the hour. Audrey appeared, grabbing Loren's arm and herding her down the hallway. The younger McKee turned and looked at Pitt, tossing him a smug smile. He watched them leave, feeling a touch light-headed himself, but trusting his instincts. He sniffed at his coffee, then put it down, unfinished. He returned to their room and grabbed a jacket and the car keys.

He found the corridor empty and decided to have a look around. Their room was at the manor's back corner, and he continued along the lakefront hallway. The view suites, named for Scottish clans with bronze plaques on the doors, were separated by small windows that overlooked the lake. Similar rooms lined the interior wall, with windows that opened onto the manor's central courtyard.

Pitt walked to the opposite corner, where the hallway turned and ran toward the front rotunda, passing the dining hall along the way. Near the corner, he stopped at a single side door that lacked any emblems. He tested the handle, and the door opened to a carpeted stairwell that led to a lower level. Scant lighting illumined the way as Pitt descended to the basement.

The carpeted steps gave way to a thick-planked wood floor, worn by centuries of use. The empty open room was dimly lit and unheated. Pitt realized why when he saw a large stack of oak barrels to one side. Behind them, he found a row of wooden racks filled with bottles of wine. He pulled out a bottle, blew off its dusty coating, and read the label aloud. "'Château Lafite Rothschild, 1961.' Well done, Mr. McKee."

He replaced the bottle and moved past the wine racks to a dark side room. Groping for a wall switch, he illuminated a richly decorated den with walnut paneling and a polar bear skin rug. Two huge salmon, presumably from the loch, were stuffed and mounted over the doorways. A pair of wingback chairs sat in the middle of the room, facing a side wall.

Stepping into the room, Pitt could see the wall displayed an assortment of museum-quality artifacts. The centerpiece, in a glass case, was an ancient frock and kilt, stained with dirt and blood and identified as a Highland rebel's uniform from the Jacobite uprising of 1745. A dagger, spear, and blunderbuss were mounted beside it. A small label beneath proclaimed ANGUS McKEE, BATTLE OF CULLODEN.

On either side was an impressive display of ancient armaments, from medieval battle axes to eighteenth-century dueling pistols. Pitt admired a highly engraved flintlock boarding pistol with attached bayonet, displayed in a wooden case. The case was dusty like the wine. No one had admired the collection in quite some time.

Pitt turned off the light and left the study. Beyond it, a wide corridor ran to his right, toward the front of the manor. He passed several empty storage rooms and a pair of dark offices, then reached a set of double doors. They were locked.

He backtracked and entered the first office. A plushly decorated executive retreat, it featured rich paneling, Persian carpets, and a large mahogany desk. Lining the walls were oil portraits of historical female figures, including Cleopatra, Joan of Arc, and Queen Elizabeth I. On the far wall hung a floor-to-ceiling painting of a red-haired woman with an upraised sword, leading a band of warriors in battle against a Roman legion.

The desk was clean and orderly, adorned with a single photo of Evanna McKee at the manor's entrance with Audrey and Riki. He opened the desk drawer, finding only a calendar that showed upcoming meetings in Paris, Jakarta, and Istanbul. He heard the bass thumping of music and realized he was directly below the dining hall.

He exited the office and poked his head into the next room. Modestly decorated, it was a functional working office with two standard-sized desks, each supporting a desktop computer.

Pitt stepped near one of the desks and noted a stack of binders with the BioRem logo on them. He flipped through the top one and found company profit and loss statements. Another contained shipping transportation quotes.

His fingers froze when he flipped a page and saw a pair of ship photos. The first was a stock photo of a familiar-looking tanker with a black hull and red deck. Pitt held the photo to the light to make out the name on its hull. *Mayweather.* The second photo was also a tanker, but one Pitt didn't recognize. He made a mental note of its name. *Alexandria.*

A turning door handle down the hall gave a metallic click. Pitt replaced the binder and stood against the wall. Through the crack of the half-open door he saw a figure pass through the double doors and enter the adjacent office.

Pitt thought better of hanging around and stepped quietly into the hallway. He made his way to the other end and ducked behind the armaments room. As he crossed to the corner stairwell, he noticed a short set of steps on a side wall that led to a heavy planked door.

He climbed the steps and pulled on the door, which opened onto a small boathouse built flush to the manor's lakefront façade. A sleek black speedboat floated in the narrow berth, concealed from the lake by a pair of high sliding doors. The boat looked clean and prepped for regular use, its keys dangling from the ignition. Pitt made his way out of the boathouse and up the stairwell to the main level, where he left the manor.

Outside the front door, he passed a female guard, who picked up a phone once Pitt had walked by. As he retrieved his damaged Mini, Pitt noticed two people climb into a dark BMW and start the engine. He exited the gate and turned toward Inverness.

Pitt drove slowly at first, watching in his mirror as the BMW left the manor and followed at a respectable distance.

Pitt toyed with the car, accelerating rapidly, then slowing, smiling to himself as he watched the car follow suit. He drove casually the rest of the way, passing Urquhart Castle and the village of Drumnadrochit before turning down a side road marked with a sign proclaiming MOORINGS.

The road led to the waterfront, where he found a dock mooring a half-dozen small boats. Pitt entered a wood-frame building beside the dock, where he was greeted by a short old woman refilling an urn of coffee.

She eyed him up and down. "You must be the empty-handed Yank looking to acquire some Loch Ness salmon," she said in a weathered voice.

"I am indeed," Pitt said with a smile, "though I'd prefer to catch a pike or two."

"Aye, a sporting man to boot. Sure you don't want to hire a guide? Most visitors prefer to fish with a local to improve their odds."

"Today, I'd prefer to let the fish find me."

She nodded at him with respect. "Usually the better approach. As you requested, I've got your boat all ready with a full complement of fishing gear. Here's some sandwiches and coffee, on the house." She passed him a small weatherproof bag.

She led him along the dock to a small skiff with an outboard motor. "You know how to handle yourself on the water?"

He smiled. "Since I was a kid." Pitt pulled the starter rope, and the little outboard fired right up.

"Just be wary of the wind if it starts to pick up," she said with a wink. "Best fishing is generally off the castle."

"Much obliged." Pitt gave the woman a wave as he pushed away from the dock and navigated into the loch. He glanced through the trees toward the main road and spotted the BMW pulled off to the side.

Pitt motored offshore in clear view, then turned east toward Inverness. He traveled a short distance, then cut the motor and let the boat drift as he assembled his tackle. He selected a spoon lure and began casting and retrieving his line. The BMW, he saw, had tracked his position.

He lingered for half an hour, then started the motor and cruised back to the west. Bypassing the inlet to Drumnadrochit, he fished in front of Urquhart Castle for an hour, then hop-scotched west until reaching the waters off McKee Manor. He eyed the doors to the boathouse, which were painted to match the castle's stone walls. As he studied the manor, the BMW crept along the road above, maintaining its view of his boat.

Pitt moved farther offshore, where, to his dismay, the fish began to bite his line. In quick succession he hooked a trout and two bass, which he promptly tossed back. Between strikes, he kept his eyes glued across the lake. On the opposite shore, through the trees, the lab was just barely visible. To Pitt's favor, the current was carrying him in that direction, and he gradually drifted closer.

It wasn't so much the lab he was interested in, but the off-shore activity. The tanker he'd seen was now gone, replaced by another of similar size. Like the first, it sat moored a short distance from the shore. There was no name on the ship, only the Roman numeral IX.

He spotted a pair of workmen on deck, engaged with some sort of equipment on the opposite side. After an hour the ship weighed anchor and made its way southwest down the loch toward the town of Fort Augustus.

Pitt continued to fish, reeling in a small salmon that gave a good fight. As he released the hook and slipped the fish over the side, Pitt looked up to see yet another tanker creeping up the loch from the direction the other had just sailed. It pulled up to a tiny red float and moored in the exact same spot. This ship was identified as XVII.

Pitt pulled out his cell phone and snapped a picture, then sent it to Rudi Gunn in Washington. A few minutes later, his phone rang with a call from Gunn.

"Is that a tanker of Scotch whisky you're sending home?" Gunn asked.

"You've been hanging around Hiram too much. And, no, whatever it's carrying, I wouldn't want to drink it on the rocks."

"Was the photo taken on Loch Ness?"

"About five minutes ago." Pitt explained his meeting with Perkins and the discovery of the hidden lab. "Can you tap some satellite reconnaissance on these tankers and see where they're going? They must be sailing through the Caledonian Canal at Fort Augustus and running into the Atlantic."

"Are they ocean-worthy?"

"They appear to be. They show no names, just Roman numerals."

"I'll get with Hiram and see what we can do," Gunn said.

"Backtrack imaging in that region may be iffy, but we can put in place some sort of forward coverage."

"One more thing," Pitt said. "Can you pull the history of a freighter named *Alexandria*, out of Malta?"

"The *Alexandria*."

"You know of it?"

"I'll say. A few months ago, the *Alexandria* was involved in a fatal collision with a small collier in the Ismailia Canal near Cairo. The crew all died, and a chemical release occurred. Your friends at BioRem Global were there for the cleanup."

"I found the ship documented in McKee's office, along with the *Mayweather*. That makes two ships that sank in a collision with a full loss of crew."

"I'm afraid it's a lot worse than that. Hiram and I found a significant pattern of industrial waterway accidents like the ones in Cairo and Detroit. In each case, BioRem Global ended up on-site, releasing their waterborne microbes. And in each case, cholera-like outbreaks occurred, resulting in local fatalities."

"Cholera? Perhaps that was in the water at El Cerrón Grande."

"Strictly speaking," Gunn said, "it's not exactly cholera, but something that shares its more harmful traits. We've found numerous recent outbreaks throughout the world that can't be easily explained. Even worse, the CDC is finding the same bacteria in water samples from all over. They say it's a pathogen they've never encountered before and they can't explain its sudden widespread distribution. Hiram and I have found that in nearly every instance, there's evidence that BioRem Global was operating in the vicinity. We suspect the disease has killed untold children beyond just El Salvador. The CDC thinks the pathogen is highly susceptible to mutating into a much deadlier form, and fear it could turn into an uncontrollable pandemic."

"Have there been any outbreaks in Detroit?"

"While no fatalities or illness have been reported, the CDC just tested a city water sample and found a similar pathogen. It turns out that Detroit draws most of its drinking water just downriver from where the *Mayweather* sank."

"And just downriver from where BioRem Global was dispersing their bacteria," Pitt added. "Perhaps Mike Cruz discovered they were directing their product into Detroit's water system."

"It could be a different agent than we tested in the NUMA labs," Gunn said. "None of it makes any sense. Could they really be trying to boost sales by staging environmental mishaps? And why would they allow their product into the water supply if it's so dangerous?"

"There are enough spontaneous accidents and natural catastrophes to keep their coffers full. It must be something else."

"Any idea what that could be?"

Pitt gazed from the BMW parked on the road above to the concealed laboratory across the lake. "I don't have a clue," he said. "But I intend to find out."

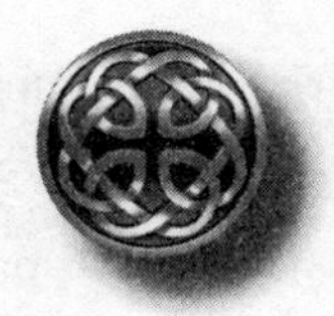

43

A half-hour drive south from Tralee brought Dirk, Summer, and Brophy to the tourist town of Killarney, near the shores of the lake called Lough Leane. Brophy guided them through the center of town and directed Dirk to park in front of an imposing graystone Victorian-era church. A placard behind a surrounding iron fence proclaimed it the FRANCISCAN FRIARY OF KILLARNEY.

"Ireland's best early historical records reside with the Christian churches and monasteries," Brophy said as they entered the grounds. "Most of the local parish records and histories are now housed at the Public Records Office in Dublin. But the good Franciscans of Killarney have a fine collection of ancient documents they never parted with. It'll be a good place to search for Falcon Rock."

Brophy turned toward the church, where an imposing arched window of stained glass faced the front grounds. Bypassing the main entrance, he led Dirk and Summer to a second doorway at the other end of the façade.

As they entered, the silver Audi pulled to a stop in front of the friary. In the backseat, Riki Sadler looked up from an electronic tablet. "The GPS signal says they stopped here."

"I see their car." The female driver pointed down the street.

"Find a place to park," Riki said. "They must be in the church."

In the friary office, Dirk, Summer, and Brophy approached a front desk, where a young man sat wearing the traditional brown robe of the Order of Friars Minor.

"Is Friar Thomas about?" Brophy asked.

"Yes, first room on your right."

They stepped down the hall and entered a small office overflowing with stacks of theology books. An older man with a beard and glasses sat hunched over a desk reviewing a donations report.

"May we intrude on you, Friar Thomas?" Brophy asked.

"Why, if it isn't Eamon Brophy." He stood and shook hands as Brophy introduced Dirk and Summer.

"I haven't seen you in Killarney in quite some time," Thomas said.

"I'm trying to retire, but these young folks won't let me just yet. They seem to think there's a pharaoh's daughter in Ireland worth locating."

"Ah, yes, our transplanted Egyptian princess. That's an old legend, one I always thought might have some teeth to it."

Brophy described their findings at the gravesite and nodded

to the statue Summer clasped in her hands. "We're hoping you have some early place-name records that might relate to Falcon Rock."

"We do indeed. We just had all our holdings copied for digitization, the files haven't yet been organized. So I think it'll be easier to browse through the books."

The friar guided them to a small stand-alone building on the rear grounds. Built of coarse stone with a high gabled roof and a thick timbered door, its rough-hewn appearance indicated it was much older than the nineteenth-century friary building.

"We keep the library out here," Thomas said. He inserted a heavy skeleton key into the ancient door's iron lock. "This was built as a granary for the first Franciscans here. We still find a few seeds in the wood floor."

The room was narrow, with a high ceiling and plank flooring. A pair of small side windows just beneath the ceiling gave the only natural light. Thomas flipped a switch to a pair of antique chandeliers, which bathed the room in a soft yellow light. The lights revealed wall-to-wall shelving on either side, filled with books. In the center of the room stood a pair of reading tables.

"Some people find it claustrophobic. I think it's cozy," the friar said, leading them inside.

"I see what you mean," Summer said. She gazed at a large pulley wheel suspended high above the doorway. "A remnant of the granary?"

"Quite right. The building used to have a second floor. The

pulley was used to hoist bales of hay and bags of grain for winter storage."

He stepped to one of the rear shelves. "Our earliest histories are in here in the back. There should be a place-names directory in here somewhere." He ran his fingers across a row of books, stopped at a brown leather-bound tome, and pulled it off the shelf.

"Friar Thomas?" At the doorway, the young assistant was poking his head across the threshold. "Your conference call with the archdiocese starts in five minutes."

"Ah, yes. Thank you, Robert." Thomas handed the volume to Summer. "Please help yourself to the collection. If you need it, there's a copy machine in the front office. I shouldn't be tied up for more than an hour."

"Thank you, Friar," Summer said. "We'll show due care."

Thomas left the door ajar with the key in the lock and followed Robert back to his office. Summer sat down, opened the book, and glanced up at Brophy. "I think you'll have to review this one. It's in Gaelic."

"Not to worry." He took a seat alongside her. "Let's see if there's a Falcon Rock to be found in these parts."

Behind them, Dirk perused the shelves, examining the titles and pulling out a dusty book or two. Most were in Gaelic and dealt with the history of Killarney and the surrounding area. He found a book in English on the fauna of Ireland and took it to the table.

"Well, there's a Falcon Field near Kilgarvan to the south, and a Falcon Cove at Ballylongford up north," Brophy said. "But neither is close to the sea."

"This might help." Dirk read from his book. "'The peregrine falcon is pervasive in Ireland. This fierce bird of prey is partial to coastal cliffs and crags, particularly in the temperate months.'"

"That makes sense." Brophy flipped through the pages of his book. "Unfortunately, I see no references to a peregrine."

"Perhaps the hieroglyphic translation has room for interpretation," Summer said. "Maybe it's a raven. Or it means a high cliff where the falcon lives."

Brophy searched for places so described and pointed at an open page.

"Sceillec!" His droopy eyes turned bright. "*Sceillec* is an Old Irish term meaning 'steep rock or crag,' or 'splinter of pointed stone.'"

"Does that relate to a coastal cliff?" Summer asked.

Brophy nodded. "The modern word is *skellig*. There's a pair of well-known islands off the Kerry coast called the Skelligs."

Dirk turned back to his book. "I saw that name in the peregrine falcon listing." He ran his finger down the page. "Here it is. 'Skellig Michael is one of the best-known coastal eyries, or nesting grounds, for the peregrine falcon.'"

A broad smile crossed Brophy's face.

"Could that be the place?" Summer asked.

"Skellig Michael is a rugged, towering pile of rock out in the ocean. It's also one of the most mystical places in Ireland. I should have remembered. The *Book of Invasions* tells of Meritaten losing two sons in a shipwreck on the island in a magical storm."

"Sounds like the place," Dirk said. "If Meritaten's sons had already died on the island, she may have wanted to be buried with them."

"Where is the island?" Summer asked.

The answer never came. Crowded around a table in the back of the room, none of them had noticed the door ease partly open. A man in dark glasses appeared long enough to hurl a large object into the room. The door banged closed, and the lock turned. Turning at the sound, the trio saw only a large glass jug arc toward the ceiling before plunging down, a small burning wick trailing like a yellow tail.

The jug struck the floor a few feet from the door and shattered in an explosion of glass, smoke, and flame. Its contents were a hastily conjured mixture of gasoline, powdered sugar, and laundry detergent meant to act as a crude form of napalm. The sticky solution splattered everywhere, carrying gooey fireballs across the floor and onto the shelves.

Summer, Dirk, and Brophy were spared direct contact, gazing in shock as the front of the room burst into flames.

"I'm going for the door," Brophy shouted. He pulled his tweed jacket over his head and burst past Dirk. Disappearing through the black smoke, he reached the door and grabbed its iron handle. He pushed and pulled at it without effect. Realizing it must be locked, he pounded and yelled for help, but the door was four inches thick.

Smoke inhalation began to make him dizzy, and he staggered backward. A strong arm grabbed him by the collar and dragged him to the back of the room. He collapsed on the table as Dirk let go of him to pat out the places where his own clothes were smoldering. Smoke began to fill the air.

Summer coughed as she grabbed Dirk's arm. "We're trapped. What do we do?"

Dirk pointed at the ceiling.

The roar of the fire made it difficult to hear, yet there was no mistaking his peculiar words.

"Make like a bale of hay."

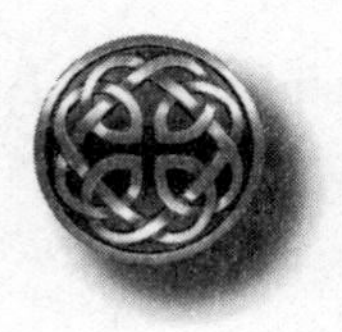

44

Wisps of black curled off the stone roof, but with the building tucked away at the rear of the grounds, no one at the friary seemed to notice. Inside, the smoke was as thick as fog, acrid and burning to the lungs.

Dirk and Summer dragged Brophy to the very back of the building and set him on the floor.

Brophy coughed and waved them away. “Leave me be and save yourselves.”

“Stay down on the ground with him to avoid the smoke,” Dirk yelled to Summer.

He flipped over a table to provide a modest heat shield, then stepped to a sliding shelf ladder. The bookshelves were ten feet high, the arched ceiling rose another five. He scrambled up the ladder and pulled himself onto the top side shelf.

With the smoke collecting at the top of the room, Dirk could barely see. Hunching over, he felt his way along the wall-mounted shelves. The smoke swirling toward the roof inflamed his eyes and made it near impossible to see. With the air growing hotter, it was like standing downwind from a barbecue.

The heat rose in waves that took away his breath. He stumbled down the line of shelves, then dropped to his knees when he almost stepped off the last bookshelf.

The front wall and doorway were another four feet beyond and beneath him. But his focus was up, not down.

The large, rusty pulley above the doorway hung from the ceiling's center beam. Just beyond it, he strained through the smoke to see what he prayed was still there.

It was. A short pair of plank doors in the front wall had allowed additional access and ventilation to the granary's upper floor. Now Dirk hoped they would still open. It wasn't grain he wanted to offload.

He backed up, took a quick step forward, and leaped off the shelf. With his long arms he stretched for the pulley, easily grasping it with both hands. The pulley was hot, the fire below even hotter. Dirk swung his legs back and forth, building momentum. He raised his feet as he swung forward and kicked the small doors. His feet bounced off, the doors just rattling. He swung and kicked again on the next forward swing. The result was the same.

It was too late to question the wisdom of his actions. If the doors didn't open, he would plunge into the fire. His arms began to ache as he swung again and again, mashing his feet against the doors. The heat and smoke were intense, and he could barely see or breathe, as he swung once more, throwing all of his weight forward.

And then the doors gave way. Not with a crack or a splinter, but with a loud bang, nearly flying off their hinges.

Dirk felt a cool gust as he rebounded. He swung forward once more and let go of the pulley. When his legs and torso slid over the doorframe, he caught himself with his arms. He clutched the lower sill, let his body dangle down the front of the building, then let go.

He landed on the balls of his feet and rolled across the ground to break the fall. Friar Thomas's assistant came running up.

"What's happened?" Robert stared at Dirk.

Dirk's face was black and his clothes were smoking. He rushed to the library door. It had been locked from the outside, and the key was now gone.

"The key!" he shouted. "Do you have another?"

Robert gave him a blank look and shrugged.

"Go get help!" Dirk yelled, then took off at a sprint. He looked around, spotting a small white car pulling into a parking lot at the far end of the complex. Racing across the lawn, he headed for the car as it pulled into a space. A young woman wearing an apron climbed out with the keys in her hand as Dirk approached, coughing and covered in black.

"Excuse me, miss." Dirk plucked the keys out of her hand and flung open the door. "There's a fire, and I need to borrow your car."

The woman backed away, gasping, as this aberration hopped behind the wheel and started the car. Dropping the transmission into reverse, Dirk floored the accelerator, and the car screeched backward. He braked, turned, and pulled forward, bounding over a curb and onto the lawn. Something thunked, and the exhaust began to roar. He glanced in the mirror and saw the car's muffler and tailpipe lying against the curb.

He found he was behind the wheel of a tiny Fiat 500. On the passenger seat sat a stack of strawberry pies for a church bake sale. Ahead, black smoke poured from the library roof. A small crowd had gathered around. In the distance, a fire truck's siren sounded.

Dirk kept applying power as he angled the Fiat toward the corner of the church. Reaching an imaginary apex, he whipped the car to the right. The tiny car skittered across the grass, then found traction on the pathway to the library door. Dirk pressed the gas pedal to the floor and braced himself against the steering wheel.

The Fiat was just a fraction narrower than the doorway and it struck the thick wooden door head-on. The car's front end crumpled, and Dirk was flung into an exploding airbag. The heavy door hung still for a moment, then its ancient hinges gave way and it collapsed to the floor.

The open doorway exposed a raging inferno inside. Dirk shook off a pain in his chest and realized the Fiat was still idling. He touched the accelerator, and the car crept forward, its front tires scraping against its mangled wheel wells.

Over the fallen door, he drove into the library. The first ten feet was through fire, but he emerged from the flames. Slowing in the dense smoke, Dirk stopped in front of the overturned table. He honked the horn and held his breath. A second later, two sets of blackened figures peered over the table's edge.

Dirk beat down the airbags and crawled to their side.

"A fire truck . . . might have been . . . more appropriate," Summer said, coughing.

"Wouldn't fit through the door. Hope you don't mind sharing a seat."

He guided Brophy to the passenger seat. Summer squeezed in with him. The stack of pies was now nothing more than strawberries, pie tins, and smashed boxes. Dirk retook the wheel and backed the car through the smoke and flames, onto the lawn.

The Killarney fire department arrived a moment later. They attached hoses to a nearby hydrant and doused the library. Paramedics checked the trio for smoke inhalation and, as a precaution, administered oxygen. Friar Thomas approached as they sat on a stone wall, watching the firemen.

"Thank the Good Lord you're all right. I swore I left the door unlocked, with the key in it. I'm so sorry you became trapped. How did the fire start?"

"Arson," Brophy said. "Somebody thought we'd enjoy an extra-large Molotov cocktail and locked us in with it."

The friar's face turned pale. "Arson? You can't be serious. Did you see who it was?" He gazed around, studying the faces gathered at the scene.

Brophy shook his head. "We had our backs turned to the door."

"It may be our fault," Summer said. "We were attacked in Egypt while pursuing the same line of research. They must have tracked us here." She turned to Dirk, and he nodded in affirmation.

"Who would try to kill you over some dusty old books?" Friar Thomas asked. "And why?"

"We don't know who they are," Dirk said, "but they sent a

pretty clear message. For reasons unknown, they don't want us to find Meritaten."

Summer turned to Brophy. "We didn't mean to put you in danger, Professor. Dirk and I can carry on from here."

Brophy stood and began pacing. "Why, those cowards are not going to deter me. Mind you, if it's a fight they want, that's what they'll get. I dare them to stop us."

Summer smiled, and Brophy turned to her and winked. "Besides, they were a bit too late. We've already got the key to the princess's whereabouts. Skellig Michael."

The firemen finally shut off their hoses. Friar Thomas walked to the doorway and peered inside, shaking his head. The walls and roof had survived, the interior was a mess. A black mass of charred debris filled the front of the room. Miraculously, the shelves at the back of the room remained standing, their books slightly blackened, showing only light water damage.

Summer joined him at the door. "I'm so sorry the library has been destroyed."

"The rare books in the collection look to have survived," Thomas said, pointing at the intact rear shelves. "I think only the modern parish records have been lost, and those we have on digital files." He gazed upward in reflection. "We thank the Lord. It could have been much worse. We could have lost all of you."

The friar led them back into the main building to wash up. As Summer and Brophy thanked the friar for his help and turned to leave, they noticed Dirk had disappeared. They found him outside, walking away from an angry young woman. He had a long face and carried a smashed pie box.

"Helping with the bake sale?" Brophy said. "Kind lad."

"Sort of," Dirk said. "It was thrown in as part of the transaction."

"Transaction?"

"I just bought a car."

"Then why so glum? That should be a happy occasion."

Dirk pointed to the mangled Fiat. "Not if you can't drive it."

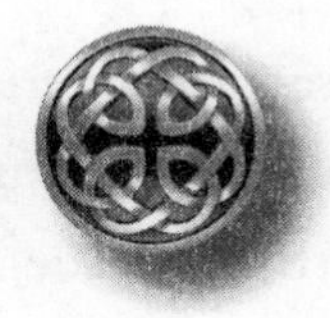

45

It was near dusk when Pitt piloted the fishing boat back to Drumnadrochit. He thanked the lady at the marina and tipped her for use of the fishing gear. As he made his way to his car, he pretended to ignore the black BMW parked on the road above, which had tracked him up and down the loch all day. He turned onto the shoreline road and drove to the McKee estate.

As he approached the manor, he quickly pulled off the road well ahead of the entrance and parked. The tailing BMW was caught off guard and had to drive past Pitt and the manor and stop around the next bend. Pitt walked to the guard at the entrance and pointed at his car.

"I got in a fender bender. A tow truck is supposed to fetch it this evening. I told them to pick it up just outside the residence."

The guard looked at the car, then back at Pitt. "I understand, sir. It will be safe there." She motioned for Pitt to proceed.

Inside the gate, Pitt saw the interior parking lot was nearly empty. At the main entrance, a handful of women with suitcases were preparing to depart. He made his way to his room and found Loren in front of a mirror, applying makeup.

"There you are," she said flatly. "We're due to dine with Mrs. McKee in twenty minutes."

"It looks like everyone is leaving," Pitt said. "I thought there was another day of conferences."

"Only the new attendees are invited to stay an extra day."

There was an unusual hardness in Loren's voice, and her eyes appeared glassy.

"Are you feeling all right?" He put his arms around her.

She immediately brushed him away. "I was fine until now," she snapped. "You better get ready."

Pitt stared at his wife with worry, but said no more. He cleaned up quickly and slipped on a sport coat. Together they walked to the formal dining hall, where a single table overlooking the courtyard was set for dinner. McKee and Audrey stood talking with Abigail Brown, each holding a drink. McKee's tall companion Rachel stood in the background, eyeing Pitt.

As Loren introduced Pitt to the former Australian prime minister, a servant offered them champagne. McKee ushered everyone to the table, where she took the seat at the head, opposite Pitt.

"I'd go easy on the drinks," Pitt whispered to Loren as they took their seats. She shook her head and took a sip of champagne.

"Where is your other daughter this evening?" Brown asked McKee.

"Riki had to fly to Ireland for a business project." McKee

turned her attention to Pitt. "I understand you tried your hand at fishing today. Did you have any luck?"

"A few bites, nothing worth keeping. It was pleasant to be on the water. The loch is quite intriguing."

"My late husband used to love to fish," she said. "He has some record salmon mounted in the basement." She looked at Pitt with a penetrating gaze.

He stared back at McKee. "I'd love to see them. I understand your husband was killed in a boating accident on the lake."

"Yes, he had an Italian speedboat that he liked to race about at high speeds." She spoke in a casual tone, as if discussing the weather. "It's believed he struck a rogue wave and flipped the boat."

"How unfortunate. I hear he was a man of high morals and intellect."

The servant reappeared and delivered a smoked salmon salad to each place setting. As Pitt and McKee conversed across the length of the table, the other women remained uncomfortably silent, picking at their food.

"Frasier was indeed a brilliant man. He loved science, archeology, and the outdoors. But like most men, he had his flaws."

Pitt saw Audrey nod in agreement. "I've noticed some artifacts on display," he said. "I presume his love of archeology included ancient Egypt?"

McKee unconsciously stroked the ever-present cartouche dangling from her neck.

"Father had a fascination with all things Egyptian," Audrey said. "He loved to visit and participate in archeological digs there."

"He found inspiration for his research in the desert," McKee added. "Incidentally, Dr. Perkins tells me you provided a water sample for him to analyze. I'm afraid he says there was nothing unusual in the sample."

"I hadn't heard."

"He said it came from El Salvador . . ."

"Yes. Cerrón Grande, a reservoir near San Salvador. I understand your firm was involved with some work at a nearby gold mine."

"We have projects all over the world," McKee replied dismissively. "What were you looking to find in your sample?"

"Something that might account for the death of several children in the neighboring villages."

"Sadly, disease outbreaks occur with too much regularity in the less developed countries. Local water purification is not always effective."

"How do you ensure there are no harmful effects from your products?" Pitt asked.

"We thoroughly test and monitor our products on a continuous basis. As it is, most of our deployments occur in the ocean, rather than fresh water. Our microbes are no more harmful than the bacteria on a block of blue cheese. I'm sure you, as the Director of NUMA, would appreciate our safeguards for the protection of the oceans."

"Without a doubt," he said. "Is that your research lab across the lake?"

The coolness vanished from McKee's face, replaced by a spasm of anger that nearly melted the table. It was a look, Pitt thought, of pure derangement. Nearly a minute passed before she calmed herself enough to respond.

"Our facilities are located in Inverness," she said in a low, gritty tone.

The table fell silent as the entrée was served—braised lamb shanks with barley, rosemary, and root vegetables.

Loren tried to break the chill. "This is delicious."

"Yes, quite good." Pitt gazed toward McKee. "It's kind of you to allow us an extra night after your other guests have departed."

"We like to have our new attendees stay an extra day," McKee said. "We'll have something of an initiation ceremony in the morning."

"Initiation?" Pitt asked.

"Into the Sisterhood of Boudicca," Loren said. "The women's organization that Mrs. McKee started here."

"I didn't realize there was a secret society at work," Pitt said with a humorless grin.

"There's nothing secret about it," Audrey said. "Just a group of like-minded women supporting their mutual empowerment."

McKee looked to Pitt. "Are you familiar with the story of Boudicca?"

He nodded. "A Celtic queen who led a bloody revolt against the Romans in Britain after her husband, King Prasutagus, died." He gazed at Audrey. "As I recall, she had two daughters."

"You are correct," McKee said. "We desire to embody the Celtic strength and spirit of Queen Boudicca in our public and private lives."

"She was a fierce warrior. I hope your sisterhood doesn't involve hanging, burning, and crucifying."

"We reserve that for those who oppose us," she said with a cold grin.

"What are the criteria for membership?"

"All our members are accomplished women who have made significant achievements in the worlds of science, business, or politics. We are dedicated to the support of one another to attain even higher levels of influence. Women make up half the world, Mr. Pitt, but remain sorely underrepresented in roles of leadership. It is time for a new global order, with female leadership across all countries. We believe the world would be a safer and a more just place with women at the helm. Wouldn't you agree, Mr. Pitt?"

"It could be, with the right women." He patted his wife's arm.

The conversation drifted to politics, which held little interest to Pitt. When the focus was off him, he reached for a saltshaker at the center of the table and intentionally knocked over his wineglass. He stood, dropped his napkin on his plate, and grabbed the upended glass. A servant rushed over and wiped up the spill.

"Agnes," McKee ordered, "bring Mr. Pitt another glass of wine."

As Pitt sat down, he scooped up a large chunk of lamb with his napkin and brought it to his lap. When the conversation resumed, he folded the meat in the cloth and slipped it into his sport coat pocket.

A dessert of berries and cream was served, and the guests grew increasingly quiet. Pitt noticed a listless look from both Loren and Abigail Brown.

"I think we've all had a tiring day," McKee said. "Get a good night's sleep, ladies, and we'll resume in the morning with your official welcome into the sisterhood."

Everyone said their good nights, and Pitt escorted Loren to their room.

"How about you skip the Celtic warrior ceremony in the morning," he said, "and we leave first thing?"

"I can't do that after all her hospitality," Loren murmured as she suppressed a yawn. "She wants me to run for president." Her words came out slurred.

She slipped under the covers of the bed without another word and was asleep in seconds.

Pitt tucked Loren in and gazed at her with rising anger. The odds were high that she was drugged by McKee, to aid some sort of manipulation. He could only guess at the purpose.

Stroking her hair, Pitt stepped to the nightstand, opened her purse, and removed a box of Dramamine she carried for airsickness. Turning off the lights, he took a seat by the window and calmly waited for the time to pass.

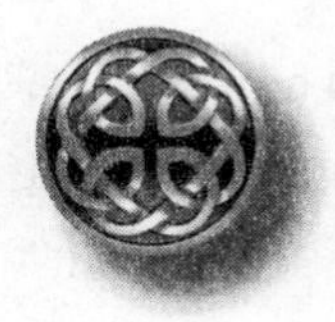

46

Riki crouched low in the backseat of the Audi as a fire truck raced by with its siren wailing. She watched with horror as it stopped in front of the Franciscan Friary. Above a line of brick row houses across the street, a curl of black smoke rose into the sky.

She took another look at an electronic tablet in her lap. The signal from the GPS transmitter placed on Dirk's rental car indicated it was still parked in front of the friary. She pulled out her phone, then convinced herself to wait another two minutes. At last, she spotted a man and woman in dark clothes walking down the street. One carried an empty duffel bag as they approached and climbed into the front of the Audi.

"What on earth did you two just do?" she asked.

The man, a balding, overweight tough named Gavin, gave a devious smile. "We tracked them into a small building behind the church. It had only one door, and someone left the key in the lock. Ainsley had seen a petrol station up the block, and we found a glass jug at a garden shop, so we made an extra-large Molotov cocktail." He grinned. "Those people should be charred to the bone by now."

Riki felt a momentary pang that ignited into anger. "I told you to follow them and see where they went. I didn't tell you to kill them. What were you thinking?"

Gavin's satisfaction turned to spite. "Mrs. McKee told us to take them out at the first reasonable opportunity."

"Mrs. McKee?" Riki said. She forced herself to take a deep breath. "I wanted to find out what they knew." She stared at Gavin and shook her head. "Carrying a jug of petrol down the street and starting a blaze at a historic church doesn't sound reasonable to me."

"It was a self-service petrol station," Ainsley replied. The woman's high-pitched voice didn't match her plain face and large frame. "We carried it in a duffel. Nobody saw anything suspicious."

"Let's not bank on that," Riki said. "Get us out of here. Now!"

Ainsley drove them out of Killarney. Outside of town, Riki yelled to the driver, "Pull over! Pull over!"

Ainsley braked hard and pulled to the shoulder. She turned to the backseat and saw Riki with her nose to her tablet. The young woman studied the screen a moment, then looked up at the two thugs. "Their car is moving."

Gavin shrugged. "Maybe the police are moving it."

Riki shook her head. "No, it's leaving town." She pointed to a barn a short distance down the road. "Go park on the other side of that."

Ainsley did as she was directed, backing the car along its far side so they wouldn't be seen by traffic from Killarney. Riki watched on the tablet as the car approached a few minutes later, then she gazed out the windshield.

The little rental car zipped by with Dirk at the wheel, Summer alongside him, and Brophy in the back. None of them seemed to notice the Audi parked by the barn as they rounded the next curve and headed north. And none of them appeared charred to the bone.

It was nearly dark when Dirk pulled up to their hotel in Tralee an hour later.

Brophy begged off an invitation to dinner. "It's been quite an harrowing day. I must be getting home to the missus," he said. "Let's plan on meeting first thing in the morning at Portmagee. It's less than an hour from here. I'll arrange for a boat, and we'll pay ourselves a visit to Falcon Rock."

"We'll be there," Dirk said. "Hopefully, our clothes won't still smell like a barbecue grill."

He and Summer showered and changed, then walked to a nearby Italian restaurant. After they received their wine, Dirk noted his sister stared at the doorway every time someone entered. "Expecting company?"

"The people that tried to kill us in Egypt have tracked us here."

"Possibly. But I doubt they'd want to join us for dinner, unless the gnocchi here is really good."

Summer shook her head. "Not funny."

"We don't know for a fact there's a connection."

"Of course we do. That's why you parked the rental car behind the hotel."

"Touché. Yet at this point, they have to suspect we died in the blaze."

"I suppose." She sipped her wine. "They must know we've made the connection between Meritaten and Ireland. Perhaps Dr. Brophy mentioned it to someone."

"It must be the grave of Meritaten they're trying to protect—or find before we do," Dirk said.

"It can only be for two reasons. Either there's treasure associated with the site or it's the Apium of Faras."

"This far from Egypt," Dirk said, "the treasure potential would be minimal. I suppose any relics from that age are still valuable to an artifact thief."

"What can we do tomorrow if they're onto us?"

"We'll make a roundabout drive to Portmagee and watch for a tail. On the small roads around here, it shouldn't be too hard to tell if we're being followed."

Having eaten their salad of burrata with tomatoes finished with pesto sauce, they finished their dinner of pappardelle with lamb ragu, then made their way back to the hotel. Dirk was preparing for bed when someone knocked at his door. Expecting Summer, he opened the door and found Riki standing there with a travel bag over her shoulder.

"I'm told the hotel is full," she said with a seductive smile. "Any chance you have room for a stray boarder?"

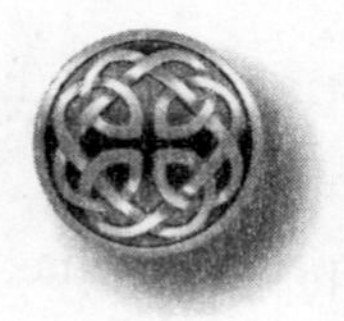

47

Pitt quietly dressed in black clothes and waited in his darkened room until midnight. He kissed his sleeping wife on the cheek and slipped out the window, lowering himself from the sill and dropping to a rocky knoll. He moved away from the illuminated manor and made his way up to the driveway. Crossing the road, he threaded his way through the trees, working his way, unseen, past the guard at the front gate.

He found the Mini where he'd parked it, still within view of the manor. Pitt put the transmission in neutral and pushed the car onto the road. With the aid of a downhill grade, he was able to shove the car around a curve and out of the guard's sight. Pitt jumped in and started the car, driving slowly toward Drumnadrochit, using only the parking lights. Once he'd put a mile between himself and the manor, he flicked on the headlights and increased speed.

He'd traveled only a short distance when a set of headlights appeared in the rearview mirror. Pitt maintained a healthy speed until he approached Urquhart Castle. Then he braked hard, pulled into the visitor parking lot, and turned off the Mini's lights. With an open view down the road, he watched as the car following him approached. A quarter of a mile away, it stopped and sat idling in the road.

Pitt flicked on his lights and hopped out. He stepped to the back, crouched, and ran his hands beneath the rear bumper. At the far end, his fingers touched a small metal box, attached with a magnet.

"Gotcha," he said, examining the GPS tracking device. He debated about tossing it into the lake, but climbed back in the car and set it on the passenger seat. He pulled out of the lot and zipped down the road, not stopping until he entered Inverness a few minutes later. He didn't have to look behind to know the other car was still tailing him.

Inverness was quiet at that hour, save for a handful of spirited pubs near the center of town. Pitt drove randomly through the city, searching for a decoy. One presented itself in the form of a late-night street sweeper. Pitt circled around, approached the vehicle a block ahead of its oncoming path, then turned down an alley. He parked the Mini behind a dumpster, grabbed the tracking device, and walked to the street.

He spotted a bike rack near the curb and stood next to it as if fumbling for a lock. As the street sweeper churned alongside, he slapped the magnetized tracking device to its back. Then Pitt returned up the alley and crouched behind the trash container as the sweeper moved to the end of the block. He had to wait only a minute before the black BMW crept by, a man and a woman visible inside.

Once the car had passed, Pitt got into the Mini and drove back down the alley. He turned left and wound his way out of town. Once he found Dores Road, he traveled south, leaving his pursuers behind.

Pitt drove the shoreline road to the small village of Foyers, where he turned at the old church. He wheeled around the building and again parked behind its high stone walls. Near the water he spotted an empty flatbed truck with a built-in crane. Pitt made his way down the hill, passed the truck, and stepped onto the small darkened dock. The glow of a lit cigar at the far end signaled he wasn't alone.

Pitt stepped along the creaking dock and found Al Giordino lying on a large coil of rope, puffing a cigar, and gazing at a clear patch of night sky.

"Nice heavens here," he said. "I've spotted Venus, Mars, and a shooting star."

"Did you make a wish?"

"I wished I was viewing the Southern Cross from a Tahitian beach." He ground out the cigar and rose to his feet. Like Pitt, he wore dark clothes.

"Any problem with the *Nymph*?"

"Not a one," Giordino said. "Rudi tested her. I grabbed her in Liverpool and transported her to the dock, here." He waved an arm around. "Finding this place in the dark was the hardest challenge."

Pitt had to search the dockside waters to spot the turquoise submersible tied up a few yards away. Lying low in the water, the tiny two-man craft was barely visible.

"Her batteries are fully charged," Giordino said. "I take it we don't have an official invite?"

"Not exactly." Pitt relayed his suspicions about the lab.

"Rudi mentioned a potential global plague. He sounded pretty panicked. You think this is the source?"

"Could be." Pitt climbed onto the submersible. "The place is heavily secured by land. I figured the best way to take a closer look was by water."

Giordino nodded. "With the *Sea Nymph* we've got both stealth and the ability to see through black water." He cast off the mooring lines, followed Pitt inside, and sealed the hatch.

Pitt took the pilot's seat, ran through a quick safety check, then engaged the thrusters and propelled the submersible to the center of the lake. He submerged the vessel just beneath the surface, allowing only a thin masthead near the stern to rise above the water.

It contained both a rotating video camera and a GPS receiver. Linked to a pair of screens on the center console, it allowed Pitt and Giordino to view the lake's surface alongside a digital map that relayed their exact position. As Pitt adjusted the light level on the image, Giordino activated a set of multibeam sonar units at each corner of the submersible's base frame.

The *Sea Nymph* was designed for deepwater survey projects in restricted environments, so it was compact with high maneuverability. The combined sonars allowed for a three-hundred-sixty-degree acoustic view, which complemented mineral, sediment, and water sensing devices.

Giordino adjusted the sonar to a range of one hundred meters, but with the *Sea Nymph* far above the lakebed, his monitor showed only a circle of green snow. He glanced at a digital fathometer and whistled. "Seven-hundred-foot depth here. Not a good place to drop the car keys over the side."

"The loch is narrow, yet quite deep." Pitt dialed up the thruster speed. With a thin prow for improved hydrodynamics, the *Nymph* could easily cruise at better than five knots. Pitt navigated by the digital map, keeping one eye on the video feed for potential lake traffic.

They hadn't traveled far when he spotted McKee Manor along the northern shore, and he reduced power. Farther ahead, he saw the lights of another vessel sailing away on the same heading as the tanker he'd seen when he was fishing.

"The site is ahead on the south shore," Pitt said. "I'd like to see how they are loading their tankers."

"Roger that. I'll keep our belly from scraping the bottom."

As Pitt angled the submersible toward the southeastern shoreline, he kept his eyes on the video monitor. At night, the camouflaged research building was all but invisible. The floating dock appeared as a black line on the water, and Pitt headed toward it. He reduced speed and nudged the *Nymph* to a twenty-foot depth, relying on the sonar to guide them.

"Bottom coming up fast," Giordino called out. "Passing under a hundred feet."

The sonar reading from the forward units crystallized into an image of the lake bottom ahead and beneath them. Pitt toggled on the *Nymph*'s exterior floodlights, which revealed a murky soup of dark green water.

"So much," Giordino said, "for the crystalline Highlands water in my Scotch whisky."

"It's the peat in the soil. The same stuff that gives your whisky that smoky flavor is also in the water."

"Tastes better than it looks." He tapped a finger on the sonar screen. "Just passed a target of some sort off to the left. Depth at thirty meters."

Pitt glanced at the screen. A linear shadow with a rounded end signified an object protruding from the lake bottom. He turned the *Nymph* toward the target and descended, leveling off when the bottom appeared. He inched the submersible ahead until the target appeared beneath the floodlights.

"A boat," Giordino said. "And a nice one at that."

Even covered in silt, the object carried the rakish figure of a large speedboat. Pitt drew down its length, allowing the thrusters to blow away some of the sediment, then hovered over it for a better look. Cleared of its muddy coating, the boat appeared to be built of mahogany. Polished brass fittings still gleamed under the lights.

"Nice ride for these parts," Giordino said.

"It must be McKee's boat. He's said to have died in the accidental crash of an Italian speedboat." The submersible's lights revealed a chrome script that spelled out RIVA.

"An accident?" Giordino said. "I'm not so sure. Look at the cowl and windscreen."

Pitt turned the *Nymph* and hovered over the boat's cockpit. A scattering of small round holes pockmarked the windscreen, cowl, and cockpit seats. On the opposite side, a large jagged gouge appeared, open nearly to the hull.

"Possible earmarks of an explosion," Pitt said.

"The wrath of a scorned wife?"

"I wouldn't bet against it."

Pitt surveyed the boat once more as Giordino shot video with an exterior camera, then he turned the *Nymph* toward shore. He followed the rising lakebed until Giordino called out again.

"Approaching the dock and what appears to be some related infrastructure. Possible pipeline and valve arrangement to our left. There's also a strange shadow ahead."

Giordino felt the submersible halt its forward progress. "See something?"

Pitt didn't answer. His attention was focused on a moving object at the limit of their field of vision. Giordino followed his gaze, leaning upright in his seat.

Slithering past the viewport, with jaws open and eyes aglow, was a long green creature of the deep.

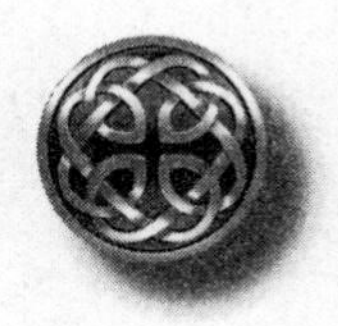

48

It wasn't a monster, but a European eel, nearly five feet in length.

"He's a big one," Giordino said.

"Look how he's swimming," Pitt said. He nudged the submersible ahead. Its lights revealed the eel was weaving in and out of a heavy cable net strung from the underside of the dock to the seabed below.

"Our slithering friend highlighted their security system," Pitt said.

"No divers allowed," Giordino replied. "Or submersibles."

"Possibly supported by surface sensors or video monitoring. Hopefully, no one's watching at this hour, especially since a tanker just departed a short time ago."

A few feet to the side, Pitt spotted a framed stanchion rising from the lakebed. He approached for a closer look.

"I'm spotting several of them on the sonar, in an L-shaped

configuration coming from shore," Giordino said. "They must be supports for the dock."

The *Nymph*'s lights illumined a pyramid-shaped latticed support bolted to a concrete base. The steel security netting hung in front of it. Pitt angled the submersible for an upward view of the surface dock, revealing a large hydraulic apparatus extending from the support.

"The great Loch Ness disappearing dock," Pitt said. "They can raise and lower it several feet to keep it out of view."

"A lot of trouble," Giordino said, "just to keep some transport activity quiet. Seems more like the workings of a Central American drug cartel."

Pitt guided the submersible along the dock and its supports, until they turned and angled to shore. At the bend, a large flexible hose stretched across the bottom. It rose along the corner support, suspended by a valve assembly on the dock that provided the means to load the visiting tankers.

Pitt followed the dock supports toward shore as the depth receded. He slowed the *Nymph* when the dorsal camera poked through the water and provided a surface view. Little could be seen. Both the dock and the lab facility were pitch-black.

"Looks like everyone is asleep," Pitt said.

"Then let's go have a look. Though I must confess, I wish I hadn't left my night vision goggles in my other suit."

Pitt surfaced the submersible and nudged it alongside the outer dock as Giordino opened the hatch, hopped onto the dock and tied up the *Nymph*. A minute later, he jumped back inside.

"Afraid we've got company," he said, shaking his head in bemusement. A loud dog's bark sounded through the hatch.

"Yes, I met him earlier," Pitt said. He reached into his pocket and pulled out the napkin-wrapped lamb. "Try offering him this."

Giordino unwrapped the napkin and looked inside. "The way to a Rottweiler's heart?" He poked up through the hatch just long enough to toss the meat on the dock. That set off another round of barking, until the dog stepped over to investigate the treat.

"I'm not sure a truckload of filet mignon would satisfy that guy," Giordino said.

"Those tidbits should do the trick." Pitt smiled. "We'll just have to give him a few minutes to digest his meal."

"Did you add a secret sauce?"

"About a dozen Dramamine tablets pressed into it. Loren always carries some when she travels. The best I could do on short notice."

He adjusted the exterior video camera to view the dock. They watched a dim image of the dog devour the lamb, then peer at the submersible.

"What about a handler?" Giordino asked.

Pitt swiveled the camera toward shore, saw no activity. "He appeared to be roaming the grounds freely and alone when I saw him earlier."

"Unless you have a sheep stashed aboard, I hope he doesn't have any friends." Giordino poked through a toolbox and pulled out a wrench for self-defense.

They watched on the monitor as the dog lay down on the dock and eventually closed his eyes. Exiting the dock, they took a few steps up a stone pathway, then stopped. In the faint starlight, they saw it led to the building's main entrance and a pair of high steel doors. It wasn't the imposing entrance that made them pause. It was a small descending set of stairs to their right that led to an underground doorway.

Giordino followed Pitt as he stepped down to the side door and twisted the handle. It turned easily. He opened the door a fraction to peer in, then stepped inside.

He found himself in a small control room cut into the hillside. A narrow window at eye level overlooked the dock. A large console below the window contained a smorgasbord of dials, switches, and controls. Video monitors showed live feeds from either end of the dock. While the moored submersible sat too low to be detected, one of the cameras showed the snoring Rottweiler.

"Must be their control room for piping the product from the lab to the tanker ships," Giordino said. "Glad nobody was around to watch our arrival."

Giordino noticed a back door to the control room and gave it a try. It opened to a narrow tunnel, dimly lit with overhead lights. "This looks like our kind of entrance." He ducked under the archway and stepped in.

Pitt followed him down the narrow passage, its walls and curved ceiling lined with smooth concrete. The tunnel extended over a hundred feet to the main building, ending at a narrow stairwell. They climbed a level to another door, which they found ajar. Giordino was about to look around it when a phone rang on the opposite side.

"Maguire," came a weathered voice that answered the phone. "No, there've been no unauthorized vehicles approaching the site." The man listened a moment. "Aye, Richards is in the housing unit. I'll wake him, along with one of the other guards, then take a look around." Another pause. "Right," he said, then hung up.

The man made another phone call, slipped on a jacket, and stepped away. When Pitt and Giordino heard a distant door open and close, they entered from the stairwell.

It was a security station, just inside the building's front entrance. A row of video monitors above a single desk provided live feeds from hidden cameras around the complex. One focused on the exterior entrance, where the armed security guard was seen moving toward the driveway.

"Something tells me," Giordino said, "that getting out of here may be more difficult than getting in." He reached over to a video monitor that showed the main corridor and adjusted the camera so that it pointed at the ceiling.

"I'm sure we can arrange some sort of diversion when the time comes," Pitt said. "Let's get moving."

They entered a wide central corridor that ran the length of the building. The bright white concrete floor, walls, and ceiling gave it a sterile feel. The doors along the hallway had glass inserts, allowing a view inside. Small offices gave way to working laboratories occupied by one or two people in lab coats. They hesitated in front of one door, which opened to a kennel. Cages lined the walls, each containing a beagle or other medium-sized dog.

"Lab-testing on Snoopy," Giordino said in a low voice. "I dislike these people already."

They continued down the hall until a door handle clicked

behind them. Pitt saw a dark room to his left and rushed in. Giordino followed quickly and closed the door. They froze in the dark, listening as someone continued down the hall. Another door opened and closed, then Pitt flicked on the light switch.

Overhead LED lights revealed a medical operating room. Worktables with computers, microscopes, and chemical solutions lined the rear and side walls. Several X-rays were posted on a corner viewing monitor. In the center, a gurney stood beneath a rack of bright operating lights, sided by a tray table containing an array of scalpels and probes. More disconcerting, a small figure lay on the gurney, covered by a sheet.

Silently, Pitt and Giordino approached the operating table. Pitt stared at the draped figure, then grabbed a corner of the sheet and drew it back. He wasn't sure what to expect, perhaps one of the test dogs from the kennel.

Instead, he exposed the well-preserved body of a thirty-five-hundred-year-old Egyptian mummy.

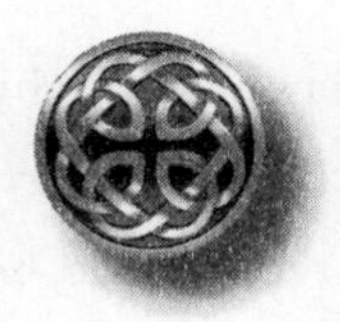

49

To Pitt's untrained eye the size of the ancient linen wrappings around the legs and torso suggested a mummified child of ten or twelve. The shaved skull indicated a male. The head was tilted back, and a small rubber block was wedged inside to keep the mouth open.

"I wasn't expecting to find King Tut," Giordino said.

"Whoever he is," Pitt said, "he's a long way from home."

Giordino rubbed his chin. "Didn't Summer and Dirk just find an Egyptian tomb along the Nile?"

"Yes. And it contained a child's coffin that was snatched." He leaned close and studied the skull. "Take a look at his mouth."

Giordino gazed at the teeth, then the tray of medical tools. "Looks like they extracted one of his lower molars, on the right side."

"Trying to retrieve his DNA." Pitt placed the sheet back over the body and studied the room. A closet door at the back with its adjoining electronic panel caught his eye. He opened the door to find a temperature-controlled bay lined with thick shelves and illuminated by dim red lights. On one side lay a half-dozen wooden coffins carved in Egyptian fashion, gilded and painted with the features of their late occupants. Across the aisle were more mummified remains, each housed in a Plexiglas box.

"A collection of coffins and mummies," Giordino said. "That's a hobby I'd forgo for golf."

Pitt motioned toward the mummies. "I don't see any adults. They're all very young males."

Giordino noted gaps in their exposed teeth. "And they all look like they've had a recent visit to the dentist."

"McKee's interest in ancient Egypt apparently goes beyond her husband's passion for archeology."

The men backed out of the storage room and searched the lab for further evidence. Pitt noticed a white lab coat and slipped into it. Finding nothing more of significance, they turned off the lights and stepped back into the corridor. They bypassed a pair of small offices and opted to enter a large conference room. Thick binders lay scattered about a long central table, while the walls were covered with charts, maps, production schedules, and shelves with more binders.

Pitt picked up one of the binders and found a detailed history of various commercial products.

"Dirk, take a look at this."

Giordino stood before a large global map. Stick-on labels were posted next to various major cities or regions. Each was coded with the prefix BR- or EP- followed by 1, 2, or 3.

Pitt read a few of the labels. "'Gulf of Mexico, BR-1.'

'Mumbai, EP-2.' 'Detroit, EP-3.' Must be the product applied on jobs at those locations."

"If so, check out where they applied a batch of EP-2." Giordino pointed to Central America. Pitt followed his finger to a label that read CERRÓN GRANDE, EP-2.

"Well, well," Pitt said. "I think I'd like a sample of this EP product. Then we can think about exiting stage left."

As he spoke, the door opened. A young woman with short black hair and wearing a lab coat entered the room carrying a yellow binder. She gave Pitt and Giordino an odd glance as she shelved the binder. Turning back toward the door, she looked at Pitt and hesitated. "I'm sorry to intrude, Dr. Andrews. Is there anything I can help you with?"

Pitt didn't hesitate at the question. "I was just looking for the outgoing transportation schedules."

She crinkled her nose and shrugged. "Sorry, I work in research. They might be in the production bay."

"No worries. Thank you, Miss . . ."

"Thompkins. You're welcome." She exited the room.

"A friend of yours, Dr. Andrews?" Giordino asked.

Pitt glanced at the identification badge clipped to his lab coat. In block letters, it read DR. EUGENE ANDREWS, above a photo of a dark-haired man who bore a faint resemblance.

"Apparently, I have a forgettable face."

"Do you think she'll report us?"

"We should probably bank on it." He turned back to the map. "They're shipping the stuff all over the world. Be nice to know exactly where." He tore down the map, folded it, and put it in his pocket.

"That's a starting point," Giordino said.

"Let's find the production bay."

The corridor was empty as they left the conference room. They nearly skipped the next room, when Giordino spotted a man seated at a desk. Pitt hesitated when the man turned and looked out the door's cutout window. He was older, with a round bespectacled face and thinning brown hair. He gazed at Pitt with a look of fear and resignation.

"Al, I know this man."

Pitt tried to open the door, but it was locked. The man inside shrugged, indicating he couldn't open it. Pitt noticed a card reader by the door, then remembered his lab coat badge. He waved Dr. Andrews's ID card next to the reader and heard a click. He turned the door handle and stepped into the room with Giordino following.

The man looked at them expectantly, said nothing.

"Dr. Perkins?" Pitt asked.

"Yes."

"My name is Pitt." He glanced about the room. It was laid out on the order of a dorm room, with a built-in bunk and a small side bathroom. "Are you being held against your will?"

Perkins hesitated, then nodded as he studied the two men. "Who did you say you were?"

"We're with NUMA," Pitt said. "We're investigating some deaths that may be linked to the deployment of a BioRem product."

"Thank God someone finally noticed," Perkins said. "How did you get in here?"

"We sneaked in through the lakeside back door," Giordino said.

Perkins popped up and peered out the window for any activity in the hallway. "They'll kill you," he whispered. He looked at Pitt with desperate eyes. "They forced me to help them."

"Can you help us obtain a sample?" Pitt asked.

Perkins shook his head. "Too late. It's already deployed everywhere. They've been mass-producing it for months. Millions will be afflicted."

"Then help us stop it."

The biochemist stared at his feet and shook his head. In a low voice he muttered, "There's no way to stop it."

"Help us try."

Perkins looked into the eyes of Pitt and Giordino. An analytical scientist, he scrutinized the two men before him. What he observed was not a hapless pair on a crusade of folly. Instead, he saw two men who had defied the odds their entire lives. They radiated toughness, morality, and an unfailing sense of determination.

For the first time in a long while, Perkins felt a sliver of hope. "Aye," he said with a faint nod.

Pitt flashed the card reader again, opened the door a crack, and stepped into the hall. "All clear."

Perkins followed him, with Giordino behind. As Perkins cleared the doorway, a shrill alarm sounded. The scientist pulled up a pant leg, exposing an ankle monitor.

"I'm terribly sorry. Been wearing it for so long, I forgot all about it."

Giordino pushed him forward. "Don't worry now. Just don't let it slow you. Any thoughts on a quick way out?"

The scientist thought a moment. "There's an external freight door in the production room that locks from the inside." He pointed down the hallway, then took off at an awkward run.

Pitt and Giordino followed him to the end of the corridor, where he burst through a set of double doors.

Inside was a large, high-bay production room where the company's bacterial solutions were grown in nutrient-filled vats. Bathtub-sized stainless steel tanks near the door gave way to larger ones along the side wall, which were dwarfed by a half-dozen huge tanks positioned in the center of the bay. A maze of pipes crisscrossed the high ceiling, connecting the various containers. Along the near wall, a raised platform housed the operating controls and monitoring systems.

A wiry man in a dark jumpsuit stood on the platform with a clipboard, examining a computer monitor. He looked up as the three men stormed into the room, accompanied by the blare of alarms.

"Hey!" He jumped off the platform and rushed over to the men. He raised a hand to Perkins's chest and shoved him to a halt.

"You don't have authorization to be in here." He gave Pitt and Giordino a suspicious look.

"Our authorization is right here." Giordino stepped between his companions and threw an overhand punch at the technician, tagging him hard on the chin. The man's eyes rolled back in his head.

Pitt caught him before he crumpled to the floor.

"Growing soft in your old age?" Giordino asked as he rubbed his knuckles.

"Sympathy for the workingman." Pitt eased the technician

onto the ground. He stood and looked at Perkins. "The back door, Doctor?"

"This . . . This way." Perkins snaked through the center tanks to the back wall and a large drop-down door. A small panel at the side controlled its operation, and Perkins pushed the lift button. Nothing happened.

"It's probably secured by a reader," Pitt said. "Let me try my key card." He waved his stolen ID in front of the panel, but it made no difference.

Pitt turned to Giordino. "We may need your sleeping buddy's assistance."

They turned to retrace their steps when gunfire sounded, and the concrete floor exploded in small chunks in front of them.

They froze as two guards with raised assault rifles appeared at the center of the bay. A third man, the Perkins imposter, emerged behind them. Stepping between the guards, he raised an automatic pistol, aimed it at Pitt, and smiled.

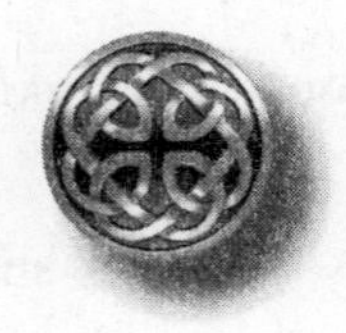

50

Dr. Perkins, so nice to see you again," Pitt said to the security man named Richards. He waved a hand toward the real scientist. "I believe you know Dr. Perkins?"

"Shut up." Richards took a step closer, leveling his pistol at Pitt's chest. He nodded at one of the guards, who searched the three men. The map was taken from Pitt's pocket, and Giordino was relieved of his wrench.

They were then held at gunpoint, backs against the wall, for nearly twenty minutes. When the production room's doors again swung open, Audrey McKee walked in, escorted by an armed man and woman. Pitt recognized her companions as the assassins who had killed Dr. Nakamura in Maryland.

Audrey approached Pitt with a look of bemused annoyance. "Mr. Pitt, you've been wandering around in places you don't belong."

"I thought you told me to make myself at home."

She shook her head. "I saw your submersible at the dock. Very sly."

"We heard that Nessie was in the neighborhood," Giordino said, "and stopped by to see for ourselves."

"It'll be the last thing you'll ever see."

"They had this with them." Richards passed her the map. She took a quick look and handed it back to Richards. "You should have let things go in El Salvador," she said to Pitt.

He regarded her for a moment, then made the connection that she'd been the fake doctor in Suchitoto who'd tried to kill Elise. "Dr. McKee, is it now? I didn't know that testing your bacteria on innocent Third World children and small dogs was condoned by the medical profession."

She began to speak, but Perkins interrupted her. "They know what you are making here."

Audrey stuck her nose in the air. "We make environmentally friendly remediation products for pollution control. Should anyone come to inspect our facility, we can quickly purge any products in development to the bottom of the loch. No one outside the facility shall ever know otherwise."

Perkins gave a somber nod. "Your father would never approve."

"My father . . . My father was a beast."

"Not compared to your mother."

As Audrey's face flushed in anger, Pitt spoke up. "Your tanker ships are being tracked. It will all be traced back to you."

"I don't believe you. But even if what you say is true, it's too late. We've deployed EP-3 in nearly a dozen locations around the globe. Even under your nose in Detroit. We're changing the world, Mr. Pitt, and there's nothing you, or anyone else, can do about it." She gave him a thin smile. "Now if you'll excuse me, I have to make plans for entertaining your wife in the morning."

She rapped her knuckles on the large stainless steel tank next to her and turned to Richards. "Since our guests are so curious about our production methods, perhaps they can be a part of the next batch. Tie them up inside one of the growth tanks and let them enjoy the process firsthand."

She gave the men a parting gaze. "You are the last of a dying breed. Good-bye, gentlemen."

As she departed with her armed escort, Richards sent one of the guards to find some bindings. He returned with a knife and a spool of heavy nylon rope. While the others kept their weapons trained, he went from one captive to the next, expertly tying their wrists and elbows behind their backs. His handiwork completed, the guard grabbed Perkins by the shirt and yanked him forward. "This way."

He led Perkins to the far side of one of the large tanks, where a hatch door stood open. "Inside," he ordered.

Pitt and Giordino were marched at gunpoint behind and forced to duck inside the hatch, joining Perkins. Richards and the two guards followed, and one flicked on a flashlight.

The tank was dark and empty, its only feature was a steel ladder welded to the internal wall for inspection purposes. The captives were prodded to the ladder, where they were tied by their elbows, facing outward.

Richards let the two guards depart, then stepped to the hatch and faced the bound men.

"The drinks are on me." He laughed as he shoved the hatch closed with a clang and spun a locking wheel.

The tank's interior fell pitch-black, the air damp and stagnant. Pitt and Giordino began struggling with their bindings, but the ropes were secure. Perkins gave a sigh and sagged against the ladder.

"Feel for a rough spot on the ladder that might cut the rope," Pitt said. His movements were limited, and he could feel only a small section of the ladder.

"I think there's a rusty gap at the corner of one of the rungs," Giordino said. "I can't get my rope against it."

The interior fell silent as the men wrestled with their ropes. Then they heard the mechanical rumble of a valve turning. Moments later, a torrent erupted from an overhead pipe, splashing down around them. Within seconds, the cold liquid flooded the floor and began a slow climb up the men's legs.

51

I take it we're in for a cold bath, Doctor?" Giordino asked.

"Indeed," Perkins said. "The bioremediation product is initiated in small batches, then grown in ever larger tanks. These big ones are used to load the ships that come up the Caledonian Canal from the Atlantic."

As the liquid splashed about their lower legs, Giordino asked, "Is this stuff toxic?"

"Not at all. Right now they're just pouring in a nutrient solution for the bacteria. It's mostly water, glycerol, and nitrates. They'll fill the tank about ninety-five percent before adding a microbe solution from one of the smaller vats. We'll be long drowned before that happens."

"What goes into the microbe solution?" Pitt asked.

"Until a few years ago, the firm made a small variety of petroleum-degrading bacterial organisms for use on oil spills. They were genetically engineered, but under the safest conditions and according to the strictest standards. The microbes were actually designed to self-destruct if deployed in any environment other than the pollutant field for which they were designed." He sighed. "Frasier McKee was a man of high ideals, and all of his research products were for mankind's betterment."

"Somewhere, he slipped off the rails." Giordino strained his thick arm muscles against his bindings to no avail.

"It wasn't him," Perkins said. "It was his wife, Evanna, who was always unhinged. To be fair, Frasier's drinking and marital infidelities didn't help matters. But something else happened, and she finally snapped. Killing him wasn't enough . . ." His voice fell away.

"On the way in, we discovered the remains of his boat," Pitt said. "It didn't appear to be an accidental sinking."

"It wasn't. And the authorities couldn't prove otherwise, so it went down as an accident. They never even bothered searching for the boat. I always suspected Evanna paid off someone."

"Her killing hasn't stopped there." Pitt thought of Mike Cruz and the children in El Salvador.

"I know," Perkins said. "She became a different person after his death. Obsessed and deranged. She surrounded herself with hired thugs, brainwashed her two daughters, and turned the lab into a secret compound—all while pursuing her crazed version of the world. Now she's spreading death everywhere."

"What's it all about?" Giordino asked. "And what did that woman mean about us being the last of a dying breed?"

"It was Frasier's and my fault, really," Perkins said with a defeated voice. "He was obsessed with ancient Egypt. He used to sponsor digs there all the time. Even dragged me along a few times, though the heat was dreadful. He was fascinated by a pharaoh named Akhenaten and excavated a number of sites associated with his reign. At several digs, he discovered the tombs and mummies of children, boys mostly. He correctly assumed they all died from disease."

"We saw the collection near the conference room," Pitt said. "Quite impressive."

"Yes, though I'm sure the Egyptian Antiquities Ministry would not be happy. Frasier was a scientist first, and he wanted to know how they died. So he smuggled the bodies to his laboratory."

"Wouldn't that be rather speculative after thirty-five hundred years?" Giordino asked.

"Typically. But if the subject died from a disease of any duration, then DNA can capture the evidence. And in the case of Egyptian mummies preserved in the desert, the answer lies in their teeth."

"From lack of brushing?"

"The dental pulp will often contain trace elements of blood—with the genetic code of the bacteria or virus that caused death. And in the case of the male child mummies from the time of Akhenaten, the cause of death from a plague."

"Plague?" Pitt asked.

"The Evolution Plague—that's what McKee called it."

"A predisposition of first-born males?" Pitt said.

"It seemed that way, but it was really just all young males."

"I'm told it may be related to cholera."

"It is. Frasier concluded it was a waterborne bacteria carried in the Nile. He theorized it may have been the result of warring neighbors, upriver in Nubia, dumping dead animals into the river. There are some physical similarities to the cholera bacterium," Perkins said. "And also some unusual genetic differences.

"After we were able to reconstitute the bacteria, we spent a considerable effort studying it. We found a variation in the pathogen that has the ability to modify its chromosomal structure, specifically targeting the male Y chromosome. That seemed to account for the great proportion of male deaths."

"So this plague is alive today?" Pitt asked.

"I'm afraid so. Frasier thought it might hold the key to developing a vaccine for the modern form of cholera. That's why he decided to revive it. We were very controlled about the process, especially once we discovered its resistance to chemicals such as chlorine that's used to treat tap water. Of course, that all changed when Evanna took over and discovered what we had."

"So she is dispersing the Evolution Plague under the guise of pollution-control bacteria?" Pitt asked. "We saw the map showing the deployment of products marked EP and BR."

"The 'BR' is our primary bioremediation commercial product, used primarily for oil spills. It is perfectly safe and effective. But 'EP' represents the 'Evolution Plague.'" Perkins's voice fell low. "She forced me to genetically recombine it, maintaining the chromosome-altering characteristics in a more benign form. I had no choice. She threatened my wife and locked me in here. My wife probably thinks I'm dead . . . if she's even still alive."

He fell silent as the solution in the tank reached their knees.

"How is it," Pitt asked, "that the cholera symptoms varied in the deployments?"

"After the first deployment where we could study the side

effects, it's taken three more adjustments to dilute the power of its immediate lethality. McKee wanted to distribute it without attracting attention. The first two production runs, EP-1 and EP-2, produced strong cholera-like symptoms in weakened males, primarily the young. This was a direct carryover from the original plague. There were terrible deaths in Cairo and Mumbai," he said, his voice falling low again. "From what I've heard, the third product run has not proven deadly on dispersal."

"If it's not killing people," Giordino asked, "then why is she spreading it?"

"Because of its influence at the DNA level to block virilization," replied Perkins. "You see, the unique thing about the Evolution Plague is not simply its tenacity. New strains of antibiotic-resistant bacteria are emerging all the time. What sets it apart is its impact at the microcellular level. The bacterium is carried in the cytoplasm and contains a mechanism that barricades the SRY gene in the Y chromosome."

"Can you try that again in English, Doc?"

"It means that during reproduction, no male embryos are formed. Once infected by the Evolution Plague, a woman will bear only female offspring. It's why there were no male heirs on the Egyptian throne for fifty years after the death of Akhenaten's son Tutankhamun. If all the women on the planet were infected, then males would vanish. As Audrey McKee put it, we're 'the last of a dying breed.'"

"So that's what's behind the Sisterhood of Boudicca," Pitt muttered.

"Yes, the Sisterhood," Perkins said. "It seeks the very extinction of men."

"But wouldn't females follow suit?" Giordino asked.

"Advances in genetic reproduction will assure that doesn't happen," Perkins said. "Human asexual reproduction is already possible in the laboratory. Women will be able to breed without men. It's just a matter of time."

"And, I'm sure McKee is positive that all women are in favor of this new world order," added Giordino.

"With their tankers deploying the Evolution Plague all over the globe," Pitt said, "it would seem they are well on their way."

"They've focused on dispersing it into freshwater lakes and waterways that provide drinking water for large metropolitan areas."

"Staging marine accidents in the process," Pitt said.

"That's right. It allows them to appear on-site to clean up the spill with the firm's bioremediation product, then secretly disperse the Evolution Plague on the side. Cairo, Mumbai, Shanghai . . . At all the locales, it's released near the induction for the main water treatment plants. The bacteria can withstand the water treatment process and infect women right out of the tap. There's no telling how widespread it's already become."

"They can't possibly reach all the women on the planet that way," Giordino said.

"No, yet we could still be talking hundreds of millions of women already infected. The gender balance could be permanently altered. More frightening, however, is the fact that this is a brand-new organism. We don't know its propensity to mutate into a more lethal form."

Another valve opened, and a second flood of solution began pouring into the tank. The men felt the liquid rise rapidly up their legs as they continued to struggle against their bindings.

"I can't say I'm making any progress with the rope," Giordino said. "You?"

"None," Pitt said. "But I've got an idea."

"Sure. Why don't you call that dark-haired girl from the conference room to come untie us?"

"Actually, I had someone else in mind," Pitt said. "My friendly counterpart, Dr. Eugene Andrews."

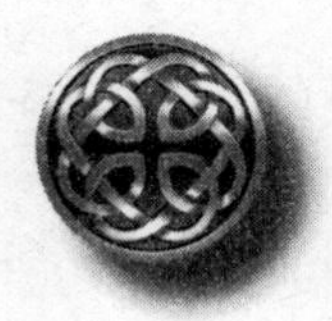

52

Dr. Eugene T. Andrews, with a Ph.D. in biochemistry from the University of Glasgow, had retired from Bio-Rem Global a few weeks earlier after discovering how the company was distributing its dangerous pathogens. Evanna McKee agreed to pay him a large severance to keep him silent, but no disbursement had been necessary after he was found dead in a suspicious one-car road accident.

Pitt wasn't counting on a resurrected Dr. Andrews to save them, just his lab coat. Or more precisely, his name badge. With it still clipped to his outer pocket, there was no way Pitt could reach it with his arms tied behind him. He coaxed Giordino to bend his way. After an initial poke in the eye, Giordino grabbed the badge with his teeth and yanked it off the coat.

The hard part was transferring it to Pitt. While his wrists and elbows were tied, his hands were free. He turned and extended his fingers past the ladder as Giordino twisted toward him and released his jaws to drop the badge.

The watery solution had risen to their waists, and Pitt heard a splash after the badge grazed his fingertips. He was just able to grab it before it floated away.

"Got it?" Giordino asked.

"Just barely. We'll have to see if I can sharpen it."

"I'd be grateful if that's done sooner than later." Almost a foot shorter than Pitt, Giordino could feel the water rising up his chest.

Pitt turned the plastic card flat in his hand and slid it across the ladder rung to the vertical support. There was a small rough spot at the joint, and Pitt scraped an edge of the card against it. He briskly rubbed the card multiple times, then flipped it over and sharpened the back edge. Because he was working the card underwater, he couldn't tell if his actions were effective. He paused and ran his thumb over the edge. It was noticeably thinner and sharper.

"Any luck?" Giordino asked as the water approached the base of his neck.

"Getting there," Pitt said in a calm voice. He could feel his friend begin to squirm to gain more height. On his other side, Perkins began exuding quiet sighs, apparently accepting his fate.

Pitt didn't. He continued to work his blade, pressing the card fast and furious against the makeshift whetstone. He sampled it again and found the plastic edge surprisingly sharp. The test would come with the rope.

He twisted his hands to align the card against a taut section of rope and began to saw. Though it wasn't a hot knife through butter, he could feel the sharpened badge slowly cut through the nylon fibers.

"I'll be taking a rather large drink soon, just so you know," Giordino said as the water splashed about his chin.

Pitt stepped up his efforts. He could feel the rope begin to give and he pressed harder. Finally, the rope snapped free.

"Got it, Al," he said.

It was only one section of rope, and he struggled to loosen the wrist bindings and slip his hands free. Then he pulled his arms clear of the rope that pinned his elbows to the ladder.

Giordino said nothing, but Pitt could hear his strains and gasps to keep his face above water.

Pitt reached around to Giordino's elbows and felt for a free end of the wet line. It had been drawn tight. Pitt, ducking underwater to get better leverage, quickly freed it from the ladder, then untied the remaining ropes, freeing Giordino's hands.

"Thanks . . . brother . . ." Giordino said, coughing and gasping. "I was almost pickled."

Pitt had already moved on to Perkins, who stood a head taller than Giordino. Pitt released the scientist's bindings as the water approached his chin. The three men clung on the ladder, recuperating, for a few moments.

"Now we need to get the door open," Pitt said.

They swam to the far wall, probing with their hands to find the hatch. Pitt felt it first and again ducked underwater to reach the wheel lock. He rotated the dog lever to unlock the hatch, then pulled on it. The door didn't budge. He popped back to the surface to take a breath.

"The hatch is here. I need some additional leverage against the force of all this water."

Giordino splashed alongside an instant later. "Ready when you are."

They ducked under and grabbed the lever. Pitt braced a foot against the tank wall, and together they pulled on the hatch. The door inched open, then slammed back from the force of the liquid. They returned to the surface to catch their breath.

"We need," Pitt said, "to wedge something inside the opening until the pressure can be relieved."

"Not much to work with in here," Giordino said.

Perkins had returned to the ladder and had seen a flash of light when the hatch briefly opened. "I'm wearing a stout pair of work boots," he said. "If you can open it again, I can try slipping a toe in. A foot in the door, so to speak." He swam over and joined them.

"You could lose it," Giordino said.

"A foot for a life seems a fair trade."

Pitt and Giordino plunged underwater once more. Both braced against the tank wall and pulled on the lever. The door nudged open a fraction, then again slammed shut. Their hope was dwindling, and both knew it.

Pitt tapped Giordino's arm with one, then two, then three fingers, and they heaved once more. The hatch sprung open a few inches as they strained with maximum effort. They held it until their strength waned, then released their grip and burst to the surface.

The tank had a different look. A sliver of light shone through, creating wavy shadows on the ceiling. Near the source of the light, Perkins stood with a twisted look. Around him came a deep rushing sound.

"I've got it," he said.

The thick leather sole of his boot started to buckle, but held the door open, allowing a rush of water to escape. Perkins struggled to keep his foot steady, flattening his body against the side of the tank to minimize the suction.

The water level was slow to drop, and Perkins had to hold his position for a minute or two until it reached waist level. Pitt and Giordino then forced the door fully open, allowing the remaining fluid to gush out.

Perkins stumbled into the outflow, thankful to exit the tank even as he lost his footing and sprawled onto the wet floor. Pitt helped him to his feet, then pulled him aside.

Alarms were sounding as the water sloshed across the floor. Too late, Pitt heard a yell and saw an armed man run toward them from the control station. A younger replacement for the earlier technician, he wore a brown jumpsuit and held a pistol in front of him. He stopped well short of Pitt and Perkins and, with a shaky hand, aimed the gun.

Pitt could see he was no trained guard and stepped toward him with Perkins, following the curved wall of the tank.

"Stay where you are!" the man said.

Pitt raised one arm, but kept walking, helping Perkins along with him.

"We need medical assistance," Pitt said as he closed the gap.

"I said to stop where you are." The man backed up a few steps to keep his distance. It was enough, Pitt gauged, to place him out of sight of the tank's door.

"Can you call a doctor?" Pitt said. "My friend's foot is broken."

The technician glanced at Perkins's mangled shoe. He reached for a radio at his hip and pressed the transmit button. "Assistance needed in the production room."

He turned to Pitt. "Where's the other man? Wasn't there three of you?"

Pitt shook his head and stared at the ground. "Drowned."

When he looked up, he had to force himself to focus on the man with the gun. It wasn't easy, as he saw another man moving behind the technician. As he had hoped, Giordino had slipped out of the tank and circled around the back.

Between the alarms and the sloshing water, there was enough noise to mask Giordino's approach, yet Pitt kept talking to hold the man's attention.

"May we put our arms down?" Pitt slowly lowered his arm. "There's been a misunderstanding. We're part of the tank inspection crew, assigned to make repairs. We found a number of leaks."

"Keep your arms up!" The man motioned with his gun toward the ceiling. He saw the reflection of movement on the side of the tank. Before he could turn, Giordino lunged and clasped him in a bear hug.

The technician struggled to break free, but he had no chance against Giordino's grip. Pitt stepped forward and finished the job, throwing a left and right to the head that left the technician barely conscious. Giordino ripped away the man's gun and let him slump to the floor.

"You're not liable to land a job here if you keep treating the employees so harshly," Pitt said.

Giordino shook his head. "I hear their retirement plan is crummy anyway."

They gathered up Perkins and started for the back door.

The old scientist held up a hand. "Just a minute, if I may." Perkins hobbled to the control platform and began flipping levers and twisting dials. Overhead valves opened across the room, dumping more fluid onto the floor. Perkins rejoined Pitt and Giordino carrying a twinkle in his eye. "Some additional mayhem to keep them busy a while."

They hurried to the back freight door, where Giordino pumped two shots from the pistol into the locking mechanism.

Pitt pushed the door open, revealing a paved lane that curved toward the entrance. In front of them, a yard filled with shrubs extended to the shore of the loch.

Giordino grabbed Perkins's arm and helped him through the door, then hesitated. Pitt wasn't moving. "Getting sentimental about leaving this place?" he asked.

"The plans. We need to know where the Evolution Plague has been deployed and what ships are carrying it."

"I believe they keep that information in a green binder in the conference room," Perkins said.

"Don't forget, our sleeping pal over there just called for help," Giordino said. "Someone more adept with a weapon will likely be here shortly."

Pitt simply nodded.

Giordino knew there was no point trying to change Pitt's mind. He handed him the pistol he'd taken from the technician, a SIG Sauer P320. "We'll wait for you at the *Sea Nymph*."

Pitt grabbed the gun. "I'll try and beat you there."

Both moved at a hustle, Giordino leading Perkins out the back door toward the dock, Pitt crossing the production room to its front door.

Water was seeping into the hallway as Pitt exited the bay. General chaos pervaded the facility. Alarms were sounding, people were rushing up and down the corridor. Escaping the kennels, the dogs began running across the yard, barking up a storm.

"What in bloody hell is going on?" cursed a man in a white coat, who rushed past Pitt into the flooded bay.

Thankful for his own lab coat, Pitt hurried down the hall, his wet appearance drawing only a few odd looks. Near the end of the hall, several men in dark clothes sprinted in his direction. He ducked into a vacant office and watched as Richards and two guards ran to the production room.

Pitt exited the office and made his way to the conference room. Thankfully, it was empty. Crossing the length of the room, he searched for the green binder. It took a few minutes, but he found it on the very last shelf. A simple label on the front cover said EP DEPLOYMENTS.

"That'll be staying here," came a deep voice from behind. "As will you."

Pitt looked over his shoulder to find Richards entering the room, a pistol extended in his hands in front of him.

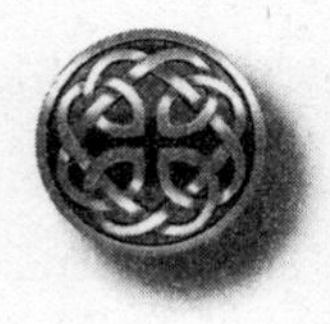

53

Pitt slowly turned toward the doorway, holding the binder in front of him. Richards stood there breathing hard, but with a steady grip on his weapon.

"Don't you have some water leaks to attend to?" Pitt asked.

"I'll stuff them with your dead body," Richards said. "Put the book down and come with me. I don't care to dirty our conference room."

That was all Pitt needed to hear. Richards had not seen the compact SIG Sauer pistol Pitt concealed behind the green binder. But he was in no position to aim and fire. Not yet.

Pitt took a step forward, better aligning himself. "There are some interesting details in this book," Pitt said. "Enough to put you and your boss away for quite some time."

"I'll tell you just once more. Put the book down."

"Here, you take it." Pitt extended the binder in front of him with his left hand, despite the distance across the room. As he did so, he pivoted the SIG Sauer in his right hand and fired two shots through the cover.

Both nine-millimeter slugs struck Richards in the chest, pushing him backward. He squeezed off two of his own shots as he collapsed, firing into the ceiling. Falling against the conference room door, he slid to the floor and didn't move. His eyes were glazed in a vacant stare as Pitt stepped over him.

"Next time, shoot first and talk later," Pitt said.

Figuring that the other guards were occupied in the production room, Pitt turned down the hallway toward the entrance. He passed more lab workers rushing toward the production bay. Most gave a wide berth to the man in the wet lab coat toting a green binder and a pistol.

The front guard desk was empty as Pitt stepped passed it and out the main door. The first rays of dawn were streaking across the sky, revealing a gray mist over the loch. The landscape was still and quiet, save for the sound of a motorboat somewhere on the lake.

Pitt followed a stone walkway that meandered between low hedges toward the waterfront. As the dock came into view, he detected movement ahead. It was Perkins and Giordino, angling across the grounds from the back of the building. Perkins was still hobbling, his foot in more pain than he'd let on. They were well ahead of Pitt as they stepped onto the dock.

The motor had grown louder, and Pitt could tell it was running at high speed on an approaching course. A few seconds later, the black speedboat he had seen in the McKee boathouse burst out of the mist.

As the pilot cut power, the sound of its motor was replaced

by the staccato report of an assault rifle. Muzzle flashes erupted from the boat, and Perkins crumpled to the dock alongside Giordino.

Pitt took off at a dead run. He raised the SIG Sauer and squeezed off four rounds at the boat. The slide locked open on the last shot. He tossed it aside as another muzzle flash flared from the boat. The walkway in front of him exploded in small chunks. Pitt dove to the side, clearing a hedge and rolling behind a small tree.

A few seconds later, gunfire swept across the dock and shoreline. Giordino had pulled Perkins off the dock, and the two men were crouched behind the thin cover at the water's edge. They were out of the gunman's sight for the moment, but all bets would be off once the boat reached the dock.

As the boat came closer, Pitt noticed the small control room they'd entered earlier was just off to his left. He stripped off the white lab coat, which made for an easy target, and sprinted for the building. He went unseen, diving down the steps and into the doorway. The gunman continued to fire short bursts toward Giordino and Perkins as the boat idled closer to the dock.

Pitt entered the room and scrambled to the control panel. Eyeing the buttons, he toggled on a switch labeled POWER. Several green lights blinked on, along with a split-screen video monitor. The left side showed a live feed from the dock's transfer hose mechanism. The right showed an animated side view of the dock facility, complete with a simulated image of the approaching speedboat.

Pitt eyed a lever marked TRANSFER PUMP beside a row of dials labeled with tank numbers. He glanced at the video screen as the black speedboat came into view. The boat had been approaching the dock head-on, but now swung parallel and drifted alongside. In the gray morning light, he saw three people on the boat—a woman at the helm, a man with an assault rifle, and another woman seated behind him.

Pitt recognized all three.

The pilot and gunman were the assailants who'd tried to kill him and Elise in Dr. Nakamura's office, and presumably had tracked him in the BMW. The woman was Audrey McKee.

The boat was docking directly in front of the transfer hose assembly. He reached to the console, randomly selecting a button marked TANK #3, and then activated the pump control lever. A whir of electric motors could be heard beneath his feet as a row of panel lights flicked on. Somewhere in the production bay, Pitt hoped, Tank #3 had something to give.

The speedboat bumped against the dock, and the pilot reached over and secured a stern line to a cleat. The gunman rose from his seat, placing a foot on the dock, when a loud gurgle erupted from the transfer assembly. He looked up as a firehose spray of bioremediation liquid came blasting out of the open end.

Standing directly in its path, the flow struck the gunman in the chest, knocking him backward. He tumbled into Audrey, both falling flat onto the floor of the boat.

As the boat filled, Pitt made his next move. He stepped laterally to a simple lever control that manipulated the dock's elevation. He pushed up on the lever, eyeing the video screen to see the results.

Built to adjust to fluctuations in the lake, the hydraulic

system allowed for an additional ten feet above the existing water level. Pitt held up the lever as the dock rose vertically in the air, drawing the security net above the surface with it. Secured tight by its stern dock line, the rear of the speedboat rose as well.

Realizing what was happening, the pilot tried to free the line, but fell forward before she could succeed. As the boat tipped forward, the pilot staggered into Audrey and the gunman. All three clung to the flooded interior as the boat nearly stood on end.

As the bow became more heavily weighted by the fluid, the boat twisted slowly toward the dock. The open cockpit collided with the dangling security net, entangling the bow and the windscreen.

Seeing the boat caught like a fly in a web, Pitt reversed the controls, sending the dock to SUBMERGE. The contracting hydraulics moved quickly, dropping the platform beneath the surface. Even from inside the control house, Pitt could hear the cries of the speedboat's occupants as the entangled boat plunged vertically into the frigid water. Pitt caught a fleeting glimpse of Audrey on the monitor, struggling to break free of the netting, before the boat disappeared into the murk below.

The video suddenly faded to black, along with the lights on the control panel. Beneath Pitt's feet, the electrical motors ceased their whirring. Somewhere inside the main facility, the power had been cut. Pitt abandoned the control room and ran down to the dock.

"You boys okay?"

Giordino was standing with Perkins at his side, watching a

rising froth of bubbles on the water offshore. He turned at Pitt's approach.

"Was that your handiwork?"

Pitt nodded. "I guess their security system works after all." He scanned the nearby waters. There was no trace of the boat or its occupants.

Giordino looked at Perkins, and both men smiled.

"That it does."

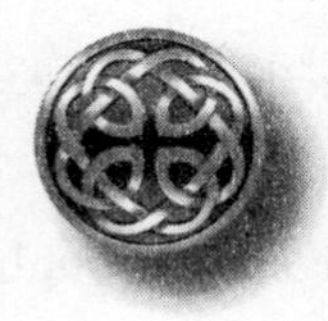

54

The laboratory's alarms punctured the still morning air as Pitt and Giordino attended to Perkins's wounds. He'd caught a grazing bullet to his shin and a clean perforation through his thigh. Pitt retrieved the lab coat and used its sleeves to bind the wounds.

Despite his injuries, Perkins remained alert, splashing across the flooded dock with an arm around Giordino's shoulder. They spied the groggy guard dog, awakened after falling into the loch, paddling to shore nearby. Pitt retrieved the submersible's painter, which had snapped during the dock's gyrations, and they all crammed into the vessel. With seating for only two, Giordino gave Perkins the copilot seat while he perched on the hatch ladder just behind.

Pitt's face was tense as he navigated the sub away from the dock. Giordino knew the reason why.

Loren.

Pitt kept the craft on the surface at maximized speed as he made a beeline for McKee Manor. The boathouse door was open, and he guided the sub through its narrow entrance and against the dock. Giordino opened the hatch and hopped to the deck with the painter as Pitt climbed out.

"Nice digs," Giordino said. "Where to from here?"

"You best get Perkins to a doctor with the *Nymph*. Follow the shoreline to the east. There's a town called Drumnadrochit about five miles from here. Look for a marina in the cove."

"You'll be okay?"

Pitt nodded.

"I'll come back with help as soon as I can."

A minute later, Giordino motored the *Nymph* out of the boathouse with Perkins. Pitt made his way to the boathouse door. He entered the manor's basement and climbed the corner steps to the main floor. The corridor was empty as he went to his room. With growing unease, he opened the door. The room was empty.

He crossed the front rotunda and checked the dining hall. It, too, was empty. Pitt followed the hallway back toward the loch, returning to the corner stairwell, where he descended to the basement. He stepped past the wine racks, entered the small den, and stopped in the rear doorway. The hallway it opened on was lit, and faint voices came from beyond the double doors at the end.

Pitt hesitated, glancing at the weapons on display in the armory case. Among the bladed weapons, one caught his eye. It was a British flintlock boarding pistol with a spring-loaded bayonet that extended beyond its octagonal barrel. The gun was displayed in a presentation case with a black powder flask, pads of cotton wadding, and a tray of lead balls.

Pitt opened the case and checked the powder flask. It was full. He poured a load down the barrel, wrapped a lead ball in a patch of wadding, and tamped it down the barrel with an attached ramrod. Then he held the gun up, checked the flint, poured some priming powder into the flash pan, and closed the frizzen. He tucked the loaded weapon into his back waistband, then stepped down the hallway.

The side offices were dark as he passed on his way to the doors at the end of the hall. He placed his palm on one of the knobs and turned it in tiny increments. McKee's voice was clearly audible on the other side. Taking a breath, he shoved open the door and stepped inside.

He was surprised to find a tastefully decorated lounge outfitted like a spa. Potted plants and an indoor waterfall surrounded a large sofa and reclining chairs. A row of raised-back massage tables stood in the center, perched under a bank of violet mood lights. Loren reclined on one of the tables next to the Australian woman, Abigail Brown.

Any sense of casual relaxation was undermined by the arm and leg straps that secured the women to their tables. Each wore a set of earphones and had large virtual reality goggles strapped to their heads. Beside each woman stood a small surgical table with an array of vials and syringes.

Pitt's sense of revulsion was completed by the sight of the truck-driving receptionist named Irene. She looked up from a computer workstation wired to the bound women and glared.

Standing beside her, Evanna McKee bared her teeth and smiled at Pitt with the warmth of an Arctic wolf. "Hello, Mr. Pitt. I was expecting you. But not alive."

He took a step toward her, then froze as the cold steel of a gun pressed against the back of his neck.

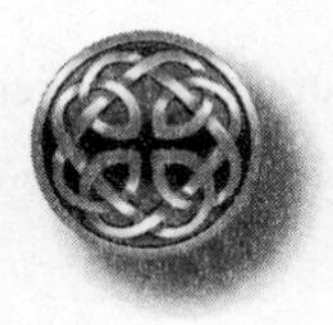

55

Rachel had been standing behind the door, waiting for him to enter.

Pitt noticed too late that a monitor on Irene's workstation carried video feeds from throughout the manor. They had watched his every move from the moment he had entered the building.

"I must have misplaced my invitation to the torture session," he said.

"You were never invited," McKee said. "And there is no torture taking place. At least not yet. Just a little psychological re-education, as I like to call it."

"I believe you know a thing or two about altered minds."

The gun's muzzle jabbed deeper into his neck.

"Your lovely wife is not being harmed," McKee said. "Induced to a relaxed state, she is in a virtual world filled with peace, love, and trust among her sisterhood of women. I'm afraid you may find her less appreciative of men when she emerges. But of course, you won't be with us long."

"No men allowed?"

"Not in her world right now. Nor in our world tomorrow."

"I always thought it took two to multiply."

"Science has taken care of that, Mr. Pitt. Female conception without the need for men is already a scientific reality. It won't be long before it's a widespread practice."

"I think there are many people who would disagree with your view of the world." The pistol dug into his neck once more, and Rachel leaned close to Pitt's ear. "Don't speak to Mrs. McKee in that tone."

"Your day is over, McKee."

McKee nodded at Rachel, and the big woman shoved Pitt toward an empty massage table next to Loren. As Pitt staggered forward, Rachel plucked the flintlock pistol from his back. "Mustn't be stealing the household goods either," she said. Loosely aiming her pistol at Pitt, Rachel stepped to the tray table and set down the flintlock.

The instant her fingers released it, Pitt spun around, knocking her arm to the side. Before she could react, Pitt threw a left uppercut that landed clean on Rachel's jaw.

Her head snapped back and her knees buckled as she weakly raised her free arm in defense.

Pitt ignored a rustle behind him and knocked her arm aside. He reached to pry the pistol from her other hand—and felt a prick on his back, followed by a nerve-shattering jolt of electricity.

From behind, Irene had thrust a stun gun against Pitt,

sending a brief surge of ten million volts into his body. The shock sent muscle spasms through his limbs and intense pain through his entire body. He let go of Rachel and struggled to stay on his feet as Irene pulled the device out and prepared for a second strike.

Rachel recovered enough to step forward and shove him against the massage table. Pitt fell backward onto it as he tried to regain his senses. Irene and Rachel rushed forward and strapped down his arms and legs before he had the chance. Then Rachel slapped him hard across the face.

McKee smiled. "Your insensitive behavior has gone too far, Mr. Pitt. But we still have high hopes for your wife."

Pitt said nothing as the feeling slowly returned to his limbs. He gazed at Loren and cursed himself for getting subdued.

McKee's cell phone rang, and she stepped to a corner to take the call. Her face turned ashen as she listened silently, then hung up. She approached Pitt, eyeing him with hostility. "What happened to Audrey?" Her voice teetered just above a whisper.

"I believe she went for a swim with Nessie."

McKee stared at him. She began to shake, and her cool sheen of invincibility vanished. Her eyes turned crazed, and she turned away from Pitt. Lurching over to Irene, she whispered in her ear, then motioned for Rachel, who came to her side. They left the room together, the large woman supporting the trembling McKee.

Irene stepped between Pitt and Loren. She selected a vial marked LSZ, a synthetic hallucinogen based on LSD, and filled a syringe. She turned and rolled up Loren's sleeve and injected it into her arm.

"Leave her be!" Pitt struggled against the restraints as the numbness finally left his extremities.

"She belongs to us now." Irene pulled a cell phone from her pocket and activated the camera. "Help her out with a big smile now," she said, and snapped a photo of Pitt's face.

She returned to the computer workstation and clicked away for several minutes. Pitt continued to fight the restraints, but to no avail. He glanced at Loren and seethed with anger.

She had been lying still since Pitt had entered the room, yet occasional body movements suggested she was partially conscious. Now her movements began to grow more frequent and more pained. As she twisted and tugged at her restraints, Irene stepped over, gazed at Loren's struggles, and smiled.

"The mind is an amazing vehicle," she said to Pitt. "With the aid of some mental enhancements"—she tapped the tray of syringes—"the virtual world can become very real."

Loren struggled some more, then let out a sharp cry. Her head tossed from side to side as if an invisible hand was slapping her across the face.

"Make it stop," Pitt said.

Irene gave a depraved grin. "It's not me that's harming her, it's you. Her reality is that she's being assaulted by you."

Pitt ground his teeth and strained against his bonds as Loren screamed. She kicked and twisted against her restraints, trying to pull herself away. Then she tossed her head back and began to whimper. Tears seeped beneath her headset and ran down her cheeks.

Pitt had never felt so angry or so helpless. "Stop it!" His muscles nearly burst through his skin in rage.

Irene laughed. "You shouldn't wish for it to stop, Mr. Pitt, for that's when you'll see the real power of suggestion."

She stepped to the workstation, eyed the monitor, then returned carrying the stun gun. "Your wife is done submitting to your violence—and is about ready to partake in her own."

Loren lay on the table, quietly shaking.

Irene released her arm and leg restraints and removed the earphones. Finally, she pulled off the virtual reality headset.

Pitt could now see his wife's eyes. They were hardly recognizable. Normally violet, bright, and vibrant, they were dark, barren, and sullen. She looked at Irene, smiling weakly.

Then she glanced at Pitt and recoiled with a gasp.

Irene leaned close. She clasped Loren's shoulders and whispered in her ear. "You must kill him. You must kill him now."

Loren nodded faintly as Irene helped her rise. She stood for a moment, leaning on Irene for support until she gained her balance. All the while she stared at Pitt with a look of revulsion.

"Loren," Pitt said.

The word sent her trembling.

Irene again leaned forward and whispered in her ear. "Do it."

Irene picked up the antique flintlock, cocked the hammer, and placed it in Loren's hand.

Loren looked at the pistol, then at Pitt, then back to the pistol.

"Loren."

She ignored him and lowered the pistol to her side. Loren walked in a trance around Pitt's table, approaching from the far side while eyeing him warily. When she stopped for a moment, her eyes taking in Abigail Brown, the workstation, and the table full of needles, she showed no emotion. Her focus returned to Pitt as she inched nervously toward him.

Irene approached from the opposite side of the table, nodding in encouragement, stun gun still in her palm.

"Loren."

Her face wrinkled at the sound until it was supplanted by the voice of Irene.

"You must do it."

Pitt looked up at Loren, who returned his gaze with a cold, robotic stare. He searched for a glimmer of recognition somewhere in her vacant eyes. For an instant, he thought he saw a flicker of acknowledgment, but he couldn't be sure.

Certainty came when she raised the pistol and pulled the trigger.

56

At first light, Riki checked to make sure Dirk was still asleep. She took his cell phone off the coffee table, grabbed her travel bag, and went into the bathroom. She locked the door and turned on the shower, but had no immediate intention of getting wet.

She riffled through her bag, pulled out a slim laptop, and accessed the hotel's WiFi. Pulling up the website to a company that sold phone monitoring software, she accessed an established account. Following the site's guidance, she picked up Dirk's phone and downloaded a stealth monitoring application.

After grilling him on the Meritaten grave search the night before, she had borrowed his phone under the guise that hers was dead and had made a note of his passcode. Disabling its antivirus software, she downloaded a tracking program and added a secret cell number. With that, she could silently call

Dirk's phone at any time and tap into its microphone, to listen in on nearby conversations.

After completing the download and covering her access tracks, she showered and dressed.

Dirk heard the shower and was up and dressed by the time she reentered the room. "I didn't hear you get up."

"I didn't want to wake you." She concealed his phone behind her travel bag. "I'm afraid I have a morning meeting with the secretary-general of the environment department in Dublin."

"Can you come back tonight?"

"Doubtful. There's a trade dinner I'm scheduled to attend. Tomorrow night looks free."

"It's a date, then."

As they kissed, she reached behind him and set his phone on the dresser. When she got to the door Riki stopped, turned, and looked into Dirk's eyes, then quickly turned again and disappeared down the hall.

She took her travel bag to the parking lot and climbed into the silver Audi. Motoring a few blocks across town, she stopped in front of a small hotel where Gavin and Ainsley stood on the sidewalk.

"We didn't see you in the lobby this morning," Gavin said as he slid into the passenger seat.

Riki ignored the comment. "Did you find us a boat?"

"Yes, but not at Portmagee," Gavin replied. "We found a suitable rental in Cahersiveen." He held up his phone, displaying a photo of a stout workboat. "Best we could find after receiving your early-morning text. Lucky for that, at this hour of the day."

"Where's Cahersiveen?"

"About ten miles this side of Portmagee. It's on an inlet, same as Portmagee. We can motor down and wait for them on the water. That is, if they're not too speedy. We won't be able to pick up the keys to the boat until half eight."

Riki glanced at her watch. "All right, let's be on our way," she said, punching the city's name into the vehicle's GPS system.

She drove southwest from Tralee before turning along the southern shore of Dingle Bay. In less than an hour, they reached Cahersiveen, a colorful small town that stretched along the River Fertha. Riki parked next to the town's marina, and Gavin led the way to a blue and white workboat moored between a pair of sailboats.

"This is the one," he said. "A retired gent rents it for charters. I told him we were in for a day of cod fishing."

There was no one about the marina. Ainsley checked the time. "It's shy of eight," she said. "Gavin and I didn't have a chance to eat this morning. You mind if we look for some takeaway in town to bring with us?"

Riki tossed her the car keys. "Grab me a coffee, if you would, but be quick about it. And bring me my tablet from the car when you return." She found a large storage box on the dock she used as a seat and sat down to wait.

Ainsley slipped behind the Audi's wheel as Gavin climbed in the passenger's side. Riki's tablet was lying on the seat, and he scooped it up and tapped the screen. The device illuminated with a map of the region, their present location indicated at the center.

"Do you think it will be rough offshore?" Ainsley asked, backing the car out of the lot.

"Afraid of the water?" Gavin replied with a snort.

"Seasickness."

"There's two thousand miles of open ocean pounding the Irish coast here. I bet it's always rough."

The Glasgow girl turned pale. Gavin laughed again, then studied the map on the tablet. A tiny red ball was visible moving along the road from Tralee.

"Our friends are on their way." He held up the image for Ainsley to see. "Why don't we just take care of business now and save ourselves the sea voyage."

"What are you saying?" she asked.

Gavin tapped the tablet and smiled. "Just head back out of town and I'll show you."

DIRK MADE NO MENTION of Riki's appearance to Summer as they grabbed a quick breakfast at the hotel, then made their way toward Portmagee. There was only light traffic as they left the outskirts of Tralee, which vanished altogether when they turned onto a side road leading west.

"Do you really think they would have transported Meritaten from the Slieve Mish Mountains to an offshore island for burial?" Summer asked, gazing at the flat pasturelands rushing by the window.

"It seems possible," Dirk said. "If her sons died on Skellig Michael, there is certainly logic to the notion."

The road edged along the River Fertha on their right, which expanded into a wide inlet that ran west to the Atlantic. Dirk drove past a scattering of old white farmhouses as the road curled along the shore. Reaching a short straightaway outside the town of Cahersiveen, he tapped the brakes when he spotted a car blocking the road ahead.

It was the silver Audi. It was parked crossways on a narrow two-lane bridge that spanned a river inlet. The car's flashers were blinking, and a gruff-looking woman stood behind the open driver's door waving her left arm.

As Dirk slowed, he passed a heavyset man lingering at the forefront of the bridge, seemingly unconcerned about the woman.

"Why is she blocking the road?" Summer asked.

"I don't know. She doesn't look like she's in distress. Maybe the road is out behind her."

Dirk pulled to a stop in front of the Audi. He had started to roll down his window when the woman raised a pistol from behind the car door. Aiming the weapon at Dirk and Summer, she fired three shots through their windshield.

"Get down!" Dirk yelled, ducking low beneath the dashboard.

Jamming the transmission in reverse, he punched the accelerator, sending the car screeching backward. He peeked over the dash to get his bearings as multiple popping sounds punctuated the air. The rear window shattered next, followed by the instrument cluster.

Glancing at his side-view mirror, Dirk saw the hefty man they'd passed earlier standing in the middle of the road. He had his arms raised and was firing a weapon from behind.

"Get us out of here," Summer urged, crouching to the floorboards.

"Trying," Dirk muttered.

Caught in a cross fire, he decided the best chance of escape was to blast forward. Pounding the brakes, he shifted back into drive and floored the accelerator. The little rental car, a Nissan crossover, shimmied as it regained forward traction. Dirk pointed the car at the woman ahead, sending her running to the side. As he drew closer, he spun the wheel, aiming for the narrow gap between the Audi's back end and the bridge rail.

The Nissan's front bumper struck the Audi's rear quarter panel with a bang. Both cars jolted off the ground.

As Dirk had hoped, the Audi's tail spun away, opening an escape route across the bridge. Less expectedly, his own car's back end swung laterally from the angled blow. As front airbags erupted, the rental car's tail slammed against the side rail of the bridge. The barrier was just a thin metal bracing, and the Nissan's bumper sliced right through it.

Dirk kept the accelerator pinned, but it was no use as the rear of the car burst through the railing, and the back end skidded over the edge. The car hung suspended, its rear wheels spinning madly in the air. Then gravity took hold, and the car slipped backward off the bridge.

It was less than a ten-foot drop to the water below. The car struck the surface with a bellowing splash, then flipped onto its roof. For a moment, the car floated on the surface, its drive wheels still turning. Then, with a gurgle of bubbles, the vehicle sunk beneath the surface.

Gavin ran to the ruptured bridge railing and peered over the side. Only a sporadic belch from the murky water marked the car's resting spot. Holstering his weapon, he turned to Ainsley and grinned.

"Worked out better than planned." He gazed up at the

overcast sky. "If the rains keep falling and the river stays high, they might not be discovered for months."

He reached down and bent the shattered side railing back into place, trying to conceal the damage.

Ainsley approached with a tentative gait and looked for herself. Tiny splatter waves still rocked the shore, but there was otherwise no sign of Dirk and Summer's rental car. In the distance, the sound of an approaching vehicle echoed off the hills.

"We better get going." She turned and pointed to the damaged rear fender on the Audi. "What do we tell Sadler?"

"Why, we tell her the truth," Gavin replied. "They ran into us by accident and they ended up in the drink."

57

The ancient flintlock fired more slowly than a modern gun. When Loren squeezed the trigger, the gun's hammer dropped and the piece of flint attached to it struck a metal frizzen. The impact sent sparks falling onto the flash pan below, igniting a priming charge of powder. A small flare erupted in the pan. It took another moment for the black powder to burn through a touchhole and ignite the main charge in the barrel.

As Loren fired the pistol, not at Pitt but at Irene, the receptionist had an instant to react. She lunged across Pitt with her hand still clutching the stun gun, hoping to knock away the pistol. She overreached and struck Loren in the back of the hand as the flintlock fired.

Lying beneath the action, Pitt saw the purple light of the stun gun crackle against Loren's wrist as a cloud of white smoke from the flintlock erupted over him. Both women then vanished in the haze.

To Pitt's left, Loren spiraled to the floor, falling unconscious from the combined effect of the electrical shock and the injected drugs. To his right, Irene staggered back from the table. She clutched her midsection, her eyes bulging with terror. As the smoke cleared, Pitt saw a splotch of blood soaking the clothes beneath her fingers where the lead ball had struck just beneath the sternum.

Irene tried to speak, the words didn't come. Then she tried to step away, and her legs failed her, too. She knocked over the tray table as she fell back against Abigail Brown, then sunk to the floor. Sprawling upright, she clutched her stomach and moaned softly.

To Pitt, the whole scene was surreal. Loren lay drugged and unconscious on one side, Irene dying on the other. The former Australian prime minister remained oblivious in her virtual world. Trapped in the middle of it all lay Pitt. But Loren had left him a way out. When shocked by Irene, she had dropped the flintlock and it fell at Pitt's side.

He twisted and slid his body, forcing the weapon toward his left hand. His fingertips grazed the barrel, and he pulled the pistol close until he could wrap his palm around its stock.

It wasn't the gun he was interested in, it was its bayonet blade. He twisted the gun and applied the steel edge against the strap that held his wrist. The ancient blade was dull, but it still had enough of an edge to fray the leather binding. He sawed at it for a few minutes until it gave way with a strong thrust from his arm. With his left hand free, he unbuckled the strap across his chest and a binding on his right wrist, then freed his legs.

He rushed to Loren, picked her up, and lay her on the table.

Her eyes fluttered open as she regained consciousness. She focused her eyes on Pitt and gave him a wary look that softened into a broad smile. "Did I do okay?" she whispered.

Pitt nodded and kissed her.

"I didn't drink their coffee or tea, only pretended to," she said in a slurred voice. "It was drugged, like you said. I could see the effects on Abigail." She glanced toward the Aussie, then saw Irene sitting lifeless in a pool of blood.

"I had a very bad dream when she poked me with the needle, though." Her eyes closed for a minute, then she came around again. "You need to help Abigail."

Pitt stepped to the Australian woman and removed her earphones and virtual reality headset. "Are you all right?" he asked.

She stared back in an unblinking daze, not comprehending the difference between the virtual world and the basement of McKee Manor.

Pitt tried to break her drug-induced stupor. "What do you say we go for a walk and get some fresh air?"

He removed her restraints and guided her to a stairwell, keeping Abigail turned so she wouldn't see the body of Irene. He returned for Loren, who rose unsteadily, but regained her strength with each footstep.

Pitt aided the women up the stairs, exiting through a hidden door into the dining hall. They made their way to the rotunda and out the front door without seeing anyone.

As they descended the steps, a pair of Inverness police cars rushed through the front gate with lights flashing. Giordino jumped out of one of the cars and rushed over to Pitt and the women.

"I see you brought the cavalry," Pitt said.

"Thanks to a nice lady at the marina who remembered you. She happens to be married to the local chief inspector." Giordino looked at Loren. "Is she okay?"

"Better than she was. The police will want to check the basement. Somebody was playing with an antique firearm and got hurt."

"McKee?"

Pitt shook his head. "She's gone. Might have returned to the lab."

A private jet, just departed from Inverness Regional Airport, screamed low overhead. It skimmed past the manor, then ascended and turned south, proving Pitt wrong in the process.

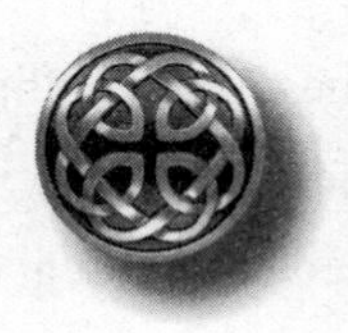

58

Cold water flooded onto Dirk's face, and he instinctively groped for the power window switch. The rental car's electronics had yet to short out, and the window slid closed, lessening the deluge. He pushed away the airbag that had inflated in his face and tried to get his bearings in the dark interior.

His neck, back, and knees ached from the rearward plunge off the bridge, and a gash on the side of his head throbbed. But the rental car's high-backed seats had held firm, cushioning against major injury. He felt his body's weight straining against his shoulder belt, and the water that was still accumulating around his head jarred his shaken senses to the fact the car was inverted. He felt the vehicle wallow a moment before striking the river bottom with a muffled crunch.

He reached to a headliner console and flicked on the switch to a map light. It cast a dull glow through a layer of murky liquid, enough to illuminate Summer sitting beside him. He noticed a dark splotch of blood on her shoulder.

"You okay?" he asked, struggling to release his seat belt.

"Yeah," came a weak and unconvincing reply. Dirk could see her dangling hair was soaked from the rising water.

Dirk unbuckled his seat belt, had to push his seat back to a full recline in order to tumble free. Rolling over and kneeling on the crumpled ceiling, he adjusted Summer's seat back, then unclasped her belt. It took some twisting and contorting, but he pulled her up and around, their heads ducking into the now overhead passenger footwell.

"Looks . . . like . . . you . . . bought . . . another . . . car," she mumbled. Even under the dim light, Dirk could see the glazed look in his sister's eyes, and he feared she would lose consciousness at any time.

"At least I have insurance this time," he said. "Can you hold your breath?"

She gave a faint nod. Water was already seeping through the damaged windshield and rear window, filling the interior to their shoulders.

"Okay, it's just a short swim. Here we go."

The map light still burned, so he reached for the passenger-side window switch. He took a deep breath as the glass slid down without protest, filling the remaining air pocket. Ducking down, he wriggled out the window. Grabbing the side mirror for support, he spun underwater and reached in for Summer.

She was limp as he reached up and clasped her under the arms. He had to pull her down to exit the window. Her upper torso was out the window when her pant pocket caught on the gearshift lever. She twisted and squirmed, her face contorted in pain, before slipping free. Dirk pulled her clear of the car and shot to the surface just a few feet overhead.

They both gasped for air. Dirk tugged his sister to shore, heading to the nearest bank, just beneath the bridge. Overhead, he heard the sound of a car—the Audi—pulling away. Another vehicle crossed the bridge a minute later.

He turned his attention to Summer, who was breathing heavily and wavering in and out of consciousness. The shoulder of her shirt was seeped in blood, and he could see a pair of small perforations in the fabric. He compressed the wound with his palm, while catching his breath, then slipped an arm around her.

"C'mon, girl, let's get up the hill."

Half carrying her, half dragging her, Dirk lumbered up the embankment with Summer, setting her down at the edge of the road. He searched for help, but the nearest house was far in the distance. Salvation appeared in the form of a panel van that approached from the east, bearing the logo DINGLE PLUMBING on its side.

Dirk waved the van to a stop as it crossed the bridge, approaching the side window of the startled driver.

"My sister has been injured in a car accident. Can you take us to a hospital?"

The plumber looked from the drenched and battered man to the crouched figure of Summer lying on the road.

"Aye, St. Anne's is just on the other side of town."

He jumped out and helped Dirk carry Summer to the rear of the van, setting her on the floor. Dirk tended to her wounds as the plumber took to the wheel and sped forward. The town of

Cahersiveen was just a mile ahead, and he raced through its quiet streets to St. Anne's Hospital on the western outskirts.

Summer was carried into the entrance, where the medical staff rushed her to the emergency room. Dirk barely had a chance to thank the plumber before a nurse dragged him into an examination room to dress his head wound. He glanced in a mirror, noting his soggy clothes were splattered with blood and his face battered. His only concern, though, was for his sister.

"You look like you jumped off a building," the nurse said, applying a bandage to his scalp.

"Not far off the mark. It was a bridge, actually."

As the nurse finished, his cell phone rang in his pocket. Even though it was a water-resistant model, he was nevertheless surprised it had survived intact. He answered the call, finding Brophy on the line.

"The boat's ready and waiting," he said. "Are you kids going to join me on the water this morning?"

"No," Dirk replied, rubbing his sore neck. "I'm afraid we already made a splash."

59

Riki was pacing in front of the rental boat when Ainsley and Gavin stepped onto the dock. With a scowl, she held up the boat keys acquired from the vessel's owner, who had already come and gone.

"What took so long? And what happened to the car?" she asked, noting the fender damage.

Ainsley passed her the tablet and a cup of coffee while Gavin shook his head and grinned.

"No need to worry. They're not going anywhere . . . for a long time."

"What are you talking about?"

"We ran into them," Ainsley said.

Gavin nodded. "Saw them approaching on your tablet, so we met them outside of town. They were a mite cooperative. Drove off the side of a bridge nearly of their own accord." He pointed to the Audi. "Well, they did nick us up a bit. But they're sunk in a creek now, not even visible. It'll look like an accident, when and if they're ever found."

Riki stared at him without speaking. She felt a surprising knot of emotions churning inside her. A prolonged silence was broken by the sound of her cell phone ringing. She saw it was her mother and answered.

The conversation was one-way. Riki listened for a minute, until her mother abruptly signed off. Putting away her phone, she turned to her companions with a pale face.

"We're to meet my mother at dusk tonight at an airfield called Abbeyfeale," Riki said in a low tone. "You can explain your actions then."

60

Brophy joined Dirk in the hospital waiting room as Summer was taken into surgery. They sat impatiently as Summer's operation was followed by a lengthy stint in the recovery room. Dirk used the time to email his father, after his phone call to him went unanswered, and to file a report with the town police. The ER surgeon eventually appeared, assuring Dirk that his sister was all right.

"She's got two puncture wounds, one above her shoulder, the other through her triceps," he explained. "Pretty lucky, actually, as there was no damage to her bones." He gave Dirk an inquisitive look. "Gunshots, I presume?"

Dirk nodded. "Range accident. We've notified the police."

"She'll make a full recovery. You can see her now, but she might be asleep for a touch longer."

He led them to a small single room where Summer was propped up in bed, asleep from her surgery medications. Dirk sat by her bedside for a short while, until his stomach started to rumble.

"Come along, lad, it's almost suppertime," Brophy said. "Let's get you something to eat. She's not going anywhere, and I spied an attractive pub just down the street."

Dirk reluctantly agreed, allowing Brophy to drive them back into Cahersiveen. At a small pub decorated with dusty crab pots, they sampled the fish and chips, then returned to the hospital just after sunset. As they entered Summer's room, Dirk was shocked to find Pitt, Loren, and Giordino standing by the bed talking with his sister.

"How did you get here?" he said, greeting the newcomers, then introducing Brophy.

"I caught your email midflight after we departed Inverness," Pitt said. "We were just flying over Galway. Rudi had sent us a NUMA Gulfstream, so we diverted to Killarney and hopped a cab here."

Dirk's curiosity about the private jet waned when he saw Loren. Her eyes had a disoriented look, and she was unusually pale. He thought perhaps she should trade places with Summer, who was now alert and talkative in her hospital bed.

"What exactly happened to you two?" Pitt asked, eyeing Dirk's bandaged head.

Dirk explained their search for Meritaten, the fire in the library, and the morning attack on the bridge.

"Sounds like everyone's had their share of fun lately," Giordino remarked.

"Troubles in Scotland?" Dirk asked.

Pitt nodded with a grim look, then described their discovery of the BioRem secret lab and the global dispersal of the waterborne plague. "Rudi said the CDC has confirmed what Dr. Perkins told us. The pathogen has the ability to alter the DNA in the cells of infected women so they will produce only female offspring. There's also the possibility that the bacteria could continue to mutate, and it could grow much worse. This much we do know—as of this moment, there is no cure."

"How many people have been infected?" Brophy asked.

"Potentially millions. They sent shiploads of the stuff around the world, distributing it into freshwater sources that are drawn for drinking. They staged accidents, in some cases, to access key locations. We believe they caused the tanker collision in Detroit, to release their pathogen into the city's supply."

"Mike Cruz was killed on account of it," Giordino said. "He likely discovered that BioRem was feeding their product into the Detroit River intake."

Summer frowned. "How could they have developed such an affliction?"

"It was derived from an ancient Egyptian plague extracted from mummies." Giordino described the coffins they found in Scotland. "They call it the Evolution Plague."

"Egyptian mummies?" Summer said.

Dirk pulled out his phone and retrieved Rod Zeibig's photos from Egypt. He held up a shot of the tomb they discovered in Amarna. "Is this one of the coffins?"

Pitt and Giordino studied the photo and nodded. "There were several children's mummies and coffins in the lab," Pitt said. "That certainly could have been one of them."

"They must have regenerated the plague that afflicted

ancient Egypt," Summer said. "It must be the BioRem people who are after Meritaten."

Pitt looked her in the eye. "You said Princess Meritaten died in Ireland after traveling from Egypt?"

She nodded. "BioRem already has the pathogen, so it must be the cure they're after. You said the CDC has no known remedy for the plague. There is a cure. It's called the Apium of Faras. It saved Meritaten, and it saved the Habiru slaves."

"So it could save those infected today," Pitt said.

"It was derived from a plant called silphium," Dirk said. "We think some of it's buried with Meritaten. That must be why they want to find her—or stop us from finding her."

"Rare plant?" Giordino asked.

"Not rare, extinct," Dirk said. "It died out during Roman times. The only hope is that some is buried with Meritaten."

"Sounds like a long shot," Pitt said.

"Maybe," Summer said, "but the mural at Amarna shows her carrying it."

"Are you any closer to knowing where's she's buried?" Giordino asked.

"I think so. We found a stone marker indicating she's at a place called Falcon Rock. Dr. Brophy thinks it represents an island off the Kerry coast."

"Skellig Michael," the Irishman said with a nod.

"You can take us there?" Pitt asked.

Brophy glanced at Summer's bandaged shoulder and nodded. "Aye. Perhaps we best get there before the competition does."

61

Riki waited with Ainsley and Gavin in a small threadbare room that constituted the terminal at Abbeyfeale Airfield. The place didn't qualify as an airport, she had quickly determined, once they had located the private facility tucked off a narrow country lane. A single paved runway with a line painted down the middle crossed an empty pasture, supplemented by a pair of hangars and a small administrative-office-cum-terminal. The lone proprietor had already vacated the air traffic control radio set and was opening one of the hangars for McKee's arrival.

Riki had opened her laptop computer and had begun tapping the keys out of boredom when Gavin pointed out the picture window.

"Here they come."

The landing lights of a small plane twinkled in the distance, and Riki watched as her mother's Learjet touched down and taxied across the tarmac. The jet halted temporarily, opening its side door to release Evanna McKee and Rachel, before continuing its journey into one of the open hangars.

When the two women entered the building, Riki could instantly see something was amiss. Dressed in a wrinkled outfit, her mother moved with an uncharacteristic slump. Her face showed both fatigue and grief as she dropped into an empty chair beside Riki.

"Mother, you don't look well. Can I get you some tea?"

"Audrey is dead," McKee said in a monotone. Her trauma at losing her younger daughter had either already passed or been muted by drugs. "The lab is damaged and possibly exposed."

"Audrey . . . dead?"

Riki grappled with the news. She'd never been close to her younger half sister, and as an adult had been dominated by her. To Audrey's lasting jealousy, Frasier McKee had always treated Riki as his own daughter, perhaps out of sympathy for her own father's early death in the Iraq War. It created resentment that Audrey never let go of.

At the same time, their mother had always shown favoritism toward Audrey. Riki knew it was because the two were more alike—deceitful, insensitive, and ruthlessly self-serving. Riki tried to emulate them, but it never came naturally.

"How did it happen?"

"The American, Pitt. He infiltrated the lab. By now he should be dead and lying at the bottom of the loch. I thought it best that we stay out of Scotland until things blow over." She gazed around the spartan room and crinkled her nose. "We took a circuitous route to get here. The pilot said our arrival at this field would not be reported to the authorities. For a price. We can fly to Italy, perhaps, for a short while."

McKee glanced at Riki's open computer. The screen showed a map of the lower side of Dingle Bay. A pair of red lights flashed on either side of a town marked CAHERSIVEEN. "What is that?" she asked.

"The younger Pitt's car and phone," Riki said. She glanced at the computer and frowned. "You said they went off the bridge east of town," she said, addressing Gavin and Ainsley. "This shows his phone on the west side of Cahersiveen."

Gavin and Ainsley looked at each other.

Riki turned to her mother with a sullen voice. "They disposed of the younger Pitts in an auto accident this morning."

"His phone says otherwise," McKee said.

"Perhaps they've been fished out of the river," Gavin said.

Riki enlarged the map on the computer. "The signal shows his phone is at St. Anne's Hospital. It must still be working. I bugged it," she added.

"Then activate it," McKee urged.

Riki pulled out her cell phone and dialed the secret number to Dirk's phone. After a click, they heard multiple voices chatting in Summer's hospital room. Riki put her fingers to her lips, as it was an open two-way line.

"It must be the BioRem people who are after Meritaten," they heard Summer say.

At the sound of Dirk's voice, Riki's eyes grew large. "They're alive," she whispered.

Gavin turned pale. "They bloody well have nine lives," he said under his breath.

They listened quietly until Pitt's and Loren's voices carried through. McKee looked perplexed, then pointed at the phone and turned beet red. "That's Pitt!" she seethed, barely suppressing her voice.

She pulled out her own phone and sent a text to the Inverness receptionist, Irene. Her anger rose as she continued listening to the voices at the hospital. When she could take no more, she stepped out the door and phoned Irene.

When there was no answer, she tried calling her other staff, finally connecting with one of the front guards.

"Irene . . . is dead," the security woman replied. "All of the guests are gone. The police are here, searching the grounds. And I can see flashing lights across the lake. They want to know where you are. What should I tell them?"

McKee hung up. Her whole world was suddenly crashing down around her.

She took a deep breath. Perhaps there was still salvation. Nobody could know for sure where the Evolution Plague had been deployed. Maybe Richards had hidden the records and dumped the solution before the police arrived. The authorities might identify a number of locations, but the deployment could still be called accidental. The Evolution Plague had yet to be identified—and a cure was still unknown. She could relocate to a friendly Third World country and continue production. The vision could endure. There was just one impediment she had to address.

She walked back into the terminal as the Pitts announced plans to search for Meritaten on Skellig Michael.

Riki disconnected the call. She turned and gazed at her mother. McKee's face wore a demented mask of rage.

Riki looked up. "Mother?"

"We go to this island," McKee said with fire on her tongue, "where we eliminate both Meritaten and the Pitts."

PART IV

SKELLIG MICHAEL

Skellig Michael

62

"Now you be a good lass and get that shoulder all healed up," Brophy said.

Summer leaned forward from her wheelchair and gave the Irishman a hug. "Thank you for all your help, Dr. Brophy. I wish I could go to Skellig Michael with you."

"We'll find her, don't you worry."

Brophy gave Summer a wave as Dirk helped her climb into the NUMA Gulfstream jet parked at Kerry Airport. Pitt was already aboard, helping Loren to her seat.

"No cartwheels until I get home," Pitt said to Summer, giving her a peck on the cheek. He stepped to the back of the plane and held Loren in his arms. "You going to be all right?"

Loren nodded as she squeezed him hard. "The whole trip seems like a bad dream. But I think the drugs are about out of my system. When I get home, I'll be due for some prolonged sleep." She gave him a kiss, held him tightly once more. "Be careful."

Before Dirk could step off the plane, Summer grabbed his arm. "Now don't you go silent on me. I want regular updates on your search."

Dirk nodded. "I'll be sure and check in."

"There's one more thing I need to tell you." Her voice fell low, and she gave him an earnest look. "When I was waiting for you at breakfast, I thought I saw Riki leave the hotel. I could have been seeing things."

"No, it was her."

"She drove away in a silver Audi. I think it was the same car on the bridge."

Dirk gave a troubled nod. "I came to the same conclusion. She was the only one who knew we were headed to Portmagee. Almost got us killed. I'm sorry for not seeing it."

"You're not the only one who missed it. At least now we know."

Dirk gave her a pat on her good shoulder and exited the plane. He joined Pitt, Brophy, and Giordino and watched the jet take off into an overcast sky. The four men climbed into an SUV Giordino had rented and drove to Portmagee, this time without incident.

A fishing village across from a large island called Valentia, Portmagee sat on a protected inlet two miles from the open ocean. Dirk easily found the waterfront and parked near the town pier, which held under a dozen boats. Brophy led them across the dock to a wide-beamed workboat, stopping alongside it to light his pipe.

"She's fueled and ready to go," he said, "but I'm not sure we'll want to be in a hurry to leave the dock."

"Why's that?" Dirk asked.

"Force 5 to 6 winds are in the offshore forecast." He waved his pipe down the inlet toward the Atlantic. "Aside from the rollers, it's also liable to be soggy. Too rough for the tour boats, they're all staying home today."

"Is there a place to tie up on the island?" Giordino asked.

"There's a small pier at the east landing. Might still be rough there."

"The boat looks stout." Pitt hopped aboard. "Let's go have a look."

He stepped into the wheelhouse and started the inboard motor. Brophy stared at him with trepidation.

Dirk approached and braced his arm. "Come along, Professor, you heard the man. No time to be afraid of a little white water."

They climbed onto the boat as Giordino cast off the mooring lines. Pitt tapped the throttle and eased them toward the inlet. He turned the boat west and increased speed. The sailing was smooth until they reached the open ocean.

The Atlantic was dark and frenzied as a stiff breeze kicked up the swells. The boat was soon pitching and rolling, but Pitt held the wheel steady.

"Are those the Skelligs?" He turned to Brophy and pointed at a rocky pair of steep islands eight miles to the southwest.

"Yes, Little Skellig is to the left and Skellig Michael to the right," Brophy said, gripping a side rail as the boat wallowed through a wave.

"What can you tell us about the island?" Dirk asked.

"Skellig Michael is a well-known place in Irish lore. As I said, *skellig* means 'steep rock' or 'splinter of pointed stone.' You'll see why when we get closer. Michael, of course, refers to the archangel. On this island, according to legend, Saint Michael appeared to help Saint Patrick banish the snakes into the sea."

"We should have had him with us in Scotland," Giordino joked.

"But the lore of the island goes back much further," Brophy continued. "I told you about Meritaten and her husband losing two sons in a shipwreck. One supposedly died at sea, while the other was buried on the island."

"Has the island been inhabited?" Dirk asked.

"That's what it's best known for. The early Christians founded a monastery there, around the sixth century. Those hearty souls lived on the rock for several centuries before the settlement was abandoned, possibly on account of Viking raiders. Remains of the monastery still exist, and people come here on pilgrimages to this day."

Pitt scanned the horizon. "They couldn't have picked a more remote spot."

"It was isolation that they were seeking. The sect was believed to be followers of Anthony the Great of Egypt."

"Egypt?" Giordino asked.

Brophy nodded. "One of the first Christian monks. In Egypt he practiced asceticism alone in the desert."

"That's an intriguing connection," Dirk said.

They pitched and swayed past the rocky island of Little Skellig and a mile later approached the shores of Skellig Michael.

The island towered out of the ocean like a slate pyramid, rising over seven hundred feet into the sky.

Sheer rock cliffs fell to the sea along a broad front, giving Pitt doubt they could make a landing. Brophy directed him to the northeast corner, where a small inlet called Blind Man's Cove appeared beyond a jagged finger of rock. Protected from the westerly winds, the water became less turbulent as Pitt guided the boat alongside a short concrete pier at the mouth of the cove. An empty blue and white workboat was already there, tied to the dock.

"Guess we're not the only storm runners out today," Dirk said, "though I can see why the tour boats stayed home." Even in the protected waters, the boat rocked and lurched.

"I'm told the winter gales can send waves ten meters over this pier." Brophy shook his head. "Not a place for the faint-hearted."

They secured the boat to the remaining section of dock and climbed ashore. Dirk grabbed a bulky backpack he'd loaded onto the boat, but was intercepted by Giordino. "Let me take that," the shorter man said, hoisting it onto his shoulders without effort. "You look like you'd have trouble carrying a balloon today."

"That obvious?" Dirk replied. His back and neck still ached when he moved, though he hadn't realized his hunched gait was apparent to the others.

The men assembled onshore and began walking along a narrow road cut into the side of the cliff. It gradually ascended, following the island's contour to the south. A thick concrete and stone wall on the outer edge protected visitors from an accidental plunge into the sea.

Giordino slapped a hand on the wall. "I see the monks weren't the ones mixing concrete here."

Brophy smiled. "The government built this little road. It leads to a lighthouse on the far south end. In the old days, lighthouse keepers were stationed here to man the light. Now it's all automated."

They followed the road a short distance until crossing a set of stone steps that rose steeply to the west. They saw at the end of the road the modern lighthouse on the island's south promontory.

"From here, we climb." Brophy motioned toward the steps. "Now we'll be utilizing the handiwork of the old monks."

The steps were rough and weathered, but spoke well, Pitt thought, of the brute labor that placed them there fourteen hundred years ago. The steps climbed to the center of the island, then angled north. The footing was wet and slippery from the rains, and they took their time.

After several minutes, Dirk stopped to catch his breath, his body feeling weak from his battering the day before. "Those monks must have been part billy goat."

"They did have a bit of a hike to haul up their supplies," Brophy said, equally winded. "It's six hundred and eighteen steps to the monastery."

As they resumed their climb, Dirk noticed an abundance of birdlife. Colorful puffins nested near the water, while larger gannets and razorbills soared overhead. He kept a sharp eye out for any peregrine falcons.

After passing a spire called Needle's Eye, they dropped down to a terraced slope and the monastery. It was a walled enclosure, tucked between a steep escarpment and the island's highest peak. Six beehive-shaped stone huts dominated the site, adjoined by the crumbled ruins of two oratories and a chapel.

"It's smaller than I expected," Dirk said, "but the huts are impressive."

"Only a dozen or so monks are believed to have lived here at its peak," Brophy said. "Let's take a look at the interiors of the huts. I'm hopeful there might be something of interest."

The nearest stone structure stood roughly nine feet square, with a corbeled roof almost twice that height. They entered through an open doorway and found the interior dark and barren. Brophy clicked on a flashlight and scoured the walls for inscriptions, artwork, or other possible clues. There was nothing to be found.

He methodically searched the other five huts, finding no markings on any of the interior surfaces. He turned off his flashlight and exited the last hut with the others at his side.

"I'd hoped the monks might have known something and left a hint," Brophy said. "There's nothing."

"Seems to me," said Pitt, "that any memorials or inscriptions would be in their prayer cloisters or chapel."

"Aye, you're right. They're in rougher condition, but worth a look."

They searched the remaining walls of the chapel and the large oratory below the huts, found only some carved stone crosses. They made their way to the last structure, called the small oratory, which stood apart from the rest of the buildings at the far north end of the complex. Slightly smaller than the huts, it retained its pyramid roof and meter-thick walls. Inside, along the back wall, they found the remnants of a stepped altar.

Brophy examined the other walls with his light, then halted at one corner. On a large flat stone, he noticed a faint carved drawing. It was little more than the image of a triangle, with an S-shaped curving line that descended to a small figure at the bottom. The lower symbol appeared in the shape of a Celtic cross.

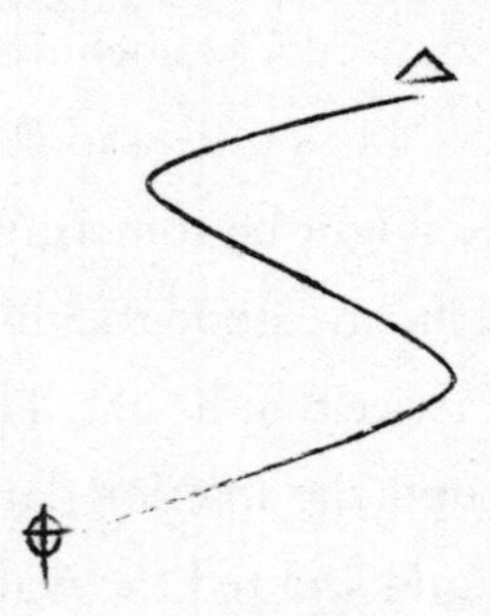

Brophy studied the diagram a moment, then turned to leave.

"Just a minute." Pitt grabbed his arm to keep the light on the image. "Take a closer look at that cross. I think the drawing has been modified."

Brophy strained to study the image under the small light. "I see what you mean. It's in the crude shape of a classic Celtic cross. The base cross and upper loop were carved with some precision, with a sharp tool. The lower semicircle was added more crudely."

"As well as the top post of the cross, above the T," Pitt said.

"Yes, I see that as well."

Brophy knelt on the gravel floor. "So if we removed the cruder carvings, we would take away the upper post and the lower semicircle, leaving this." He dragged his finger across the ground, creating a T shape with a half circle centered atop it.

"It looks like an Egyptian ankh!" Dirk said.

Brophy gave a cautious nod. "The Egyptian hieroglyph that symbolizes life. Or perhaps in the case of Meritaten, eternal life."

They studied the crude drawing, taking photos with their phones, before stepping out of the dark structure.

"If we take that to be an ankh and a representation of Meritaten's burial place," Brophy said, "then it appears to show a trail leading down from the monastery."

"The drawing doesn't resemble the path we took up," Giordino said, "which was more in the shape of a large U."

"There are actually three stairways to the monastery." Brophy took a map of the island from his coat pocket. "Aside from the main path we took, there is a zigzag path from Blue Cove on the west coast, which joins our route below the monastery. It doesn't resemble the marking on the stone."

"What's the third trail?" Dirk asked.

"It's a steep and overgrown path that leads from the landing pier. It appears to be a more direct route that doesn't match the drawing either."

Pitt leaned over a retaining wall and looked down the steep hill to the north. A postcard view presented itself of Little Skellig and the Irish coastline. Directly beneath him, remnants of a steep stone stairway descended to the landing at Blind Man's Cove. He turned and took another look at Brophy's island map. The rock inscription didn't match any existing trail or a likely lost path from the monastery. A wily look came to his eye as he gazed across the terrain.

"I don't think it represents a trail at all," he said.

"If it's not a trail," Brophy said, "then what is it?"

"Only one other thing it could be," Pitt said with a smile. "A cavern leading to a tunnel."

63

Their concealed lookout was situated on a rise above the monastery, near the base of Needle's Eye. It was more bunker than perch, a rocky uplift that jutted from the soil, creating a covered shelter large enough to conceal four people from the monastery and its main trail.

"What are they doing now?" McKee asked, sipping tea from a thermos. For once, she wasn't dressed in designer flair, instead wearing jeans, hiking boots, and a dark all-weather jacket. Around her neck was her ever-present gold scarab necklace.

After sending Ainsley back to Scotland to monitor events, McKee had joined Riki, Gavin, and Rachel in taking an early-morning voyage to Skellig Michael. They all got a dose of seasickness on the trip over, but had cleared their heads with a hike up to the island heights.

McKee had acquired the same trail map as Brophy and knew there was little to see on the island beyond the lighthouse and the elevated monastery site. Like Brophy, she assumed any clues to Meritaten would lie with her. Down in the cramped shelter, they would wait for Brophy and the men from NUMA to find Meritaten for them.

"They went around to the north side of the monastery," Gavin said. He aimed a pair of binoculars through a crevice in the rock overhang and peered down at the monastery. "They're beyond my line of sight."

He lowered the binoculars and turned to the three women. Rachel sat next to him, clear-eyed and cradling a Beretta pistol. The only one he could count on, Gavin thought.

Riki sat at the far end, quiet to the point of almost sulking. She had perked up when she spied the four men hike by, but now sunk back into somberness. Her confidence diminished, as usual, when her mother was around.

And then there was McKee. She had shown surprising spryness in the hike up the trail, and still exuded an intense energy. She sat nervous and beady-eyed, like a falcon eyeing a field rabbit for the kill. But a hint of defeat had crept into her usually composed face. Gavin had known her long enough to realize that she wasn't one to go down without a fight.

"Be patient, young man, and give them a few more minutes," she instructed. "After all, they won't be leaving the island alive."

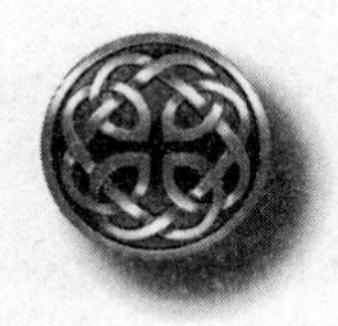

64

The three men gave Pitt a blank stare, then Brophy's face lit up like he'd won the Irish Sweepstakes.

"A tunnel. By heavens, you may be right. Local lore tells of a subterranean tunnel associated with the monastery, but it's never been found."

"Maybe no one knew how to go about looking for it," Dirk said, stepping to the large backpack Giordino had muscled up the hill. Unzipping it, he began removing components of the ground-penetrating radar system that he had broken down and packed inside.

"So that's what you have inside," Giordino said. "I was hoping it was a case of beer."

"Ah, our old lawn mower," Brophy said. "It worked for us once. Maybe it will work again."

As Giordino helped Dirk reassemble the radar, Pitt pointed

across the site. "Any hints on where the tunnel might have been located, Professor?"

Brophy shook his head. "Pure speculation, I'm afraid. Somewhere in the vicinity of the chapel, might be a guess. It likely had a peaked roof, which might be what's depicted in the stone inscription."

"Then let's start the search there," Dirk agreed.

Once assembled, the radar unit was rolled to the chapel ruins and a search made around its interior and perimeter. When nothing appeared, the search was expanded to the huts and large oratory, then on to the hillside above and below the main structures. The men took turns, in pairs, hoisting the device along the treacherous hillside. Other than some small objects and buried debris near the huts, there was no sign of a subterranean passage.

"Nothing showing up around here," Dirk said, hefting the device over a stone and stopping to rest. "The small oratory is the only area left within the walled grounds."

"Then that's where it must be," Giordino said. He took the grip of the radar unit and manhandled it toward the small structure at the end of the site. Circling the stone building without success, he worked the device up the hillside above it. He stopped at a perimeter stone wall that burrowed into the rising slope of the hill. Studying the radar's display screen, he turned to the others and raised a fist in the air.

"Underground Al has delivered."

Dirk rushed over and looked at the screen. A small tube-shaped pocket of white was visible amid the squiggly bands of gray lines.

"It's small but distinct here," Giordino said. "It seems to grow larger before fading away as you cross the hill."

He angled the unit up the hill, Dirk glued to his side watching the display.

"The radar is losing its signal strength due to increasing depth," he said.

Pitt and Brophy stepped to the edge of the oratory and waited as the two men returned with wide grins on their faces.

"Looks to be a potential passage right where the stone wall abuts the hillside," Dirk said, pointing.

"Afraid we didn't bring a shovel this time," Brophy said.

"We may not need one," Dirk replied. He followed the contour of the wall until reaching the point where it curled chest-high into the hillside. At the endpoint, he began hoisting off the stacked stones and laying them in an orderly pattern on the ground.

"We can reassemble it in the order it's taken apart," he said, as the others joined him.

"I'm sure it won't be the first time this wall's been rebuilt over the centuries," Brophy said.

Pitt and Giordino joined in with the work, exposing a wall of compressed soil behind the stacked stones. As they worked their way to the corner, they came upon a large flat boulder embedded vertically. Dirk brushed away the edges and tried to move it. It wouldn't budge. He winced at the effort.

"You take the left side," Giordino said, squeezing in beside him. Together, they heaved against the boulder. They were able to rock it back and forth a few times until it sprang forward, falling flat to the ground.

Behind it was a narrow opening.

"A small cave for storage?" Giordino asked.

"Or something much more," Brophy said.

Giordino stood aside and waved a hand at the opening. "Your honor, my boy."

Dirk nodded with a smile, activated a flashlight, and burrowed through the entrance. After a minute or two, the others heard him call to them. Giordino crawled in next, followed by Brophy, then Pitt.

Pitt found a tight crawl space that extended four or five feet in a downward slope, then gradually expanded. He shuffled forward until he was able to rise to his feet, joining the others on a narrow ledge. They congregated there, shining their flashlights into the dark depths beyond.

"What do we have," Pitt asked, "a cave or a tunnel?"

"Something even better," Dirk replied, shining his light onto a series of carved steps that led down into the black chasm before them. "A stairway to the deep."

65

I've lost sight of them again."

Gavin lowered his binoculars and turned to McKee. "I think they might have found something."

McKee peered over the top of the rock shelter at the empty monastery. "Make your way closer without being seen, if you can. Call us on the radio if there is anything to report."

Gavin nodded, passing the binoculars to Rachel. He pulled a Ruger SR9c pistol from a shoulder holster, released the safety, then tucked it back in. He then climbed out of the rocky command post and slowly made his way down the rise.

Reaching the entrance to the monastery site, he ducked behind a stone wall and listened for the sound of voices. The only noise was the rustle of wind in the grass and the cry of a nearby gull. He crept forward, slipping behind the first hut and peering around its front. There was no sign of the other men.

He made his way across the site, eventually reaching the

small oratory. He looked over the wall to see if they had climbed down the steep back side, but they were nowhere to be seen. Then he noticed the excavated wall, a large boulder on the ground, and a dark opening in the side of the hill.

He peered inside, then stepped back and retrieved a two-way radio on his hip.

"They've found a tunnel and have gone underground," he radioed to McKee. "We can finish them off in there. And they'll never be found."

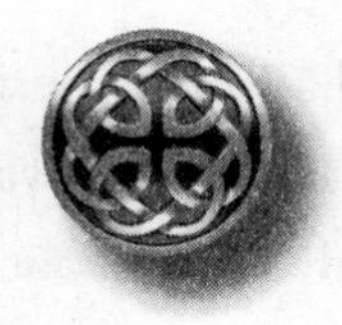

66

The steps were carved into a nearly vertical slab of rock that disappeared into total darkness below. The four men stood aside a massive underground fissure that descended several hundred feet. Pitt aimed a light at the steep, narrow steps that had been hand-carved into the rock face.

"Hope no one's afraid of heights," he said, initiating the precarious descent.

"Never an elevator when you need one," Giordino grumbled.

Dirk followed his father down the steps, Giordino and Brophy trailing behind. They walked in silence, attentive to each step they took, while in awe of the vast underground opening they had stumbled into.

The steps followed the face in a wide arc, which leveled briefly across a flat slab, then resumed descending in a countercurve. The men trekked downward, their shoes clapping against the steps and echoing across the crevice, shattering the silence of the subterranean world. Brophy periodically aimed his light over the side, but the bottom was always beyond view.

"It fits," Dirk suddenly blurted out.

Everyone stopped a moment to catch their breath.

"What fits?" Giordino asked.

"The inscription on the oratory rock. The steps have descended in the same curvilinear path as depicted on the rock." As he spoke, he motioned over his shoulder at the steps they had just descended.

The others stared past him. They weren't focused on his words. Rather, they were focused on the four small lights that now appeared at the top of the steps.

A hail of gunshots echoed through the chasm like bells in a cathedral.

"Kill the lights!" Pitt yelled, as flecks of stone burst from the wall above him.

The four men ducked onto the steps, extinguishing their lights, as Gavin and Rachel each peppered a handful of shots at them from above. Dirk looked up, spotting four figures on the upper ledge.

"Keep moving," Pitt urged in a low voice. "Use a hand on the wall."

Dirk did as his father suggested, sliding a hand along the rock face for support as his feet probed in the dark for the next step. Giordino started to follow from behind him, but then hesitated when he heard a loud gasp.

"Everyone okay?" he whispered.

The wilted body of Brophy slumped onto his back in the darkness, nearly knocking him off the stairs.

"Sorry," Brophy said. "My leg . . . I think I'm hit."

"I got you, Professor," Giordino replied. "Hang on while we get you out of here."

He proceeded to move down the steps, carrying Brophy piggyback style. Pitt led the way, whispering guidance as they descended into the abyss that materialized in the dim light.

Standing atop the entry ledge, McKee aimed her flashlight into the depths. The four escaping men appeared as indistinct shadows beyond its range.

"Go ahead, follow them down," she directed to Gavin. "They're surely not armed. Let's see where this leads."

"Yes, ma'am." Tucking his gun into his holster, Gavin waved his light ahead of him, then took a tentative step into the darkness ahead.

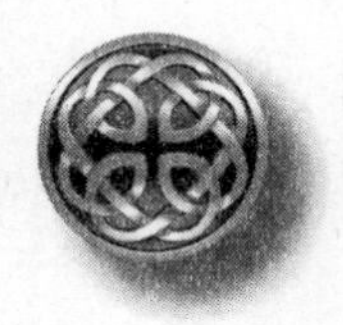

67

Pitt felt flat ground beneath his feet and halted. He activated his flashlight, pressing a thumb over the beam to allow just a pinprick of light. Scanning around him, it appeared they had reached the bottom of the fissure. The flat landing was surrounded by a trio of locomotive-sized boulders that squeezed against the sheer rock walls.

"End of the line?" Giordino grunted, as he stepped onto the landing.

"Appears so," Pitt replied. "How's the professor?"

"The buggers got me in the hip," Brophy said, as Giordino set him on the ground. His voice was noticeably weaker, but not his spirit.

Dirk joined in checking his wounds under a concealed light. Damp red spots were visible on the right hip and thigh of his trousers. Dirk stripped off a sweatshirt and passed it to Giordino.

"This will help."

"Thanks, lad," Brophy uttered, as Giordino split it into two lengths and bound it around the wounds.

Pitt gazed up, spotting the jiggling lights of their pursuers high up on the rock face. They had perhaps a five-minute advantage, and nothing with which to wage a defense.

He turned his light to the boulders, studying them up and down. Near their base, he noticed a faint path that led to the far-right boulder. He followed the vague trail to the far side, where he found a low triangular opening between the boulder and the rock wall. Shining his light in, he saw it led to a carved tunnel.

"This way," he called out quietly.

Dirk and Giordino appeared a moment later, supporting Brophy between them. On the steps above, Pitt could see the lights of their pursuers getting closer.

"You okay to keep moving, Professor?" Pitt asked.

"As long as these pack mules don't mind hauling an old bag of bones."

"I'm afraid it's a tight squeeze."

Pitt led them through the opening and into a low, narrow tunnel. He had to duck to keep from scraping his head. Gradually, the tunnel grew in height, if not width, allowing him to stand upright.

"Looks like a natural tunnel that was enlarged," Dirk said from the rear, noting sporadic pick marks in the ceiling and walls.

The tunnel sloped downhill in a long and windy path. Pitt stopped at one point and listened to a faint rumble.

"I don't think they're behind us yet," Dirk said.

"No, it's the sea," Pitt said, as the sound of pounding waves became audible. "We're near the water."

"And a way out, I hope," Giordino replied, sweat dripping down his face from carrying his human cargo.

Pitt picked up the pace, leading the group through a long sweeping curve. Then he came to a split in the tunnel. The main tunnel curved to the right. A smaller passage continued straight. Pitt shined his light into both openings, but there was no visible end.

"Left or right?" Giordino asked.

Pitt turned his light on him. The strain of lugging Brophy was showing on his face. Over his shoulder, the Irish archeologist looked pale, his eyes losing their lucidity.

"Why don't you keep moving with the professor down the less obvious route," he said, pointing to the narrower tunnel. "I'll take a quick look down the other passage."

As Dirk approached, fatigue wearing on him as well, Pitt waved him on. "You best give Al a hand with the professor."

Dirk nodded, hustling to catch up with Giordino, who had already moved down the left opening.

Pitt turned and jogged down the larger tunnel to his right. He didn't have to go far. Forty feet on, the tunnel turned and came to its end. Not at a closed or sealed wall, at a huge cavern.

Pitt entered onto an elevated rise that overlooked the vast elongated space. A natural high-domed ceiling stretched over the cavern. A dozen pinpricks of light penetrated a wall of boulders at the far end, casting a dim gray pallor over the room. The audible crash of waves just beyond told Pitt they were adjacent to the shoreline, and that the cavern may have once been a grotto open to the sea.

A large upright boulder blocked the entrance, but carved steps descended to the side. At the foot of the steps, a deep basin was cut into the floor, extending across its length. Rising from somewhere in the center of the basin was a towering wood post that rose high above the elevated entrance.

Pitt hesitated at the top of the steps when he heard the sound of voices approaching from behind. They weren't those of his companions. As he turned to descend, his light illuminated the timber, revealing a line of rope dangling from its peak. Pitt suddenly realized it was no simple wooden post, it was a ship's mast. A single rectangular sail hung in tatters. Below him was a ship, 90 feet long, with a hull made of cedar planking. Moving closer, he aimed his beam along the side of the strange vessel, revealing a sea of oars attached to the hull. He couldn't help but wonder who last touched this ship so many centuries ago.

68

The narrow tunnel that split to the left at the junction proved a far more arduous path. It snaked for a couple hundred yards, rising sharply in elevation at times. The narrow walls became constricted in places, forcing Giordino and Dirk to slide Brophy through its confines. The path leveled, and the tunnel finally reached its end in a small natural chamber that was roughly square. A high mound of boulders towered over one side of the entrance, but the chamber was otherwise open. It wasn't empty.

Along the far wall was a narrow wooden altar. A pair of bronze oil lamps flanked a high silver cross that was mounted on an ancient anchor. On the rock wall behind the cross was a faded mural, featuring a man standing in a desert setting, a pyramid to one side and a halo of gold above his head.

"Guess we found a dead end," Giordino said. He carried Brophy across the chamber and set him down in the corner. The professor looked up, his eyes crystallizing as Dirk's light splayed across the mural.

"It's Saint Anthony of Egypt," he said, sitting upright. "This must be a secret vestry, or perhaps a chapel, built for Anthony by the monks."

"Whatever it is, there's no way out," Dirk said. "Might be a good time to pray for his help."

Giordino eyed the altar, then waved his light toward the mound of rocks by the entry.

"I'm not sure who this Saint Anthony character is," he said, "but I think he might have helped us already."

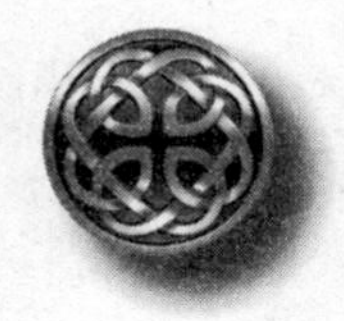

69

Gavin reached the tunnel intersection and stopped to catch his breath. Overweight and averse to exercise, the hired tough was out of his element. The initial climb, followed by the subterranean descent, had left him winded and sweaty, despite the cool temperature. Three wavering lights appeared behind him as McKee, Rachel, and Riki caught up. Like Gavin, McKee appeared fatigued from the hiking, though the two younger women showed more stamina.

"The main tunnel looks like it continues to the right," Gavin said.

McKee studied the two tunnels, then pointed her light at the ground. In the dusty gravel underfoot, she detected a partial footprint leading in the direction of the smaller tunnel.

"You take this one. Rachel and I will follow the larger one." She patted a two-way radio on her hip. "Call me in five minutes with a status."

Gavin nodded and took a few steps into the narrow passage. He stopped and turned. Excluded from her mother's commands, Riki duly stepped past McKee without saying a word and followed in Gavin's path.

Rachel took the lead down the right tunnel with McKee close behind. She moved cautiously, scanning the tunnel with a light in her left hand, the Beretta thrust forward in her right. The two women reached the end of the passage and stepped into the cavern. They stopped at the elevated landing, scanning the depths of the room with their lights. McKee eyed the tall timber at the center, a slack line of hemp angling off to a side wall. She raised a hand to Rachel, and both women stood perfectly still, their eyes and ears straining to detect another presence.

The cavern remained dead silent for a moment, then they heard a faint rustling. McKee realized it originated above them. She looked up with her light toward the top of the timber. The angled line was now taut and moving in a wide arc toward their position. She turned to the side, detecting an accelerating shadow, and jumped back.

Flung by Pitt from a nook in the side wall, a triangular limestone anchor came hurtling through the air like a pendulum. Secured to the mast line by a hole in its upper section, the ancient ship's anchor swung across the platform in a wide arc. It missed McKee, but struck Rachel, who had been peering in the opposite direction.

The stone anchor struck her shoulder and the back of her head. She instantly corkscrewed to the ground, the blow knocking her unconscious. McKee dropped low as the anchor reached the end of its extension and swung back over her head. She crawled to the fallen woman and retrieved the Beretta that had dropped at her feet. McKee rose to her knees, then turned the gun and light to the wall where the flying object had originated from.

The dangling stone banged against the wall, then spiraled toward its tethered pole with a loss of momentum. There was no sign of the person who had launched it.

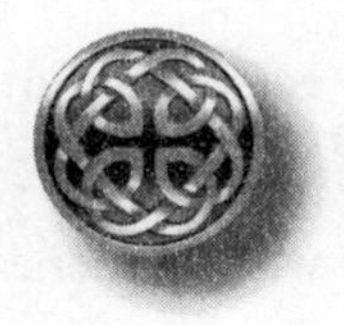

70

Help me . . . Help me, please . . ."

The cry came soft and weak, but with an unmistakable Irish accent. Gavin hesitated, holding his gun steady in front of him, then moved slowly toward the voice.

The narrow tunnel led into a larger opening, Gavin could see, the voice hailing from the pitch-blackness inside. Breathing heavily from the undulating climb, he tried to calm himself a moment before moving forward. Riki remained a shadow at his side, tucking close without uttering a word.

Stepping into the chamber, Gavin aimed his light and gun at the far corner. Seated on the ground, clutching his bloodied side, Brophy squinted into the light with a look of agony he didn't have to exaggerate.

"Can you help me?" he asked, his voice suddenly loud and firm.

His words provided a signal to Dirk and Giordino. Crouched

on the back side of the rock mound adjacent to the entry, the two men rose and heaved on the silver cross borrowed from the altar. Its lower end was wedged beneath a large round boulder perched at the top of the pile. The stone quickly rocked loose, falling down the opposite side of the mound.

Turning to the sound of the tumbling rock, Gavin looked up too late. The boulder was nearly on him when he attempted to jump back. In a moment of panic, he squeezed off a pair of shots from the Ruger that ricocheted off the rock walls. The boulder struck him on the side, crushing his arm as it knocked him hard against the side wall.

A gasp trickled from his lips as his gun and phone clattered to the ground beside his collapsing body. Then the chamber fell silent.

Dirk and Giordino climbed down the mound in the darkened chamber and turned on their lights.

"I think you got them," Brophy announced from the corner.

"You made a nice decoy," Dirk replied. "Are you okay?"

"Dandy, under the circumstances."

Giordino had already stepped around the rock pile and was aiming his light at the entry. Two bodies lay still on the ground. The nearest was Gavin, who showed no signs of breathing. Stepping closer, Giordino could see the gunman's head was bloodied beneath him. His skull had cracked when he was knocked against the wall.

Giordino felt Dirk rush past him to the second figure. It was an attractive woman, he saw, lying on her side with her eyes open. Oddly, she showed no apparent sign she had been struck by the boulder.

Dirk kneeled at her side and gently raised her torso. Riki's face winced as he did so, then softened as she focused her eyes on Dirk. He felt a warm wetness in his hand and noticed a small rip in the side of her jacket. A ricocheting bullet from Gavin's gun had found her, striking her in the side of the chest. Dirk pressed his hand against the wound, then looked in her eyes under the glow of Giordino's light.

"I didn't mean to hurt you," she said in a weak voice. "It's . . . It's all my mother's doing. I'm sorry."

"Me, too." Dirk saw she was fading quickly. He leaned over and kissed her on the forehead.

"Find it," she whispered. "Find Meritaten and what she had. Then save us all." She looked into Dirk's eyes and forced a smile, then she was gone.

71

McKee crouched at the cavern's entrance, sweeping her light across the room. She saw now that the timber holding the rope was in fact the mast of a small ship housed in the narrow basin. The ledge on either side of the basin was empty, telling her the assailant was hiding somewhere below with the ship.

She knelt next to Rachel, calling her name to see if she was alive. She was not. McKee stood and retrieved the two-way radio.

"Gavin. Are you there?"

Silence.

"Gavin. Please answer if you can hear me."

"Oh, I can hear you all right," came the irritable voice of Al Giordino. "Like the squawk of a turkey vulture."

"Where's . . . Where's Gavin?"

"He and his girlfriend are down for the big sleep. Now if you just—"

McKee let out a wail, then tossed the radio at the rock wall. Giordino's voice fell silent as the smashed radio slid to the ground.

She felt herself go dizzy, and her knees nearly buckled. She sucked in several deep breaths of air to calm herself and regain her senses. It was all too much to process. How could everything have gone so terribly wrong?

The answer came in the form of a voice from the darkness.

"It's all over, McKee," Pitt said. "It's all over."

Her despair turned to anger at recognizing the voice. Following the sound, she climbed down the steps to the topside of the basin and looked down. The naturally carved cavity was a near perfect rectangle, a dozen feet deep, and extending to the rear cavern wall. What sat inside wasn't naturally formed, however.

It was a long boat, almost 90 feet in length, but with a narrow beam. It had stem and stern pieces that rose upward in tall spires, and a single high mast with a tattered sail. A half-dozen long oars slung over either side, their tips resting on the basin floor below. Aft of the mast was a lone enclosed cabin that stretched almost to the stern. McKee knew nothing of ship construction, yet even under the weak light of her flashlight she could see the boat was ancient.

She had little concern for the boat or its construction at the moment. Her only focus was for the man hiding in the shadows. She heard a scrape of wood on the far side railing and raised her Beretta, firing three shots into the darkness. The gunfire echoed through the cavern, gradually replaced by dead silence.

Near the bow, McKee saw a wooden ramp from the top of the basin to the boat's deck. Striding to the ramp, she tiptoed across, realizing that the low-drafted boat was perched on supports, raising it well off the bottom of the basin. Taking a first step onto the deck, she heard a thunk on the side of the cabin. She turned and fired twice more at a shadow that vanished around the back end.

"It's over for you, McKee," Pitt's voice called out from the stern.

She gritted her teeth. Her heart pounded, and her hands shook with an internal frenzy. Moving across the bow, she passed the center mast and heard another sound, this time on the right side of the boat. She raised her light, catching a glimpse of a man's torso dropping to the deck. She raised her right hand and fired.

With her left hand holding the light, the pistol bucked in her right hand. She splayed a wild pattern of gunfire, kept shooting anyway, gradually zeroing in on her target. Pitt's body jerked and bounded as she pumped shells into the dark figure, until the Beretta's slide locked open with the expenditure of her last round.

She stepped toward her victim, the light in her hand finally held steady. In the distance, she could just make out the full shape of a man's jacket, shredded by gunfire. Suddenly, the jacket moved. It didn't roll about, but stood upright, elevating above the deck. McKee stared in shock, which turned to dread. The coat wasn't occupied by Pitt. Rather, it was held up by one of the boat's long oars.

Standing in the basin with his arms raised, Pitt had maneuvered the jacket about the boat, drawing McKee's gunfire. He knew the difficulty of shooting a moving target with a handgun in negligible light and kept himself out of sight while sacrificing his coat. Pitt couldn't hear the click of the Beretta clear its last round due to the echoes in the cavern, but he saw McKee's light waver on his jacket, then turn to the ground.

McKee sagged in defeat. Stepping backward, she bumped against the boat's mast and Pitt's dangling anchor at its base. She stared at the anchor a long moment, then tossed the gun aside. Setting her light on the deck, she untied the rope from the stone, then stood and carried the mast line to the side of the boat. Without a word, she wrapped several loose coils about her neck and pulled them tight. Climbing onto the side rail, she leaned forward and jumped off.

In the otherwise silent cavern, Pitt heard the snap of McKee's neck and then the tumble of her body as it unraveled from the rope and dropped to the basin floor. He slowly walked to the figure, approaching and turning on his light when he detected no movement.

McKee lay with a stark look on her face, blank eyes staring into oblivion. Her gold scarab necklace sat coiled next to her, the chain breaking with her fall. Pitt stared at the demented yet once beautiful woman a long moment. Then he gently closed her eyes that were staring at nothing. Next he picked up the scarab and reached over the boat's railing and laid it on the deck.

"Your reign is over. A world without men was never meant to be." He spoke softly. Pitt rose to his feet and peered at the thirty-five-hundred-year-old boat above him.

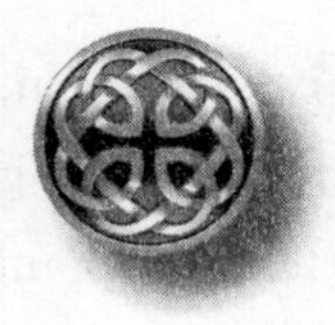

72

The high stem feature was the first thing to catch his eye. Carved lotus flowers marked the boat's prow, intertwined with Egyptian ankhs and Celtic crosses. It was an unlikely mix of cultural symbols that hinted at the boat's age and provenance.

The vessel's overall construction was crude, Pitt noted, built with uneven timbers and expanded seams. It had not been meant to sail long distances. As a funerary barge, it bore a striking resemblance to the Khufu burial ship found near the Great Pyramid of Giza.

Pitt made his way across the slim deck to the enclosed cabin. Long-dead dried flowers crunched underfoot as he approached a small door secured with a wooden latch.

Raising the latch, the door squeaked open, and he ducked through it to enter. Rising upright, he pivoted with his light to illumine the small enclosure. Ceramic jars of varying sizes lined the walls, surrounding a raised center platform. Atop it sat a painted wooden coffin, its top carved with the image of its occupant.

Pitt stepped closer. Like the boat, the coffin's features were carved with less precision than the royal tombs of ancient Egypt. Yet there was no mistaking the wide-eyed figure, wearing a striped *nemes* headdress, as anything other than Egyptian.

Pitt set his light on the deck and tested the coffin's lid. It moved without protest, so he lifted the cover and set it upright against the wall. He retrieved the light and looked inside.

Meritaten, the princess from Egypt, lay wrapped in heavy linens that covered most of her body. Her exposed head showed a thick mane of dark hair, encircled with a crown of dried flowers and clover. A rusty sword rested against her side. She wore a heavy gold necklace studded with turquoise faience beads. Clinging to the sides of her head was a pair of gold hoop earrings.

But it wasn't the jewelry buried with the immigrant Irish queen that caught Pitt's eye.

GIORDINO BURST INTO THE CAVERN with Gavin's gun drawn, nearly tripping over the prone figure of Rachel on the ground. A relieved smile crossed his face when he observed Pitt climbing up the steps from the basin.

"I see you found the grand palace," he said, gazing about the open cavern. "I think we found the antechamber. Just a small altar and some rocks."

"Everyone okay?" Pitt asked.

"Yes, the boys are right behind me." He turned his light on the body of Rachel. "McKee?" he asked.

"No, she's over here," Pitt said, pointing into the basin. "She took the easy way out when she realized she was the last one standing."

Giordino leaned over the steps and aimed his light into the basin. McKee's lifeless body was visible beneath the Egyptian boat, beside a dangling strand of rope. He turned at hearing a shuffling sound near the entrance.

Brophy entered the cavern, supported by an arm around Dirk's shoulder. The Irishman's eyes grew large at the sight of the cavern, while Dirk gave a thankful nod when he spotted his father.

"Are we late to the party?" Brophy asked, sidestepping Rachel.

"Afraid so," Pitt said. He pointed to the far rock wall and its faint glimmers of light. "I think we can dig our way out over there and save you a trip up the stairs."

"I'd be much obliged. What else did you find here?" he asked, inquisitiveness overriding his pain.

"There's a boat," Giordino answered, peering into the basin. "Come have a look."

Giordino took support of Brophy and led him down the steps and along the basin. Their flickering lights appeared on the boat's deck a moment later.

Dirk approached his father, eyeing the vessel from above.

"It looks similar to the one buried by the pyramids in Egypt."

"It's a funerary barge," Pitt replied, "with Celtic and Egyptian markings."

"Is she aboard?"

Pitt nodded. "Just as you and Summer predicted. Meritaten's in a royal tomb set up inside the cabin. The monks never touched it. They must have deemed it a sign from Saint Anthony when they found it."

Dirk stared at the boat a long while, Summer and Riki weighed on his mind. The question he was afraid to ask finally crossed his lips. "The Apium of Faras?"

Pitt opened the fold of his bullet-riddled jacket, exposing a bulging skin sack beside his waist. He gave his son a proud pat on the back.

"It would seem, son, that our days aren't numbered just yet."

EPILOGUE

QUEEN OF THE AGES

Princess Meritaten and Her Funerary Barge

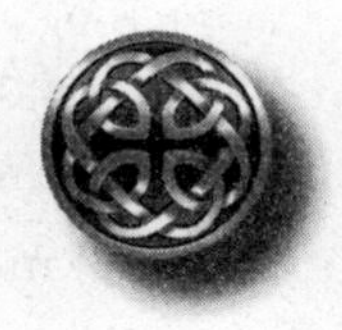

73

Washington, D.C.

Two years later

Prominently displayed on a raised platform, with bright overhead lights accentuating its every detail, the funerary boat of Princess Meritaten captured the eye like no other artifact in the Smithsonian Museum of Natural History. With its long oars and elegantly carved prow, the ancient ceremonial boat represented one of the oldest intact vessels ever discovered.

Only Meritaten's coffin and the mummy of the Egyptian princess herself, both in Plexiglas cases, could compete for the attention of the small group in the museum's first-floor special exhibition hall.

The Meritaten exhibit presented the full life of the princess, including her travels from Egypt to Spain to Ireland, and her ultimate burial on Skellig Michael. Cases displayed her sword, jewelry, and canopic jars found with her on the funerary barge. Evanna McKee's Egyptian gold scarab necklace found a place in the gallery as well.

Yet the most priceless article among Meritaten's possessions was exhibited in a small case off to the side, attracting minimal attention. It was a small gray goatskin bag, displayed with a few samples of the dried plants it had contained inside.

Pitt and Loren passed through a security station at the museum's entrance and joined the small group of dignitaries gathered for an exclusive preview of the exhibit. Museum officials mixed with politicians and international archeologists in admiring the rare artifacts.

A short, spry man with a trimmed red beard and an unlit cigar noticed Pitt and Loren's arrival and marched over, a security contingent on his tail. Vice President James Sandecker bowed to Loren and kissed her hand, then turned to Pitt.

"Outstanding discovery, my boy, simply outstanding," said the Vice President, who had once been Pitt's boss at NUMA.

"We're lucky to have the temporary exhibit," Pitt said. "Dirk and Summer worked closely with a Dr. Eamon Brophy in Ireland to track down Meritaten. Once Brophy recovered from his injuries, he was the one responsible for overseeing the funerary boat's recovery and conservation. It will ultimately remain on permanent display at the National Museum in Dublin. The museum wasn't keen to let Meritaten do any more traveling, yet Dr. Brophy insisted on a temporary exhibit here."

"The least they could do for your help in finding her," Sandecker said. "And, more importantly, putting Evanna McKee out of business."

"A truly evil woman, responsible for untold deaths," Loren said, shaking her head.

"It could have been much worse," Sandecker said. "Speaking

of evil, I hear Senator Bradshaw has admitted under FBI questioning that he accepted large, unreported 'campaign donations' from McKee."

"Influence peddling at its worst," Loren said. "Senate ethics investigators have just scratched the surface, but they've found enough to send him packing. I understand he'll be tendering his resignation this evening."

"At least he realized he was finished," Sandecker said.

Sandecker pointed to the display case with Meritaten's leather pouch. "That bag contained the extinct plant that will save our species?"

"So it would seem," Pitt said. He noticed Elise Aguilar entering the exhibit hall and he waved her over. "Here's the young lady we have to thank."

Pitt introduced the agricultural scientist to Loren and Sandecker, noting with amusement she was visibly nervous at meeting them both.

"Since the discovery of Meritaten's tomb, Elise has been working with the Department of Agriculture and the Centers for Disease Control in an attempt to revitalize the extinct plant."

"Do you have a cure in the works for the Evolution Plague?" Sandecker asked.

"Thanks to the intact DNA we recovered," she said, "we've finally been able to regenerate the silphium, the plant that was buried with Meritaten. We also found out why it became extinct. It's very difficult to grow, even in controlled settings. It seems to thrive only in a narrow range of soil and moisture conditions. The original plants, which grew wild in ancient Libya, just didn't have the ability to replenish themselves when the Romans harvested them in bulk."

"But you're able to grow it now?" Loren said.

She nodded. "There's no way to cultivate enough in a short time to help those afflicted with the Evolution Plague. Our real plan is to synthesize the compounds found in silphium that shield or destroy the plague pathogen. We've created an initial sample that we're currently testing. We hope it can be distributed soon to the places where the Evolution Plague contaminated the water supply."

"In the meantime," Sandecker said, "we're in for a surge in female births?"

"It should be only a brief spike in the birth ratio," Elise said. "A year or two deviation, then hopefully equilibrium will be restored once the treatment is fully dispensed." She nodded to Pitt. "Thanks to the records acquired from the BioRem Global lab, we have a pretty good idea of all those locations."

"Quite a few tankers were caught at sea before additional pathogens could be released," Pitt said. "Still, the company records indicate a significant dispersal in some of the world's largest cities."

"It's a bit overwhelming when you look at the number of potentially infected women," Elise said. "Thankfully, there's no reason they can't all be cured, given enough resources. And the treatment should also act against the cholera-like symptoms caused by the earlier versions of the plague. The trick will be convincing the women who don't exhibit any signs of infection to take the cure. Personally, I can't wait to get back to El Salvador to bring the remedy to the people of Cerrón Grande."

: waved his cigar toward the artifacts. "It looks like
itaten saved not only the men of her generation, but
generation."

certainly did," Elise said. "I should tell you we've
on the assistance of Dr. Miles Perkins, formerly of
al, in our project."

the University of Edinburgh has taken over the
cilities, and they're now under his direction," Pitt
good man."

Perkins has been a great help," Elise said. "In
he one who suggested the designation for the syn-
luct we hope will cure those infected with the
gue."

tion for the cure?" Pitt asked.

d. "He thought it appropriate to recognize the key
ible for the cure."

you decide to call it?" Loren asked.

d at the couple and gave a sheepish grin. "It's to be
fter your husband."

: Pitt a nudge. "The savior of the male half of the
ure you're not disappointed there won't be more
world?"

't be altogether bad." Pitt's grin was wolfish. "The
tter is, there's only one woman in the world that

ed his arm to Loren, and they turned and strolled
bition hall, his own princess by his side.

Sandecker waved his hand toward the [illegible]. "It looks like Princess Meritaten saved not only the [illegible] of her [illegible], but also our next [illegible]."

"That she certainly did," Elise said. "[illegible] we've been relying on [illegible] Dr. [illegible] for [illegible] BioKem Global's [illegible]."

"I heard the [illegible] has taken over the McKee lab facilities and [illegible]," [illegible] said. "He's a good [illegible]."

"Yes, Dr. Parsons has been [illegible]," Elise said. "In fact, he was the one who suggested the designation of the synthesized product we hope will cure [illegible] with the Evolution Plague."

"A designation [illegible]?" [illegible] asked.

She nodded. "[illegible] to [illegible] party responsible for [illegible]."

"What did he decide to call it?" [illegible] asked.

Elise looked at [illegible]. "It's to be called DP-1, after [illegible]."

Loren gave [illegible]. "[illegible] of the [illegible] species. You sure you're not [illegible] women in the world?"

"It wouldn't [illegible]," [illegible]. "The fact of the matter is [illegible] only [illegible] in the world that counts to me."

He extended his arm to Loren [illegible] down the exhibit [illegible].

KEEP READING FOR AN EXCITING EXCERPT
FROM THE NEXT NOVEL FROM THE NUMA® FILES,

JOURNEY OF THE PHARAOHS.

Aboard the trawler things had gone from dangerous to desperate. The boat had settled onto the rocks with a ten-degree list, water was pouring in down below, and the storm showed no sign of relenting.

The helmsman, feeling the sting of guilt and believing he'd failed the ship, turned to the captain. "I'm sorry. I should have swung wider."

"Nothing much you could do," the captain said. He got on the intercom, calling the chief engineer. "How bad off are we?"

"Three feet of water in the bilge. She's flooding fast. We need to abandon ship while we're still upright."

Vincennes heard this and shook his head vigorously. "No," he snapped "We cannot leave the boat. We have to get off the rocks."

"The rocks are all that's keeping us afloat," the captain shot back. He pressed the intercom switch again. "Get the lads topside. We'll go out in the rafts."

With the order to evacuate given, Vincennes became livid. He pointed an accusing finger at the captain. "If this is some kind of a trick—"

Whatever else he might have said went unheard as a larger wave crashed against the ship, slamming the trawler broadside and rolling it further over to starboard.

"You want to stay on board, you're welcome to it," the captain shouted. "My men and I are leaving."

Vincennes stared irately as men began coming up the stairs from down below. Unable to sway the captain, he waited for the last sailor to pass and then lurched in the other direction, making his way to the back of the wheelhouse and charging down the stairwell.

The helmsman went to follow, but the captain held him back. "He's my problem, lad. Get out on deck. Keep the men together. Launch the rafts as the waves crest, not before or after, or you won't stand a chance. Understood?"

The helmsman nodded, pulled on his life jacket, and pushed out through the starboard door. As soon as he was in the open the wind attempted to knock him down. He grabbed the railing and fought to stay upright on the tilted deck.

Things couldn't have been much worse. They were over nearly twenty degrees now and leaning into the rocks. The port side of the ship was raised and acting like a bulwark against the onslaught of the storm, shielding the deck from being swept by every wave. But any boat that went into the water on that side would be slammed against the trawler's hull long before it could move away.

The starboard side of the deck looked more promising. The

trawler was leaning that way, and the edge of the deck was already awash. That should have made for an easier way off, but just beyond the rail lay a field of jagged, rocky spires.

They vanished every time the crest of a wave came through, only to reappear as the trough passed, emerging from the water like teeth in the lower jaw of some hungry beast. Still, he decided, a small chance was better than no chance.

He made his way down a ladder and then along the deck toward the midships muster station. By the time he arrived, several of the men had begun inflating one of the boats.

The compressed gas charges filled the raft quickly, but the wind and the rocking deck made it difficult to control.

"Secure the lines," the helmsman shouted.

Even as he shouted, the trawler shuddered with the impact of another wave. A blast of spray flew over them and a foot of green water slid down from the elevated port side of the ship. It swept two men off their feet and took the raft into the sea.

Attached by a sixty-foot lanyard, the raft was not yet lost.

The helmsman rushed forward. "Grab the line," he shouted, wrapping his hands tightly around the nylon cable. Two of the crewmen joined him. They pulled with all their strength, but they'd only managed to drag the raft a short distance when the next wave surged through.

It flooded over the ship and around it, surging in from the bow and stern. It caught the raft square, wrenching the line from their stinging hands and flipping the raft as it carried it into the teeth of the rocks beyond.

One side of the inflatable boat was torn open on impact. The orange craft lost its shape and was soon awash with seawater.

The next wave finished it, dragging it backwards and wrapping the deflated fabric around one of the outcroppings of stone.

The crewmen had seen the destruction up close. They all knew what it meant.

"We're trapped," one of the men shouted. "Even if we get another raft ready, we'll never survive that."

"This gale has a center to it, an eye," another of the men said. "If we wait it out, we might have a chance."

"The eye of the storm is hours away," a third crewmen replied. "The ship will be scrap by then."

"Quiet," the helmsman shouted. He thought he'd heard the sound of an engine on the wind. He turned his eyes skyward, hoping to spot a Royal Navy helicopter. All he saw were churning grey clouds.

"There," one of the crewmen shouted. He was pointing toward the channel.

The helmsman turned, squinting against the wind and rain, and finally spotted a torpedo-shaped craft racing through the grey twilight. Whatever it was, it took a curving path, disappearing behind the back of a large swell and then reappearing as the wave moved on.

"Are you lads seeing this?"

Murmurs of acknowledgement came his way.

"Whoever it is, he's got to be a bloody loon."

The *bloody loon* was a man on a high-speed watercraft, similar in design to a Jet Ski but longer and wider, with an extended section aft of the seats, a noticeably broader stance, and a bulbous nose.

The craft moved with great speed and agility, and its pilot

showed no fear, racing up one wave, coming down the backside, and then heading directly toward the stricken trawler.

"He'll never make it past the rocks!"

The helmsman had to agree, but just as a bone-shattering impact appeared unavoidable the front of the next swell rolled through. The water rose, covering the spires and lifting the oncoming machine above them.

Not only did the rider cross above the rocks, but he raced straight onto the tilted deck of the trawler, ending his run in something of a controlled crash.

The crew rushed over, reaching the vehicle as the man climbed off the machine and hooked an industrial grade carabiner onto the second rung of a ladder near the superstructure.

"Are you alright?" the helmsman shouted.

He discovered a tall man in a wetsuit, wearing a waterproof headset over a well-soaked mane of silver hair. The man's face hadn't seen a razor in a week, but under the thick stubble he appeared to be smiling.

"This is no place to moor a boat," the new arrival said.

The helmsman laughed, forgetting for a split second how dire their situation was. "Can't move it now. Any chance you can tow a raft with that speeder of yours?"

The man shook his head. "Too much weight. We'd never get past the rocks before the next breaker came through."

"Perhaps you can take a few of us at a time? As passengers?"

"I could, but that would take too long," the stranger said. "We're going to get you to safety the old-fashioned way."

As the helmsman watched, the man detached a cable from the tail section of his watercraft. Pulling it with a firm grip, the line rose out of the water behind him, stretching out into the turbulent bay.

The stranger carried one end of the line to the nearest boom, which the crew used to deploy the fishing nets. He climbed a set of rungs welded to the side and upon reaching a spot higher than any sane man should have climbed to in the storm, he wrapped the cable around the boom in a figure eight, hooking it though one of the metal rungs and then onto itself.

With the line secure he pressed the microphone to his mouth and presumably spoke to someone on the other end of the line.

Somewhere in the distance, a winch started pulling in slack on the cable. As it did, the cable rose out of the water. Only now did the helmsman realize what he had in mind. "A breaches buoy," he shouted.

"A what?" one of the crew asked.

"Think of it like a zipline," the helmsman said. "It'll carry us over the water and onto shore."

The stranger climbed down, shrugged a backpack off one shoulder, and pulled out several harnesses, each of which was attached to a wheeled runner.

As he handed out the harnesses, the stranger explained what was about to happen. "The other end of the cable is attached to a trailer manned by a friend of mine down on the beach near the point. He has orders to keep the line tight and haul you in. How many on board?"

"Nine."

"Two trips," the stranger said. "Four people at a time. Then the last man goes with me."

The helmsman nodded and began directing his men to climb

into the harnesses. The first four went up the boom and, one by one, hooked their new gear onto the steel cable and then to one another like a line of freight cars. With all four dangling out over the edge and the line sagging with the weight, the stranger spoke into his radio.

Instantaneously, a smaller, secondary cable linked to the first harness pulled tight and the group began to move.

They went out across the water, dropping slightly and racing off into the distance. Between the rain, the dim light and the blowing spray, it was hard to see them beyond the first hundred yards.

For the first time since they'd run aground, the helmsman felt a glimmer of hope. He looked back up at the stranger. "I'd like to say a proper thanks, but I don't know your name."

"Austin," the man replied. "Kurt Austin."

Where did you come from?" the helmsman asked.

Kurt was the director of Special Projects for an American government agency known as NUMA, the National Underwater and Marine Agency. Now was not the time to explain all that. "McCloud Tavern," he said. "We saw that you were in trouble. Crazy to be out fishing in weather like this."

"We weren't fishing," the helmsman. "Just trying to get back to Dunvegan before the weather hit."

That sounded reasonable, except it meant sailing into the teeth of the storm. Heading south would have been far safer. Kurt filed the thought away and pressed the radio button connected to his headset. "What's the word?" he asked. "Has the first group reached you yet?"

A QUARTER MILE AWAY, close enough that an Olympic swimmer could cover the distance in four minutes, Joe Zavala stood on the back end of a trailer hitched to a powerful F-250 pickup truck. He was parked halfway up a deserted beach, watching as the winch on the trailer reeled in the cable.

Joe was Kurt's second-in-command at NUMA and his closest friend. He had a stocky build, short black hair and an easy smile that suggested things would be alright—even when that appeared highly unlikely considering the situation. This was one of those times.

Despite being less than five hundred yards from the wrecked trawler, all Joe could see of the wreck was a shroud of lighted mist around the dim outline of the vessel. He strained for any sight of the men coming in on the line.

Finally, the cable began to bend, telling him there was weight on it, and four shapes emerged from the mist. They came sliding toward Joe, pulled their feet up as a wave tried to swipe them from the line and then they crashed onto the beach in a four man pileup.

Joe shut the winch down, hopped from the trailer, and ran down to where they'd landed. He helped them out of their harnesses. "Get in the truck," he said, pointing to the crew cab of the Ford. "The heat's on. Make yourself comfortable, but don't play with the radio dial."

The men looked at him blankly, not getting the joke, and then stumbled toward the truck. As they opened the doors and climbed in, Joe pressed TRANSMIT on his own headset. "Congratulations, amigo. We've got four men on dry ground. Make that solid ground, nothing's dry around here for miles."

"Roger that," Kurt said. *"Get them out of those harnesses, so I can pull them back and send over the next group."*

Joe had already clipped the harnesses together and made sure they were secure on the cable. Heading back to the truck, he disconnected the brake on the winch, allowing the drum to spin freely and the cable to play out. "All clear," he said into the radio. "Use those biceps and pull to your heart's content."

BACK ON THE SHIP, Kurt began hauling on the guide cable, pulling the harnesses back toward the foundering vessel. He worked quickly and without a rest. Finally, with his arms burning from the effort, the harnesses came into view. When they were close enough, he reached out and grabbed them.

"Next group," he shouted.

It took only a minute for the helmsman and two other crew members to get situated in the harnesses and hooked onto the cable.

By Kurt's count they were short. "Am I confused or are we missing a couple of people?" Kurt said to the helmsman.

"What?"

"These men are five and six," Kurt shouted over the wind. "You make seven, but you told me there were nine on board. Where are the others?"

The helmsman looked toward the wheelhouse. "The captain. He went down below to get our passenger."

"Passenger?"

"When we hit the rocks, he went below. The captain went down after him."

Kurt glanced toward the wheelhouse. With the lights on, it looked warm and inviting against the grey storm, but it was no place to hide when the ship came apart. “Go with your men,” he said. “I’ll get your captain and this passenger.”

The helmsman looked as if he was about to argue. Kurt didn’t give him a chance. He hooked the harness to the cable and pressed the radio button to call Joe. “Next group ready to go. Reel them in.”

The draw line tightened, lifting the helmsman and his crew off the gantry and out across the waves. As they rode toward safety, Kurt climbed down to the tilted deck and made his way toward the wheelhouse.

As he stepped inside, the hull shifted with another wave, groaning in protest. If Kurt didn’t find the captain and the passenger quickly there would be no ship left to escape from.

CLIVE CUSSLER

"Clive Cussler is just about the best storyteller in the business."
—*New York Post*